UNDER THE GHOST MOON

ALSO BY LYN LIAO BUTLER

The Tiger Mom's Tale

Red Thread of Fate

Someone Else's Life

Crazy Bao You

What is Mine

The Fourth Daughter

The Deadly Book Club

UNDER THE GHOST MOON

A NOVEL

LYN LIAO BUTLER

LAKE UNION PUBLISHING

Published by Lake Union, Seattle

www.apub.com

EU product safety contact:
Amazon Media EU S. à r.l.
38, avenue John F. Kennedy, L-1855 Luxembourg
amazonpublishing-gpsr@amazon.com

ISBN-13: 9781662539312 (paperback)
ISBN-13: 9781662539305 (digital)

Cover design by Amanda Kain
Cover image: © Nikki Smith / ArcAngel Images

Printed in the United States of America

For my fellow Taiwanese Americans

Prologue

Ah-Hui
1980, Manhattan

Don't tell my grandmother, but the Old Man Under the Moon is a fraud. From the time I was a little girl growing up in Taiwan, my ah-ma loved to tell me stories from long ago. She would hold me close as we sat in her favorite wooden chair in the courtyard, looking out past the dirt path that led from their modest country house on the outskirts of Taichung to the single road that ran in front of their property. She told me mythical tales about gods and goddesses, monkey kings and dragons, and an old man they called Yue Lao, who appeared most often at night under the moon.

"He is the god of marriage and love," she told me, her voice dreamy as she stared out at the groves of fruit trees she tended. "Love and marriage," she whispered in my ear, "are not dictated by a goddess of beauty. Rather, they are dictated by the contents of this old man's book of fate, and the unions he records can never be broken."

"Old man," I exclaimed, my nose wrinkled in displeasure. "What would an old man know about love?" I much preferred a beautiful goddess, one adorned with gold and jewels, who would lead me to the man I was destined to be with.

But no, Ah-Ma insisted, "Yue Lao is the one who unites with a silken cord all predestined couples, after which nothing can prevent their union."

"Like you and Ah-Gong?" I asked.

Ah-Ma laughed and laughed, a booming sound from such a tiny woman. But she never answered my question. Instead, she bounced me on her knobby knees while I marveled at how my grandmother could have given birth to eight children when I, at nine years old, was almost as big as she was.

Now, at age thirty, after finding out my husband had been sharing a bed with our children's nanny right under my nose, I would look up at the moon every night and wonder: Who was this Old Man, and why was he given so much power over our destinies? Why did Ah-Ma believe in him when her own life was such a struggle and nothing like the fairy tales that she told me?

Maybe Ah-Ma already knew that the Old Man Under the Moon didn't really exist. Maybe she believed because it gave her hope when the reality of raising a large family in a country where chaos and fear reigned was so bleak. Or maybe it was easier to believe a myth than it was to face the truth. That some unions do break, and we humans are the ones who destroy them. I know the Old Man Under the Moon would understand. Because like him, I was a fraud.

1

Joey
Present Day, Kauai

A tidal wave of emotions washed over Joey the moment she set foot outside the open-air baggage claim area at Lihue Airport. A gentle breeze lifted her hair, and the bright sun kissed her skin, making it flush. A yellow helicopter thrummed in the distance, and tourists and locals streamed out of the building behind her, their happy chatter buoyed by the excitement of being on vacation or returning home. But for Joey, this homecoming trip was bathed in a wash of sorrow and grief.

Her right ear hadn't popped on the airplane's descent, and she felt as if her head were encased in a bubble of cotton. She heard everything as if underwater, the noises around her muffled and slightly out of focus. She had to ask the rental car agent to speak up because she couldn't understand his questions. When she finally had the keys, she heaved a sigh of relief and dragged her suitcase into the parking lot to find her vehicle.

She stopped in front of the designated car, staring at it in all its blinding-white glory. It glinted in the sunlight, as if taunting her. White was the color of death in Taiwan. She laughed, even though there was nothing funny about the situation.

"Okay, Sam, ha ha." She looked around, expecting to find her brother grinning at her from a few steps away. "You ordered this car for me, didn't you? Haunting me already?"

She cocked her head and closed her eyes, waiting to see if she would hear Sam's voice. It wasn't impossible that Sam's ghost was here on Kauai, waiting for her. He'd raised her since she was almost eleven, when their parents had drowned, and they were connected in a way that transcended death. She willed his ghost to tell her she would be okay, that her life would somehow still be balanced without him. It was at times like this that she wished she had her mother, Ah-Hui, to turn to when she needed guidance and comfort.

When she heard nothing but the rustle of the wind and cars pulling in and out of the rental lot, she opened her eyes. "You're really not here, are you?"

Her text alert dinged and she jumped, thinking for a moment that it really was Sam reaching out to her from beyond. But it was her closest friend, Maggie Estrada.

Get there okay?

Yes, she texted back. Just got my car.

I'm here if you need me.

Joey smiled. Thanks. I'm here for you too. Love you.

Right back at you. Xoxo

Joey took in a lungful of the warm, humid air and then threw her suitcase into the trunk. Ethan had offered to pick her up at the airport since Sam's car had been taken by the police until they could determine whether his death was indeed accidental, but Joey had declined. She hadn't seen Ethan in over eight years, and she didn't want the first time she'd see her brother's best friend again to be out in public. They had too much history, and now the shared grief over Sam's death, for her not to break down when she saw Ethan again. Better to do it in private.

She got in the driver's side, taking time to adjust the seat and mirrors, and then pulled out of the rental lot. Small white birds, cattle egrets, scattered as she accelerated, making her smile. She thought they were pretty, even though Sam had told her years ago that they were considered pests since they hunted the chicks of native birds. Thinking about Sam made her heart ache, but at the same time, with the mountains of Kauai looming in front of her and the palm trees swaying in the breeze, she couldn't help feeling comforted in the presence of all that beauty. This was Sam's favorite place on earth, where they'd lived with their parents for five years when he was eleven and Joey was one, and where Sam and Joey had moved back for her high school years.

As she drove in her funeral car up north to Sam's condo in Princeville, Joey's thoughts went to the phone call she'd received from Sam's lawyer a few days ago. It wasn't unusual for her to get messages from Victor Liao, who was also Joey's lawyer and an old family friend. But he never called without sending a text first, so when she'd seen his name on her phone, her heart skipped a beat. She was in a rural area just outside of Kuala Lumpur, working with the littlest children, assisting with their studies as well as helping build a schoolhouse. She'd been volunteering at this community project for the past three weeks.

That day, the children were working outside on a concrete patio, their happy chatter loud over the rush of the river nearby, and she'd quickly moved away from them as she picked up the call.

"Joey." Victor's voice was quiet. "I have bad news."

Her breath had caught and she said right away, "Sam?"

Victor's silence spoke volumes, and Joey moved around the corner, out of sight of the children. She sank onto the hard ground.

Finally, Victor spoke. "Yes. He drowned. His body was found at Anini Beach."

"What?" The word burst out of Joey's mouth as disbelief flooded through her.

Her brother was in prime physical shape, a triathlete and the strongest swimmer she knew. He was the last person she would ever have thought would drown. She'd bitten her lip, thinking, though, that Sam had looked like he'd lost a lot of weight when she visited him on Kauai a few weeks ago on her way to Malaysia. The meaning of Victor's words hit her, and the grief poured in, obliterating everything else.

"How . . . What happened?" she gasped out.

"They don't know. No one saw it happen. His . . . body washed up on shore around dusk yesterday." Victor's voice was laced with sympathy.

"That's impossible. He's such a strong swimmer. And he doesn't take risks." Joey's mind refused to believe her big brother was gone.

"I'm sorry." Victor didn't say anything else, waiting for Joey to process the news.

"I . . . He . . ." Tears stung her eyes, but she refused to let them fall. She wasn't going to cry for her brother because there was no way he was gone.

They'd both been busy, her life taking her around the world researching for the novels and articles she wrote as well as volunteering wherever she could, and Sam as a family practice physician on Kauai. Yet they always found time for each other, even though Joey had only visited Sam on Kauai a few times since graduating from college.

"He left instructions." Victor's voice broke through her reverie.

"Instructions?" It took a moment for Joey to understand his words. "For what?"

"In case of his death." Victor's voice was quiet.

"You mean like a will?" Her brows furrowed as she puzzled over what he was trying to tell her. He was a man of few words, which normally didn't bother her, but now she needed him to spell it out.

"Yes. But also . . ." He trailed off, and Joey wanted to jump through the phone and shake the words out of him. "He left specific instructions for you. And Ethan."

Ethan.

The object of Joey's teenage crush. Ethan was half Japanese and half white, and Joey had always teased him that he looked like a Japanese George Clooney. Nothing had ever happened between them except that one time when she'd just graduated from high school . . . She shook her head, wanting to forget the humiliating experience. Best not to think of that mistake. She hadn't seen much of him since he'd gotten married just as he started his residency at a hospital in California.

"I don't understand," Joey said when Victor didn't continue.

"He wants you to go to Kauai. And he wants Ethan to be with you when you scatter his ashes if his body is found. He doesn't want a funeral or service. Just the two of you."

"What? *If* his body is found?" *And no funeral or service? Why?*

"He was really insistent." Victor cleared his throat. "Two months ago, he flew me out to Kauai." Victor was based in New York, where Joey kept an apartment as a home base. "If anything were to happen to him, he wanted everything to be ready. He left instructions for you on his laptop."

"I don't . . . understand." Joey couldn't help but repeat this. "It sounds like he knew he was going to die. He wasn't sick, was he?" Her voice rose as she remembered how she'd asked Sam offhand one day whether he was feeling okay when he'd said he didn't feel up for a hike. Sam had brushed aside her concern, saying he'd been getting over a bout of COVID. "What's going on?"

"I'm sorry, Joey." Victor's voice was full of regret. "That's all I can say. But it'll all make sense once you get to Kauai." He paused, then said, "He was a great man. I'm going to miss him."

Tears filled her eyes now, the grief so powerful that it felt like it would swallow her whole. She couldn't fathom a world without Sam. She fought to get control of her emotions as she drove up the eastern coast of Kauai with the windows open and the wind whipping through her hair. It was hot and she should turn on the AC, but the fresh air felt good after the stuffiness of the flight.

The GPS on her phone directed her to make the next right, and she realized she'd reached Princeville already. The last forty-five minutes had passed in a blur, she'd been so lost in thought. She bit her lip as she pulled into the residential community where Sam's condo was located. She followed the road, going back toward the ocean, remembering the way since she'd been here so recently. Her eyes searched the lush greenery, filled with palm trees and big red ti leaves, not quite believing that Sam wouldn't be standing in the parking lot waiting for her, like he'd been last time. He wouldn't pull open her door as soon as she'd parked and practically drag her out of the car and into his arms, nearly smothering her with his overenthusiastic hug.

Oh, Sam. What am I going to do without you?

Joey turned off the engine and sat for a moment. Her right ear was still clogged, and she tried yawning to get it to pop, but nothing happened. She knew Ethan, who had moved to Kauai when he'd finished his medical residency to start a practice with Sam, was waiting for her in Sam's condo. Taking a deep breath, she got out of the car and made her way down the path lined with colorful bird-of-paradise flowers and yellow and red hibiscus. When she reached Sam's duplex, the front door opened before she could punch in the key code.

"Joey."

Ethan Yamaguchi stood before her. Heat flooded Joey's entire body as her breath blew out in a loud woosh. Her eyes skimmed over his face, his beloved face, and it suddenly seemed so silly that she hadn't seen him in almost a decade because she'd timed her trips to Kauai for when he wasn't here. All because she'd been hurt when he'd gotten married and then had a daughter. It seemed she'd never really gotten over her unrequited childhood crush.

"Aloha." Joey managed that one word before falling silent, drinking Ethan in.

His dark hair was tousled as if he'd run his hand through it many times, making it stick up in some places. And while his eyes were rimmed in fatigue and the corners of his mouth were turned down in sorrow, he still managed to exude a level of sexiness that had Joey swallowing hard. She was grieving for Sam, but she wasn't dead, and the woman in her appreciated the view. There was silver at his temples now, and lines at the corners of his eyes, but he still had the rock-hard muscles and lean body that had filled Joey's daydreams as a teenager.

Ethan grinned when she finally met his eyes, his surprisingly light-brown ones gleaming as he took her in. "Look at you." He held out his arms. "Beautiful as always."

She flushed again and looked down before stepping into his embrace. And then her eyes closed, relieved, because here was someone else who loved Sam as much as she did, who was mourning Sam as much as she was. A surge of emotions welled up within her. Ethan was her closest connection to Sam, and right now, she craved anything that would bring her brother back. Something pulsed in Ethan's neck, and she turned her face into it. She breathed in, his body warm against hers, and felt herself relax for the first time since hearing the news.

After a moment, Ethan pulled away but kept his hands on her arms lightly. "I'm so, so sorry, Joey. I have no words."

She could see the fatigue pulling at his eyes, the way his face drooped with grief. He met her gaze, and the look that passed between them helped ease her broken heart. He understood that the whole world had changed, that it had dimmed with the loss of her brother.

"Thank you. I'm sorry for your loss too." They looked at each other for another long moment, then he stepped back to allow her to enter.

"Do you know what's going on?" she asked.

She slipped off her flip-flops and followed him into the main living area. It was flooded with sunlight from the many windows and sliding glass doors off the kitchen. Natural rattan furniture with bright-red cushions filled the living room, along with an upright piano against one wall, and the open kitchen sported stainless steel appliances with a tan granite countertop. Artwork by local artists of the ocean, flowers, and mountains graced the walls, as well as a surfboard mounted over the door out to the lanai and small fenced-in backyard.

Ethan nodded. "I'm sorry, Joey. Sam made me promise not to call you. He didn't want you to know."

"Know what?" Joey stared at Ethan in disbelief. He didn't sit, and neither did she. How was it that Ethan knew what was happening and she didn't? Sure, Sam had always thought of Ethan as a brother, but *Joey* was Sam's blood sibling, not Ethan.

"Oh, Joey." Ethan's eyes brimmed with sympathy, and his shoulders sagged, as if he was carrying a heavy burden. "Sam left you videos. He'll explain everything."

"Why didn't he explain everything when he was still alive?" Joey's voice rose, but she couldn't help it. "I don't understand."

"I know. He never wanted you to know the truth when he was alive. But facing his own mortality, he realized it was unfair to you. You're an adult, not a young child who needs to be shielded. He ran out of time, so he made videos for you." Ethan paused, then he gestured to Sam's office. "Everything is on his laptop."

Joey gaped at Ethan for a moment and then turned and headed for the office, which was also the guest room she'd stayed in last month and where she'd stay this time. Something was very wrong about Sam's death, and she was determined to get to the bottom of it. She couldn't work out how she felt about Ethan's role in it until she understood what had happened.

Ethan followed her as she went to Sam's desk where his computer was, lid closed. Sitting down, she opened the laptop, surprised that it was on. The desktop appeared without a password, as if Sam had left it ready for her.

She turned to Ethan, who was standing behind the chair, and their eyes met for a moment before she returned her attention to the computer. Scanning the icons on the desktop, she found one labeled FOR JOEY. Her breath hitched, and Ethan placed a reassuring hand on her shoulder. Her heart tripping in trepidation, she clicked open the document, drumming her fingers against the desk in the seconds it took to open. When it finally did, she took a deep breath and started reading.

Hi, Joey—
If you're reading this, I'm probably dead. I'm sorry to leave you—you know that, right? Trust me, I'm not ready to go. But if I have to, I want to do it on my own terms. And I need to explain what has happened in my life these last few months.

I also have a confession. I've kept what really happened to our parents from you your whole life. If I had to do it again, I would do it exactly the same way. It was the best thing for you at the time, and if it were up to me, you would never have to know the truth. But I've recently begun seeing a therapist, and she has convinced me that even though I did it to protect you, it isn't right to keep this from you.

I should at least have told you our family's history, starting from when our grandfather, our mother's father, disappeared a few years after the 228 Massacre in 1947, which was the most infamous day in Taiwan history. I know you don't know much about it because I didn't discuss it with you. Back then, I tried to shield you because you were struggling so much after our parents died, and it was more important for me that you assimilated into your new life in America. But now I wonder if I did you a disservice. With what has happened in my own life, I realized I wasn't going to be here forever to protect you, and that my therapist was right. You have a right to know our family story, however awful it is.

I have our mother's journal, which I've translated for you. But before I tell you where it is, I need to explain some things to you. I've left videos for you that will explain everything. Please watch them with Ethan. And don't be mad at him. I made him promise

> not to tell you. He's the best friend I've ever had, and I'm so glad I met him in that triathlon training group when I brought you to New York after our parents died. I couldn't have survived everything without his support. He'll help you through this and answer any questions you might still have.
>
> You've always been so busy and have only returned to Kauai a few times since you graduated from college. (How was that seventeen years ago!) I blame myself for whatever it is that keeps you running around the world, but it's time you came back here and let the healing powers of Kauai help you after my death. I will always be with you, Joey, Chiao-Yi. (At least my ghost will, because you know I'm coming back to haunt you, right?) Be well.
>
> Love you always,
>
> Sam

Joey looked up from the document, her heart heavy but a laugh erupting despite herself. She'd known Sam was going to haunt her. She pushed the laptop toward Ethan so he could read her brother's words, as she thought of the time when Sam had given her the name Joey. She'd been Chiao-Yi her whole life before then, but when she'd started school in New York, her classmates hadn't been able to pronounce her name. When she'd come home in tears because a boy had called her Chow Chow the Chinese Dog, Sam had given her a nickname.

"You will always have your Taiwanese name," he'd said to her. "But why don't we give you an American one since you live here now?"

"Like you're Sam?" she'd asked him in Taiwanese.

"Yes." He'd rubbed his chin and thought. "I know, how about Joey? It's close to Chiao-Yi, and it's unique. It's usually a boy's name, but"—he reached out and pulled her braid—"you look like a Joey."

And that had been it. She was Joey from then on, and when she turned eighteen, she officially changed her name to Joey Chiao-Yi Zhang.

"Oh, Sam." Her words sounded so loud in the silent room. "What happened?"

She waited for his ghost to answer her, or at least send her a sign, like a book falling off the bookcase or a picture fluttering out of nowhere in front of her. But there was nothing, only silence and the myriad of questions his sudden death had left behind.

2

They sat in front of the laptop, having taken one of the dining chairs into the guest room. Joey hadn't even brought her luggage in yet. She needed answers now.

"Here goes," Joey said, mostly to herself. She glanced at Ethan from the corner of her eye. She'd pulled up the first video, and the cursor hovered over the play button. With a deep breath, she moved her finger over the mouse pad and started the video.

Sam's image filled the screen. He looked so alive—so vibrant and real, dressed in a green Crazy Shirts tee—that she let out a gasp. Ethan's eyes shifted to her, but otherwise he didn't react. Joey wanted to reach through the screen and touch her brother, to feel his heart beating in his chest, proof that he was alive and not dead. But her very next thought was that he didn't look well. He was too thin, and there was a sallow hue to his skin.

On-screen, Sam smiled, but it didn't reach his eyes. "Aloha, Joey. Today is Sunday, November fifth." Joey and Ethan exchanged a glance. That was only five days ago, the day before they'd found Sam's body. "If you're watching this, then I'm gone. I wish I still had years with you, to watch you grow old and decrepit." He chuckled but then sobered almost immediately. "I know you probably have so many questions right now, and I'm about to answer them all."

Joey noticed right away that Sam's speech was slow, almost hesitant, which wasn't like him at all. And there was a faint rattling sound when he breathed out. Her spine tingled and she braced herself for the bad news.

Sam continued to talk on the screen. "I'll start at the beginning. About four months ago, I started getting these strange back pains. As an athlete, it wasn't like anything I'd ever experienced. It wasn't muscular." Sam paused for a moment, his mouth twisting. "It was deeper. At about the same time, I also lost a whole bunch of weight without trying. I just didn't have my usual appetite. I ignored it, thinking maybe I'd overdone it on a workout, so I took it easy for a couple of weeks. But then I started getting stomach pains and throwing up." He stopped and seemed to be staring right into Joey's eyes. "You know I don't throw up. Ever."

It was true. Joey had never understood why Sam didn't vomit like a normal person, even when he was nauseous.

"Oh no," Joey muttered under her breath. "I knew something was off."

"I went to the doctor. And then another doctor. They ran all the tests, but by that time, my heart knew something bad was happening. When I finally got the diagnosis, I was stunned, and for days, I refused to believe it. My doctors wanted to talk options, steps forward. But I knew what I wanted to do." Sam stopped and looked dead into the camera. "I have Stage 4 pancreatic cancer. A rare cancer, squamous adenocarcinoma of the pancreas. The doctor didn't need to tell me. I knew I only had months, if that, to live."

Joey inhaled sharply, her heart seizing as both hands covered her mouth.

Sam's eyes burned with intensity. "I'm not going to let this disease get me. I don't want to do chemo or try any of the other ideas the doctors presented. I don't want to live if I can't fully live, and I know enough about this cancer to know that I don't want to spend the last moments of my life sick and debilitated." He bowed his head until all they could see was the top of his hair.

"Ethan." Joey turned horrified eyes to her brother's friend, who reached out to take one of her hands in his. She barely felt the contact, where once her pulse would have jumped.

Sam picked up his head, his hair tousled. "If I had a family, children who counted on me, a wife I loved madly, maybe I would feel different and I'd fight. But I don't. I've opted to be single, just like you have, Joey, for different reasons, which I'll get to later. I don't have anyone depending on me. You and Ethan both have your own lives. You don't need me to try to survive for a few more months, hoping for more time. That's why I didn't tell you, Joey." He stared into her eyes. "I know you would drop everything if you knew and fly here to take care of me. You'd argue with me and say I needed to stay alive, to fight and do the chemo, anything because maybe a miracle would happen and it would cure me."

"Oh, Sam." How had her brother gone through this alone and not told her? She was sick, sick to her stomach that she hadn't known.

Sam set his jaw with resolution before speaking again. "I will not let this disease dictate my life. I will not suffer more than I need to." His eyes darkened with determination and a fierceness that scared Joey. He bent down and picked up his dog, Wonton, who licked him on the cheek. He leaned in closer to the camera, his gaze so intense it took Joey's breath away. "I hope you understand why I have decided not to seek medical treatment, and why I have decided to end my life at my choosing, and not at the mercy of the cancer. Either choice is awful—terrible—but I've made up my mind. And I can't go through with it if you knew. I'm so sorry."

He sat back and stared down at Wonton while Joey held her breath, unable to take her eyes off her brother. She knew what he was going to say before he said it.

He finally looked up. "I've settled my affairs. I've left instructions with Victor. I've told the Kellys next door because I need them to take care of Wonton for me until you get here. I don't want you to be sad. I want you to celebrate my life, knowing that I've lived it the way I want. And that I'm going out the way I want, in the ocean I love so much."

The impact of Sam's words shook Joey to her core. She squeezed Ethan's hand, needing to anchor herself to someone warm and alive, to not think about her brother preparing to die because his body was failing him.

She turned to Ethan. "I need to go see the Kellys. Get Wonton." She struggled to get the words out because it suddenly felt like there was no air in her lungs.

"We will. Soon." Ethan squeezed her hand back.

Sam spoke from the video. "I've left our mother's translated journal for you in a safe place."

Joey's forehead knotted as she wondered where the journal was. She could still speak Mandarin and Taiwanese but hadn't taken Chinese classes once she moved to the States, so she could no longer read or write it.

"In the same folder as this video, you'll find a document. It's a bit from our mother's journal so you can decide after you read it if you want to know the truth about our family. And about your nanny, Ren Ren. If you do, watch the next video, and I'll tell you where to find the journal."

He let out a deep sigh and Joey's body tensed, bracing for what was coming.

"I know you think our parents had a fairy-tale marriage, and I've kept up that facade for you your entire life." Sam shook his head. "Maybe I shouldn't have. Maybe I should have told you that our father had an affair with Ren Ren right under our mother's nose. It lasted for years." He stopped, his chin trembling for a moment. "I'm so sorry to have to tell you that, after all these years. I blamed Ren Ren for their deaths."

Joey sucked in a breath, and then she was shaking, her whole body moving as shock took over. She felt as if she were fighting to stay above water that was threatening to drown her like it had Sam. Like it had her parents. Her breath came out in a loud gasp as she finally consciously realized that her entire family had died by drowning. And then she was struggling for air as her lungs closed and her vision darkened.

Ethan gripped her hand. "Joey. Look at me." He waited until she met his eyes. "Breathe. Deeply. In through the nose, out through the mouth. It's going to be okay. I'm here."

She struggled to take deep breaths, Ethan's hand tethering her to the present as her mind flew back to that awful night when Ren Ren Ayi had woken her from a deep sleep. She could still see the terrible look on her nanny's face as she told Joey softly that her parents had drowned trying to come back to Bangkok from the village where they'd gone to take care of the sick. They'd died under a full moon, which had illuminated their boat when her mother had gone overboard and her father jumped in to save her, even though he couldn't swim either. Witnesses on land had seen the accident and rowed out to help, but it was too late. By the time they pulled them out of the river, they were both gone. Joey remembered staring up at the huge moon that night and thinking it had seen her parents die. And now Sam was gone, too, in the exact same way.

Joey squeezed her eyes shut, trying to focus on the present, focus on her breath until her lungs started working again and it no longer felt as if she were trying to push air through a straw. When she opened her eyes, she found Ethan staring at her in concern, both of his hands now gripping one of hers.

"Okay now?"

She nodded, even as her chin wobbled. "I have no one left in the world."

Ethan pressed her hand between his. "You'll always have me."

No, I don't. You're married with a teenage child.

"He drowned, just like my parents." She said this out loud. "And I never saw Ren Ren Ayi again." Joey's hands were shaking.

She pressed her lips together as she was assaulted with memories of the time when her parents had died and Sam had come to get her. It was also the last time she ever saw her beloved nanny.

3

Joey (Chiao-Yi)
1996, Bangkok

"Sam!"

He turned his head when he heard her calling his name. She broke free from her nanny, Ren Ren Ayi, and ran to him, down the alley from the guesthouse that their parents had rented for their mission in Thailand. He scooped her up and held her to him, and she buried her face in his shoulder.

"Mama, Baba," she cried, fat tears rolling down her cheeks. She was sweaty from the muggy heat, but so glad her older brother was here. He'd make everything okay again.

"I know, I know," he murmured in her ear, stroking her hair and patting her on the back. Chiao-Yi heard her brother swallow hard, as if he had taken a large pill. She clung to him even more fiercely. He was all she had left.

He suddenly stiffened, and she raised her head off his shoulder to see what had caught his attention. Ren Ren Ayi stood next to them, and Chiao-Yi could feel the way her brother was practically vibrating with some strong emotion as he set her on the ground. Was it anger? She looked back and forth between them, confusion drawing her brows together. Ren Ren Ayi stood there, serene as always, her hands clasped together in front of her, worry and concern marring her features, while her brother now stood with his hands fisted at his sides. Why was he glaring at her nanny like that? As if he wanted to hit her, or worse?

"Sam?" His name came out in a small voice.

He turned to her and gave her a smile.

"Where'd they go?" Chiao-Yi blurted out, needing answers to the question that had plagued her ever since she'd found out her parents had drowned.

"You know they died, *xiao mei.*" He called her "little sister" in Mandarin, something their parents had done also. "They drowned in the river." He frowned as he put his hand on her shoulder. "Ren Ren said she told you Mama fell overboard and Baba tried to save her."

"I know." She looked at him solemnly. She would turn eleven next month, but right now, she wished she was still a little girl. "But where did they go? After they died?"

He rubbed his chin and seemed to be considering his words. "I don't know," he finally said. "But they will always be with us. Here." He thumped himself on the chest.

Chiao-Yi looked at him, her bottom lip trembling.

Before she could say anything, Ren Ren spoke. "Sam. You must be tired from the long flight," she said in Taiwanese, her voice soft. "I've prepared your parents' room for you and cooked your favorites."

He looked at her, his lip curled in a snarl. Chiao-Yi's eyes widened at the ferocious look on his face. If looks could harm, the glare he aimed at her nanny would have ripped her skin to shreds. Chiao-Yi chewed on her bottom lip, wondering what was going on. Sam loved Ren Ren Ayi as much as she did. Why, then, was he staring at her like he wished she would disappear?

Ren Ren's face flushed, and she looked away, taking a step back from them. Only then did Sam's features relax, and he reached out to Chiao-Yi.

"Come." He slipped his hand into hers. "Let's go in so I can bathe and change. We have a lot to talk about."

She nodded, gazing up at him. Her big brother was here to save the day. He would make everything okay again. He gave her a small smile, and they went inside, leaving Ren Ren Ayi in the heat by herself.

⁂

Five hours later, Sam sat next to Chiao-Yi in her antique platform bed, an arm around her shoulders as she snuggled into his side. After dinner, he'd searched their parents' room, turning it upside down while Chiao-Yi watched. She'd asked what he was looking for, and he said only that he wanted to put their affairs in order. She'd gotten bored after a while and went off to read a book before bed. But an hour later, she'd heard a choking sound from their parents' room and had crept out into the hallway to see what it was. She'd found her brother on the floor in their room, retching over the garbage can, an open notebook on the floor beside him. It had scared her to see her big brother like that, and she'd fled, back to her bed and under the covers, before he knew she'd spied on him in a vulnerable moment.

"You're coming back to New York with me." Sam's words brought Chiao-Yi out of her reverie.

"I am?"

He nodded. "Our lawyer, Victor Liao, gave me a copy of our parents' wills. They want to be cremated, their remains scattered wherever they died." He paused and looked at Chiao-Yi as if to see whether she understood.

She nodded. "Mama and Baba weren't close to their family in Taiwan." She thought for a moment and then said, "Victor is the one who brought Ren Ren Ayi to our family, right? He's really big into all that political stuff."

Sam drew back and stared at her. "How do you know that?"

"I heard Mama and Baba whispering about it one night when they thought I was sleeping. Mama didn't want Baba to get involved." She turned to look at her brother. "Get involved in what?"

"You don't have to worry about that now." Sam reached out to draw Chiao-Yi tight against his side, and she rested her head on his shoulder, so grateful she wasn't alone.

"What is New York like?" Chiao-Yi changed the subject, as she could see her brother was getting agitated again.

Chiao-Yi had been born in New York like her brother, but when she was barely one, their parents had relocated to Kauai because the island was in need of qualified physicians. They'd eventually moved on to Asia as traveling physicians, and Chiao-Yi had lived all over the continent, primarily in Southeast Asia, and didn't remember the city of her birth. She was used to the nomadic lifestyle, with Ren Ren Ayi there to take care of her and a tutor for her schoolwork.

"You'll like it. It's a busy city. Lots of different kinds of people, different kinds of food. I know how much you like to eat." He pulled her closer. "Good thing you already know how to speak English." The smile he aimed at her wobbled. Their parents had wanted them both to be fluent in Mandarin and English, spoken and written, as well as Taiwanese, which they used at home.

"Will Ren Ren Ayi come live with us and take care of me?" Chiao-Yi looked at her brother and was surprised when he seemed to balk at the question.

"No." He shook his head hard. "She's not coming."

Chiao-Yi pulled back from him. "What? Why?" Panic tinged her voice, making it go up an octave. Ren Ren Ayi had been with their family ever since Sam was born. As busy doctors, their parents had hired Ren Ren to take care of their baby. When Sam was ten, Chiao-Yi had come along, and Ren Ren became her nanny too.

"I can't bring her." He pressed his lips into a thin line.

"But . . ." She paused, her eyes stinging. "I need her. Baba and Mama are gone. I can't—" She broke off, biting her lip to keep from crying again.

"Chiao-Yi." He looked at her helplessly.

A movement outside her room had them looking up in time to see Ren Ren hovering in the doorway.

Before either could say anything, Ren Ren ducked her head and glided out of view like a ghost melting into the mist. Sam turned his attention back to her.

"Listen. I know things are hard right now. I miss them too. But we'll be together, and I'll take care of you. I promise." He pulled her into his side again. She resisted at first but then softened against him. "You're going to go to school in New York; won't that be fun? You've always said you wanted to go to a normal school. You can make new friends."

"But Ren Ren Ayi . . ."

"I'm sorry, Chiao-Yi. She can't come." His voice was firm.

She pulled her lips into her mouth, wondering why her brother was being so mean. Ren Ren was part of their family. She should go wherever they went.

He kissed her on the top of the head and then stood, pulling the covers up. She snuggled down in bed and reached her arms up for a hug.

"We'll talk more tomorrow, okay?" He gave her a smile.

She returned it even though she was filled with worry at the thought of going to New York without Ren Ren Ayi. She turned on her side, hugging the stuffed dog their parents had given her, which she was never without. Her brother turned off the light and walked out of her room. He shut the door behind him but left it open a crack, just the way she liked it.

Chiao-Yi closed her eyes, but she could hear her brother moving around in the main room. What was he doing? A few minutes later, she heard him coming back toward her room, but he didn't come in. Instead, she heard him go past her room to Ren Ren's, which was next to Chiao-Yi's. She could hear them speaking, but not what they said. Getting out of bed, she tiptoed to the door, staying behind it so that they wouldn't see her there, spying on them. Her brother went past her room again and then out the front door. A moment later, Ren Ren followed, and when the front door closed, Chiao-Yi knew she was alone.

Quietly, she opened the door to her room and slipped out into the main room. The house was decorated in the traditional Thai style, with red sofas, lantern lights, richly textured red-and-gold wallpaper, and Oriental rugs on the floor. Decorative screens painted with Thai gods and goddesses sectioned off parts of the main room. The upright piano that their father always insisted on in whatever home they rented stood in a corner, and a tear slid down Chiao-Yi's face. She thought of the many evenings when she and her father used to play duets together, singing at the top of their lungs while her mother sat and listened, tapping her foot.

She moved to the front door and, very slowly and very carefully, turned the knob and eased it open, a little bit at a time. She needed to know what her brother was saying to Ren Ren Ayi. With both her parents gone, she felt like she was drowning too. She needed Ren Ren, who knew everything about Chiao-Yi: that she liked savory food more than sweet, that she loved to wear dresses and hated jeans, and that she was scared of the dark and loved to sing like her father. Ren Ren was like a second mother, and Chiao-Yi couldn't imagine losing her too.

She stuck her head toward the crack she'd made, wide enough for her to put an eye to it and see out, but not so wide that her brother and Ren Ren would know she was lurking. She was immediately hit by the scorching heat, so muggy even though the sun had gone down. April was the hottest month in Thailand, and the temperature was still over 90 degrees. Chiao-Yi knew if she stepped outside, sweat would immediately gather on her forehead and roll down her back. She was grateful for the air-conditioning keeping her cool.

She could see her brother sitting on the bench at the front of the house, with Ren Ren standing by his side. Her nanny was saying something, but her voice was so soft Chiao-Yi couldn't hear what it was. She leaned closer, in time to catch her brother's words.

"You might be seven years younger than our mother, but you could never hold a candle to her. My mother, she was the most beautiful, the smartest person I knew, even smarter than my father, and now they're gone forever. Because of you."

Chiao-Yi almost gasped out loud at the cruel words coming out of her brother's mouth. It was true that Ren Ren was plain-looking compared to their mother. She had a wide face, her eyes set far apart with an expression that always looked startled, no matter her mood. Her long black hair was held back in a low bun, and her skin, her best feature, glowed, even in the dark, lit only by a light over the door. But he didn't have to be so mean and point that out.

"I want you to leave." Her brother spoke again, and she opened the door a little bit wider. "Now. I want you gone before she wakes up in the morning. You'll never see her again, or me."

"No, Sam . . ." Ren Ren's voice pleaded, even as a note of resignation tinged her words. "Please, don't do this. I love Chiao-Yi like she's my own."

"She's not yours." His voice rose and Chiao-Yi cringed. "She's ours."

"Please, don't do this." Ren Ren raised her palms in supplication.

"You know what you did." He stared at her, hard.

"You don't understand," Ren Ren pleaded. "It's not what you think."

"I know what you did. I found my mother's journal."

Her eyes widened and she froze in shock, her gaze on his. "You . . . What do you know?" she finally whispered.

His jaw clenched. "I never want to see you again. You killed my parents. You've taken enough from this family. I don't know why my mother put up with it all these years." He stood, turning his back on her. "I begged her before I left for college to leave him. But she refused."

"You knew about . . . ?" The tremor in her voice made Chiao-Yi's stomach churn.

Her brother turned and skewered Ren Ren with his gaze, causing her to shrink back. "I know what you did with my father. Even worse, I know you lured him into helping you and Victor with Taiwan's fight for independence, even though my mother begged him not to get involved. It was you. It's all your fault."

She gasped. "No, it's not . . ."

"It is." Sam gave a dry laugh. "You betrayed us. And now . . ." He shook his head as Chiao-Yi scrambled to understand what he was saying. "I don't . . ." His voice broke and Chiao-Yi wondered if he was crying.

Her heart picked up speed, and even though she didn't understand his words, she knew something was happening, something that would mark the end of her innocence, of her childhood.

"I'm sorry. I didn't mean . . ." Ren Ren's voice was barely a whisper, her entire body trembling.

Sam clenched his jaw again. "What did you say to them before they left on that boat?"

"I . . . It wasn't me . . ." She faltered and then took a breath, seeming to gather strength. "I loved him. And her. I loved both of them so much."

"They didn't need your love," he ground out, his voice rising. "You ruined our family!" He blinked furiously, and now Chiao-Yi could see tears shining in his eyes. The sight of them shot terror through her heart. She had never seen her brother cry. Never.

"I didn't mean to." Ren Ren reached a hand toward Sam.

He paced in front of her. "You lived with us, made me love you, made my sister love you, like you were family. And now what you've done has killed them."

She shrank away from him, biting her lip. "I'm sorry. So sorry."

"Sorry isn't going to cut it," he roared at her, making Chiao-Yi jump. His entire focus was on Ren Ren, and he didn't notice when she eased the door open more. "You're the one responsible for killing my parents, as sure as if you'd been on that boat with them and thrown them over, knowing they couldn't swim. You will never see Chiao-Yi again, you understand? You have one hour to clear your things and get out."

"No!" A voice shrieked and it took Chiao-Yi a moment to realize it had come from her. "No, Sam! Why are you sending Ren Ren Ayi away?" She flung open the door and stepped out into the muggy night.

"Chiao-Yi." Sam rushed to his sister, intending on gathering her against him, but she pushed him away, pounding her fists against his chest.

"No, don't touch me! What's going on?" She looked wildly from her nanny to her brother. "Why are you being so mean to her?"

"Chiao-Yi," he said again, taking her firmly by the shoulders. "Listen to me. There are things you won't understand now, things that Ren Ren Ayi has done. Please believe me."

"No, no, no!" she shrieked, fighting against her brother.

Ren Ren flew to her side, and with a questioning look at Sam, drew Chiao-Yi into a fierce hug. "I'm sorry, *xiao mei*. Your brother is right. I've done wrong to your family. I need to go." She hugged her close again. "I love you."

With one last look, Ren Ren pulled away and faced Sam. "I'll gather my things. I'll be gone as soon as I can." And she whirled and ran into the house, leaving brother and sister staring at each other in a standoff.

"Sam, please. Stop her." Her eyes pleaded with him. "I don't want her to go." Her words ended in a sob.

"I'm sorry." His voice softened with sorrow. "She has to."

When Chiao-Yi realized her brother was serious, she let out a scream that echoed in the alley and launched herself at him. "You're so mean; I wish you hadn't come here. Baba and Mama are gone, and now you're making Ren Ren Ayi leave too? I hate you. I hate you, I hate you!" Her voice rose with each word until she shouted the last, her face heated and tears leaking out of the corner of her eyes. People passing by the alley glanced at them with curiosity before their gaze slid away, embarrassed for them.

Sam picked her up, even as she flailed against him, still screaming. She didn't want him to touch her. She didn't want him to be taking her far away to a city she didn't remember. And she didn't want her parents to be dead. Not her lovely mama, or her strong baba.

She fought him with a strength that she didn't know she had, but he managed to carry her back into her room, where she continued to scream and wail, weakly fighting him until her sobs turned into hiccups and she collapsed against him. They both heard Ren Ren quietly leaving the house, and Chiao-Yi buried her face in her pillow, sobbing as if her heart would break. Her entire world had been drastically changed forever.

4

Joey
Present Day, Kauai

Joey's ears rang with the echoes of her screams from all those years ago as she looked up. Ethan must have stopped the video during her panic attack because Sam's image was frozen on the screen. She reached out and touched it, wishing it was her brother's real face under her fingertips.

She turned to Ethan. "Did you know my father had an affair with Ren Ren? Did Sam ever tell you?"

Ethan nodded. "About two years after he brought you back to New York. Right around when he finished medical school and was about to move the two of you to Hawaii for his residency. He was really stressed out—overwhelmed, I think. We went for a run that day, and he suddenly started talking, telling me things that he'd always kept inside."

A stab of hurt ran through Joey, but she tried to tamp it down. Ethan had known about the affair, too, and neither ever told her? She'd idolized her parents, held their marriage up as the perfect fairy-tale romance. She'd been so mad at Sam in the early years for taking her away from her beloved nanny. Now she understood why he'd done so, why he'd felt he had to protect her. And apparently, Ethan had always thought of her as a little sister. Except for the night of her high school graduation dinner. But even that had turned out to be a mistake.

Not wanting to wallow in self-pity, Joey pushed those thoughts away. "I never knew how Sam managed to graduate from college two years ahead of schedule and then complete medical school in only three years." Her brother had been brilliant, just like their mother.

"I know. And he was raising you at the same time." There was a faint smile on Ethan's face. "He was so smart. He could have been a surgeon, or a cardiologist. But he wanted to go into family medicine, to open a practice on Kauai."

"I'm going to miss him so much." Grief rose in her again, making her heart ache.

Ethan placed a hand on her arm, and her skin tingled. She quickly moved away, reminding herself that he was married.

"He was so worried about you at the end. He wanted to see you one last time. So you'd remember him the way he'd always been and not ravaged by the disease." Ethan took a few steps back from Joey, as if sensing her need for space.

"That's why he insisted that I come for five days before leaving for Malaysia." Joey had fought him on it at first. She'd only relented when he'd told her Ethan would be out of town for a medical convention in California. How she wished she could rewind time and go back. She wouldn't have hesitated and would have stayed longer, had she known it was the last time she'd see Sam alive.

She looked up, out the window at the palm trees visible in the distance. Her head reverberated with the echoes of their laughter as she'd paddleboarded at Kalapaki Beach, Sam cheering from shore as she'd fought against the wind that pushed her back; sharing a gigantic mound of shave ice drizzled with passion fruit, lychee, and guava flavors, as they'd laughed again about how it was called *shave* ice in Hawaii but in Taiwan was referred to as *shaved* ice; and chasing her brother down the beach at the water's edge when he'd stolen her hat and threatened to throw it into the waves. They'd spent the nights taking turns playing the piano in his apartment, singing all the old showtunes and popular songs they knew, just like they used to do with their father.

"It was a good five days, when I was just here. He was happy and we—" She broke off, choking back the tears, not wanting to mar her memories with sorrow. "He was so thin. But I . . ." She trailed off, thinking of how self-absorbed she'd been. "It didn't register enough for me to ask him about it."

Ethan nodded slowly. "It's all right, Joey. He didn't want you to know."

They stayed quiet for another moment, and then Joey reached out to start the video again, but it was only Sam saying, "Bye for now." She opened the document containing the first part of their mother's journal, and her heart jumped a little, seeing her mother's words translated by her brother.

She started reading and was soon engrossed, not looking up when Ethan stood and quietly let himself out of the room. She devoured her mother's words like a hungry ghost during Ghost Month. With each word she read, her curiosity grew until she knew without a doubt that she needed to know the full story. It was time to stop hiding in the safe bubble Sam had created for her after their parents drowned. It was time to finally figure out who her parents were, and who Joey herself really was.

5

Ah-Hui
1968, Taipei

I looked around the tiny room that was going to be my home, at least for the next few years as I began my studies at National Taiwan University. My heart was nearly bursting with excitement because I knew how proud my mother and grandparents were of my achievements. I was about to start medical school at the best university in Taiwan, following in my father's footsteps. But sadness also shrouded my heart as I looked out the window, knowing this was the city where he had disappeared from when I was only six months old.

My mother had come to Taipei with me to help me get settled. I would be living with a distant aunt and uncle, who had offered this room in their home when they heard I'd gotten into NTU. I wished we had money for the dormitories, but I was grateful for my own room. When I was eleven, my mother had sent me off to live with an older cousin in Taichung City to attend the middle school at Taichung Girls' High because I'd scored so high on the middle school exams that they thought I'd cheated. I only went home on the weekends when she could come get me.

"Remember when you moved me to Taichung?" I turned to my mother, who was busy making the bed.

Her hands stilled on the cotton quilt she was smoothing. "You didn't want to go." She sent me a rare smile over her shoulder. "But you were too smart for the country schools. Aren't you glad I made you?"

I nodded. The competition for admission into middle school, high school, and then university was fierce in Taiwan, and it had been an honor for me to get out of the rural school I had attended on the outskirts of Taichung. But I remembered how frightened I had been to be left alone with a stranger in a small dark apartment, where I'd slept behind a makeshift curtain in the living room on a single cot.

"I cried the entire first month." I made a face, thinking about how lonely and homesick I'd been back then. I'd wanted to be in my grandmother's arms, listening to her stories. I had missed being able to roam around the farm freely or curling up to read a book with my friend Ing. I hadn't liked that dark apartment, and even though my cousin was kind to me, we were two strangers who were forced to share a space and make the best of it.

My mother made a noise with her tongue. "You don't get anywhere by crying. Look at you now. Eighteen and studying to be a doctor, just like your father." She reached out to smooth the hair away from my face. "He'd be so proud."

I looked down to hide my smile, delighted to be compared to my father. School came easily to me. I was always at the top of the class and had made a few close friends in Taichung. I thought back to the many adventures I'd had in middle and then high school: going to the night markets, where we'd eat our way from stall to stall; enduring the cram schools, or *buxibans*, together; meeting for shaved ice on hot, sweltering days, giggling over the giant bowls of fluffy ice drizzled with a sweet syrup and loaded with toppings like tapioca, taro balls, coconut jelly, mangoes, and red beans. Sometimes we'd stop at food stalls on the way home from school, forking over coins in exchange for fish balls on a stick, or a pig's-blood cake coated in peanut powder and cilantro, served with a brown dipping sauce. We'd walk home, arm in arm, our hair cut short in the typical student style. I got used to living on my own, away from my family.

"I hope I make some friends here." Even though I was excited for this chapter of my life, I was worried because I didn't know anyone in Taipei.

"Isn't that rival of yours from high school, what's-her-name—didn't she get into NTU too?" My mother sat at the edge of the bed.

I gave her a pointed look. "Yes, but like you said, she's a rival. Not a friend." I was going to miss the good friends I'd made in Taichung, most of whom had stayed there for university or had found jobs because they didn't get into a good school.

"Ah-Hui." The sudden change in my mother's tone had me looking up. She sounded so serious. "Let's go for a walk."

"Don't you have to go soon?" I looked at the small clock on the table, noting that she should probably leave now if she wanted to catch the over-two-hour-long train ride back to Taichung and arrive before dark.

She shook her head. "I've decided to stay in Taipei tonight." Her spine straightened and she took a breath, as if gathering strength. "I think it's time you knew more about your father, now that you're all grown up."

My heart picked up speed as I waited for her to finally tell me about the father I'd never known. I'd wondered all my life what had really happened to him. But whenever I'd ask, she always brushed me off, unwilling or unable to tell me the full story. All I knew was that he had been here in Taipei at the scene that fateful February day in 1947, which came to be known as the 228 Massacre. And then three years later, six months after I was born, he disappeared without a trace.

"I know I don't talk about the past much, but now that you're here, in Taipei, maybe it's time you knew what happened." She paused and looked down at her hands.

"I want to know." I tried to keep my voice level, even though inside I was brewing with impatience.

"I can show you where we used to live. It's not far from here." She gestured with a hand, pointing out the window.

"Yes." I tried to keep the eagerness in check, for fear she'd change her mind if I was too enthusiastic. My mother had transformed over the years, and the soft-spoken mama I remembered from my early childhood was now a hard, bitter woman who often didn't have time for me. For her to be showering me with this much attention made me feel grown up, as if I were finally an equal, someone she could talk to.

"Before we go, let me tell you about that day." She paused, as if choosing her words carefully. "You know your father witnessed the incident that instigated the violence, when tens of thousands of Taiwanese lost their lives at the hands of the Kuomintang, the KMT, who ruled our island at the time." My mother's voice was shaky, as if she was reluctant to allow the memories to resurface.

I nodded. "He happened to be there when that widow, who later became infamous for unwittingly starting the massacre, was being harassed."

"Yes. It was a chilly night. He was hurrying home to me . . ."

I closed my eyes as my mother continued, and it was as if I could see the scene unfolding before me. I saw how my father's breath formed misty clouds whenever he exhaled, how he must have rubbed his hands together to warm them up. He was hurrying down the street when he came upon the widow, who had set up her cigarette stand in front of the Tian-Ma Teahouse. She was minding her own business when Tobacco Monopoly Bureau agents accused her of selling black market cigarettes and confiscated them. She protested, and

I imagined how her cries had brought my father out of his reverie of getting home to my mother. He would have turned his head sharply toward the scene.

By then, the people around her had drawn closer as some shouted for the agents to stop harassing her. I can imagine the horror on my father's face as my mother recounted how he'd watched an agent strike the widow on the head with the butt of a gun, prompting the bystanders to retaliate. In the confusion that ensued, the crowd, with my father in its midst, swept angrily forward, and the agents fired into the throng.

"Your father was not a fighter." My mother's voice was stronger now, clearer. "He was a gentle man, a peacemaker, and a healer. He told me how he could feel his heart pounding with fear as people screamed and chaos swarmed around him. We had only recently gotten married, and he said all he could think of was getting home to me."

My mother paused, and I could see him in my mind, fighting to break loose from the crowd, to escape the massacre, which was only just beginning.

"Was he shot?" I held my breath, since I'd never known the details.

"No. He was able to break free from the throngs, and he got home safely to me. He didn't know at the time that another bystander had been hit by a bullet, or he would have stopped to help." My mother sighed, shaking her head. "It was a chaotic time. People's tempers against the government were flaring, and your father was an intuitive man. He felt that our country was on the brink of violence. He came home that night and ordered me to pack a bag because he sensed our neighborhood was no longer safe."

I gasped, bringing a hand to my mouth. "Did you get out in time?"

"Yes, but only because he told me we needed to leave right away. We went to my parents' countryside home, which as you know, is about twenty miles outside of Taichung City. It was just far away enough to feel relatively safe."

"I'm glad you had a place to go." I gave a shudder, imagining my parents fleeing from Taipei all those years ago.

I knew that the assault on the widow had led to widespread protests and uprisings all over Taiwan, which were violently suppressed by the KMT. On February 28, 1947, and in the days that followed, approximately eighteen to twenty-eight thousand (depending on who you asked) Taiwanese were killed, making it one of the most momentous dates of Taiwan's modern history.

"We stayed with my parents for many months before he felt it was safe to come back here." Her words stopped and she stared off into the distance, as if reliving that time.

I tried to be patient, to wait for her to continue, but finally I couldn't stay silent. "Tell me more about when you and Baba went to live with your parents."

She glanced my way, a small smile on her lips, which made my heart glow to have put it there. She didn't smile often, and it felt like I'd accomplished a major feat.

"Well, you know my parents' house is pretty remote, but still, every once in a while, we could see KMT officers racing by on the lone road in front of the house, chasing whichever unfortunate soul they were after."

"My uncles must have loved that." My mother's younger brothers were full of mischief even as adults, so I could imagine how they must have pressed their noses to the window, excitement lighting their faces as they watched the KMT at work.

"My youngest brother, who was at Taichung First Senior High at the time and happened to be home when the violence started, made the mistake of saying he wanted to join in the fight against the KMT." The mirth in my mother's voice made me smile too. "He tried to sneak out the front door to chase down the officers, but your ah-ma caught him. She grabbed him by the ear and dragged him howling away from the door and ordered me to sit on him."

I burst into laughter, and my mother joined me. We looked at each other and my heart warmed. I was imagining my tiny grandmother, her face in a scowl and hands on her hips, threatening to skin my uncle alive with Ah-Gong's belt if he dared to join in the uprising or get into politics of any sort. She may be tiny, but she was fierce.

My mother stood and gestured to me. "Come, let's take a walk and I'll show you where we used to live."

We went out into the busy street, the air stifling from the late-August heat, so oppressive that I almost wished we were still inside, where it was cooler. But this rare chance to hear about the past she never spoke of had me matching my mother's stride as she took off briskly down the sidewalk.

My mother pointed to her left. "We lived close to Tian-Ma Teahouse at the time, but after we had you, we moved to a building over there in the Da'an District."

I nodded, my eyes scanning in the direction she was pointing. "How far away is our old apartment?"

"About fifteen minutes from here." My mother paused and looked at me. "You sure you want to go in this heat?"

"Yes." She'd become so distant with me the older I got, and I craved any attention she was willing to give me. This was the most time we'd spent, just the two of us, in years. I'd walk through burning fire for any attention from her.

We strode down the sidewalk, keeping the conversation light, as you never knew who might be listening. After a while, we walked in silence, the sweat trickling down my back. Soon, we turned into a side street that I could see was filled with residential buildings. They stood one right next to another, of varying heights, looking like blocks that had been stacked by a young child. Cars were pulled right up to gates with scooters and motorcycles crammed in wherever there was space.

After a moment, my mother stopped in front of a gray five-story building that looked like it had seen better days.

"We lived here." She pointed at the building. "On the fourth floor."

I stared up, trying to imagine myself as a baby, living in this apartment with my parents. It was surreal to be standing in a place where I'd been before but had no recollection of. In that moment, I wished my father hadn't been a doctor. Because it was my father whom they all feared for back then. The KMT had been targeting the country's elite, which included lawyers, professors, and doctors like him. My father knew enough to keep a low profile, but I wondered whether there was a part of him that itched to fight for freedom and democracy, like so many others. That had wanted to help the wounded and stop whatever suffering he could. Was there a rebellious part of him that wanted to defy my mother and grandparents and do what he believed was right? I couldn't help wondering whether he had secretly gotten involved somehow, and that was why they had eventually captured him. My heart swelled with pride for this supposed bravery of my father's, who had been so much stronger than me, because I'd never had the courage to go against my mother.

I'd thought about my father a lot over the years. Was he like me, born with a fire in his belly that he had to constantly suppress in order to be the dutiful son, husband, brother? Had he lain awake at night, staring up at the moon like me, aching for something, that elusive something that was always just out of reach? After all, I must have gotten my hidden defiance from someone, and it certainly wasn't from my mama. I liked to imagine that my father and I were similar in temperament and in our beliefs, even though I never knew him.

"You were our miracle baby." My mama's voice broke into my thoughts.

"What?" I turned to her, my forehead creased.

"We had trouble conceiving, even though your ah-ma kept giving me herbal supplements and teas." Mama looked away, back up at the building, as if trying to remember our lives here. "We lost four babies before we had you." She turned back to me. "We were happy, Ah-Hui. Just the three of us, a happy little family living in this building." Her smile dropped, and her expression hardened. "Until they took him away."

"Were you home, Mama?" I asked. I looked at the metal front gate and wondered whether they had come for him in the middle of the night, as we had slept. Maybe they'd stormed the building up to the fourth floor and pounded on the door until my father answered it. Had they grabbed him as soon as the door opened and dragged him out in his night clothes? Or had they allowed him to change? Had my mother held me and cried and wailed, or had she been silent, standing stoically aside because she knew there was nothing that she could do to stop them?

My mother didn't answer, so I tried again. "Or did they get him at his doctor's office?"

"Hush, Ah-Hui." My mother shushed me and turned her head away, but my imagination was already at work.

Maybe he'd been dragged away by the police from his doctor's office. That three, maybe four young men, silent and dark, had barged in and grabbed him as his patient cowered in a paper gown on the examination table. No one would try to stop them, because everyone was afraid that they would be next. I could see his nurse running out of the office when he was gone, all the way to our apartment to inform my mother.

"Not here." My mother gripped my arm, and her fingernails dug into my skin.

I knew my mother was cautioning me because a group of men had just walked by us in the road. They were loud, boisterous as they teased each other, and didn't seem to notice us, but even still, I knew my mother was right to be cautious. With one final look at the building, my mother turned and retraced her steps back toward the main street. I hurried to catch up, so many questions still running through my mind about what happened after they took my father. But I knew better than to ask. We walked in silence all the way back to my aunt and uncle's place, and by the time we arrived, we were both sweating profusely. I let my mother use the bathroom first while I sat on my new bed, thinking of all she'd just revealed to me. When she finally came back to my room, I turned to her, determined to get more answers.

"What happened after Baba was taken?" This one event had shaped my entire life, and yet I knew next to nothing about it because my mother had refused to speak of it until now.

She pursed her lips, and at first I thought she would refuse to answer me, but then she sighed and sat down in the desk chair.

"I spent days, weeks, months searching for him. First at the police stations, where I was told they had no record of him and knew nothing of what happened to him. They were sorry, but there was nothing they could do." She shook her head, and the familiar stubborn expression I was used to seeing these last years came over her face. "I asked around, called in favors from anyone with connections to the government, the police, who might know something. But no one did. He had disappeared without a trace, and no one knew where they'd taken him or if he was still alive."

We fell silent, so still I could literally hear my heart beating in my ears.

"I waited for months for him to come home," she finally said. "I was all alone with you, a tiny baby who screamed and cried no matter what I did. You wanted your baba, and I couldn't give him to you. I consulted fortune tellers, prayed to the gods with incense and offerings for your father's safe return. I followed every lead, every rumor that was whispered among the Taiwanese as to where they took the men who had disappeared over the years. But I couldn't do it anymore." She turned to me, her mouth in a firm line. "I had to go back to my parents' house. I only intended to stay until your father came home."

But he never did.

6

Joey
Present Day, Kauai

Joey jumped off the chair after reading her mother's translated words, too agitated to stay still. She had so many questions for Sam, but he was no longer here. She went out into the living room and found Ethan there, watching a game on TV.

"I wish Sam were here." She jammed a fist against the ear that still wouldn't pop. "It was always me and Sam against the world. I don't understand why he didn't tell me he was sick." She started pacing the small room. "I would have done everything I could to help him. Looked into treatments, made things better for him. Cooked for him. Whatever he needed." Joey's voice rose. "Why didn't he tell me?"

Ethan let her rant and pace for a few more minutes, and then the next time she passed him, he reached out and gently took hold of her forearm. She stopped, startled, and stared at his hand on her arm.

"Joey." He let go.

She stared at him for another moment before shaking her head slightly. She sank onto the couch, propping her elbows on her thighs and dropping her head into her hands.

He gave her a moment and then said, "This is exactly why he didn't tell you. He didn't want to be defined by the cancer. It's a brutal one, Joey. There is no miracle cure, no cure at all." He blew out a shaky breath. "I understand his choice, why he didn't want to wait for the cancer to devour him."

Joey burst into tears, burying her face in her hands. He let her cry for a moment and then placed a hand tentatively on her back.

"He wouldn't have wanted you to drop everything to see him deteriorate. You heard him in the video. He didn't want pity. Look at his life. He was one of the most vibrant, physically active people we knew. It would have killed him to not be able to do everything he's always done." Ethan stopped, but his hand on her back radiated warmth to her chilled skin, comforting her as she tried to control her sobs.

He hesitated and then drew her against him. She stayed still, allowing Ethan to absorb some of her pain, feeling as if she would break into pieces if he let go. She needed his comfort, yet she couldn't forget that he was married. She'd thought she was over her childish crush, but seeing him again after all this time only made her realize she'd never really gotten over him.

She pulled away, embarrassment coursing through her at thinking these thoughts when Sam was gone. She needed to focus on what her brother had revealed.

Agitated, she stood, her thoughts tumbling around in her head. She turned to Ethan.

"We need to get Wonton." As much as she wanted to watch the next video Sam had left for her, she needed the warmth and love of his dog even more in that moment.

She ached to hold the little dog in her arms, to breathe in her special doggy smell, hoping some part of Sam still lingered in Wonton's fur. How Sam had loved that dog. Wonton was the last connection to her brother, and Joey would take care of her as she knew Sam would have wanted. She would go and get Wonton and bring her home.

⁂

"Joey, oh, you poor thing. Come here, give me a hug."

Linda Kelly reached out and enveloped Joey in her arms. Joey allowed herself to be smothered by Sam's next-door neighbor, a woman in her early seventies with short, cropped silver hair and a body tanned and toned from daily walks and swims. Her ample bosom cradled Joey's head, and tears sprang to Joey's eyes again. She needed the comfort Linda provided, needed the connection to the very last people who had probably seen Sam alive who knew him. They had been the ones to call the police when Sam hadn't come home from Anini Beach that day and taken Wonton home with them. They were the ones to call Victor when Sam's body had been found.

Linda let go and hugged Ethan too. Then she gestured for them to come in. "Wonton is going to be so happy to see you."

As if on cue, a brown-and-white Chiweenie came dashing into the foyer and launched herself onto Joey's legs and then Ethan's, her tail wagging so fast it was a blur.

"Wonton!" Joey bent down to pet the dog, and Wonton jumped into her arms, frantically licking whatever part of Joey she could reach. Joey laughed and then hugged the dog to her, tears stinging her eyes as she held the dog that Sam had considered his child.

"Joey. You're here."

Joey looked up at the deep voice and saw Mac Kelly standing by the screened-in door that led to the backyard. Mac was as lean as his wife, with a full head of white hair and a white beard. His tan made his blue eyes even bluer.

He walked over to Joey and opened his arms wide, wrapping them around both Joey and Wonton in a hug that had the tears dripping down her cheeks again. "We're so sorry about Sam."

"We are, honey." Linda's voice was full of sympathy.

"Thank you. For what you did for Sam. For being here for him and taking care of Wonton." Joey pulled away from Mac so that she could look him in the eyes.

She clamped her lips together to keep the emotions in check. Sam had told her how kind his neighbors were, always looking out for him, bringing him food, and offering to watch Wonton when he traveled to the mainland to visit friends or overseas to see Joey.

"You okay?" Linda asked, peering at her.

She nodded. "As okay as I can be, finding out what was happening to Sam."

Mac ushered them into the living room, and they sat down. Wonton came over to Joey and claimed a spot on her lap. She was glad for the warm weight of the dog, who was keeping her grounded at a time when she felt like she might splinter into a million pieces.

"I'm glad you finally know." Linda clasped her hands over her knees.

Mac leaned toward Joey. "I have to say, I tried to convince him to tell you. But he was adamant. He didn't want you to know until he was gone. He wanted to decide when he would leave this world without placing any guilt or worry on your shoulders."

Joey nodded. "That sounds like Sam. He was always so stubborn when he made up his mind about something." Even so, she was grateful he'd had the Kellys and Ethan in his last days. "Can you tell me more? How was he, really?" Joey laid a hand on Wonton's back as she looked from Linda to Mac.

"He was resigned." Linda's voice was firm. "His diagnosis made him sad because he loved life. Loved you two and wanted to grow old with you."

"He told us one night, a few months ago." Mac's kind eyes met Joey's.

"Do you know how we met Sam?" Linda interjected.

Joey shook her head.

"This was years ago, when he first bought the condo after he sold the house he lived in with you. He was sitting at the bar by himself at Lemongrass Grill, down in Kapaa. Mac and I walked in and sat next to him to have a drink before dinner. We started talking and then found out he was the one who'd just bought the unit next to ours." Linda beamed at the memory. "How's that for a coincidence?"

"Really?" Ethan's voice held amusement. "All the way down in Kapaa, and you happen to walk into the same bar at the same time?"

"Yup." Linda smiled. "You know how some people just come into your life at the right time? That was Sam for us." She looked over at Mac. "We don't have any kids, so having Sam in our lives has been like having a son."

Joey's breath hitched. "Thank you," she said when she could talk. "You don't know what that means to me that he had someone—" She broke off and cleared her throat. "He was my everything—brother, father, mother. But I forget sometimes that he lost his parents too. He didn't have anyone watching over him."

"He had us." Linda's lips quivered and she pressed a hand to them.

"I'm so glad." Joey gave Wonton's belly a rub when she flipped onto her back.

"He had Ethan too," Linda said.

Joey nodded, her eyes brimming with tears. "My head understands why he didn't want to tell me, but my heart hurts, knowing he had you all with him at the end but not me. I wish I'd been here." Joey swallowed down the sob that threatened to escape. "I wish I'd been able to give him a final hug, to tell him in person that I love him more than he knows and thank him for taking care of me all these years."

"He knew," Linda said. "He didn't want you to see him like that." She paused, then added in a gentle voice, "We should be getting his ashes back in a few days."

"Oh." Joey was at a loss for words. Part of the reason she was here was to scatter Sam's ashes somewhere on the island at his request, but the reality of spreading what was left of her brother made her balk.

They sat for a moment in silence until Wonton started scratching at her legs, making her laugh. "What, Wonton?"

The dog gave a yip, and stood up on her hind legs, making them all chuckle.

"You think she misses Sam?" Joey asked.

"Definitely." Linda reached over to pat Wonton on the head. "Every time we take her for a walk, she tries to pull us back to your brother's condo. She keeps staring at the door and then back at us, wondering why she's with us and not home with Sam."

Joey cuddled Wonton against her chest. "What's going to happen to her?"

"Sam wanted you to have her, but if you're not able to because of travel, we'll take care of her." Linda laughed as Wonton licked her hand. "She'll always have a home with us if needed."

"Thank you." Joey kissed Wonton on the top of the head and stood, cradling the little dog in her arms. "Is it okay if I take her for now? I don't know what my plans are, if I'm going back to Malaysia or home to New York. But I'll be here for at least a week." Holding Wonton in her arms already made her feel better, as if she had a part of Sam with her.

"Of course, take her." Mac stood and went to get the harness and leash hanging on a hook by the front door. He put them on the little dog and handed the leash to Joey.

She looked at Ethan. "I want to go to Anini Beach. Where Sam loved to swim." Where his body was found. She needed to see it, to see where her brother was when he'd taken his last breath.

Ethan nodded. "We can take Wonton there now. Then get something to eat." He looked at his phone. "It's past lunchtime. You must be hungry."

Joey paused, thinking maybe she should watch the next video Sam had left her so she could find her mother's journal. But she needed time to absorb everything, and her stomach was grumbling. The journal could wait.

"That's a good plan." She nodded. "I can find out where my mother's journal is when we get back."

They said goodbye to the Kellys, Joey promising to have dinner with them the next night, then went out to the parking lot.

"You want me to drive?" Ethan gestured to a dark-green SUV parked in a visitor spot.

"Sure."

They got into the car, Joey holding Wonton in her arms. Linda had given her a roll of poop bags, which she tucked into her purse, and then she snuggled the dog against her chest, wishing so much that her brother was still here. She started to say something to Ethan, but the blocked ear made her wince. She opened her mouth wide, hoping that would help.

"What's the matter?" Ethan looked at her in concern as he backed out of the spot.

"My ear. It didn't pop when the plane landed. I feel slightly deaf." She fake-yawned again, but nothing happened.

"Take a deep breath and hold your nose shut with your fingers. Then try blowing out, as if forcing air out of your plugged nostrils."

She did as he suggested, but nothing happened except the left ear popped.

"We'll go to the store later for Sudafed. It'll help clear up the congestion." Ethan reached out and touched her briefly on the side of her head.

She bit her lip, trying to ignore the tingling where his fingers just were. Suddenly, being in the enclosed space of a car felt far too intimate. She struggled to focus on the task at hand, going to see the last place where her brother had been alive, and not on how her body seemed to yearn for Ethan. She looked out the window and said little during the ten-minute drive.

Ethan parked along the side of the road, and they got out, walking Wonton across the grass and toward the beach. They stopped at the edge of the sand, and Joey looked out over the ocean, imagining Sam going into the water for his last swim, knowing he wouldn't be coming back out. How had he done it? How had he found the courage to swim out there and . . .

Joey shook her head, unable to continue the thought. It was so beautiful, the waves crashing and rushing up to the sand, families gathered together under colorful umbrellas, swimmers bobbing in the water as children played on the shore. The sun was warm on her skin, and a light breeze lifted her hair, tickling the back of her neck. How could this be the place where her brother had died? Was this where Sam had wanted his ashes scattered? He hadn't specified, and she wondered how she was supposed to know.

Wonton pulled on the leash, wanting to go on the sand, and Joey followed with Ethan trailing behind. They went to the right, away from where most people had set up on the sand, until all they could hear was the roar of the ocean and the rush of the wind.

Joey stopped to gaze out at the blue, blue water.

"Bye, Sam." She finally spoke as she imagined seeing her brother's strong form swimming out to sea until he disappeared into the horizon. She turned to Ethan. "Where was his body found?"

"On the other side of the boat launch." Ethan pointed back the way they came.

"Oh." Tears dripped down her face, and she closed her eyes for a moment, letting her grief wash over her without trying to suppress it. She felt Ethan move closer to her side, and his presence soothed her, made her feel less alone.

When she opened her eyes, Ethan had a tissue in his hand, and she took it from him with a grateful nod. Once she'd used it, she turned to him.

"Did Sam ever talk to you about our parents and what happened when they died?"

Ethan shook his head. "Not really. He was angry in those early years. That's why he joined the triathlon training group. He needed to burn off some of that stress. He only said he had to protect you from whatever it was that killed your parents. I got the feeling that it was something horrible."

Joey stared out at the ocean. "He wouldn't tell me why he made my nanny go away. You know how stubborn he was. Eventually, I stopped asking. And we never spoke of her again."

"You weren't curious?"

"I was. But I was also so sad. I had so much to deal with back then. And I trusted Sam." She pulled her hair away from her face, wishing she had an elastic to tie it back.

"And now?"

"I need to know everything." Joey turned toward Ethan. "I only knew my parents through the lens of a child. I never wondered what their lives were like. What they felt, what they dreamed about. I always held out hope that I'd find a relationship like theirs." She gave a dry laugh. "Now I find out it was all a lie. That the nanny I idolized was flawed, too, not who I thought she was."

"I'm sorry." Ethan spoke quietly.

They turned and walked back the way they came, closer to the spot where Ethan had said they'd found Sam's body. There was so much she wanted to ask her brother. So much they never talked about and she'd let slide because Sam would get that stubborn look on his face and refuse to talk whenever she asked about their parents or their past.

She let out a sound of frustration, and Ethan shot her a sympathetic look.

"Do you know I grew up not knowing anything about the history of Taiwan?" She had to talk, had to get some of the thoughts inside her head off her chest. "I knew my grandfather had disappeared during the White Terror, but it was a distant thought, as if it had happened in a history book, not connected to me at all. As I got older, I knew that Taiwan had been under martial law until 1987, but again, it was so far from my reality that I never thought about how it affected my family."

As an adult, Joey had learned about the Japanese occupation of Taiwan from 1895 to 1945, and that the KMT had taken over after that in a reign of terror that had ensued until too recently. She'd read about how the people who had fought for Taiwan democracy had been thrown in jail, disappeared, or tortured, or their families had been killed. It froze her blood at the turmoil the Taiwanese had lived through and the fight that continued to this day for Taiwan democracy. But it was all so far removed from her reality. She'd been safely cosseted in the cocoon and life Sam had carved out for her, never returning to Taiwan or wondering about her ancestors. How had she become so Americanized?

"Sam wanted to keep you away from Taiwan politics as much as possible." Ethan's voice brought her back to the beach. "Victor kept trying to get him involved. That was one of the reasons Sam decided to do his residency in Hawaii. He wanted you as far away from all that as possible."

Wonton stopped to sniff at a rock, and Joey paused, digging her toes into the sand. "I don't know if you know, but I have an apartment in New York that I keep as a home base between my travels. Victor once invited me to a rally in Union Square in Manhattan, an event where hundreds of Taiwanese marched and gathered, calling for Taiwan's inclusion in the UN." She looked at Ethan out of the corner of her eye. "I declined, not understanding what the fuss was about. I never equated what I knew about Taiwan history with my own family. Never wondered what it was like for my mother to live during that time."

She sat in the sand, and Wonton flopped down next to her. Ethan also sat, so close to her that she could feel the warmth radiating off his skin. She willed herself not to notice, not to move an inch closer so that their skin touched.

Joey stared out at the horizon, so many thoughts running through her head. Sam, her parents, the mysterious something that Sam alluded to, that he had kept from her all this time. She thought also of Victor and decided she would give him a call soon to ask him more about Taiwan. He was still heavily involved in Taiwan's fight for independence, and maybe it was time she learned more about it.

"Are you okay?" Ethan's voice startled her out of her thoughts.

She turned to look at him, her breath catching at how handsome she still found him. How she yearned for him to see her, really see her, and not just as his best friend's little sister. But he wasn't available, and she forced herself to look back at the ocean.

"I'm not." She couldn't lie to him. "I want Sam back. I want my parents back. I want to be with my mother, making the *zongzi* she and Ren Ren Ayi used to make for the Double Fifth Festival."

Joey's mouth watered, remembering even all these years later the sticky, glutinous rice that her mother had stuffed with shiitake and wood ear mushrooms, bamboo shoots, peanuts, and salted duck eggs, all wrapped in a bamboo leaf and tied up with string. She remembered the long pole of a mop that Ren Ren Ayi used to prop up between two chairs, and the way her mother had hung up the many *zongzi* bundles when they came out of the giant steamer. Joey had loved to poke at the bundles all strung up on the pole like decorative green lanterns swinging in the air. It would take days to make them all, and she had loved opening one up when it was cool enough to eat, the fragrant steam of the rice and savory stuffing wafting out, tantalizing her.

"Is that also known as the Dragon Boat Festival?" Ethan asked.

She nodded. "It begins on the fifth day of the fifth lunar month, marking the start of the summer solstice." She turned to Ethan, being careful not to meet his eyes. "I wished I'd learned to make the *zongzi* from my mother. I've had them since, at a little stand in Flushing, Queens, and all over Asia, but they are never the same as my mother's."

"Did she cook a lot?" Ethan shifted in the sand, stretching his legs out in front of him.

Somehow, their shoulders were now touching, and Joey had to work really hard not to lean into him, not to drop her head on his shoulder.

"Not really. She was so busy working as a doctor. But she liked to make things for special occasions. When she had a day off, she'd sometimes make big batches of wontons and dumplings that we would freeze and take out whenever we needed a quick meal."

How Joey used to love to help pinch together the dumplings after her mother had dropped a dollop of the filling in the middle of the wrapper. Her heart longed to be at the kitchen table with her mother again, ringing the edges of the wrapper with her fingers, wet from where she'd dipped them into a bowl of water so that the dough would stick together firmly. The oyster omelets her mother and father used to make together, sweet potato starch mixed into the egg mixture to give it a thick chewy consistency, as well as the oyster vermicelli noodle soup that had been her father's favorite. Regret coursed through her at all she'd missed from her parents, and the loss of them felt again like a fresh wound, splitting open and spilling blood.

"That sounds really good."

"It was." Joey stood and picked up Wonton's leash from where she'd dropped it in the sand. "I'm starving. Let's go eat, then I want to find out where Sam put the journal."

She squared her shoulders, trying to ignore Ethan's presence next to her. It was time she stopped hiding her head in the sand like an ostrich. It was time to find out what Sam had left her, as soon as she had a meal and could think clearly again.

7

They sat at a high top on the lanai of a small family-owned restaurant, sipping on Mai Tais while they waited for their food to arrive. They'd decided to drive to Hanalei after leaving Anini Beach because Joey had good memories of spending the day there with Sam the last time she was on Kauai.

"Here." Ethan handed Joey the box of Sudafed he'd picked up from the Big Save Market down the road while she waited for a table, and she nodded her thanks. "Don't take these until bedtime, since you're having a drink now."

She nodded and gave him a small smile, realizing with embarrassment that she'd cried more today than she'd done in years.

"Thanks for being here." She reached out to touch him lightly on the forearm.

He nodded. "Of course."

Joey took another sip of her drink before looking at Ethan. "How is your daughter? Rory, right?"

"Yes. She's great." Ethan's face lit up at the mention of Rory. "She's a moody, dramatic teenager, but she's got a good head on her shoulders."

"The last time I saw her, she was just a small thing." Joey remembered a pretty little girl with curly light-brown hair and big brown eyes. Ethan's wife was also half Japanese like him.

"And now she's a sixteen-year-old who thinks I work too much." Ethan rolled his eyes. "Rory thinks I'm wasting my potential."

"Wasting your potential?" Joey laughed. "What does that mean? And how's Naomi?" She slipped that in casually, remembering the sting to her heart when Sam had told her Ethan had gotten engaged. Ethan knew about Joey's childhood crush on him. Once she reached high school, though, she'd hidden it from him well, or so she'd thought. That was when she'd started to avoid Ethan, determined to move on and find her soulmate like her mother had found with her father. But true love had always eluded her.

"She's good. Although I haven't talked to her in a while, except in matters regarding Rory." One of Ethan's shoulders lifted and then fell. "And Rory and I have very different ideas of what I should be doing with my life."

"Oh?" Joey tried to keep her tone neutral, even though she was dying to know more about Ethan's family and life. And then the meaning of his words hit her. "Wait, what do you mean you haven't talked to her in a while?"

"Naomi?" Ethan put down the water glass in his hand. "You know we separated, right?"

"What?" Joey felt her eyebrows rise in surprise. "When?"

"About two years ago. When Rory started high school." He paused. "Sam didn't tell you? The divorce was finalized a couple of months ago."

Joey's jaw dropped and all she could think was, *Ethan's not married.* And then her next thought was, *Why didn't Sam tell me?*

When she could finally speak, she said, "I didn't know."

In all fairness, she'd told Sam when Ethan had gotten engaged that she didn't want to talk about Ethan ever again. She'd sensed Sam knew how she felt about Ethan, but they'd never discussed it. Joey had assumed Sam didn't want to get in the middle of anything between his sister and his best friend.

They were silent as the waitress put a plate of coconut shrimp between them. Joey picked one up and dipped it into the sriracha aioli as soon as the waitress left. She was starving, and the appetizer smelled so good. Ethan took one, too, and it wasn't until they'd eaten them that Joey spoke again.

"What happened?" She stopped, embarrassed. "You don't have to tell me. Sorry. I'm being nosy."

"It's okay." Ethan gave her a crooked smile before picking up another shrimp. "Naomi didn't like Kauai. The schools aren't the greatest, even though Rory had some amazing teachers. Naomi wanted to move back to California where we lived before we came out here."

"Oh." Joey widened her eyes at him. They'd divorced because Naomi didn't like Kauai?

"It was more than that." Ethan seemed to read her mind. "We realized we were better as friends than as husband and wife. It was all very civil." Ethan took a bite of the shrimp before he continued. "We tried a separation for a while, and she took Rory back to California. I visited as much as I could, and Rory came here for the summer. About a year ago, Naomi and I realized we were happier apart than together."

"And Rory lives with Naomi?" Joey didn't have kids, but she could imagine how hard it would be not to see her child every day.

Ethan nodded, his eyes sad. "I don't like not being in Rory's life every day. I thought of going with them, getting an apartment by Naomi's place so I could see her more. But Sam needed me here. Our practice is thriving, and to be honest, I love it here." He looked away and picked up his drink. "It was a hard decision, and some people might think I'm selfish—"

"Hey." Joey cut him off. "You're not selfish. And you see her as much as you can, right?"

Ethan nodded. "Yes. I go back at least once a month, and she now spends every holiday with me." He smiled, and for a moment, Joey was mesmerized by the dimple that appeared in his left cheek. "We have a great relationship, except that she thinks I should be dating and getting back out there. That I'm wasting away living for my job and nothing else."

"You're not dating anyone?" Joey looked down at her Mai Tai, not wanting Ethan to see the red tingeing her cheeks. But why should that matter to her? After her last disastrous relationship, she'd come to the realization that maybe she wasn't fated to fall in love. That she'd never have what her parents had. Which she now knew was a lie.

"No." There was laughter in his voice. "I'm happy with my life. I have a wonderful daughter, I love my job, and I love this island."

"You're not . . . lonely?"

"Are you?" Ethan gave her a pointed look. "Sam said you never seem to have any long-term relationships. Except with someone named Oliver."

Joey's eyes widened. "You know about Oliver?"

Ethan shook his head. "I only know that Sam was spitting mad about that guy. Kept cursing him and saying he wanted to kill him for hurting you."

"Oh." Joey took a long drink of her Mai Tai, feeling the alcohol warming her insides as it slid down her throat smoothly.

"What happened with Oliver?" Ethan raised an eyebrow at her. "We can drop the subject if you'd rather not talk about him."

Joey blew out a breath. "Oliver." His name on her tongue tasted bitter. "I don't want to get into the whole drama, but basically, Oliver was the man I thought was my soulmate, the man I've waited for my whole life. But I found out eight months into the relationship that he was married. And he wanted to stay married. And keep seeing me." She let out a harsh laugh. "Can you believe that? He said he loved both of us and didn't want to let me go."

"Ouch." Ethan's face was full of sympathy.

"I couldn't believe how stupid I was. He was married." Joey's cheeks flamed, just thinking about that humiliating day when she'd called Oliver.

"A woman answered his phone one day. I thought it was his assistant. But then the woman said she was Oliver's wife. I thought it was a joke at first and I laughed." She scrunched her nose in disgust. "Because

I thought Oliver and I were in love. We were soulmates, just like my parents; Oliver had said so himself." She shook her head, thinking again how stupid she'd been. "I thought he was the man that I'd waited my whole life for, the only man that had made me put my lifelong wanderlust on the back burner, turning down assignments so I could spend more time with him in New York."

"I'm so sorry." Ethan didn't reach out to touch her, for which Joey was grateful. "That must have been such a blow."

"Yes." She gave a wry smile. "He kept encouraging me to take assignments, go on my trips, and now I know why. Because he was hiding a whole other life the entire eight months we'd been dating."

"You must have been devastated."

Joey nodded. "Devastated beyond words. I never wanted to be 'the other woman.' And yet, I was. I was not only crushed by his betrayal but also felt guilty for causing his wife pain. I called Maggie right away and she consoled me."

Joey looked out onto the road, watching the cars going by as she thought of how Maggie had found her in a heap on the ground. She'd literally felt her heart breaking in her chest as tears clogged her throat and she tried to wrap her mind around the fact that the man she thought was her destiny was already married to someone else.

Maggie had been livid and demanded that Joey take out all the framed pictures of Joey and Oliver and throw them away. "He doesn't deserve you. I will cut off his balls if he comes near you again. Stay away from him."

Joey had sputtered out a laugh, thankful that Maggie always had her back. But she hadn't heeded Maggie's warning. She needed to hear from Oliver himself that he was married, and that their entire relationship was a sham.

"What did Oliver have to say for himself?" Ethan's face was a stony mask, and he looked like he was about to jump up and find Oliver.

Joey gave a small laugh. "He told me he loved me. And he kept apologizing, saying how he hadn't meant to lie to me, but he'd fallen for me hard and couldn't stop his feelings. He loved me, nothing was a lie. His feelings were *so* real." Joey drew out the word "so" the way Oliver had done.

"But he loved his wife too?" Ethan's eyes narrowed and he looked ready to murder Oliver.

"I asked if he was going to leave her. And he couldn't say yes. He said he loved her in a different way." Joey took a sip of water to soothe the ache in her throat. "I lost it after that and told him never to contact me again. But he persisted and texted and left messages for me constantly." She put her glass down, playing with the shrimp on her plate. "And then his wife, Mara, started calling me. She told me she was leaving Oliver, that I could have him. He threatened to kill himself if she did that, and she wanted me to take care of him. Make sure he didn't do as he threatened."

"Oh god." Ethan stared at her in disbelief. "That's a horrible thing to put on you."

Joey ran a hand over her face. "I know. I ignored it at first, still refusing to take his calls or answer his texts. Until he left a message telling me that he was going to shoot himself that night if I didn't take him back."

"Joey. I'm so sorry." Ethan's face reflected his shock.

"Yeah. I guess he couldn't convince Mara to stay, so he tried me instead." She sighed. "That was when I realized Oliver was a master manipulator. I knew he wouldn't do it. He's too vain, too sure of his entitled place in this world. I called his bluff, and sure enough, he didn't do anything. I told him I'd get a restraining order if he kept bothering me, and he finally stopped. That was over three years ago."

The thought of Oliver no longer made her angry, but it was still a pang in her heart that she'd been so easily duped by a man she'd thought she loved and trusted deeply. They sat in silence until the waitress had set down their main courses. Joey picked up a slice of the veggie pizza she'd ordered but didn't take a bite.

Ethan finally spoke. "What an awful thing to go through."

She bit into her pizza, swallowing before answering. "It was tough. I swore off relationships after that. If I couldn't have what my parents had, then I didn't want it at all. And now I find out that was all a lie."

"It doesn't mean there isn't someone out there for you." Ethan's voice was gentle, and Joey looked away, not wanting to be sucked in by Ethan's expressive eyes.

"I don't know." Joey gave a careless shrug. "Maybe my family is cursed when it comes to relationships. Look at my parents. And Sam." She gestured with one hand. "He never had a long-term relationship, as far as I know."

Joey thought back to a conversation she'd had with Sam last month when she'd visited him. They were lying on the sand on giant colorful towels at Kalapaki Beach after Joey had gotten back to shore on her paddleboard. She'd wondered then why Sam hadn't gone out with her, but now knowing about his diagnosis, it made sense.

"Why have you never married?" She'd asked him with her eyes closed.

"What?" She felt Sam sitting up next to her.

"I was just thinking about why neither of us ever got married." It would have been nice to expand their family, to have a sister-in-law, and nieces and nephews.

"I have my reasons." His voice was hard.

She opened her eyes to see her brother looking away from her. "What are they?"

She used to think it was her fault that Sam never had a serious relationship, that the women he was interested in had been scared off because he was raising her. But over the years, Sam never introduced her to anyone special. She knew he dated, but none ever lasted more than a few months.

He hadn't answered her question. His jaw had tightened, always a sign that he didn't want to do something. Joey waited, hoping he'd tell her. But he hadn't and she'd let it go as she'd always done in the face of Sam's stubbornness.

"I think what happened to your parents had a profound effect on Sam." Ethan's comment brought Joey back to the restaurant. "Not just the fact that your father had an affair but also whatever it was that happened that's been torturing Sam all these years. It made him not trust relationships."

"And now he's gone." Joey looked down at her hands. "I don't have any family left. Both my parents were estranged from their families. They never told me why, and Sam didn't either. The closest person we had to family is my father's old friend, Victor."

Ethan drummed his fingers on the table and then said, "Sam once told me that your mother was promised to some other man but she ran away to New York with your father, causing the rift in her family."

"Really? I didn't know that." Joey sat back in her chair and put her hand on Wonton's back, thinking about this. "Like an arranged marriage?"

"Kind of. I think they met, so it wasn't completely blind." He jerked a shoulder. "He didn't say much about it."

"We need to get back. I need to read the rest of my mother's journal." She was suddenly impatient to find out where it was.

"Okay, let me get the check and we'll go."

Joey stood, Wonton next to her, shifting impatiently until the check was finally paid for. She didn't speak in the short car ride back and went right into the office as soon as they arrived. She found the next video and clicked it open before she even sat down. Vaguely, she was aware of Ethan coming into the room, but her entire attention was on Sam.

"Aloha, Joey." Sam's smile on-screen was sad, but Joey's heart lifted all the same. It was so good to see him, even if it was only in a video. "I know you think I'm a control freak, and here I am, proving you right again by dictating when you get to read our mother's journal."

Joey barked out a laugh because Sam was right, of course.

"But you know why I do that, right? Our lives were blown up, so much out of our control. If I didn't keep a tight rein on the things I *could* control, I felt like everything would spiral. And I couldn't have that happening. I needed everything to be good for you."

"I know, Sam," Joey whispered. "I know."

"Since you're watching this, I assume you read the snippet I left you from our mother's journal and you want to know more. Our mother's translated journal is in a binder where I keep my cookbooks. I figured I'd hide it in plain sight, since I know you don't cook at all." His condescending grin on camera made her heart ache, as it was so real, so Sam. At the same time, he nailed it since Joey hated to cook and would never have thought to browse through Sam's cookbooks.

She was about to jump off the chair and run into the kitchen when Sam's next words stopped her.

"Before you get it and start reading, I wanted to tell you a bit more first. So settle down." He wiggled his brows, and she couldn't help the laugh that escaped. Even in death, her brother knew her too well.

"When I was seventeen and graduated from high school on Kauai a year early, our parents decided to become traveling physicians in Southeast Asia." Sam stopped and made a face. "It was our mother's idea. She never said, but I think she hoped to leave Ren Ren behind and just be a family of four again. But as you know, that didn't happen. Ren Ren came with us." He paused and then looked back into the camera. "Before I left for college in New York, I confronted our father about the affair."

"But how did you know?" Joey asked out loud.

As if reading her mind, Sam said in the video, "I saw them together when I was sixteen. At home, when our mother was working at the clinic." He scrubbed a hand down his face. "I used to idolize our father. He was the whole world to me. But then I saw them together when they thought no one was home—" He broke off and took a deep breath. "It ruined me. It wrecked my trust in him. I couldn't believe what I was seeing. They didn't know I was home. They were out on the back lanai and Ren Ren was sitting in his lap. He had a hand down her pants and . . ." Sam trailed off, as if unable to continue.

Joey drew in a sharp breath and her heart hurt for her mother all over again. How could their father have done that? How could he have been so selfish?

"I confronted him later that night, after everyone had gone to bed. I told him it was disgusting what he was doing, and that he had to stop." Sam's face was set in a scowl. "Do you know what he said to me?" He blew out a breath. "He told me I didn't understand. That he loves our mother very much but that there were things I couldn't comprehend." Sam shook his head. "He said he often felt inferior to our mother. She was so smart, so brilliant. Ren Ren looked up to him, and her fire for Taiwan filled a void inside him. I told him to send Ren Ren away. But he refused. My opinion of our father was forever altered after that."

Joey brought her hands up in front of her chest, her heart breaking at what her brother was saying. She, too, had idolized their father, thinking he was the best man in the world. Now she was finding out he wasn't.

"I knew then that our father was weak." Sam continued to speak on-screen. "He wasn't the hero that I thought he was. He was a product of his generation, growing up in Taiwan in a time when women were basically owned by men. It didn't matter that he went to university in New York. Our Taiwanese culture was ingrained in him, and he thought it was his right to have a wife and a mistress."

Joey could only shake her head.

Sam stared into the camera. "I think he knew my opinion of him changed, because he tried to talk to me before I went to New York. He told me he'd stayed away from Ren Ren for eleven years. As if I should give him a medal for that . . ."

Sam trailed off and Joey held her breath, wondering what else he would reveal.

"I saw him for what he was: a flawed, entitled man who thought it was okay to sleep with the woman who was taking care of his children and living in his home." Sam blew out a breath. "A few weeks before I left for New York, I tried to convince our mother to come with me.

But she wouldn't. She said he'd never let you go, and she wouldn't leave without you."

"Oh, Mama." Joey's heart hurt thinking she was the reason why their mother had stayed.

"I knew then that I was never going to get married. I saw what it did to our mother and how it made our father think he had all the power in the relationship. It isn't right." Sam clenched his jaw. "I know there are relationships that are equal, and people who have happy marriages, but I knew it wasn't for me. That's why I have never had a serious relationship. I never wanted to do to another person what our father did to our mother." He looked down for a moment. "I think I was afraid there was some part of him that's in me, and I didn't want to take that chance."

Joey's nose stung as tears gathered behind her eyes. What a mess their whole family was when it came to relationships. Joey was following right along in their footsteps.

Sam looked back up on the screen. "There's more to this video, but wait until you've read our mother's journal to watch it. I'll help you try to make sense of it and of what our mother did." He gave a small, sad smile. "I'm sorry, Joey. For everything."

Joey wasn't sure what he was apologizing for—his decision to keep everything from her? Or what happened to their family? Whatever it was, she could see the sincerity in her brother's eyes, and even though she wished he'd trusted her enough to tell her all this while he was alive, she knew he'd had his reasons for not doing so.

She reached out to stop the video and then ran from the room, past Ethan, who stood aside to let her pass. Once in the kitchen, she spotted the stack of cookbooks on the side of the microwave and scanned the spines. Finding three binders, she pulled them all out and saw that two contained recipes he'd printed out but the third contained their mother's journal.

"I'm going to go, let you have privacy." She looked up at Ethan's words.

"Thank you." Her heart melted at how considerate he was, but she didn't have time to dwell on that. Right now, all she could think of was her mother's words.

Without putting the rest of the binders back in place, Joey took the journal and settled on the couch, Wonton next to her. She heard Ethan leaving the condo as she began to read.

8

Ah-Hui
1972, Taichung

I stood in the dirt road in front of my grandparents' house, taking in a deep breath and feeling a wave of calm wash over me. I was home. It didn't matter that I hadn't lived here full time since I went away to attend middle school. Whenever I thought of the word "home," my mind always conjured up images of this house on the outskirts of Taichung. A simple structure in the middle of acres filled with fruit trees, it had wooden slats over the windows to keep out the sun but let in the breeze. There was always dust everywhere, stirred up by the wind or by the dogs, cats, chickens, and ducks who roamed freely on the grounds.

A gust of wind made the dirt swirl, and some of it got in my eyes, stinging them before I squeezed them shut. I kept my mouth closed tightly, remembering how the grit would fill my mouth if I was laughing when the wind blew. When I opened my eyes again, I smiled to see the resplendent fruit trees I used to help Ah-Ma tend: lychees, apple pears, and star fruit, along with grapes that my grandmother grew on vines. A dog walked by me toward the house, and I could see another one curled up under the giant tree in the front. A chicken came up to me, clucking and trying to peck my feet as I danced away, laughing. I'd missed the animals, living in the city. It was so good to be home.

The front door opened, and my tiny grandmother stuck her head out the door. Her face lit up at the sight of me, and she let out a girlish squeal.

"Ah-Hui! You're home."

She came barreling toward me, and I dropped my bag, opening my arms to pull her close. My mother rarely hugged me, and it was always my ah-ma who comforted me if I hurt myself or held me tight when I had a nightmare. I'd missed her so much. I'd been so busy with my studies at NTU for the past four years that I hadn't been back to see my family in over a year.

"Come, come." She grabbed my arm with one hand and my bag with the other, practically dragging me inside. "Everyone's waiting for you."

"Everyone?" I asked before I stumbled over a rock. I would have fallen if not for the firm grip my grandmother had on my arm.

"You'll see." She turned and winked at me, and a knot of worry lodged itself in my stomach.

I didn't like that look. It told me she or my mother (or both) were up to something. I'd hoped for a quiet time at home, to recharge before I returned for my fifth year at NTU. I didn't want to entertain company. But when I walked in and saw only my mother and grandfather in the main room, I let out a sigh of relief. They greeted me but didn't embrace me as my grandmother had. That had always been their way.

"Come sit." My mother gestured to the spot next to her on the old brown couch that had been there for as long as I could remember.

When I was settled at her side, she turned to study me, her eyes running over my hair, which was cut short and neatly combed, my navy skirt and white blouse, clean and only slightly wrinkled from my train ride, and the black sensible shoes I'd left by the door. She gave a nod of approval and poured me a cup of tea from the porcelain set on the table in front of us.

I sipped the oolong tea, closing my eyes for a moment as the familiar taste lingered on my tongue. Tea elsewhere never tasted as good as what my grandmother served in this house. When I opened my eyes, I found three other sets studying me.

"What?" I looked from one face to the other, wondering what was going on.

"We have good news." My mother spoke with a hint of pride. "We have found you the perfect match."

"Match for what?" I put my cup down, slow on the uptake.

"Your future husband." My mother announced this as if I should break out into applause, but I sat unmoving, trying to understand her words. "I consulted a fortune teller, and she has finally found an auspicious match for you."

"Oh." My eyebrows rose as I looked from my mother to my grandmother and then my grandfather. I'd known this day would come, for my mother had talked of finding a good match for me from the time I was little, but I was so busy with my studies that I hadn't given marriage any thought in the last few years. Sure, boys had flirted with me, and sometimes I flirted back, but I was too focused on my schoolwork to be distracted by the opposite sex.

"They'll be here any minute." My mother's words made my head snap up.

"I'm meeting him now?" I didn't know whether to be terrified or elated.

"Yes. No time like the present. You're so busy with school." My mother patted me on the leg. "We're so proud of you."

I dropped my gaze, murmuring something in agreement, and picked up my cup of tea. I'd been a good daughter, very filial in my duties and responsibilities. My future had been planned out since middle school. Medical School at NTU for seven years, and somewhere in there, marriage to a man they would pick for me with the help of a matchmaker, then children. I accepted it all, even though that fire in my belly continued to burn with a need I didn't know how to fill.

I wondered whether my father would have understood. What words of advice he would have had for me, had he been around to watch me grow up.

A knock came at the door and my grandmother jumped, almost dropping her cup. Her hands were shaking, and when I tried to catch her gaze, she avoided me by turning away. I narrowed my eyes. What was wrong with her? My mother was the one who answered the door and came back with a woman about her age who looked vaguely familiar and a young man that I assumed was her son hovering behind her.

My mother came to my side and proudly presented me.

"Huang Tai Tai, please meet my daughter, Hui-Zhong. We call her Ah-Hui. She has just returned from medical school at National Taiwan University to visit us."

Was it my imagination or had my mother's voice gotten louder when she said the name of the university?

Huang Tai Tai, who I now recognized as the wife of a prominent and well-respected businessman in Taichung, gave me a polite nod and the faintest of smiles. She had her hair pulled back in a bun so severe it made her eyes look like slits, and she was wearing a red *qipao* that looked way too fancy for our country home. Something about their family name niggled at the back of my mind, but I couldn't think of what was bothering me in that moment.

"She's very pretty," Huang Tai Tai said, her eyes roaming over my body, making me feel like I was being inspected for sale.

"And smart," my mother put in. "She consistently ranks at the top of her class at NTU."

Huang Tai Tai nodded. "So we've heard." She pushed her son in front of her. "This is Li-Jie, our second son."

He reached out to shake my hand, and I had to stop myself from cringing at the limp, slightly damp appendage that clasped mine so weakly it felt like I'd put my palm out to grasp a dead fish. He didn't say anything, only looked down as if searching for money on the ground.

"Go." My mother made a shooing motion with her hand. "Take a walk. Get to know each other while Huang Tai Tai and I work out the details."

I looked at Li-Jie, and with a slight shrug, he gestured for me to precede him. I was very conscious of four sets of eyes following our every move as we walked out of the door. Once we were gone from their sight, I heaved a sigh of relief and headed into the fruit groves, eager to see them again. Li-Jie trailed behind me without a word, and as I couldn't think of anything to say, either, we walked among the trees in silence.

The sound of birds chirping and chickens clucking filled the air. I inhaled deeply, wondering why I hadn't come back more often. But my life in Taipei was busy, and I was always studying, working hard to keep my top placement in my class. And when I did have a free moment, I enjoyed walking through the street markets with my friends or catching up over bowls of noodle soup from a streetside cart. I never seemed to find the time to make the trip home, but now I was glad I'd taken almost the whole week off.

Li-Jie wandered away from me so that for a moment, I was alone. I closed my eyes and was transported back to my childhood, working in these orchards with my grandmother. I could taste again the apple pears my grandmother used to slice for me, the juice dripping down my chin as we grinned at each other, enjoying a midday snack. The sweet lychees we'd pick right off the tree, peeling off the hard shell to get to the white plump fruit, always searching for those little worms that liked to dwell in the nuts. If we found one, we'd pluck it out and drop it to the floor for the chickens to devour before popping the fruit into our mouths. In my mind, I felt the wind whipping through my hair as I pedaled furiously on the red bicycle that I used to ride all over the property, pretending I was on a horse galloping through a field. I opened my eyes, realizing this was the one place where I was content, where I'd always felt carefree and unburdened.

I turned and saw Li-Jie walking toward me. I knew I had to make an effort, as it seemed he would remain silent unless I started the conversation.

"Are you still at university?" This was all I could think to say.

He shook his head. "I work for my father's bank. In Taichung."

"Ah. That's good." I snuck a peek at him out of the corner of my eye. He was a nice-looking man, if a bit skinny, and he had a good job and came from a respected family. All my life, I'd been enthralled by the fable of the Old Man Under the Moon that my grandmother had told me and had waited impatiently for my destiny to appear. Was this him? Was this the match that Yue Lao had written in his book for me? Determined to find the zing I'd heard about in all the romantic stories Ah-Ma and I used to read together, I touched him on the arm, hoping to feel a spark.

There was nothing, except the puzzled look he shot my way. I pretended to stumble, and he reached out to steady me. I clung to him for a moment, desperate to feel something, anything. But again, there was nothing. I let go of him and walked a little faster, staring out at the fruit trees as my heart plummeted in disappointment. Where was the burning, eternal love that would make me want to throw myself into an ocean for him, like the stories Ah-Ma had told me? Staring into his benign face just a few seconds ago, I couldn't even imagine wetting my toes for him, much less drowning in an entire ocean. But maybe it was too early. We'd only just met. Maybe I was rushing things. After all, I'd never been in love, never felt that relentless need to be with someone. I decided to be patient, to give Li-Jie a chance.

He caught up to me and after a moment, he started talking about the political climate of our country. I tuned out at first because I usually avoided such topics, but when I caught the name Chiang Kai-shek, I looked over at him.

"What did you say?" I asked.

"I was saying that I'm so glad he got reelected for a fifth term."

"Really?" I lifted my eyebrows and then realized what it was that I was trying to remember about their family when I first saw them. "Your family is . . ." I trailed off, catching myself. "Yes, really good that he got reelected."

It had been drilled into me from the time I was little not to talk about politics to anyone, and never outside of the privacy of our own home. I went to school with both KMT students and those who were from *benshengren* families, who had been in Taiwan long before the KMT took over.

"I'm glad you agree. My father is a high-level KMT official." Li-Jie's chest puffed out, and I tried to keep my frown from him.

He continued talking, but my mind was in an uproar. My mother was betrothing me into a KMT family? After the KMT had taken my father and probably killed him? What was she thinking? She despised the KMT.

My ears rang as my heart started beating too fast. I needed to confront my mother, find out what was going on.

"We should get back," I said when Li-Jie paused for breath. I thought he was the quiet type, but apparently all I had to do was bring up politics and he came alive.

My mother and Huang Tai Tai both beamed as we rejoined them inside.

"Come, Li-Jie. Have some tea and I'll tell you more about Ah-Hui." My mother gestured to a chair that was normally reserved for my grandfather, who was no longer in the room. I wondered vaguely where he'd gone. How could I make the Huangs leave, too, so I could question my mother?

My grandmother brought out a tray of pineapple cakes and sun cakes, with their honey-filled, flaky layers, as well as a variety of dried meat jerky. She offered it to our guests before sitting down, and then the conversation turned to my achievements.

"You know most students in Taiwan have to take an entrance exam to get into high school, but at Taichung Girl's, there's a policy that if your ranking is high enough, you would automatically gain entrance without taking the exam. Only the very top of the top ever achieve this, and our Ah-Hui was the only one in her year who got accepted into the high school without having to take the exam." My mother leaned back and gazed at me with pride, while heat bloomed in my cheeks and I focused on the sun cake I was currently shredding, layer by flaky layer.

My mother and grandmother continued to regale Huang Tai Tai and Li-Jie with all my accomplishments until my eyes glazed. Finally, the visit was over. They were returning to Taichung City that night, and I was only visiting until the end of the week, so my mother was lamenting the fact that we'd have to get to know one another through letters and phone calls. But Li-Jie pulled me aside as my mother was saying goodbye to Huang Tai Tai.

"I can come up and see you in Taipei after you get back to school?" This was the first time he'd shown interest in me since we met.

I nodded, because I didn't know what else to do. I couldn't imagine being married into a KMT family, but at the same time, I didn't want to regret letting my destiny slip away by being foolish and not accepting my fate. If my fate was to marry this man, then I trusted the Old Man Under the Moon to know what he was doing. I walked with Li-Jie out the door and watched him and his mother get into a black sedan, driven by a chauffeur. When I married him, I knew that would be my life too. My own driver, instead of having to catch a train or walking or biking. Could I see myself living that kind of lifestyle? Maybe the passion that was missing between us would come later, once we were comfortable with each other.

My mother and grandmother were waiting for me inside.

"Well?" my mother asked. "What did you think?"

"He seems nice." But was nice really what I'd been waiting for all these years? "But there was no zing. Nothing like the love stories Ah-Ma used to tell me."

My mama scoffed. "Bah, there is no happily ever after." She turned to my grandmother. "I wish you hadn't filled her head with all that big talk when she was growing up. She thinks marriage is about true love and passion."

"Isn't it, though?" I turned to her, my eyes burning with questions. "Isn't that what you had with my father?"

"Ha." She practically spat out that word. "And look what that got me. I found my true love, only to have him taken away from me." Her mouth hardened and her eyes took on a faraway look. "Studying hard is better than some folktales."

"It was love, though, wasn't it?" I didn't know why I was pressing the matter, but I suddenly needed her to tell me the love I'd always thought bound my parents together was real. "It was just like the fairy tales."

She turned her head away, and for a moment I thought she wasn't going to answer. But then she whipped back to face me, her eyes flashing. I pulled away from her instinctively, as if she would strike me if I stayed too close.

"What good are fairy tales when we live in a country where innocent men and women are being persecuted?" She stood and started pacing in front of me, while my grandmother sat still, wringing her hands together. "Even out here in the country, we hear the rumors that abound of the men, most of them political and intellectual elites like your father, who have disappeared. Some were sent to Green Island, where they were held prisoner and tortured. Tortured, Ah-Hui." Her eyes blazed and I gave an involuntary gasp. "What if that was what happened to your father? What if he's right this moment a prisoner somewhere, beaten, tortured, living in his own filth or worse, and forced to endure what we could never imagine?"

I stayed still, suddenly afraid to breathe. She'd never spoken this honestly with me before. And her words scared me. Terrified me down to my marrow.

"Our country is under martial law, and the KMT persecute anyone who criticizes or opposes the government. Or anyone who they think criticized or opposed the government. Innocent people like your father." She gestured to me with one flailing arm. "Basic human rights have been completely disregarded, and everyone is under mass surveillance. Do you know how terrifying the rumors of what is happening on Green Island are? Have you heard what they do to prisoners? What your father may have been enduring all this time?" She gave a shuddering sigh and turned her head away. "I hope he died right away. I hope he's not still alive, held prisoner somewhere, his days an endless string of pain and suffering. I'd rather he be dead than know that he's been held against his will all this time, tortured daily, beaten, forced to drink his own blood . . ." Her voice broke, and I looked away, unable to bear her pain.

"Then why are you marrying me into a KMT family?" I cried. "The Huangs are KMT. If you hate them so much, why are you giving me to them in marriage?"

My mother spun around to face me. "Because it's the only way to keep you safe. You're going to be a doctor, just like your father. We've taught you not to discuss politics in public, but what if they come for you one day, just like they did to him? What if they throw you in jail?"

My heart pounded at the thought. I'd always known that was a possibility when I decided to study medicine, but I had been more focused on learning how to save lives and ease suffering than on the political implications of my chosen profession.

My mother and grandmother exchanged a look that was heavy with meaning. Unease prickled at the nape of my neck, sure that there was something they weren't telling me. But before I could ask what it was, my mother spoke again.

"If you marry into a KMT family, they will protect you. The Huangs have a good reputation. Li-Jie is a nice young man. He'll treat you right. Huang Tai Tai and her husband are really impressed with your ranking at NTU. They want a doctor in the family." My mother clasped her hands together. "Ah-Hui, this union would be the best for everyone."

I looked away, thinking about her words, not sure how I felt. I turned to my grandmother, and she got up to come to my side. "Listen to your mama. She knows what's best." She stroked a hand down my hair, yet the look on her face told me she felt otherwise. Why? What did she know about this union that I didn't?

Despite my doubts, I would do as they said, just like always. I would get to know Li-Jie and trust that he was the man I was destined to be with. Because I had to believe he was the one if our parents were setting us up.

But then I met Zhi Wei at the stinky tofu stand at the Shilin Night Market a month later, and my entire future was rewritten in that moment.

9

Ah-Hui
1972, Taipei

I rushed into my dorm room, throwing my bag full of textbooks onto the floor because I wanted to change before heading to the night market. I'd been studying hard all day and had forgotten to eat. My stomach was now grumbling, and I was craving stinky tofu. The weather had finally cooled off a bit, still hot but at least with a breeze, and I wanted to put on something more casual before taking my scooter fifteen minutes north to my favorite stand.

As I brushed my hair, I looked around my dorm room, so grateful that I could finally afford to live here instead of with relatives. While my aunt and uncle had been kind, I'd always felt like an intruder in their home. This was the first time I'd had a space all to myself, and even though it wasn't much, really just a square box with a bed, desk, and a small table, I loved it.

I headed back out into the night, thinking about Li-Jie. He'd come to visit me a couple of times since we met at my grandparents' house. Each time, I kept hoping for my heart to leap, for electricity to pass from his hand to mine, but so far, there was nothing. He was a nice man, but we didn't have much in common. Was this really the person that the Old Man Under the Moon had destined for me? Or could the matchmaker have been mistaken and my true destiny was still waiting for me out there somewhere?

When I got to the Shilin Night Market, I parked my scooter in a small space crammed between two cars and headed for the stinky tofu stand I loved the most. As I got closer, the pungent aroma of fermented bean curd was like a siren song calling me across the crowded, noisy night market. My mouth watered at the thought of biting into the crispy exterior and sinking into the light, creamy texture of the tofu on the inside. When it was finally my turn, I ordered, paid the vendor, and got a cardboard box in return. I didn't know it yet, but my destiny was standing behind me, tapping his foot impatiently. I was blocking his way because I had to have a bite as soon as I got my tofu. It was too hot, and I fanned my mouth as he muttered under his breath.

I turned to give this impatient man a piece of my mind, then my breath caught, the piece of tofu lodging itself in my throat. I couldn't breathe. His piercing dark eyes held mine while I took in his long lashes and full lips that would have been considered beautiful on a girl. His hair was longer than those on the men in Taiwan who I associated with. A flush crept over my skin. I managed to swallow that bite (because I was too stubborn to expire right as I met my fate), and what I said next horrified me.

"You're too pretty to be so grumpy and impatient," was what flew out of my mouth.

His eyes widened for a moment in disbelief, and then he threw back his head and laughed. Deep and coming from his belly, it was a laugh of pure enjoyment, like that of a child with a new coveted toy. It pierced right to the core of me, and my entire body buzzed with electricity. It knew before I did that my life was about to change.

When he could speak, he fixed me with an amused smile, stepping out of line so that the next person could place their order. "I've never been called pretty before."

"Well, you are." I gave an insolent shrug, my eyes never leaving his face.

"I've been looking forward to stinky tofu all day." He eyed my cardboard box. "I haven't had really good ones since I left Taiwan."

"You don't live here?" My heart lurched.

"I did until I went to New York for university and medical school." His eyes were still fixated on my tofu, and I held the container out to him.

"Want one?"

"Seeing as how you've made me lose my place in line . . ." He used one of the toothpicks provided and speared a piece, along with a bit of pickled cabbage and stuck the whole thing in his mouth. His groan of pleasure had heat rising in my cheeks, and I looked away; it was too personal of a sound for me to be witnessing, even as a primal part of me awakened.

I cast about for anything to take my mind off that sound. "Are you a doctor?"

He nodded, still chewing. "I am. Came back to visit my mother." He grimaced. "And to tell her I'm not moving back to Taiwan. I just accepted a permanent position in New York."

I was surprised at the tug of disappointment in my heart. "What about your father?"

"He passed away when I was ten." He was eyeing the stinky tofu again.

"My father disappeared when I was six months old," I said, thrilled we had something in common even if it was the loss of our fathers.

"Oh." His eyebrows rose. "Was he . . ." He didn't finish his sentence.

I nodded, understanding what he was asking. You didn't talk about such things out loud in a public place like this, for fear someone was listening. "He was a doctor too. I'm in medical school right now."

"Oh," he said again. But this time, his eyes gleamed with interest. I held out the box. It seemed I was fated to share my stinky tofu with him.

He took another piece, and when he closed his eyes in rapture, I caught my bottom lip between my teeth. I was mesmerized, watching him enjoy a snack I took for granted.

"Which medical school?" he asked when his eyes opened.

"NTU." I said this proudly, having learned not to downplay my own worth.

"Wow." Admiration gleamed in his eyes. "National Taiwan University. I'm impressed."

I smiled and looked down. And then we stood there in companionable silence, sharing my stinky tofu. The sounds of the market and the shouts of people all around us faded away.

When we'd split the last piece, laughing as we fought over it, he gave me a bemused smile. "What now?" he asked.

"What do you mean?" My heart pounded. I didn't want my time with this man to end.

"I ate half your food. It's only right I get something and share it with you." He gestured around the market. "What'll it be? Grilled squid? Pork blood cake? Sweet potato balls?"

"Hmm." My eyes darted around, taking in the stalls lining both sides of the street, delectable treats and tantalizing aromas all around us. "I'm thirsty. How about shaved ice?"

Too late, I realized that sharing shaved ice would be intimate—too intimate between virtual strangers. I blinked, flustered. I was used to men paying attention to me, but I wasn't used to feeling something back.

"Shaved ice is perfect." He gestured ahead of him. "Lead me to your favorite stall."

"Wait." I held up a hand. "I don't even know your name."

"I am Zhang Zhi Wei." He gave a slight bow, and I hid a giggle. "And you are?"

"I am Lin Hui-Zhong. But everyone calls me Ah-Hui." I lowered my lashes, suddenly shy and uncertain. What was I doing, flirting with a complete stranger when I was already promised to someone else?

Zhi Wei gallantly took the cardboard box out of my hands and threw it away. And then with a grand motion, he took my arm, and we proceeded into the crowd in search of shaved ice.

I knew then the old man Yue Lao had come through for me. Something had been missing with Li-Jie, and now my true destiny had arrived. I felt bad about Li-Jie, but I knew my grandmother would understand. This was the man I was destined to be with. This was the man I was *predestined* to be with, to whom I was united with a silken cord, and nothing would get in the way of our union. Not even a prearranged marriage.

I spent as much time as I could with Zhi Wei for the next two weeks, and it was the happiest I had ever been. For the first time in my life, my schoolwork was no longer my number one priority.

I skipped classes to spend time with him. We explored Taipei, and he took me to a new little eatery with only four tables called Din Tai Fung, where we dined on exquisite *xiao long baos,* soup dumplings. We went to an exclusive shopping mall, and when he saw the white grand piano sitting in the lobby, he sat down and gave me a mischievous look. I thought for sure he was just sitting there for show, but then he launched into the most rousing, rambunctious rendition of Mozart's "Rondo alla Turca" I'd ever heard, complete with exaggerated hand lifts and comical winks at me as his fingers flew over the keyboard.

"I thought you're a doctor." I looked at him breathlessly after he'd bowed to the audience and returned to my side. "You never told me you're a concert pianist."

He threw back his head and laughed. "I've always loved to play. It's a hobby."

On the third day, we kissed for the first time at another night market, hidden in the shadows of an alley. When his lips touched mine, I knew I would follow him to the ends of the Earth. This was every love story Ah-Ma had ever told me. He was my destiny, my future, and he breathed sweet words into my ears about how he'd been waiting for me his whole life. The next night, he rented a real hotel room, and not a love hotel that couples who needed privacy in Taiwan used. It was at once the most beautiful night I'd ever had, and also the most heart-breaking. I cried and Zhi Wei gathered me in his arms, kissing away the tears. What were we to do? His life was in America and mine in Taiwan.

Two nights before his flight back to New York, he picked me up from NTU on a moped. We wove through traffic, and I hugged him close from behind. The wind blew my hair back, and the roar of traffic and the smells of a city with over two million people assailed my senses. I felt so alive. We arrived ten minutes later, breathless, at a small alleyway that held a stall with what he proclaimed was the best *orh ah mee sua* in the world. He'd told me he had dreamed about this oyster vermicelli soup while he was in New York.

We balanced on rickety stools, and the vendor put steaming bowls of the thick soup, topped with plump oysters and slices of pork intestines, in front of us. It was garnished with cilantro and a homemade chili sauce. I leaned over my bowl and inhaled the intoxicating fragrance. We dug in, smiling at each other over our bowls, and he was right. It was the best bowl of soup I'd ever had. Maybe it was made more so because of the magic between us.

We finished the soup in silence, and then he reached over and took my hand in his. "Ah-Hui. I can't live without you. Come with me." His serious eyes bore into mine.

I laughed. "How can I? I can't leave Taiwan."

"Why not?" he insisted, his tone urgent but low, only for my ears. "What's keeping you here? Our poor country is suffering. The KMT rule everything, and anyone who dares to take a stance, to make a statement, lives in fear of being on their list." He squeezed my hand. "With America adopting the 'One China' policy, Taiwan has basically been pushed to the periphery of international affairs. We don't exist to these nations. That's why I'm staying in New York."

My heart sank, thinking of never seeing him again.

He squeezed my hand again. "Come to America with me."

I tugged against him, but he held fast. "I'm in the middle of medical school. I can't just leave." And what about my family? What about Li-Jie? I'd yet to break the news to him that I couldn't marry him, even if I never saw Zhi Wei again.

"You can transfer to a medical school in New York. Any school would be lucky to have you." His eyes shone and I couldn't look away. "Think of what the two of us could do together. You wouldn't be confined like you would here, being watched all the time."

"Zhi Wei," I protested weakly. "I can't leave my family."

"We can visit them." He gave me a quick kiss on the mouth. "I can't live without you."

I wavered and my resolve weakened as he talked about what our life could be like in New York. I suddenly couldn't bear the thought of being separated from him by thousands of miles.

"Okay." The word popped out of my mouth in English.

"What?" He stopped talking and sat back. "Wait, you mean it?" His eyes lit up, then he stood and swooped me into his arms.

He twirled me around as I squealed, almost knocking over the rickety stools. "You'll need a visa. I have to go back first, but I'll make arrangements for you." Plans spilled out of his mouth, and all I could do was laugh. I couldn't believe I'd agreed. I'd known this man for only two weeks. Two weeks! I'd never done anything spontaneous like this in my entire life. The laughter died on my lips, because I knew my mother wasn't going to be pleased.

I was right. My mother was livid. Zhi Wei went back to the farm with me the next day so he could meet my family. He thought he could win over my mother, but I knew better. The years of hoping my father would come back, each one passing in disappointment as she tried to adjust to life without him, had hardened her. She no longer resembled the gentle and kind mother I remembered from my childhood. She was now a bitter woman who frowned more than she smiled, placing all her hopes and dreams on me. Sometimes the pressure of her expectations threatened to crush me, and I was ashamed to admit I was relieved not to be living with her.

"Wah!" my mother wailed when we told her our plans. "You cannot throw away everything we worked so hard for, just for this . . . this . . ." She sputtered, pointing to Zhi Wei.

"Mama, I thought you'd be happy for me." I begged her with my eyes to calm down.

"You are promised to Huang Tai Tai's boy." She waved her hands at me, her eyes sparking with anger. "You cannot run away to America with . . . him."

My grandparents didn't say anything, but my grandfather sank into a chair, his lips moving in prayer and his head bowed, as if someone had died. Why did he care who I married?

"Lin Ayi," Zhi Wei addressed my mother, a deferential tone in his voice as he addressed her with the honorific of "Aunt." "I promise . . ."

"Don't you 'Ayi' me," Mama shouted. "I forbid you to go. Your family needs you." She glared at me, and if looks could start fires, I would have combusted into a shiny ball of flames.

I knew she fully expected me to acquiesce as I'd always done my entire life. I had never let her down before. But for the first time, I was about to disappoint her.

I drew myself up to my full height and conjured the ghost of my father, hoping he would give me the courage to defy my mother. I said, my voice firm, "I'm going, Mama. I'm sorry if you don't like it, but I love him, and I will go." I turned to Ah-Ma, thinking she would be our ally. "You were right about Yue Lao. Zhi Wei and I are destined to be together."

"Aiya," Ah-Ma muttered. "Not like this, Ah-Hui. You'll destroy our family."

I looked at her, confused. What was she talking about?

"See!" Mama turned her fury on Ah-Ma. "You filled her head with fantasies, and now look what you've done! Baba will be ruined!" With one last glare at me, she stormed out.

"What is she talking about?" I turned to my grandmother after exchanging a puzzled look with Zhi Wei.

Ah-Ma wrung her hands together, her face screwed up in pain. My grandfather let out an anguished cry and rushed from the room, knocking over his chair in the process.

We stared at the overturned chair in silence before my grandmother spoke quietly. "Ah-Hui, your ah-gong was tricked." Her eyes flared then, and dread dropped over me like a shroud. "They took our money and disappeared. They told him it was a good investment, and he believed them. He thought they were his friends."

My forehead scrunched in confusion. "What does that have to do with me?"

She sighed and looked like she'd aged ten years. "The Huangs said they would cover our debt when you marry Li-Jie. If you don't marry him, we will be ruined. We will lose this house."

My mouth dropped open, and I could only stare at my grandmother in shock. At my side, I heard Zhi Wei's sharp intake of air, but I didn't turn to him.

"You bartered me to get out of a debt?" I said, when I could finally speak.

"Ah-Hui, it's not like that." My grandmother's hands waved in the air, and her feet shuffled on the ground. "It's a good match. The matchmaker said so."

"But . . ." I sputtered. I couldn't believe they would do this to me. This was the action of desperate people, willing to marry their granddaughter to anyone who would save their family.

Ah-Ma shook her head in despair. "Wah! This is a big mess. What are we going to do?"

I looked at her until she met my eyes, and then I knew. They expected me to marry Li-Jie. It was all on my shoulders, and at that moment, it became too much for me. I'd been a good daughter and granddaughter my whole life, but I couldn't do this. Didn't Ah-Ma understand that Zhi Wei was my destiny and there was nothing we could do to prevent our union?

"Ah-Hui . . . your grandfather needs you. We all need you." Her words ended in a whisper, and I saw the desperation in her eyes.

I turned away, my heart breaking. I didn't want to be responsible for my family's downfall, but I couldn't give up my love, even if it destroyed my family. Zhi Wei grabbed my hand, then we were walking away, out of the one place that had always meant home to me, as my grandmother let out a wail behind us.

My heart led me all the way to New York and a new life with Zhi Wei. I started sending money to my family as soon as I could, but I never heard from them, even though the money I wired was never returned.

Despite that, I was happy, so happy to be with the one I loved. I believed our love would last forever, that we could face anything as long as we were together. But then the cracks in our marriage appeared. At first, I didn't notice. The wife is always the last to know, the oblivious one, thinking all is fine. Because I believed in Zhi Wei. I believed the myth that we were bound to each other forever, that nothing could break the thread between us, not another woman, and not Taiwan's fight for independence.

How naive I was. I should have known nothing lasts forever. I should have known our love story would turn rotten, like a piece of durian left out in the sun.

10

Joey
Present Day, Kauai

"Maggie, how are you?"

Joey was still sitting on the couch, her mother's journal in her lap. She'd called her best friend on FaceTime as soon as she'd read a chunk of the journal.

Maggie sighed. "Holding on. Who knew divorce could be so draining?" Maggie lived in Alaska and was in the middle of a messy divorce.

Joey's heart hurt for her best friend. "Ben's family still giving you two trouble?"

"Yes." Maggie heaved out a breath. "Good news is, we finally settled the child custody battle. I've got joint custody of Kristy, no thanks to Ben's parents."

"I'm so glad for you!" Joey knew how terrified Maggie had been when Ben's parents, both lawyers, had fought for Ben to get full custody of their seven-year-old. His parents had dug deep into Maggie's background, trying to bring out any "skeletons" that might hurt Maggie's chances of getting joint custody. Of course, they'd found nothing, but it had been a harrowing year for Maggie.

"I am relieved." Maggie didn't sound happy, though. "But now they're coming for me financially. They want me to give Ben spousal support because I make more money than he does."

"What? Are they insane? Ben makes plenty of money." Joey was indignant on Maggie's behalf.

Joey had not liked Ben's parents, even when Maggie and Ben were happily married. They hadn't wanted Ben to marry Maggie, who was half Filipino and half Japanese. They'd tried to convince Ben to marry someone of "their own kind"—that is, white, from a "good" family. Having grown up on Kauai, which was very diverse and where white people were the minority, usually referred to as *haoles*, Maggie had been shocked by the treatment she'd received from Ben's family. It was partially why they'd broken up after eight years of marriage. She hadn't felt supported by Ben, who'd never stood up for her in front of his family. Ben wasn't a bad person, but he lived under his parents' thumb, and eventually Maggie had had enough.

"Well, apparently, according to our last tax return, I made about a thousand dollars more than Ben. So yeah, they're using that against me."

Joey scoffed. "That's the most ridiculous thing I've ever heard of. God, why can't they just leave you alone? They got what they wanted, didn't they? You, no longer a part of their family. I wish I could beat some sense into them."

That finally got a laugh out of Maggie. "Thanks, Joey. How're you holding up? What's going on over there?"

"Boy, I've got a lot to tell you." And Joey proceeded to fill Maggie in on all the unbelievable things she'd found out in the past few days.

"Poor Sam." Maggie's face was full of grief when she heard about Sam's illness and how he'd decided to take his own life. "I don't know if I'd have had the courage to do what he did." Maggie leaned closer to the camera. "I'm so sorry, Joey."

"There's more." And Joey told Maggie about her father's affair with her old nanny and her mother's journal.

"Oh my god." The shock was clear in Maggie's voice. "I have no words."

"I spent most of my life kind of mad at Sam for making Ren Ren go away. Turns out, he was trying to protect me. And now I can't help being angry at Ren Ren for what she did to our family. And my father! I adored him, loved him so much, and now finding out what he did to my mother, I just don't know what to feel."

"What can I do?" Maggie's face was full of concern.

"Just listen to me rant." Joey let out a dry laugh. "I miss you."

"I can't believe you've been handling all this on your own." Maggie's forehead furrowed. "I'm coming to Kauai. You can't go through this by yourself."

Joey knew her face reflected her gratitude for her best friend. They'd always been there for each other ever since they met in high school. When they'd graduated from college, Maggie had found a job as a marine biologist in Alaska. They tried to see each other at least once a year, but it had been almost two years since they'd met up in Napa Valley for a long weekend of wine tasting and catching up.

"In the meantime, rant away," Maggie said.

"I thought my parents had the perfect marriage. You know that. I used to love hearing about how they met. When I was little, I begged my mother to tell me about meeting our father at a stinky tofu stand at a night market all the time."

"I remember." There was a hint of laughter in Maggie's voice.

"Yes." Joey smiled, looking off into space, having forgotten about that detail until reading about it in her mother's journal. "Sam pretended he was too old whenever my mother told me the story, but I'd see him secretly lurking in the doorway of my room, listening to our mother. She had such a melodic voice. It's the one thing I remembered distinctly about her. I loved hearing about how the Old Man Under the Moon had led her to our father."

Maggie sighed. "You should hold on to that. The good memories."

"Yeah."

They chatted a bit more, then Maggie said she had to pick up Kristy.

"I'm going to look into flights. Try to get time off," Maggie said. "I want to be there for you."

"Thank you, but you have so much on your own plate right now." Joey didn't want to add to Maggie's stress.

"I need a break from Alaska. And Ben's family." Maggie rolled her eyes. "And Kristy's due for a visit with her other grandparents. The ones who truly appreciate her."

"Let me know if you can swing it." They said goodbye just as the doorbell rang.

Joey walked to the front door and opened it to find Ethan standing there with a grocery bag in his hand.

"You okay?" His eyes scanned her face before he came into the condo.

"I don't know." Joey gave a little shrug. "But I guess I'm going to have to be. What do you have there?" She gestured to the bag in Ethan's arm as she closed the door.

Ethan held it up. "You know Sam cooks for Wonton, right? He's told me many times what a terrible cook you are, so I went to the store to get things for Wonton's dinner."

"Hey." Joey wanted to reach out and swat Ethan's arm, but ever since finding out he wasn't married or attached to anyone, she'd felt something shift within her. And she was afraid to get too close to him.

"Only stating what your brother told me." He shot her a grin over his shoulder as he made his way to the kitchen, Wonton at his heels. "This is one spoiled dog."

"I know. Sam always said he didn't want children, that he'd rather have a dog." Joey followed them and leaned on the counter. "How do you know what to cook for Wonton?" She watched as Ethan pulled ground turkey, a slab of salmon, broccoli, carrots, green beans, kale, and a carton of eggs out of the bag.

"I've seen Sam make her meals many times, even helping sometimes, like that time when he broke his arm." Ethan pulled out a cutting board and after washing the vegetables, started peeling the carrots.

"Thanks for doing this." Joey looked down at Wonton. "She's very appreciative too. Because she would have gotten kibble and canned food if it were up to me."

"I'll just make the food and then leave you to it." Ethan glanced up at her. "You look exhausted and you probably want to read more of your mother's journal." He started cutting the carrots into chunks and then dropped them into a pot of boiling water. "Oh, and I ran into Linda on the way in. She said they're making lasagna for dinner, and she'll drop off a portion for you."

"That would be great." Joey looked in the fridge and pulled out two cans of POG—passionfruit, orange, and guava juice. "Want one?"

"Sure." Ethan stirred the ground turkey in a large pan with a bit of water and then added the broccoli and kale he'd chopped.

Joey opened the cans and filled two glasses with ice from the fridge. She poured the juice and handed one to Ethan, who clinked his glass against hers. Sitting at the breakfast bar, she admired the way Ethan brandished the knife and scooped the vegetables into the pot.

"Sam told you about our parents?" Joey took a sip of her POG before placing the glass on the counter.

"The gist." Ethan looked at her briefly before focusing back on his task. "Enough to know why he didn't want you to know when you were younger."

"This changes everything I knew about my parents." Joey dropped her face into her hands for a moment. "I feel horrible, loving my father so much but now knowing what he did to my mother. And my nanny." She looked at Ethan, the anguish making her wish she was comfortable enough with him to ask for a hug. But if he touched her now, she was afraid all her defenses would crumble and she'd cling to him and never let go.

He looked at her and put the knife down on the cutting board. Coming to her side, he reached one hand out to touch her cheek briefly. "Hey. It's a lot to take in. I'm sorry Sam never told you."

Her skin tingled where his fingers had been, and she put a hand up to the spot. Suddenly, the kitchen felt too small, and she searched for something to take her mind off the man standing inches away from her.

"I just spoke to Maggie." Her friend, always a savior even when she didn't know it.

"Maggie." Ethan's lips curved. "I run into her father from time to time in Kapaa. He tells me she lives in Alaska? Some sort of marine biologist?"

"Yes." Joey nodded. "She loves her job but misses Kauai. She's going through a nasty divorce right now, but she finally got joint custody of her daughter."

Ethan's eyebrows rose. "That's terrible. I'm lucky mine was amicable."

Thinking about Ethan's divorce reminded Joey once again that he was single. Available. She flushed, looking away and hoping he couldn't see how flustered she was. What would it be like to kiss him again, after their one stolen kiss all those years ago? Her ears burned with humiliation, remembering how he'd responded when she'd boldly kissed him after he'd dropped her off from the dinner Sam had hosted to celebrate her graduation from high school. They'd gone to Hualani's, high on the cliffs above Kalapaki Bay, and she'd been drunk on success and happiness. Sam had been on call and had responded to an emergency, so Ethan had driven her home. When he'd walked her to the door, she'd been sure of the strong chemistry that crackled between them. The look in his eyes told her he didn't see her as a little kid anymore.

After years of yearning for him, she'd decided to be bold. She felt beautiful because of the way Ethan was looking at her. And she'd leaned in and kissed him, and for a few glorious moments, he'd kissed her back. His hands had gone to her face and pulled her closer, and he'd kissed her in a way she'd dreamed about for so many years. She could still remember the way she'd radiated with happiness that Ethan was finally seeing her as a woman. Ethan was attracted to her. Then seconds later, he'd shattered her heart.

"Joey?" Ethan's voice brought her out of her thoughts. "Are you okay?" His eyes scanned her face, each glance like a caress on her skin.

"I'm, um . . ." She looked down, bringing a hand to her cheek and finding it burning hot. "I'm fine. Just . . . overwhelmed."

He looked at her closely, as if he didn't believe her. "Do you want me to stay here tonight?" He took a step closer until mere inches separated them, making Joey's pulse jump and her heart race out of control. "I could sleep in Sam's room upstairs."

"No!" The word came out more forcefully than Joey intended. But the thought of Ethan sleeping here when her attraction toward him was growing again horrified her. As did the thought of Ethan sleeping where Sam had last slept, his sheets still rumpled and a T-shirt thrown across the bed. Joey had peeked in there and didn't have the heart to change a thing.

"Okay." Ethan backed away, hands up. "I just want to make sure you're fine."

"I am. I need to be alone, absorb all this." She gave him a quick smile and then looked away, not wanting him to see how red her face was. "Plus, I haven't quite forgiven you for keeping Sam's secret instead of telling me."

"I really am sorry about that." Ethan's voice was full of remorse. "But I promised Sam."

"I know." She let out a breath. "You were being a good friend."

"I tried many times to get him to change his mind, to call you and give you a chance to say goodbye." Ethan shook his head. "He wouldn't budge."

"Thank you for trying." She watched as Ethan walked back to the stove and turned it off. "Thank you for everything."

"Of course. You're family, Joey."

No, I'm not, her mind screamed. *I don't have any family left.*

They stood in silence until Joey finally broke it. "I'm tired."

Ethan reached out to pull her into a hug, but she took a step back at the same time, so he ended up side-hugging her shoulders instead. She walked him to the door with Wonton tagging behind, which broke some of the tension.

"When the food cools, just put it into the containers I laid out on the counter and freeze all but one. Wonton usually eats around six."

Joey nodded. "Thanks."

The Kellys' door opened and Linda stepped out, a takeout container in her hands. "Joey. I was just bringing this lasagna to you."

She accepted the food and gave Linda a warm smile. "Thank you. You're a lifesaver."

Linda squeezed her shoulder. "If you need company, pop over anytime. We don't go to bed until around eleven."

"I will. Thanks, again."

Linda waved at them and went back inside, leaving Joey and Ethan together. She stood there hugging the container, wishing he would stay yet needing him to be gone. Her want of him was growing too strong for her to deny, the longer he stayed in her presence.

"Call me anytime, even if it's the middle of the night." Ethan broke the silence. "I'm serious, Joey. If you wake up or can't sleep, if this is all too much, just call and I'll be here."

She nodded, looking down. "I will. Thank you."

With one last worried look, Ethan left, and Joey stood at the door for a few moments before collapsing against it. She blew out a breath, letting go of all the tension that had gathered in her body while in Ethan's presence. She was embarrassed by her reaction, yet she couldn't deny how aware of him as a man she was now that she knew he was single.

Pushing off the door, she went back inside, glancing at the clock in the kitchen. It was only five, but she would feed Wonton as soon as the food had cooled. She wanted to read more of her mother's journal. Having her illusions of her parents shattered was a shock, and she knew eventually, the grief and possibly even anger would set in. She needed to understand what had happened before her emotions took over.

She couldn't imagine how her mother had felt, knowing for all those years that her husband was sleeping with their nanny. That the issues in their home country were tearing their marriage apart, like the petals of a plum blossom blowing away in the wind.

11

Ah-Hui
1975, Manhattan

It was late, but my bladder was full, and I had to get up before I wet the bed. I was eight months pregnant, a pregnancy I hadn't planned as I'd yet to finish medical school. I was in despair, but Zhi Wei had been over the moon and convinced me it would be fine. He would find a way for me to finish my studies as well as have our baby.

As I sat up in bed, I realized my husband wasn't next to me. He often stayed up late, but I saw by the bedside clock that it was three in the morning. What was he doing? After I relieved myself, I stood still in the middle of our two-bedroom apartment on the Upper West Side of Manhattan. That's when I heard it. My husband's voice coming from what would become the nursery once our son was born. What was Zhi Wei doing in there in the middle of the night, and who was he talking to?

I crept to the partially closed door, being careful to stay out of sight. I held my breath until I could understand some of his words.

"She can come to us, Victor . . . perfect timing . . ." Then words I couldn't make out before I heard, "Get her out . . . father has gone underground?"

I knew he was talking to a friend of his who'd recently arrived in New York from Taiwan. I'd met Victor Liao only once and had liked him despite knowing he'd had to flee Taiwan to avoid the repercussions of the KMT. We'd taken him to dinner in Flushing, Queens, where a large population of Taiwanese had established a foothold recently, mostly descendants of soldiers from the KMT, but also refugees from Taiwan seeking a safe place to start a new life. Over *niu rou mien* and multiple glasses of beer, Victor had charmed me with his quiet intelligence, making light of his plight by saying how lucky he was to have friends like Zhi Wei and me. He complimented the beef noodle soup we were eating, saying it reminded him of home. He was a man of few words, but what little he spoke was full of meaning, and even I, someone adamantly opposed to his cause, softened in his presence.

But now my nerve endings lit up, wondering what Victor was getting my husband into. I tiptoed back to bed, and when Zhi Wei finally slipped in beside me, I turned to him.

"What were you and Victor talking about so late at night?"

"Did we wake you? I'm sorry." He reached out to stroke my hair.

I closed my eyes, reveling in his touch, thinking again how lucky I was to have met him. If I hadn't been craving stinky tofu that day, would we have met? I liked to believe so, since our love was destined to be.

"Victor has found the solution to our problem." My husband's voice was full of tenderness.

I opened my eyes to stare at him. "What problem?"

"He's found a nanny for us so that you can focus on your studies." Zhi Wei leaned back against his pillow and crossed his arms over his chest with satisfaction.

This was indeed good news, because I'd been stuck in my own worries of how I was going to finish medical school with a newborn baby. With only a month to go, I'd begun to wonder how I would be able to juggle it all. Even though I knew English before I came to New York, having to think entirely in English all day long had been a hard adjustment. For once in my life, I wasn't at the top of the class. I'd slipped in the first year as I'd adjusted to life in a new country, a new language, and a whole new culture.

Manhattan terrified me at first, even though Taiwan had it beat when it came to crowds, noise, and drivers who didn't pay attention to traffic rules. I was afraid to take the subway by myself, afraid to walk outside at night by myself. I was no longer the number one student favored by the professors, envied by the other students. Even though Zhi Wei still bragged about me to everyone we met, even though he told me every day how proud he was of me, I vowed to work harder, to get back to number one, and I was slowly getting there. I hadn't wanted to be distracted by a baby, but at the same time, I couldn't help loving our son already as he did flips in my belly and kicked me when I least expected it.

"Who?" I turned on my side, so that I was facing Zhi Wei.

"A young girl whose family was killed during a break-in at their house. She has nowhere to go. We're going to bring her here to take care of our baby."

I stared at my husband, sure there was more to the story than what he was telling me. "She lives in Taiwan? How do you know her?"

"They're family friends of Victor's. With her whole family gone, we need to get her out of Taiwan."

"We?" I sat up, my skin prickling. "Do you know them too?"

He looked away from me for a moment. "No, but I'm going to help bring her to New York. She will be safe with us. And we need her." He gave me an encouraging smile. "It's the perfect solution."

My internal radar went up. "Who is her family? What's their name? And was it a random break-in, or were they targeted?"

Zhi Wei didn't answer and at first, I thought he was going to ignore my questions. But then he leaned down and kissed my cheek. "Don't worry about it. I'll take care of everything. It will be fine, you'll see."

I wanted to protest, but then a big yawn overtook me. I had to be up early, in just a couple of hours. Zhi Wei pulled me close, and my fatigue won out over my need for questions. I'd get my answers the next day.

But I didn't. When I asked my husband again who this girl was, he deflected, only saying her given name was Ren Ren.

"Is her family involved in the fight for independence?" I stood next to his chair, having waited until we'd finished dinner before my questions began again. "Was that why they were targeted? Will her being here put our family in danger?"

"Ah-Hui." My husband dabbed his mouth with a napkin before putting it down and turning to me. "Don't worry so much. I'll take care of all the details. You need to rest, stay calm for the baby. Focus on your studies. It will be fine."

"Are you involved in some way?" I put my hands on my hips, trying to stop the quavering in my voice. "Did Victor pull you in?"

"No." He sighed and got up to put his dish in the kitchen sink. "Everything will be fine." He refused to speak about it more, no matter how I pleaded.

That weekend, while he was on call at the hospital, I started digging. I looked through his papers and read the Chinese newspapers, and what I found out about Ren Ren's father scared me to death. Zhi Wei had lied to me. He was involved in the movement, no matter how marginally. Because Ren Ren's father was a major leader of the democracy movement, often praised for his bravery and conviction. He'd been arrested recently during a crackdown on pro-democracy demonstrations but had escaped with the aid of fellow activists. They'd helped him go underground, and a few months later, his family had been massacred. The sole survivor, Ren Ren, had disappeared after she got out of the hospital. My eyes widened in fear as I read, and my heart bled that Zhi Wei would do this to us when he knew how I felt. How could he put a target on our backs by bringing this girl into our lives, after knowing how my family had suffered when my father had disappeared?

I missed my family so much, even though they had tried to sell me out to save themselves. I especially missed Ah-Ma. How I wished I could talk to her in the way I'd never been able to with my mother and ask her what I should do about Zhi Wei bringing this refugee into our home without asking me. On one hand, my heart yearned to help Ren Ren since she obviously had no one left, and I could imagine how petrified and traumatized she was, witnessing the slaughter of her family. But on the other, I knew the danger taking her in would place us in, and I wanted to be able to return to Taiwan one day and reconcile with my family. This was why I didn't want to do anything to draw attention to us, even though we were in America. I'd heard of too many Taiwanese, even those who were American citizens, who were blacklisted or arrested when they went back to Taiwan, thrown in jail for the smallest infractions, or sometimes for no reason at all.

I cried when my husband came home that night. "I read about Ren Ren's father. I know who she is." Tears streamed down my cheeks as I confronted him.

"Ah-Hui." He shook his head, a sad but determined look on his face.

"How could you do this to us?" I was terrified for not only us but also our unborn child. I wanted our son to grow up without fear, to live life the way he wanted. "You know how I feel. I want nothing to do with Taiwan politics."

Zhi Wei reached out and held me tenderly in his arms, but I twisted away.

"No. You can't make this better. I don't want her in our house. I don't want to be targeted." He pulled me to him again, and I beat my fists against his chest. "I came to America with you because you said we could have a new life here, one without fear of persecution. Yet you're willing to risk our safety for that of someone you don't know?"

"Ah-Hui, stop. It's going to be fine."

I struggled against him and called him all the bad names in English that I'd learned from fellow students. Asshole. Fucking bastard. Shithead. Then I collapsed in his arms, and he held me as I cried. When I finally quieted, he kissed my tearstained cheeks.

"We have to help her, Ah-Hui. The poor girl isn't safe in Taiwan. She's so traumatized by what happened that she's barely spoken a word since. Victor knows someone who has volunteered to smuggle her out, get her here to Manhattan. She needs us. And we need her. She'll take care of our baby so you can concentrate on finishing medical school. We'll help her get over the loss of her family. It's the perfect solution."

I looked into his eyes, and I knew he'd already made up his mind. Nothing I said was going to convince him to turn the girl away. This was the first time since I'd met Zhi Wei that he hadn't listened to me. He'd done what he wanted, without any input from me. I tried for days to convince him otherwise. He kept saying everything would be fine. I knew it wouldn't be. But what could I do? Some days, as I walked down the streets of Manhattan, I would think, We're safe here. We're on American soil. Zhi Wei was an American citizen, and I soon would be too. Could the government really reach us all the way across the world?

Then finally, a few days before my due date, Ren Ren arrived. Victor brought her to our apartment in a taxi, and she stood in our doorway, only one suitcase at her side. I was prepared to harden my heart against her, but one look at her terrified face and all my reservations dissolved. She had the saddest expression I'd ever seen in my life.

I thought she looked like a dumpling. And I didn't mean that in a negative way. She was cute, with a round head like a soup dumpling, dimples in both cheeks that winked when she tried to smile at us. Her skin was so smooth, like porcelain, and I longed to run my hand over it, wondering whether it was as silky as it appeared. She was only seventeen years old and had never lived anywhere but her parents' apartment in Taipei. I could see she was scared, clutching her shoulder bag tightly against her body, her wary eyes darting around as if looking for assassins who would jump out at her. I didn't blame her, because her entire life had been violently disrupted on the day when unknown assailants had broken into their home and shot her, her mother, and two brothers in cold blood.

I couldn't imagine the horror this poor girl had gone through. To watch your family being killed in front of your eyes while you lay helpless, bleeding from multiple gunshot wounds and unable to help yourself, much less them. Her two younger brothers were only thirteen and ten, and I could imagine the grief that had torn through her body as she'd watched them bleed out. She'd spent months in the hospital, fighting for her life and struggling to heal from not only her physical injuries but also the psychological ones, with no one to visit her.

"Welcome," my husband said to her in Taiwanese.

She looked behind her, as if contemplating escape. But Victor stood there, a reassuring hand on her shoulder. She was like a scared little mouse, and I knew then I couldn't turn her away. She wasn't safe in Taiwan, and even though I still feared for my family's safety, this traumatized girl pulled at my heart. We needed to protect her, to let her know that no one was going to get her. As much as I hated to admit it, Zhi Wei had done the right thing. We were doctors, or he was and I was about to become one, and our mission was to heal those who were sick and broken. This girl standing before us was broken from something that wasn't her doing, and it was up to us to help her.

In those first few years, she slowly came back to life. I was glad to have her with us as I struggled between completing medical school at the top of the class and taking care of a newborn baby. Our son was perfect. Slowly, we developed a routine, me waking early to take care of the baby and then handing him to Ren Ren as I rushed out of the apartment to my lectures. Even though I had been against having her, I couldn't deny she was great with Sam. We had given him a Taiwanese name, but since we lived in America, we called him Sam. He always quieted whenever Ren Ren took him in her arms, and she treated him as if he was her own, with awe and care and gentleness. I didn't like to be away from my baby, but I was able to leave the apartment, knowing he was well cared for. Ren Ren still didn't speak much, in either Mandarin or English, but her face always lit up whenever she looked at

Sam. For that, my heart relented toward her. I knew I could trust her with our baby.

Zhi Wei doted on Sam, and our household was a happy one for many years. I still longed for my family and mourned the fact that no one had reached out to me. Zhi Wei would often find me sitting in the rocking chair in the nursery, our son in my arms, as my eyes stared out the window.

"Thinking of your family?" he asked one day late at night when I couldn't sleep and had gotten up to quiet the baby when he cried.

I turned to him, nodding. "They took the money I sent. But no one has answered any of my letters." I kept my voice soft so as not to wake our son. "I keep writing to them, hoping my mother or my grandmother will write back, tell me how they are. How could they cut me off like this? I'm their flesh and blood."

"You have me now. I'll always take care of you. And our son." He leaned down to kiss the top of my head, and I took his hand, grateful for his presence.

I didn't tell him how I longed for my ah-ma so badly that I'd often weep in grief when Zhi Wei wasn't home. The one thing that made all this worthwhile was Zhi Wei's love for me. He helped me adjust to my new life, and my heartbreak over my family slowly subsided over the years. Waking up with him every morning and falling asleep in his arms every night was everything I'd dreamed of.

I finally completed medical school, confident that my son was getting the best care as I embarked on a career to help others. If my husband disappeared for hours with Victor some days, I chose not to dwell on it. On my graduation day, my eyes were wet because I wished so much for my mother to see what I had accomplished. I wished she was out in the audience, clapping her hands as hard as she could, my ah-ma and ah-gong at her side as they all beamed proudly at me when I accepted my diploma. But only Zhi Wei, Ren Ren, and Victor were there. My husband and Ren Ren sat side by side with Sam in his nanny's lap. I glanced at them after I held my diploma in my hand, and Ren

Ren made Sam clap his hands as she stared up at me with a smile on her face. I smiled back, not realizing then what she would eventually do to our family.

If I had known the day she'd arrived on our doorstep, scared and frightened out of her mind, how she was going to destroy my marriage, I would have slammed the door in her face.

12

Joey
Present Day, Kauai

Joey woke with a start, realizing she was still on the couch. One hand groped the coffee table, and when she found her cell phone, she turned it on. It was four thirty in the morning. She must have fallen asleep while reading her mother's journal.

She sat up, seeing with relief that the journal had fallen onto the floor and she hadn't ruined it. Wonton lifted her head from where she was snuggled at the end of the couch and then dropped it again when Joey stood. She went to the wall switch and turned on the lights. Blinking, she looked around, suddenly wide awake. Her eye landed on the piano on one wall of the living room. She was glad Sam had kept their upright piano when he'd sold their house and bought this condo soon after Joey graduated from college.

Wandering to the piano, she sat and opened the lid. She played a little tune softly, her thoughts on Sam and how they'd inherited their love of music from their father. Even though neither of them had pursued careers in music, they were both accomplished on the piano and could each play at least three other instruments plus sing.

The notes died and Joey lifted her hands off the keyboard. She sighed, wishing she could break out into one of the concertos with crescendos and crashing chords to match her mood, but it was too early in the morning, and Sam's neighbors wouldn't appreciate it. Whenever she was sad or mad, she used to pound out her feelings on the piano. She'd play later, once the sun was up.

Knowing there was no way she'd be able to go back to bed, she made herself a strong pot of coffee. She took a mug out onto the lanai, Wonton settling in the grass in front of her. They sat in silence as Joey stared out at the papaya tree with fruit hanging overhead and the lilikoi vine that entwined the wrought iron fence at the back of the yard. The plumeria tree in the corner gave off the most heavenly scent, as did the pikake vine and gardenia shrubs dotting the edge of the yard. Joey marveled at how much beauty Sam had managed to create in the small space.

When she finished her mug of coffee, she decided to go inside and look through Sam's paperwork. What better time than now when she couldn't sleep. She stopped in the kitchen to refill her coffee and took it with her into the room where she should have slept. Setting it down on a coaster on the desk, she sat on the floor and pulled out the bottom drawer where she knew Sam kept his files. They were neatly labeled: Passport, Birth Certificate, Bank Information, Will and Power of Attorney, plus various other documents relating to the condo and to his practice. In the back, she found a photo album from when she was a baby, and she pulled that out first.

Flipping through the pictures, she searched for her mother's image, and now knowing what she knew, could see the pain in her mother's eyes. Her lips smiled, but it didn't reach her eyes. The one thing that was evident, though, was the love she had for her children. The way she gazed down at baby Joey in her arms, or posed with Sam, their cheeks smooshed together, her face beaming with pride, showed Joey that the love she remembered from her mother was real. Whatever she'd been going through in her life, she hadn't let it detract from her love and care of her children.

"I'm sorry, Mama." Joey whispered the words as she traced a hand over her mom's beautiful face.

How hurtful it must have been for her mother, living with the "other woman" and feeling as if she had no say in the matter. Joey had always adored her father, but now, in light of what she'd discovered, she realized he must have had a cruel or selfish streak to do that to his wife. She hated that her feelings for her parents, for Ren Ren, had been changed by what she'd learned. Now she understood why Sam had kept the truth from her all these years.

Hearing about her father's infidelity made her feel even more guilty about her involvement with Oliver. It made her sick, thinking of what that had done to Oliver's wife, Mara. It made Joey even more certain she never wanted to get married. Marriages destroyed relationships, in her experience. She would rather be independent and answer only to herself than give someone the power to hurt her beyond words.

What about Ethan? A voice whispered inside her head.

"No," she said out loud. "I can't get distracted by Ethan."

Wonton came into the room and put her head on one of Joey's legs. She reached down to rub the little dog behind the ears.

"It's just you and me now, Wonton." The dog yawned, making Joey laugh softly. "I'm not going back to Malaysia. I might stay here for a bit, decide what I'm going to do next." Wonton's ears wiggled as if she was listening. Joey sighed and leaned down to give the dog a kiss on the top of her head. "I need to figure out where I fit in this world."

Not wanting to get melancholy, she started sorting through the files of documents. Victor had told her Sam had left everything to her, and she knew she'd need to go to the bank with Sam's death certificate to get everything transferred into her name. As well as take care of the life insurance Sam had. There was a myriad of paperwork she'd need to get through, but right now, she focused only on the immediate things that she could do.

Looking at the clock on her phone and calculating the five-hour time difference between Kauai and New York, Joey knew Victor would be awake by now. She dialed his number.

"Hello?" Victor's familiar voice came over the speakerphone on her cell.

"Victor. It's Joey."

"Are you okay?" She could hear the concern in his voice.

"No." She knew Victor would understand. He knew how much Sam meant to her. "I still can't believe Sam is gone."

"I'm sorry." Victor was quiet for a moment. "I know it's not the same, but if you need anything, you can always come to me."

"Thank you, Victor."

"You also need to deal with the paperwork. You're going to need to obtain certified copies of the death certificate and file the will with the probate court to get that process started."

"Oh god." Joey's head throbbed. "Can you help me with that?"

"Of course."

"Thank you." She changed the subject to the reason for the call. "I need to ask you something. Please be honest with me."

"Okay." Victor's voice was cautious.

"You must have known about my father's affair with Ren Ren, right?"

"Ah." Victor paused. "Yes, I knew."

Joey's heart sank. She'd suspected that, but hearing him confirm it made it even more real.

"Did you ever confront my father? Tell him it was wrong?"

Another pause before Victor said a simple, "No."

"You thought it was okay, then?" Joey's voice rose. "What about my poor mother? Did you ever think of how she felt? I thought you were friends with both of them."

"Joey." Victor's voice was quiet, but her name sounded like a gunshot to her ears with the way adrenaline was pumping through her veins. "What happens between a husband and wife was not my business. Yes,

I was friends with them. I tried to look out for your mother. But there was nothing I could do." He took a breath. "Ren Ren came to me about a year after she arrived in New York. She was so fired up, wanted to get involved, to get justice for her family, her father. We needed her passion, her fire. She was very much her father's daughter. And she convinced your father to join in the fight for Taiwan independence."

This was the most Joey had ever heard Victor speak at one time, and it took her a moment to absorb the meaning of his words.

"But my poor mother. What must have she gone through, living with them both? How could my father have done it, both the affair and his involvement in your movement, when he knew how opposed to it my mother was?"

"I did what I could for her. I tried to shield her from the truth."

Joey snorted, and her clogged ear suddenly released. Her eyes widened with surprise, and she opened her mouth wide, making her ears pop. "I can hear again."

"What?" Victor's voice was confused.

"Never mind. And my mother didn't need to be shielded." Joey couldn't help the way her voice caught on the last word. "She needed her husband to be faithful to her."

Victor sighed. "I know it's hard to understand. It was a different time. My focus was on Taiwan, fighting for our freedom. Would I do things differently now? Probably."

"Was she sad? Angry?" Joey had never been able to understand why her mother had stayed with her father after finding out the truth.

"She was sad. And betrayed." Victor paused. "I was worried about her. I thought she'd do something drastic."

Joey gasped. "You mean . . ." She couldn't bring herself to say the words, but Victor filled in the blanks.

"I was afraid she would take her own life at one point."

13

Ah-Hui
1980, Manhattan

The taxi pulled up in front of our building, and I got out first, then reached in to help my son. He was burning up with a 103-degree temperature, and the school nurse had called me to come pick him up. Had Ren Ren known he was sick just a few hours ago when she took him to school? I assumed not, as our nanny loved our boy as much as we did.

"My throat hurts," Sam said as I took his hand. We had moved into this building a year and a half ago, so that Ren Ren could have her own room once Sam got too big for a crib.

"I know; I'll make it better once we get upstairs." I had tried Ren Ren when I got the call from the school, but she hadn't picked up. Since I had a break in my appointment schedule, I decided to get Sam myself and take care of him. Too often, it was Ren Ren he turned to when he was sad or hurt, so I was glad for this opportunity to spend time with my five-year-old.

He was growing up too fast. My grip on his hand tightened as we got on the elevator, and I vowed to spend more time with him.

"I'll make you the special soup to soothe your throat, okay?" We spoke a mixture of Mandarin, Taiwanese, and English to each other, as both Zhi Wei and I wanted to make sure Sam was fluent in our native languages.

"Okay." Sam beamed a happy smile, despite the flush in his cheeks and the feverish sheen in his eyes.

When we got home, I sent Sam to wash his hands in his bathroom, and then he curled up in bed. I tucked the blanket around his small form. "Get comfy. I'll heat up the soup."

I always kept a stock of the Chinese herbal chicken soup in the freezer for emergencies like this. Whenever I had time, I made a big batch of it using ingredients like ginger, astragalus, and white fungus, which reminded me of my grandmother. She was the one who used to cook it for me whenever I was sick, and she taught me to make it when I was older. I'd freeze the stock and add fresh chicken and green onions. As I pulled out the cooked chicken I had in the refrigerator, my longing for my grandmother made me double over as I thought again of how my family had disowned me.

I was dumping the frozen soup stock into a large pot when I heard a noise from Ren Ren's bedroom. I froze, the hair on the back of my neck rising up. Was Ren Ren home? She hadn't answered the phone when I called earlier. Maybe it was Zhi Wei? But if so, what was he doing in the nanny's room? He'd told me earlier he was on rotation today at the hospital, which would keep him busy all day. My heart raced as I wondered whether we had an intruder in the house.

I closed the freezer softly and took a few careful steps toward Ren Ren's closed door. There it was again—a whimper of some sort. Was there a cat in there? My heart pounding with fear, I took a few more steps until I was standing outside the door. I was about to twist the knob open when I heard a noise that was very familiar to me. My husband, groaning.

My mouth dropped open, thinking I'd caught him in a moment of self-satisfaction, as heat flooded me with embarrassment. I was about to turn and go back to the kitchen when I heard another noise. Ren Ren's voice, crying out in ecstasy.

My entire world spun. I couldn't deny what I was hearing, but my mind refused to believe it. My husband was in there, doing things to our nanny that he should not be doing. Tears sprang to my eyes as my head filled with images that I didn't want to see. There was no way; Zhi Wei would *never* do that to us. He loved me. Me. Not Ren Ren. And he would never betray my trust and love like that. Would he?

I didn't know what to do. Should I open the door to confirm what my mind already knew? Should I go back to the kitchen and pretend nothing happened? Or should I grab Sam and leave right away? But my little boy was sick, and he needed to rest. Yet how could I stay, knowing that the two people closest to me were betraying me right this moment?

I clasped a hand to my mouth to keep back the sob and stumbled toward Sam's room. We couldn't stay. We needed to leave, right now. I was too humiliated to think of confronting them, not when my heart was breaking.

"Sam, why don't we visit Auntie Pippa? I know you love to play with her dog."

Sam blinked at me, his cheeks flushed. "But I want to stay in my own bed."

"Please." I reached out a hand, desperate. He must have seen the look in my eyes, because he climbed out of bed willingly with his stuffed dog in his arms.

"Okay, Mama. Can we bring the soup?"

I kissed him on the top of his head, then we walked out of his room. I moved quietly back to the kitchen to grab the pot after dumping the chicken into it, and we slipped out the front door. Pippa was our upstairs neighbor, a grandmotherly type who would sometimes watch Sam if Ren Ren had an appointment and couldn't be back in time to get him after school. She had a miniature dachshund named Winnie that Sam loved, and I knew she would foster us until I felt it was safe to go back to our apartment.

Pippa answered within seconds when I knocked softly on her door.

"Well, look who came to visit me. Mr. Sam and his mom." A broad smile on her face, Pippa stood back to let us in.

She was a tall, fit woman in her seventies, her pure-white hair in a long braid down her back. She made the best brownies, and I could see Sam's eyes scanning Pippa's counter, looking for the treats.

"Can we . . ." My voice faltered, and I cleared it and tried again. "Can we stay here for a bit? There's a . . . situation . . ." I couldn't finish my sentence.

Pippa gazed into my eyes and a knowing look came over her face. "Of course you can crash here anytime."

"Sam's sick. He's got a temperature. I had to get him early from school. And when we got back—" I broke off, not sure what I was babbling or how much I wanted Pippa to know.

On one hand, I longed to unload what I'd just witnessed on her, needing someone to comfort me, tell me everything would be okay. On the other, I was a very private person, and the thought of anyone else knowing about my husband's infidelity skewered me to the bone.

"Well, let's get you comfortable on the couch, young man. I just might have a brownie with your name on it." Pippa hurried to the couch, and once Sam had jumped on, she tucked the blanket she always had on the back of the couch around him. She picked up her dog and settled Winnie in the crook of Sam's arms, and the joy that spread over my son's face made me feel as though all was not lost.

"I brought soup. Can we heat it up for him?" I still had the pot in my hand, my feet frozen to the ground where I stood. I felt as if I was having an out-of-body experience. I could feel my physical being grounded here in Pippa's apartment, yet my soul seemed to be floating above us, watching all this as if in a dream.

Pippa took the pot from me and then patted me on the shoulder. She leaned in close to my ear. "It'll all be okay. Everything will work out," she whispered, for which I was grateful. I didn't want my son to know anything was wrong.

I nodded, not sure what she thought she knew but needing to hear her words of comfort. "Thank you."

She gave me one final pat and then took over preparing the soup as I collapsed at the end of the couch by Sam's feet. He was chatting happily with Pippa about the book his teacher had read to their class today, while petting Winnie. I sat staring off into space, trying to grasp the idea that my husband was sleeping with Ren Ren.

Tears sprang to my eyes, and before I could break down in front of Sam, I sprinted for the bathroom. I closed the door and then slid to the floor, my grief and hurt and anger flooding through me and releasing in a torrent of tears. I stuffed my fist against my mouth, not wanting to make any noise that would scare my little boy. I didn't know how I was going to live with what I'd just found out, but for the time being, I let myself cry, let myself feel all the things, and let myself wallow in my anguish because I knew my little boy was safe with my neighbor.

Pippa gave me a questioning look when I finally came out of the bathroom. I knew she could see my red and puffy eyes, but I averted them, putting on a cheerful demeanor for my son. When we left an hour later, after Ren Ren had called me at Pippa's to ask how Sam was once she saw the note I'd left, then told me she was at a doctor's appointment and hadn't been able to pick up the phone (liar), Pippa pulled me back.

"You can always come here. Anytime. I'm here for you. Whenever you're ready."

Ready for what? I wanted to ask. But I didn't. I only nodded and thanked her again for taking us in.

I didn't confront my husband or Ren Ren that day or even that month. I was too humiliated, and I think part of me believed if I didn't say anything out loud, it wouldn't be true. I stopped sleeping. Every night, once our little household was asleep, I'd sit by the living room window and stare up at the moon, the same moon I used to look at while in my grandmother's arms, listening to her stories. I wondered how my life had turned out like this. In none of the old fables did the husband sleep with the nanny. Nowhere in the stories did it tell me how I was supposed to handle this situation. I longed for my grandmother, to ask her what I should do. I longed for my mother, for wasn't it the mother's job to prepare her daughter for life?

But I had no one. They'd cut me out of their lives for running away with Zhi Wei and marrying him instead of my intended. Now I wondered whether I'd made a mistake. Wasn't Zhi Wei my fated, predestined love? Did that love come with a lover on the side? I shook my head, wanting to get the images of him and Ren Ren together out of my mind. I couldn't take it, yet I knew I wouldn't say anything. Because what good would it do? Would he stop just because he knew I knew? I wasn't prepared for the answer and decided I would watch them, gather more information before taking any next steps.

The first thing I had to do was pay more attention to Ren Ren. I realized I'd underestimated her, my little dumpling of a nanny. I thought she was a shy, scarred young woman, but in reality, she was a backstabbing husband stealer. I started spying on her. I usually left before she took Sam to school, but I started going in later, saying I had things to take care of before going to the hospital. I'd wait for five minutes after everyone left, then I searched her room. She was surprisingly trusting, leaving everything out in the open, nothing hidden or locked away. For why would she think I would ever snoop through her stuff? I told her all the time how lucky we were that she'd come to us, how she was like family, and how much I appreciated her. And look what she'd done in return.

I found her planner, and saw notes jotted inside, all relating to her work for Taiwan: protests to oppose the KMT authoritarian government and to raise awareness of its human rights abuses, local town hall meetings and events with members of Congress to educate them on relations between the US and Taiwan, and articles she'd written in prominent US publications under a pen name to win public support for the rights of the Taiwanese people. The initials "ZW" were all over her planner, which I knew referred to my husband. I ignored the thorn in my heart and forced myself to focus on the task at hand. Here was proof that my husband had been accompanying her to these meetings and protests. And from her notes, I also saw VL, meaning Victor.

I stopped by Victor's office, unannounced. I couldn't confront my husband or Ren Ren, but I could try to get information from Victor. He'd always been honest with me, and I knew I could ask him the hard questions.

"What have you done?" I didn't even sit down when he showed me to his office before I launched into my questions. "Are we in danger?"

"Ah-Hui." Victor gestured to the mini fridge behind him. "Do you want some water?"

"No. I need answers." I wanted to ask him about the affair, but I didn't know if I wanted to know what he knew, so I stuck to politics. "Ren Ren is neck deep in your movement. And she's dragged my husband into it."

Victor studied me for a moment before sitting down in his chair. "You know what they did to her father. Her whole family."

I nodded. About a year after she came to us, news broke out that Ren Ren's father had been captured and killed in Taipei. I still remember Ren Ren's grief, how she'd collapsed to the ground when Victor had come over to tell us the news. I'd comforted her then, taken care of her as if she were my child. She'd stayed in bed for weeks and I'd let her, knowing she needed time to heal even as I needed her to watch my child so I could focus on my career. I'd been kind to her, and now I wish I hadn't been.

"She is filled with fire. Her whole family perished because of the KMT."

"I know that." I brushed at the air with impatience.

"She is passionate about advocating for a free Taiwan. She wants Taiwan to change from a one-party dictatorship into a multiparty democracy. I only put her in touch with the right people." Victor leaned back in his chair.

"And my husband?" My question was laden with meaning. What was his involvement? Did Victor know about the affair?

Victor looked at me, as if asking if I really wanted to know. "Have you not asked him?"

I lifted my chin. "I have. And he keeps saying not to worry."

Victor nodded and stroked his chin. "He's been going with Ren Ren to rallies. They volunteer with various groups. It's not a secret."

I blew out a breath. "Then why has my husband kept it from me? He knows I don't approve. That I don't want us to be involved."

Victor nodded again. "I know." He looked at me. "He loves you, Ah-Hui. He doesn't want to hurt you. But he believes this is the right thing to do."

"He didn't do anything about it until Ren Ren got involved, though, did he?" I stared hard at Victor, willing him to tell me the truth.

He sighed and I could see in his eyes that I was right. Ren Ren was the one who got my husband riled up enough to go against my wishes. My already broken heart cracked even more. Zhi Wei had chosen Ren Ren over me in more than one way.

I sat there, looking down at my hands, fighting tears. I didn't want to break down in front of Victor, yet I had no one else to turn to. I had made some friends, fellow doctors and one or two mothers of Sam's friends, plus Pippa upstairs, but they were all casual friendships. No one I could trust enough to tell them my deepest thoughts, and certainly not about my husband's infidelity. But Victor was my husband's friend first, even though I'd always thought he had a soft spot for me. His allegiance would be with Zhi Wei, not me.

Victor blew out another breath and then leaned toward me. "Ah-Hui, he loves you very much. He would do anything for you."

I turned my head away. "No, he wouldn't. Otherwise, he wouldn't have taken up with Ren Ren and helped her." Or gotten into bed with her. I could no longer sleep next to Zhi Wei, remembering how I'd heard their moans of pleasure. I'd taken to wandering around the apartment at night instead of sleeping, catching a few hours on the couch when I could no longer keep my eyes open. Zhi Wei had been concerned, offering advice about taking herbal supplements or trying warm milk, and I had wanted to scream at him that he was the reason I couldn't sleep.

Victor studied my face, then he sat back in his chair and steepled his fingers together. "He loves you. Whatever else is happening with him, you and Sam are his number one priority."

I snorted, a most unladylike sound, but I was past caring. How were we his number one priority when he was carrying on with Ren Ren right under my nose? Where were his priorities when he didn't make it to Sam's end-of-the-year concert because he'd gone to a protest instead? Or when he didn't come home to play the piano with Sam like he'd promised because he was off with Ren Ren, spreading their pro-democracy work? I didn't know how I was going to continue to live like this.

I left Victor's office, feeling worse than when I'd gone in. I wanted to die. My whole life that Zhi Wei and I had planned was slipping away between my fingers. For the first time in my life, I couldn't see a future, couldn't fathom how we'd come out of this still married.

And if I couldn't be married to Zhi Wei, then I didn't want to live.

14

Ah-Hui
1981, Manhattan

All I wanted to do was sleep, to burrow under the blankets and close my eyes to what my life had become. Six months after finding out my husband was sleeping with Ren Ren, I was no longer the strong, brilliant doctor my husband used to be so proud of. I was broken in spirit, and even though I loved my son, I couldn't muster the will to do anything for him.

I'd taken a leave of absence from the hospital when I'd come down with pneumonia so severe I'd ended up in the hospital for over a week. It had taken me three weeks to recover, and even though I was finally feeling like myself, I'd yet to get out of bed. I couldn't. I was so down-trodden that I didn't think I'd be able to move even if our apartment was on fire. All I wanted to do was wallow in bed, my eyes closed to shut out the pain and humiliation that plagued my every day.

Our front doorbell rang but I ignored it, hoping whoever was out there would go away. But then they started pounding on the door, and I heard Pippa's voice calling out to me.

"I know you're in there, Ah-Hui." Her voice was loud. "Open the door or I'm coming in."

I closed my eyes and hoped that Pippa would go away. But then I heard the key in the lock, and I turned my face away from the bedroom door. We had given Pippa a key in case of emergencies, and I guess she thought this was an emergency.

I heard her footsteps in our apartment, and then they headed for my bedroom, which I still shared with my husband. She pushed the door open and then there was silence. I opened my eyes and turned to find her gazing at me, sympathy shining in her eyes as she took in my disheveled state and unwashed hair. My nightshirt was stained, and I knew I smelled bad. Zhi Wei had tried to convince me to get up and take a shower before he'd left the house this morning with Ren Ren, doing who knew what, but just knowing they were together fighting for a free Taiwan made me even more depressed.

"Ah-Hui. Don't let them do this to you." Pippa took a step into the room. "You're a brilliant, strong woman with your whole life ahead of you. Don't let them bury you and make you think life isn't worth living."

I pushed myself to sit up in bed, surprised at her words. What was she referring to? Could she possibly know about my husband's affair with Ren Ren?

Pippa came to my side, her face soft. "I know, dear heart. It's all I could do to keep my words to myself when I saw them leaving the building this morning, his hand on her lower back."

I groaned and hid my face in my arms. "Does the entire building know? The doormen?"

"I don't know." There was so much compassion in Pippa's voice that I wanted to weep. "But I know you, and I know them. It wasn't hard to figure out."

"I hate her." I whispered the words, but I knew Pippa had heard by the breath she expelled.

"What about him? Do you hate him too?" Her tone was fierce.

My breath caught at her question. I should hate him too. So why did I still love him with a ferociousness that scared me whenever I thought of life without him?

"Ah-Hui." Pippa's voice was stern when I didn't answer. "It's the eighties. You don't need to stay with a man who is unfaithful. And bringing his mistress into your home." She *tsk*ed and made a noise of disgust. "You can leave him. Get custody of Sam."

"No." The word came out more forcefully than I'd intended. "I can't ever leave him." I pushed the hair out of my eyes and turned to face her. "He loves our son so much, he'd never allow me to take him. And he still loves me." I looked down, knowing how pathetic my words were. If he truly loved me, then why was he still carrying on with Ren Ren after all these months? I thought I could wait it out, that it would run its course and he'd soon grow bored of her. But the opposite was true. Didn't he know he was hurting me, slowly killing me day by day?

"Is that what you want?" Pippa sat at the edge of the bed. "You want to stay in a marriage with a man who brought his mistress into your home? Taking care of your child? Ah-Hui, I'm serious. If you want to leave him, I can help. I know a very good divorce lawyer. She'd help you get custody of Sam."

We were silent for a moment, and then I looked up at Pippa. "I still love him." Tears dripped down my cheeks and my eyes lowered in shame. "I just can't be that modern woman and leave. I love him. I want *her* gone."

"Have you told him that?" Pippa laid a hand on my forearm. "Have you given him an ultimatum?"

I looked up with fear in my eyes. "You mean, like, either she leaves or I do?" I shook my head so hard my vision spun. "I can't take that chance." Because deep in my heart, I feared he would choose her over me. And that would kill me. "I'm stuck, Pippa. I have to stay. I won't lose my child, and there's no way he would let Sam go if I left him."

Pippa didn't say anything, but I could tell by the way she pressed her lips together that she didn't approve. The shame rose in me again, as I'd often heard my patients talking about standing up to a man, being an independent woman, not being owned by their husbands. This concept was new to me, having grown up in a culture that gave men all the power, even in this modern day.

We sat in silence for a while, and even though I knew Pippa didn't approve of my decision, I was comforted by her presence. Whenever I was alone, all the fear and paranoia would overcome me to the point I wondered how long I'd be able to stay sane.

"Stand up to him, Ah-Hui." Pippa leaned forward and took my hand. "Be strong. Tell him you know, and that you want him to stop."

I gave her a pointed look. "You really think my husband will agree?"

She shrugged. "You won't know until you ask."

I looked at her, this kind neighbor who had taken me and my child under her wing ever since we moved in, and for the first time since finding out about the affair, hope bloomed in my chest. Was there a possibility I could get my marriage back? I knew Pippa thought I'd be better off alone, but I couldn't fathom a life without him. It was *her* who I wanted gone.

"But first, I think you should take a shower and eat something." She held her nose with two fingers and grinned at me. "You kind of smell."

I wrinkled my nose at her but then laughed, relief filling me that someone understood and was standing up for me. "I guess if I'm going to win my husband back, this isn't the way to do it."

"Nope." She stood and reached down to help me out of bed. "Go shower. We can make your bed after you've changed."

I nodded, wishing I could show her how grateful I was. She was right. No wonder my husband was carrying on with Ren Ren. They were out there, side by side, fighting for a cause they believed in deeply, while I'd been hiding here in our home, a stinky shell of my former self. I needed to show my husband the woman he'd fallen in love with, who he'd married and had a child with. He was *my* husband, and it was time I remembered that.

That night, after Sam and Ren Ren had gone to bed, I asked Zhi Wei if he would go for a walk with me. He looked at me in surprise. When I'd first arrived in New York, he used to take me for a walk around the neighborhood every night to show me New York wasn't a scary place. I'd clung to his hand, practically glued to his side as we'd circle the block, widening our path as time went by. Even though I'd been filled with fright, I looked back on those walks with a sense of nostalgia. I'd been truly happy with my husband then, trusting him to protect me and always be by my side. I needed to find that man again, to remind him of everything we had and everything we'd built together.

We strolled in silence at first, the noise of the city enveloping us: the beeping of car horns, the screams of sirens, and the chatter of a group of young people as they jostled past us on the sidewalk. I took a breath, trying to compose myself and slow the beating of my heart. I felt as if I was preparing to fight for my life.

"I know, Zhi Wei," I said, not sure how else to start the conversation. I hadn't wanted to have it in our apartment, where Sam or Ren Ren could overhear.

"Know what?" He turned to me with a chuckle, but any trace of amusement left his face when he caught my expression.

I willed my voice not to shake and fisted my hands, feeling my nails digging into my palms. The pain reminded me I was alive.

"About Ren Ren." That was all I could say, and I dug my nails even deeper into my flesh.

"Ren—" He stopped, and for a moment I was relieved because at last, he was going to admit to his infidelity.

Yet he turned away, and we walked a few strides in silence. I thought he was going to ignore me, but then he glanced over at me. "What exactly do you know about Ren Ren?"

I blew out a breath, unable to believe that he was going to make me say it. But Pippa's words echoed in my head, and my chin lifted in resolve.

"I know you're sleeping with her. I know you broke our marriage vows. And I want you to stop. Now." My lips quivered, but I was proud of myself for having spoken my mind. I wished Pippa were here, because she'd give me a reassuring squeeze and tell me I was doing just fine.

"Me and—" My husband broke off, and I thought he was going to laugh, but then he stopped walking.

I halted, too, and turned back to him, my eyes meeting his stricken gaze.

"Yes." I forced myself to hold his stare, to channel Pippa and stand up for myself, even as my knees threatened to buckle and tumble me to the ground. "If you love me, you'll get rid of her."

I couldn't believe I'd said it. I'd uttered the ultimatum that Pippa had talked about, and I didn't know whether to cheer and clap my hands or turn and run all the way back to our apartment, jumping into bed and never getting out again.

We stood there, like two statues in the middle of Columbus Avenue on the Upper West Side of Manhattan as New Yorkers and tourists pushed past us on both sides. It felt like an eternity, and I was ready to crumble to the ground and tell him I took it all back, that nothing was wrong, everything was just great, when he moved. He reached out his hand and with his thumb, gently rubbed away the tear that I hadn't known trailed down my cheek.

"Okay." His eyes were on mine. "I'll stop."

My eyes widened but other than that, I didn't move. Had he just agreed? I was so elated I wanted to jump up and down, but I forced myself to remain calm.

"Really? You'll make her go?" I needed to hear him say the words before I believed they were true.

"No." He shook his head for emphasis, and my heart literally tumbled out of my chest. "I'll stop, but she's not going anywhere. We need her to watch Sam."

My mouth dropped open, and it took a few moments to find my voice. "What . . ." I cleared my voice and tried again. "What do you mean then?"

His hand dropped to his side. "I won't be with her anymore. But she stays in our household."

We stared at each other as the meaning of his words washed over me. Did I believe him? What was to say if she stayed that this wouldn't happen again? That whatever had drawn him to her wouldn't overcome him again? Yet this was more than I'd imagined. Perhaps there was hope for our marriage. Perhaps there was a way we could find our way back to each other.

Slowly, I reached out a hand, and he met it halfway. We intertwined our fingers like we used to do when we first met, and without another word, we headed back to our apartment. For the first time since finding out about the affair, I had hope.

⁂

1984, Manhattan

I ran for the bathroom, barely making it before my breakfast came back up. I hovered over the toilet, waiting for the queasiness in my stomach to pass, then collapsed on the tiled floor, leaning against the wall. I closed my eyes, knowing in my heart what was wrong but not ready to acknowledge it yet.

"No." I whispered the word out loud, praying I was wrong. But I knew I wasn't.

"Ah-Hui?" My husband knocked on the bathroom door. "Everything all right?"

"I'm fine." I got off the floor and rinsed my mouth, then looked at my image in the mirror. There were bags under my eyes, and my face was too pale, as if all the blood had been drained out of it. I looked terrible.

I waited a few minutes, hoping my husband would leave, but when I opened the door, he was waiting for me. His eyes filled with concern, and he reached out to pull me to him. I was too weak to resist.

"What is it? You don't look good." He stroked a hand down my hair, and I melted against him, wondering what he would think of this new development.

The past two and a half years had been tentative ones for us as I'd tried to put the affair behind me. Pippa had been so proud of me when I told her I'd stood up to him, told him he had to stop the affair. But she'd frowned when I told her he wouldn't ask Ren Ren to leave.

"You can get a new nanny. I'll help you until you find one." Her mouth was pursed, and I knew she itched to say more but was restraining herself.

"He won't do it." And the truth was, I was afraid to ask again. It was already such a big step for me to stand up for myself, for our marriage. I didn't want to push him right back into her arms.

Pippa hadn't said anything more, for which I was grateful. And true to his word, Zhi Wei had stopped sleeping with Ren Ren. But also true to his word, he didn't ask her to go. So she was always there, a constant reminder of that rift in our marriage, even as I tried to find a way back to the happy marriage we'd had before she arrived.

"Ah-Hui?" Zhi Wei asked, when I didn't answer. "What's wrong?"

Tears leaked out of my eyes, and I turned my face into his shirt, soaking the front of it. I'd always thought I was so strong, so smart. I thought I could do anything. But I'd realized in the past few years that I was a fraud. I couldn't make my husband do something he didn't want to. Part of me still believed Zhi Wei and I were destined to be together, and there had been so many good moments recently, yet I couldn't ever forget his transgression because she lived in our home, a daily reminder that I wasn't enough.

I didn't have the courage to demand she leave. So instead, I ignored the situation, pretending everything was fine. And if I kept thinking that, then I could convince myself that our marriage was perfect and my husband loved me and only me. Because whenever I let myself wallow in the knowledge that I hadn't been the only one sharing my husband's bed, I wanted to dissolve in tears and die. And I couldn't do that to my son.

Sam was the only thing that kept me going on the days when I wanted to wallow in self-pity. When I would catch a look between

Ren Ren and Zhi Wei that was way too intimate. When I saw the way Zhi Wei caught Ren Ren when she tripped on the sidewalk, and the way she clung to him for far too long after she had righted herself. The doubts would come then, even though Zhi Wei reassured me often he had stopped the affair. But I felt as if I was always living on the edge of collapse, just waiting for them to start up again.

Only Sam could make me smile in those times. He would jump into bed with me on my days off, when I didn't have to leave the house so early to tend to my sick patients. I was at my happiest then. I'd snuggle under the covers with him, listening to him tell me all about what he was going to do that day, or about his friends, and my heart was full. This was why I stayed. For my little boy.

He was so smart and had started reading by himself when he was four. He was curious and peppered me with questions that I didn't always have answers for. I loved him with a ferocity that scared me, and I knew if it were not for him, I'd have taken my life soon after finding out about Zhi Wei and Ren Ren's affair. Even though the two were no longer in a physical relationship, what they'd done hung over my head like a sword ready to strike. But for Sam, my little boy, I kept getting up every morning and going through the motions of life.

"Ah-Hui." My husband's voice brought me back to the present. "You're scaring me."

I pulled away from him and wiped my eyes with the back of my hand. "I think I'm pregnant," I whispered and then burst into tears, for I knew this pregnancy would hinder the freedom I'd recently been dreaming of.

"What?" Zhi Wei stared at me for a moment, and then he whooped and swept me up in his arms. "For real? This is amazing!"

He spun me around and I protested weakly, my poor stomach rebelling and almost making me throw up again. He put me down and started talking about all the plans he had for a new baby, how he hoped it was a girl and what he'd do with her. Something twisted inside me. I was relieved he was happy, but could I trust him? I wanted so much to believe we could become a happy family, with two beautiful children. But with Ren Ren constantly in our lives, how would that work? I still loved him and craved his touch, yet after each time, I'd be filled with remorse and self-disgust. It was exhausting and I didn't know how much longer I could keep up this charade of a marriage if he insisted on keeping Ren Ren in our home.

When we broke the news to Ren Ren a week later after the doctor confirmed my pregnancy, I watched her face closely. There was a moment of shock in her eyes, but then she smiled and congratulated us.

"Another baby. For me to take care of." A dreamy look crossed her face, and I wanted to scratch her eyes out.

"*I* will take care of this baby." I couldn't keep the defiance out of my voice. "Sam is almost ten years old. We won't need a nanny anymore." And it was then I fully realized why I was so unhappy about this pregnancy.

With Sam getting older, I had dreamed that soon, we would no longer need Ren Ren and she could finally leave our household. But now with a new baby on the way?

"Ah-Hui, don't be silly." My husband laughed, confirming my worst fears. "You're busy with your job at the hospital. Ren Ren will take good care of her, just like she did Sam." He gave her an affectionate pat on the shoulder, and I had to turn away.

I didn't often spend much time with the two of them, having learned how to avoid them when they were together. I may have lost the battle to banish Ren Ren from our home, but I wouldn't watch them together. I'd had so many daydreams of running away, taking Sam and starting over somewhere where I didn't have to live with the woman my husband had bedded. I was an excellent doctor. I could get a job anywhere. I'd heard that they were in need of physicians on Kauai, a place I'd always wanted to visit. But now with a baby on the way, how could I do that? Zhi Wei was right. If

I was to keep working, I needed someone I trusted to take care of the baby. And as much as I hated her, I had to admit I *did* trust Ren Ren with my children.

I held it together more or less for my entire pregnancy, even as I kept dreaming of Kauai. Yet I couldn't deny I still loved Zhi Wei and knew I wouldn't do it. I wanted Ren Ren to run away, not me. She was the interloper in our marriage, not me. I hated her with a passion some days, yet I couldn't feel the same for my husband. And because of these conflicting thoughts, I was always highly stressed at home.

When our baby arrived, I fell in love all over again. She was beautiful, so perfect I was in awe. I touched her little bow lips and then her forehead, and knew I would protect her with everything I had.

"She's an angel," Zhi Wei whispered next to me. He reached out his hands as if wanting to take her from me, but I wasn't ready to give her up yet.

"I want to name her Chiao-Yi." I didn't look at my husband when I said this. My grandmother was named Chiao-Li, and I wanted a part of my daughter to have something of my grandmother. I still missed my ah-ma so much, and tears fell from my eyes as I wondered whether she was still alive and if she would ever meet her great-granddaughter.

"Okay." Zhi Wei stroked a finger gently over the baby's cheek. "Chiao-Yi."

Sam was absolutely enthralled with his baby sister. At ten years old, he wanted to help and often took her out of my arms.

"Here, Mama. I'll take her. You eat." He cradled his sister in his arms as Ren Ren hovered behind him, ready to catch her if Sam dropped her.

"Thank you." I gave my son a small smile, for even though I loved the baby, a fog had descended over my mind ever since I'd brought her home from the hospital.

I couldn't clear my head. I felt as if I were swimming underwater, fighting to break through the surface so I could breathe, feel alive. Most days, I wouldn't get out of bed in the morning until Ren Ren brought the baby to me to nurse. Sam often had to cajole me out of bed and into the shower, and I got up only because I didn't want to disappoint my little boy. I no longer had the will to do anything. All I wanted to do was sleep. Stay in the cocoon of my bed, all my worries far away.

I thought I would feel better once my body healed, but I only got worse. One day, when Chiao-Yi was four months old and she and I were home alone together, our home phone rang. I was in bed, with the baby snuggled at my side, even though I knew I shouldn't do that. I feared I'd fall asleep and roll over on her or accidentally smother her with a pillow. But I had no energy, no desire to get up. I was supposed to have returned to work, but I couldn't do it.

I ignored the phone, and it stopped ringing. But then it started again, and then again, until I couldn't take the noise anymore and finally reached across the bed to Zhi Wei's night table where an extension was.

"What?" I said, instead of hello. I knew my voice was crabby, but I couldn't help it.

"It's me, Pippa."

"Oh." My voice softened and I cleared my throat. "I'm sorry."

"I'm coming down. Please open the door for me."

"I'm not . . . I . . . It's not a good time." I was at a loss for words. I didn't want to tell her I was still in bed, even though it was after one in the afternoon.

"Ah-Hui. I'm coming in, even if I have to use my key like last time."

I paused, thinking about the day she made me get out of bed and confront Zhi Wei. "Fine. I'll let you in."

Five minutes later, Pippa was sitting on our couch with me next to her, Chiao-Yi snuggled in my arms.

"You can't go on like this." Her voice was gentle, even though the look on her face was not. We'd grown close in the time since she'd told me to stand up to my husband, and she knew me better than I knew myself sometimes.

"I know." There was no use denying anything to her. Pippa saw right through me, and I often wondered how she was able to do that.

"I never told you about my husband, did I?"

It wasn't really a question since both of us knew she'd never even told me she *had* a husband. But I shook my head, nevertheless.

"He was a serial cheater, had been from the time we were dating, but I didn't know it back then. All I knew was that this handsome firefighter was in love with me and wanted to marry me. I felt so lucky." Her voice was dreamy and there was a sad smile on her face.

"Oh." I breathed out that word. No wonder she'd been so perceptive when it came to my situation.

"I had no idea until our second anniversary, when a woman stormed into the restaurant where we were having dinner, a baby in her arms. She claimed it was his and tried to give the baby to him. They argued, right there in public, and I wanted to die of shame."

"What happened?" I couldn't help leaning closer, feeling like we were in this together.

"The woman left without her baby. I left, too, and he ran after me, all the way with the baby in his arms." Pippa turned to smile at Chiao-Yi, where she cooed from my arms, waving her fists in the air. "He told me that night, about all the women he'd slept with. He cried, said he loved me, that I was the one for him, but he couldn't help it. It was an illness, he said, like getting cancer or having allergies." Pippa turned to me, her mouth twisted in a smirk. "That was the first time I've ever wanted to smack anyone. In fact, I did smack him, hard across the face. Then I took the baby from him and told him to get out."

"You did that?" I marveled at her bravery. "You got divorced then?"

"No." She shook her head, a small smile on her lips. "He had a heart attack two weeks later, at the age of twenty-seven. Turned out he'd had a heart murmur his whole life, and I guess the stress of me finding out about all his affairs strained his heart." Pippa turned to me with a laugh. "At least I like to think it was my fault."

A laugh escaped from me, and I clapped a hand over my mouth. I couldn't help it.

"I adopted that baby and raised her as my own because her mother had disappeared. She's now a wife and mother, with two little ones of her own."

"You're amazing." I admired her, even though I couldn't do the same for myself.

"What if you left New York?" Pippa turned to me, her expression suddenly serious.

"Without my family?" My mouth dropped open. "I can't do that."

"I meant *with* your family. Not her." Pippa's expression darkened, and I realized I'd never heard her call Ren Ren by name. "Start somewhere new. Just the four of you. Maybe if you got away from the Taiwanese political climate here in New York, go somewhere where it's not as prevalent, you and your husband could come together again."

"Oh." I couldn't help the gasp of surprise that Pippa had read my mind. "I've been thinking about that," I admitted. "They're hiring physicians on Kauai. I've always wanted to go there." I looked off into space, thinking of taking my family minus Ren Ren, living in paradise away from the rallies and protests, the newspapers, and the rumors that abounded in the Taiwanese American community here as they fought for independence.

"There you go." Pippa sat back, a satisfied look on her face. "Take your family to paradise. Leave the nanny behind."

I smiled, the fantasy filling my heart. But then I thought of the way Zhi Wei had always protected Ren Ren, how he'd refused to ask her to leave, and I knew it was just a pipe dream.

"He'll never agree to leave her behind." I shook my head, looking down at the baby, sleeping so peacefully in my arms.

"Plan it carefully." Pippa's voice dropped into a conspiratory tone. "Make him think it's his idea to start over somewhere new while helping the community but without her. Find an excuse, anything to make him believe that this is necessary for your family. I'll help you brainstorm."

I nodded, even though I didn't have any faith that we'd come up with a plan. But Pippa was right. I had to get rid of Ren Ren somehow. I couldn't allow her to destroy my marriage and my family any longer.

15

Joey
Present Day, Kauai

Joey's phone dinged, bringing her out of her mother's world and back to Sam's apartment. She looked down to find a text from Ethan.

> Heading into work but I can come over later if you need company.

Joey smiled, thinking about him. While she'd love to see him, she needed to be alone today. She had a lot to think about and couldn't deal with the distraction that was Ethan. She intended to take Wonton and visit her old haunts, places where she had good memories of Sam.

> I'm fine. I need time to myself. What about lunch or something tomorrow? Oh, and by the way, my clogged ear finally released! Thank you for the Sudafed suggestion!

He sent a reply right away. Okay, but if you get lonely, just reach out. You're going to have dinner with the Kellys tonight, right? And yay for the ear.

Yes. Joey typed back. I'm going to wander around Kauai today with Wonton. Remember my brother.

Okay. Talk soon.

Thanks. She almost sent a heart emoji but stopped herself at the last minute. She needed to eventually figure out what she was feeling for Ethan, but now wasn't the time.

She stood and stretched, her body cramped from sitting so long on the couch, reading. She was proud of her mother for standing up to her father. It broke her heart at all her mother had been through, and anger at her father had made her curse a few times as she'd read. And Ren Ren Ayi? Joey wanted to spit at what her nanny had done. What kind of woman was she to come into their home for a job and then destroy the family by sleeping with the husband while living with them? Ren Ren was the type of woman Joey had always hated—women who were either too insecure to find their own boyfriends and instead preyed on married men or who knew exactly what they were doing and got pleasure out of destroying families. Funny how Joey had found herself as the other woman, even if she hadn't meant to be.

She shook her head, the anger at her beloved nanny and her father too fresh to examine right now. She had things to take care of today. Number one on her list was getting the death certificate and asking Victor to help her with the process of getting the will into probate court.

But before she could do anything, her phone rang and she picked it up.

"Maggie! You always know when I need you."

Her best friend laughed, and something loosened in Joey's chest. "Guess what. I cleared my schedule, and I'm coming to Kauai tomorrow to see you. And I'm bringing Kristy."

"No way." Joey's heart leaped. "I didn't think you could get off work that fast. And Ben's family is letting Kristy come with you?"

"They can't stop me from bringing her to see her other grandparents. Ben is fine with it, so there's nothing they can do. I have to pull her out of school for one day, but it's an emergency." Maggie's voice was light. "You need me."

"I do. So much has happened. I have so much to tell you." Joey shook her head. "I feel as if my head is going to explode."

"Keep your head on," Maggie chided softly. "I'll be there in the afternoon, and with Kristy spending time with my parents, you can tell me everything."

"Thank you." Joey was so happy her best friend was coming. "And if you need to vent about Ben's family, I'm all ears too."

Maggie laughed. "Thanks. I already booked our flights." She paused for a beat. "How're you doing about Sam being gone?"

"I'm holding it together. Mostly because I've been distracted by our mother's journal and finding out all our family secrets." Joey gave a sigh. "But there's so much I have to do to settle his estate."

"I'll be there soon." Maggie's confidence made Joey feel better.

"Thanks, Maggie." Joey thought for a moment and then blurted out, "Did you know Ethan got divorced a few months ago?"

"What? No way." Maggie's voice rose in surprise. "I've only been back to Kauai for a quick visit at Christmas last year, and I didn't run into Ethan. Sam didn't say anything and neither did my parents."

"I guess the subject never came up. Ethan told me yesterday. They'd been separated for a while."

"Wow. What're you going to do about it?" Maggie teased.

"Nothing," Joey said firmly. "I can't get wrapped up in all those old feelings for him."

"Oh. Your graduation dinner." Her best friend's voice was thick with sympathy.

Maggie knew about that kiss all those years ago and how wrong it had all turned out. Joey had been so elated that Ethan was *finally* kissing her, seeing her as a woman. But then he'd suddenly pulled away and looked so shocked. He'd muttered something that sounded like an apology, making Joey's heart drop. And then he'd turned and walked so fast back to his car he'd practically been running. She'd stood there on the doorstep, staring after him, embarrassment and despair warring within her. And then the humiliation had hit, and she'd run into the house and into her bedroom, burying her face under a pillow.

Ethan had tried to talk to her the next day when he'd found her at the pool about to start her shift as a lifeguard. "I'm sorry. I shouldn't have done that. You're only eighteen, and I'm eight years older than you. I shouldn't have taken advantage of you."

She'd stared at him, devastated that he thought she was too young. She wanted to scream, *Look at me. I'm about to go to college. I'm not a little kid anymore.*

But the guilt in Ethan's eyes had stopped her. He regretted the kiss, and she would not let him see her cry.

"It's fine, Ethan. It didn't mean anything. I was just carried away from graduating and that fabulous dinner." She'd turned away and started slathering on sunscreen before she went up on the lifeguard stand.

They'd never spoken of it again. Joey acted like nothing had happened when she came home for breaks from college. And then two years after that kiss, she found out Ethan was engaged to Naomi. She'd vowed that day she'd never think of Ethan again and had started avoiding Kauai because of him.

"Uh-huh." Maggie's voice brought Joey back to the present. "You know I'll get the full story out of you."

Joey smiled. "I'm sure you will. But there's not much to tell."

"I can't wait to see you." Maggie's voice grew softer. "I'm really sorry about Sam."

"I know. And I can't wait to see you too. To give you a big hug for everything you've been through," Joey said. "Do you need me to pick you up at the airport?"

"No. My dad will get me. I'll text you as I'm landing."

"Okay." Joey nodded. "I'll start heading down as soon as you land."

When they hung up, Joey sat for a moment and then realized she was hungry. It was one in the afternoon, and she decided to take Wonton and go to the food trucks at Hanalei. She'd done that with Sam the last time she'd seen him, and she wanted to relive the experience. After, she and Wonton would take a walk on the beach, and she would bring the binder with her mother's words to read at lunch and on the sand.

"Come on, Wonton." She held up the dog's harness after she'd changed into a bathing suit and put on sunscreen. Wonton willingly stuck her head through it.

Joey picked up the water bottle she'd filled with ice water and grabbed a beach towel from the shelf in the entryway on her way out. Her heart lifted when they were in the sunshine, and she closed her eyes for a moment to feel the heat of the rays on her skin. She'd missed the way Kauai smelled, so sweet and clean, unlike anywhere else she'd ever been. She missed the sense of community, the way drivers always let each other go first, and the aloha spirit, so different from the frenetic city life she was used to.

The drive to Hanalei was short, and she pulled into the parking lot down the street from where the food trucks were set up. She picked Wonton up as she made her way back to the trucks, because there were no sidewalks and cars passed dangerously close. Once she'd gotten past that stretch of road, she put Wonton back on the ground, and they made their way into the *U* of the food-truck area. She went immediately to the first truck, a farm-to-beach one, and ordered a salad bowl made of locally sourced vegetables and other ingredients. She'd had one with Sam last time and had enjoyed how fresh and tasty it was. While she waited, she wandered farther in with Wonton and decided to get a donut from Holy Grail. She figured with how healthy the salad was, she could indulge. But then she couldn't decide and ended up ordering both a guava and a lilikoi one.

"Oh well." She shrugged at Wonton as they made their way back to the first food truck to pick up her salad. "We'll burn this off with a nice walk on the beach."

They found a picnic table and Joey settled Wonton under the table with a bowl of water and a liver treat. Then she dug into the food, closing her eyes to see if she could feel Sam's presence next to her. She really wished his ghost would come back and haunt her, make her feel less alone in the world. But there was nothing, not even a whisper of a breeze or a sound that could have been Sam sending her a signal.

"Joey?" The high-pitched voice made her eyes pop open to find a tall, skinny woman staring at her.

"Um, yeah." She flipped her sunglasses on top of her head to get a better look. The woman looked familiar, but Joey couldn't place her.

"It's me. Makayla. From high school?" The woman smiled, lighting up her face.

"Oh, right. Hi, how are you?" Joey stood and they hugged, just as a girl around ten came running up to them.

"Mommy, I want a donut." The little girl had long dark hair and the same dark skin as her mother. She was joined by a boy who looked a bit younger, who also asked for a donut.

"Meet my two oldest." Makayla pushed them in front of her, even though they squirmed and kept looking back at the donut truck. "We also have a one-year-old at home. My husband stayed back with her."

"Wow, you have three kids?" Joey couldn't have felt more inadequate in that moment.

"Yes." Makayla beamed at her, her long hair blowing in the breeze. She and her daughter were nearly identical. "They're a handful but we love it."

Joey nodded. "That's great."

"What about you? Any kids?" Makayla kept a firm grip on her daughter's shoulder when she tried to run back to the donuts.

"No." Joey shook her head. "No kids or husband." She gave a short laugh. "Just my work to keep me busy."

"Oh." Makayla's eyes softened in sympathy, and Joey suddenly felt truly pathetic about not having a family at the ripe old age of thirty-nine. "I get it about work. I'm a freelance editor, and when we had our first child, my husband wanted me to quit. But I knew if I did that, I would regret it. I love my job. I need it to balance my home life, you know?"

Joey nodded, even though she didn't know. Now she felt even more pathetic. The woman was not only a wife and mother of three but she also had a career? Joey wanted to shrink into herself and disappear, but Wonton took that moment to shoot out from under the table.

"Mommy, look at the cute dog!" Makayla's son pointed at Wonton. "Can I pet him?"

"Why don't you ask my friend Joey?" Makayla nudged him forward.

"Can I pet your dog?" The boy looked away shyly.

"Sure. And Wonton is a girl. Hold out your hand like this." Joey leaned down to supervise the introduction.

The two children delighted in petting and playing with Wonton while Joey and Makayla caught up on the people they knew. And when Joey told her why she was back on island, Makayla's face crumbled in sadness.

"I'm sorry, Joey. I remember how close you were." She put a hand on Joey's arm. "If there's anything I can do, please call me. Here, let's exchange numbers." She pulled out her phone.

"Thank you. I may stay on island for a bit." Joey swallowed the lump in her throat.

"I'd better get these two the donuts we promised them for doing well at school." Makayla rolled her eyes. "Before they kidnap your dog. They've been begging for a dog for a while now." She leaned in closer and whispered, "We're finally caving and adopting one from the shelter. It'll be their Christmas present, and we're going to let them pick out the dog."

"That's great." Joey smiled at the utter delight the kids had in Wonton. But a wistful feeling passed through her, something she wasn't used to feeling.

In her world, she was a strong, independent woman, someone who always got the story and wrote them in a compassionate yet powerful way. Her volunteer work had people looking up to her, and the small fame from her books hadn't hurt her image either. But now suddenly, she wondered whether she'd been missing out on this part of life. She'd sworn off men after the Oliver debacle, thinking having a family just wasn't for her, that she was fine being independent, able to travel to wherever she wanted at the drop of a hat. But was that enough?

She said goodbye to Makayla and turned back to her food. Opening the donut box, she bit into the guava one, needing the sugar rush to fuel her flagging morale. She let herself enjoy the donut, one of the best she'd ever had, as she thought about how much Sam had loved these and his delight in introducing them to her. And thinking of Sam made her think of Ethan. She couldn't deny how much she was still drawn to him. Did she want to pursue this? She'd always gone after everything she wanted, not afraid of rejection. But now, she was tired, her whole world turned upside down. She didn't even know who she was anymore.

Finishing the treat, she stood, deciding she'd had enough of her maudlin mood. She wanted to go to the beach, feel the sand between her toes and hear the roar of the ocean. They made their way back to the car, where Joey put the extra donut in the cooler she'd brought, then drove down to the Hanalei Pier parking lot. Grabbing her bag, which contained her towel, water bottle for both her and Wonton, and her mother's journal, she got out. Picking their way carefully through the gravel of the parking lot, they made their way across the lawn toward the sand, the pier rising in the distance. It was a beautiful day, the temperature just right and the sun shining brightly in the sky. Once she stepped onto the beach, she stood for a moment, taking in a deep breath and feeling her toes sinking into the fine sand. The breeze lifted her hair, and the smell and sounds of the ocean immediately calmed her.

She allowed herself to just be and looked out over the water at the magnificent emerald-green mountains rising across the bay. Waterfalls cascaded high up on the mountains to her left, and the view of the sweeping shoreline took her breath away. Up ahead on the right, the pier stretched out over the waters of Hanalei Bay, where tourists and locals gathered, some jumping off the pier into the water below. This was where she'd learned to surf, in the calmer waters to the left of the pier. She remembered how terrified, yet exhilarated she'd been when Sam had taken her out and held on to the back of her surfboard, keeping her steady until she felt confident enough to go by herself.

Wonton scratched in the sand, making Joey look down with a smile. "You want to walk, huh? Let's put the towel and bag down and claim a spot."

They started walking to the left and found a spot against the back of the beach. Joey anchored the towel with the water bottle and sunscreen but took the bag containing the binder along with her phone and keys. She wasn't about to let her brother's translation of their mother's journal out of her sight. It was the last thing Sam had given her.

"Ready, Wonton? Let's walk by the water, okay?" Wonton jumped forward eagerly, leading the way down to the shoreline.

Joey had always loved to walk this beach, which was about two miles long. She used to come here when she needed to clear her head, and she'd had many dates here also, holding hands with her boyfriend at the time and kicking up sand as they'd frolicked at the ocean's edge. She remembered her giggles and how carefree her high school years had been, all because of Sam.

A scruffy dog passed, and he and Wonton sniffed, tails wagging for a moment before they continued on. With each step she took in the wet sand, with each breeze that kissed her skin, and with every sunbeam that bounced off the ocean, making her glad she had her sunglasses on, Joey felt her shoulders relax a bit more. Locals and tourists alike had made camp on the beach, huddled under umbrellas or giant awnings, or lying out in the sand. Joey's strides lengthened and her calves pulled in a pleasing way against the soft sand. Sam was right to make her come back here. Nowhere on Earth felt like home to her as much as Kauai did.

She turned around when they reached the lifeguard stand, not sure how much of a walk Wonton could handle. Her tongue was hanging out and she was panting, but she was also trotting along, looking like she was thoroughly enjoying the outing. Joey let herself forget everything as they walked, all the doubts and anger and fears that had warred within her since finding out Sam was gone. She would deal with them later. For now, she was going to enjoy the beauty of Kauai and get in touch with the island again.

When they made it back to where Joey had left their towel, Wonton immediately flopped down on it. Joey poured water into her travel bowl, and the dog began lapping it up, spraying water everywhere. Joey laughed and took a drink herself, enjoying the cold water as it slid down her throat. Thirst sated, she flopped onto her stomach and pulled out the journal. Turning to where she'd left off, she stared at the ocean for a few moments, wondering what she was about to discover.

Sighing, she turned back to the journal and began reading.

16

Ah-Hui
1987, Taichung

It'd been fifteen years since I left Taiwan as a wide-eyed romantic, thinking the Old Man Under the Moon had finally found my predestined one and joined us with a thread that could never be broken. Why had no one told me this thread could also bind in a cruel way, forcing me to stay with a man who had broken our marriage vows and disrespected me?

I held my twelve-year-old son's hand tighter as we crossed the wide street, darting between cars and scooters that came at us as if they were aiming for us. Sam shouted at my side, the thrill of being in this foreign land making him cling tighter to my hand, when back on Kauai, where we'd finally moved to the year before, he wouldn't have allowed me to hold his hand in public.

"Where're we going?" he yelled over the roar of the traffic. We ran until our feet hit the sidewalk, then we looked at each other in relief that we'd made it to the other side safely.

"We're going to try and find my family." We entered the train station, and I stood for a moment, overwhelmed by all the people rushing from one side to the other.

Sam stopped short and pulled his hand from mine. "What family? I thought you don't have any?"

I turned to look at him, my bright, handsome boy who always stood up for me no matter what. He was like my own personal cheerleader. On the days when I felt as if I couldn't go on, he'd be there with his tight hugs, his words of praise, his undying love for me shining through. I could do no wrong in his eyes, and on the rare occasion when Zhi Wei and I disagreed in front of him, he always took my side.

"My family didn't want me marrying your baba." I started walking with him keeping pace by my side. "They stopped talking to me. I never heard from them again. But unless something happened to them, I think they're still there somewhere on the outskirts of Taichung. We're going to try and find them today."

"Oh, wow." Sam's voice was awed and his steps slowed. "You mean like cousins and stuff?"

"Maybe." I looked over my shoulder at him. "But today we're going to try and find out what happened to my mother and my grandparents."

"Why didn't Baba and Chiao-Yi come with us?" He hurried at my side, looking around at all the people and activities with wide eyes.

Because I didn't tell him what I was going to do.

Out loud I said, "Your sister is still a bit sick from the flight. Baba volunteered to stay at the hotel and watch her."

Zhi Wei had announced a month ago that he needed to return to Taiwan. He didn't say why, and no matter how I asked, he only gave me vague details about doing something for his family. Which I knew was a lie as he had no contact with his family either. When I found out Ren Ren would not be going because she couldn't risk showing her face back in Taiwan, I jumped at the chance for us to be a family of four again.

"The children and I will go with you," I told him.

No matter how Pippa and I schemed, we couldn't come up with a plan to make Zhi Wei fire Ren Ren. I'd been tearful the day I'd said goodbye to Pippa, when we left Manhattan and headed to Kauai to our new life. With Ren Ren.

He stared at me and then shook his head. "It's not s—" He broke off, but I knew he was going to say, *It's not safe.*

"Why?" I challenged him. "You said you're not involved in Taiwanese politics. So why would it be dangerous for us to go back to Taiwan? You told me I could visit my family."

"Ah-Hui." He ran a hand down his face. "They haven't responded to any of your letters. Why would you want to visit them?"

I set my jaw, debating my answer, but I knew I wasn't going to back down.

"I need to see them. Hear for myself that they really want nothing to do with me. If that's the case, then so be it; I can move on. But until I hear it from them, I'll always wonder." I took a breath, knowing I couldn't get emotional. "I'm going, Zhi Wei. I think it would be a good thing for us to go as a family." *Without Ren Ren,* I didn't add.

Zhi Wei had finally acquiesced, and our family of four had flown to Taipei from Kauai two days ago. How wonderful it'd been to be just us again, with no interloper taking up space and driving us apart. How I wished Ren Ren would disappear, but no matter how much I asked and pushed, Zhi Wei refused to let her go. She was right now back at our house, looking after things until we returned.

I clenched my jaw, grinding my teeth at the thought of Ren Ren. Every day, I wished something would happen to her. I wanted her gone because I knew as long as she lived with us, the threat of my husband starting his affair with her again would always be there. I forced myself to relax as I headed for the train that would take us to the country town and my grandparents' house. My nerves were so revved up, and I was at once looking forward to seeing them again, as well as apprehensive of the reception I would find. I thought that bringing Sam would make the reunion easier, for how could anyone resist the charm of my son? I refused to let myself think what I would do if they weren't there.

Less than an hour later, we were walking down the lone dirt road that ran in front of my grandparents' home. My steps slowed as I looked at all the changes around me. The trees were bigger, the homes older, but some familiar landmarks jumped out at me, like the fences that marked the boundaries of my grandparents' farm from their neighbors, and the fields that stretched for miles behind their house. As we came up the hill that would lead down toward my grandparents' place, my steps slowed until Sam looked at me.

"Are you nervous? Do you think they won't like me?" He looked so worried that I forced myself to smile.

"They're going to love you. How could they not?" I would have said more, but we'd crested the hill, and as we started going down the other side, my grandparents' property came into view and my eyes darted to the house.

My hands flew up to cover my mouth and I gasped, staring at the derelict building that used to be the place I called home. It looked like no one had lived there in a long time. One side of the building was sagging, as if it had sunk into the ground beneath, while a large hole in the roof on the other side looked like a tree had fallen on it at one point. The beautiful fruit groves my grandmother had tended were wild and overgrown, and tears came to my eyes at the state of the property that I'd been dreaming of for fifteen years.

"Is that the house?" Sam pointed at it. "It doesn't look like anyone lives here."

I closed my eyes, hoping that when I opened them again, I'd see the house and grounds I remembered before I left Taiwan. But the same broken-down home and neglected grounds greeted me, and I had to stifle a sob. What had happened? Where was my family?

I don't know how long I would have stood there staring at the depressing scene if a woman hadn't come walking up the dirt path from the other side. She stopped as she got near us and asked in Taiwanese, "Can I help you? Are you lost?"

I hadn't recognized her, but I remembered the voice. "Ing?" I asked, my mouth flying open and my eyes roaming over her features, seeing my best friend from when we were children.

"Yes, I'm Ing. How do you know—" She broke off, and a look of recognition crossed her face. "Ah-Hui? Is that you?"

"Yes." I nodded because my voice failed me after that. She took a step closer, then she was smiling, laughing, and grabbing me for a hug. I embraced her back, and then we were both talking at the same time, trying to ask our questions as laughter made us stop.

"I thought I'd never see you again." Ing was deeply tanned, probably from spending so much time outside. She hadn't attended university, but rather had decided to stay on her parents' farm and help them. "What are you doing here?"

I gestured to the house behind her. "I was hoping to find my grandparents and my mother. What happened? Where'd they go?"

Ing turned to look at the house, then her gaze swung back to me, her lips pressed together and a sorrowful look on her face. "You don't know what happened to your grandparents?"

"No," I whispered. "I sent them money, wrote to them after I left for New York. But they never answered any of my letters or calls."

"Oh." Ing stared at me, her eyes filled with sympathy. "I'm so sorry."

"Sorry for what?" I felt my stomach drop, as if I'd stepped off the side of a cliff.

She looked as if she was about to speak but then shook her head. "Not here, on the street. Why don't you come to our place, sit down, have some tea and a snack. I can tell you all I know."

I looked at Sam, who had perked up at the prospect of food and drink. He nodded, and I knew he was hungry again, a never-ending eating machine now that he was twelve years old.

I turned back to her. "Are you sure? I don't want to put you to any trouble."

Ing waved a hand in the air, and we headed toward her property. "No trouble at all. I was just going for a walk, but I'd much rather catch up with an old friend." She beamed, and I was hit with remorse that I hadn't kept in touch with her once I went off to NTU. "I'm in charge now," she said over her shoulder. "My father had an accident, lost part of his right arm. He decided to pass the farm to me, and even though he helps out once in a while, it's now my responsibility."

"That's great." I knew she'd never aspired to live in the city. She'd been content here and had often told me she hoped to take over her parents' vegetable farm when they retired. She looked happy, which was more than I could say for myself.

Once we were settled inside her modest home, with cups of hot tea in hand and biscuits for Sam to snack on as he played outside, she turned to me.

"You're saying you've had no contact with your family since you went to New York?"

I nodded. "I kept hoping my grandmother at least would write to me, tell me how everyone was doing. But I never heard from anyone. Tell me what you know."

Ing sat back in her chair, a grim look on her face. "Your grandfather was imprisoned by the KMT soon after you left." She stopped when I gasped.

"Oh no. Why?" My eyes widened in shock.

"I'm not positive, but something about him owing money to someone in the KMT." Her face softened and she looked like she wanted to reach out and touch me, but then she drew her hand back. "Ah-Hui, I'm sorry to tell you this, but he died in prison a few months after they took him."

"No." The word escaped from my suddenly cold lips, and horror washed through me.

I'd known he owed money, but not that he owed it to the KMT. No wonder they'd wanted to marry me into a KMT family. They were not only trying to save face but also trying to save my grandfather's life. And I'd left them and gone with Zhi Wei to New York, and the KMT had gotten my grandfather. No wonder no one ever wrote me back. They must have surely blamed me.

Ing was still talking about all the people we knew who were imprisoned or disappeared, but I barely registered her words. All I could think was that I had killed my grandfather. Would I have stayed and married Li-Jie if I'd known my grandfather's life was in jeopardy? Would I have stayed and been the good daughter I'd always been, if I'd known he would be thrown in jail and killed? He was an old man when I left, and I couldn't imagine how he'd endured the torture I knew was bestowed upon prisoners. My stomach heaved, and for a moment I thought I'd be sick all over Ing's clean floor. I doubled over, one hand clamped over my mouth.

"Are you okay?" Ing was suddenly by my side, a glass of cold water in her hand.

She rubbed my back as I took a few careful sips. I couldn't stop the chant in my head: *You killed your grandfather. You killed your grandfather. And all for someone who cares so little about you that he was sleeping with his mistress right under your nose.*

"What happened to my mother and grandmother?" I finally asked when I could speak again. "Where are they now?"

Ing lifted a shoulder and let it fall. "I have no idea where your mother is. When your grandfather was taken, she left the farm—I think to find out what happened to him. She never came back." Ing looked out the window toward the direction of my grandparents' old house. "Last I heard, your grandmother was living with one of her sons in Tainan. But I have no idea if she's still there." *Or if she's still alive,* Ing didn't say out loud but I heard anyway.

I took in a deep breath, trying to calm my heart. I knew my mother would never forgive me. I'd killed her father, or at least had been the reason he was imprisoned, and she would never forgive me for this. But I still longed for her, longed for my grandmother, wondering whether she blamed me too.

"I'm sorry to be the one to give you such terrible news." Ing stood and sat back down in her chair.

"I . . ." I couldn't think of what to say. I wanted to thank her, but for what? I wanted to ask her more questions, but I knew she didn't have the answers.

"How long are you here for?"

"Just until the end of next week." I was still reeling from the news about my family. "My husband is here on business."

"What are you going to do?"

"Look for my grandmother and my mother." I took in a deep breath. "I'm sure they blame me for what happened to my grandfather, but I need to see them. To reconcile with them. Do you have a last address or phone number for my grandmother?"

Ing shook her head. "You're not in touch with any of your family?"

"No." I couldn't meet her eyes. "I didn't even know one of my uncles was living in Tainan. I guess I should start there."

"I'll ask around, see if anyone I know has been in touch with anyone in your family."

I smiled at her, gratitude in my heart. "Thank you, Ing."

We spent the next hour catching up, with Sam running in and out, telling me all about Ing's dogs. He'd been asking for a dog for the past two years, but with us moving from Manhattan to Kauai, it had been too hectic. Maybe once we got back to Kauai, we could finally adopt one.

When it was time to leave, I embraced Ing.

"Keep in touch." We'd exchanged our contact info, and Ing promised again to reach out if she heard anything about my family.

"I will." She squeezed my arm and then walked out with me to get my son.

She waved from the front of her house as we headed back up the dirt road. I paused in front of my grandparents' house, sadness filling me at what had become of our family home. Sam halted at my side, silent. I wondered why none of my aunts or uncles had taken over the house. Why had they let it go into such disrepair?

I decided to ask Victor to help me find my mother and grandmother. He had many connections in Taiwan, and he did say I could come to him whenever I needed help. I wasn't going to tell my husband, because he was no longer someone I confided in. I gazed at the courtyard where I had spent so many happy years and vowed that I would never turn my back on my children.

They were the most important things to me in my life, and I would protect them, no matter what.

17

Joey
Present Day, Kauai

After getting home from the beach, Joey took a quick shower, fed Wonton dinner from the food Ethan had made, and then headed next door. She showed up with a six-pack of Kona Longboards, which Ethan had told her was Mac's favorite, and a bottle of sparkling rosé, which was Linda's happy hour drink of choice.

"You didn't have to bring anything, dear," Linda said as she ushered Joey and Wonton into their unit. "Mac's out back tending the grill. Hope you like smoked black cod. He has a friend who was a fisherman in British Columbia, and whenever he visits us, he brings us giant slabs of the fish that he smoked himself."

"Yum." Joey sniffed the air, the tantalizing aroma of the fish on the grill making her mouth water. She relinquished the drinks to Linda and followed Wonton out to the lanai.

"There you are. Food's almost done." Mac waved the tongs in his hands as he sipped from a glass of beer in the other.

"I brought you more Longboards." Joey looked up as Linda came out with two glasses of the sparkling rosé in hand.

"Thanks, Joey." Mac's eyes twinkled at her before he turned back to the grill and plated the fish.

Linda handed a glass to Joey, and after clinking their glasses together, Joey took a sip of the refreshing wine. She sat at the table and watched Wonton run out onto the grass, chasing after a bird that Joey knew was a myna, with a yellow beak and legs. It alighted in the Kellys' yard and then flew off again once Wonton got too close. The air was fragrant from the plumeria tree in the corner, mingling with the aroma from the grill. It would have been an idyllic evening, if only Sam were there with them.

"So, Joey." Linda sat in the chair next to her. "How're you doing?"

"I've been better." Something about Linda made Joey want to talk to her, to tell her how she was really feeling. She hadn't had a mother or mother figure since she was ten, and now all the emotions inside her begged to be let out.

"Oh, Joey." Linda reached over to pat her hand.

"It's like my whole life was a lie. I thought my parents had the perfect marriage, but it turns out they didn't. I adored my nanny and was mad at Sam for making her go away, and yet she was in the wrong and Sam was right. I just feel angry right now. At my father, my old nanny, even at Sam for dying. And then I look at my best friend, Maggie. Yes, she's getting a divorce, but she had a husband once, and they have a beautiful child. She has a mortgage." Joey paused, thinking of Makayla, who really put her to shame. "And then there's me, wanderlust making me always on the move, never able to settle down anywhere for too long." She stopped and let out a breath. She had no idea why she'd just told Linda all that when Linda probably didn't know half of what she was talking about.

"Oh, Joey," Linda said again. "Sweetheart. It's okay to be feeling the way you are. You've had a big shock. Your life isn't the way you thought. And you have no family left to guide you, hold you up." She looked at Joey with so much sympathy that Joey wanted to weep. "You can come to me anytime, okay? If you need an unbiased opinion."

"Thank you." Joey looked down at her drink, suddenly shy but surprisingly not embarrassed by her outburst.

"Sam told me you're a writer?"

"Yes." Joey looked up, grateful to the older woman for changing the subject. "I freelance and write articles for anyone who wants to commission me, but I've also written two novels. My editor has the option for my next book, but I haven't been able to come up with a concept yet."

She didn't add that she'd had a block since the whole debacle with Oliver. It was as if finding out that she'd been dating a married man had dried up all the creative juices in her brain.

"I love to read. I must get your books." Linda pulled out her phone. "What're the titles?"

Joey told her, and Linda ordered the books right there.

"Thank you." She smiled at Linda. "I know I said this already, but I'm so glad Sam had you two in his life."

"And now you have us too." Linda took a sip of her wine before focusing her attention on Joey. "The funeral home called. We can pick up Sam's ashes tomorrow."

Joey inhaled sharply, reminded once again that her brother was gone.

Linda patted her on the arm and didn't say anything, letting Joey get control of her emotions. Mac put the plate of smoked fish on the table in front of them, next to the cucumber-and-tomato salad Linda had put together and the roasted potatoes Mac had made on the grill.

"This looks and smells amazing," Joey finally said.

Wonton came running over, putting her front paws on Linda's legs and sniffing the air enthusiastically.

Joey laughed and tried to get Wonton back down. "I already fed you."

"Wonton is a foodie," Mac said, sneaking her a piece of the fish. "She appreciates my cooking."

They helped themselves to the feast, and after tasting the fish, Joey hummed in approval. "I appreciate your cooking too."

Mac raised his beer glass, and Joey clinked her own against his. Once they'd taken a drink, she turned to Linda. "Should I . . . get Sam's ashes tomorrow?"

"We can do it for you, if you want." Linda cut her potatoes before putting a piece in her mouth.

"You don't have to do that," Joey protested, even though she dreaded the thought of going to the funeral home.

Linda met Joey's eyes. "If it's too hard for you, we really don't mind."

Joey swallowed and then nodded. "Okay, yes. That would be better. I appreciate it."

"No problem." The matter settled, Linda asked questions about Joey's travels, and she relaxed, enjoying the older couple's company.

She slept like a rock that night. Maybe the fatigue had finally taken over, or maybe it was knowing the Kellys were there to help her, but whatever it was, she didn't remember falling asleep. When she woke the next morning, she was disoriented, and it took her a few minutes to realize where she was. She looked at the bedside clock and saw it was already ten in the morning. She'd never slept so late before, especially not on Kauai, where she was used to getting up with the sun.

The doorbell rang, making her jump. She got out of bed, realizing it was probably the Kellys back with Sam's ashes. They had said they would leave at nine that morning for the funeral home. Joey rushed to the door, not believing she'd slept so late. When she opened it, Linda stood there holding a bag.

"Oh." Joey's hands went to her mouth, her eyes glued on the dark-blue bag. After a moment, she met Linda's eyes. "That's . . . Sam?"

Linda gave her a gentle smile and held the bag out to Joey. With trembling hands, Joey accepted it and then stood there, not sure what to do.

"Will you be all right?" Linda tilted her head, studying Joey's face.

"Yes. It's just a lot." Joey swallowed hard, trying not to freak out over the fact that she was holding what was left of her brother in her hands.

"Do you want company? Or would you prefer to be alone?"

Joey gave a tremulous smile. "I think I need to be alone."

"Okay." The older woman nodded. "You know where to find us if you need anything."

"Thank you." Joey reached out to clasp Linda's hand in hers for a few seconds. "Really. I don't think I would have gotten through this without you."

Linda squeezed her hand and then let go. "We're here for you." And then she returned to her own unit.

Joey went back inside, closing the door softly behind her. She placed the bag on the kitchen table and then just stared at it. What was she supposed to do with it? Put it in a closet somewhere? That didn't seem right. But at the same time, the thought of putting it on display made her want to laugh. She eyed the bag as if it were a bomb and would detonate at any moment.

Then she shook her head and chided herself out loud. "Don't be silly. It's not going to bite you." She walked over to it and peered inside. There was a velvet bag, the same deep blue as the heavy paper bag. Gingerly, she pulled it out and opened the drawstring of the velvet one. Inside was a metal urn, in shades of blue and tan. It resembled the waves at the beach, and Joey knew Sam must have picked it out himself.

She carefully pulled the urn out of the velvet bag. She clasped it tightly against her body since her hands were shaking and she didn't want to drop it. She took the urn with her to the couch and sank down onto it because her legs wouldn't hold her up anymore.

She stared down at it, still clasped tightly against her chest, and was suddenly overcome with grief.

"Why did you have to die and leave me, Sam?" she said aloud, her voice cracking. "I still need you. I can't do this . . . this thing, this life without you. You're the only family I had left, and I don't know how to move on by myself."

She rocked the urn against her body and fought back tears. She was sick of crying. She, who hadn't cried in so long, not even when Oliver had betrayed her. Yes, maybe she had shed a few tears, but those had been in anger, not in grief like this that threatened to pull her under.

"I get it now, Sam." Her voice trembled as she spoke to the empty room. "I get why you wouldn't let Ren Ren come with us. I used to love her so much, but now I'm so mad. Mad at her for what she did to our parents. Hate her for how she betrayed me too. I loved her so much. Do you remember that day when I was seven or so, and I had slipped and called Ren Ren 'Mama' right in front of our mother? Even though I was so young, I still remember the hurt on our mother's face. I didn't understand it then, but now I do, and I wish I could take it back. I must have wounded her so bad that day."

Joey would have dissolved into tears despite her resolve not to cry if Wonton hadn't come up to her right then and put her paws on her legs.

"Wonton." Joey let the urn go and placed it carefully on the coffee table before picking up the small dog. She held her against her chest and buried her face in Wonton's back, needing the warmth and comfort the dog offered. And even though it helped, it wasn't enough. She needed human comfort. She needed someone's arms around her, holding her close. Because without it, she felt like she would float away.

Impulsively, she pulled out her phone and dialed Ethan's number.

18

Two hours later, Joey waited in the parking lot of the Wai Koa Loop Trail in Kilauea with Wonton. Her breath released as she watched Ethan's car pull up. She felt guilty for dragging him away from work, but she needed him. Holding Sam's remains had weirded her out, and she hadn't wanted to be alone. When Ethan had suggested a walk on this trail, a place Sam and Joey used to come to in the past when they wanted to escape, Joey had agreed.

"Hey." He got out of his car and looked at her for a moment. Then he closed the distance between them and hugged her close. She inhaled, finding comfort in his familiar scent.

"Thanks for meeting me early." They'd had plans for happy hour later.

"Of course. I told Sam I would look out for you."

Joey pulled away sharply. "I'm not a little girl anymore, needing to be looked after."

They stared at each other, the air crackling between them. And then Ethan smiled. "I know you're not, Joey. You've turned into a beautiful, smart, accomplished woman."

She had no comeback for that. Her chest heaved as she tried to contain her emotions. To distract herself, she gestured to the dog park behind the lot. "Can we let Wonton play first?"

Ethan nodded and followed her in through the gate. There were only two other dogs there, but Wonton ran straight to them, her tail wagging. They were just as interested, and Joey let out a breath, watching her brother's dog—her dog now—happy and playing. She and Ethan didn't speak, but he stayed close to her and she was grateful for his presence. She was glad she'd called him, but she had to keep her temper in check. Because she needed to finally settle things between them.

Half an hour later, when both dogs had left, Joey clipped Wonton's leash back on her harness. They walked out the gate and then started down the path. They were quiet, for which Joey was grateful. She wanted to enjoy the majesty of the trail, with the mountains off in the distance and trees, wildflowers, and other vegetation all around them. They followed the dirt path, going past a field that stretched out toward the horizon and into the woods. Birds chirped up high, and the only other sound was the crunch of their sneakers on the ground. When there was nothing but trees and plants surrounding them on both sides, so green and lush, Joey finally spoke.

"I need to ask you about that night. After my graduation dinner at Hualani's." She was afraid to look at Ethan.

He drew in a breath but didn't say anything.

She kept walking, following the sign for the stone dam, her body remembering the way even though it had been years since she'd been here. When they made their way into a grove of trees that were so tall they formed a canopy high above them, Joey stopped but didn't turn to Ethan.

"Why did you say you were sorry? Why did you run away from me?" She refused to look at him. "You made me feel so bad that I've been avoiding Kauai and you ever since. Especially when I heard you got engaged to Naomi."

"Joey."

She turned to find him staring at her, a devastated look on his face.

"I never meant for you to feel that way. I'm so sorry." He took a few steps until he was at her side. "I just felt so guilty. You were only eighteen. I'd helped Sam take care of you since he brought you to New York, and it felt wrong, like I was taking advantage of you." He took another step closer. "I felt guilty because I had feelings for you, and I knew Sam would kill me if he knew."

"Oh." Joey's eyes widened. Her heart fluttered as she let the meaning of his words seep in. She hadn't imagined it. He *had* felt something for her all those years ago.

Wonton tugged on the leash, breaking her eye contact with Ethan. They started walking again, Joey filled with so many emotions she didn't know how to voice them out loud. But it was okay. The silence between them no longer felt uncomfortable. They walked through an enchanted forest so breathtakingly beautiful that Joey kept stopping to absorb the nature all around her. She'd missed this, all the years she'd spent away from Kauai. She missed this trail, missed being here with Sam, missed the Buddha statue that sat amid a grove of bamboo up a hill near the stone dam. Taking in a deep breath, she inhaled the sweet scent of the yellow ginger lily flowers all around them. The stone dam waterfall was just ahead, and Joey stopped before the narrow ledge that would lead them to the dam.

She sighed, looking at the rush of water. "Sam and I used to come here all the time."

Ethan nodded. "We still did every once in a while, when we had a bad case or something horrible happened with one of our patients. We'd come here to get away."

He gestured with his hand, and she and Wonton walked onto the narrow ledge single file. When Joey slipped on the slick ground, Ethan reached out to steady her. And then somehow, his hand found hers and she linked her fingers around his. She didn't look at him, afraid if she did, he'd disappear. But he didn't let go even once they reached solid footing, and they climbed up the wet stone steps like that, as if it was the most natural thing in the world for them to be holding hands. At the top, the waterfall fell to their left, while a swimming hole sat on their right, complete with a rope swing.

"We used to swim here sometimes." Joey looked into the murky water, imagining that she could see Sam's head bobbing on the surface.

They stood on the raised dock overlooking the swimming hole for a while, both lost in thought. This was the end of the trail, and after a while, they made their way back the way they'd come, going down the slippery steps carefully. When they were back on the path, Joey started to tell Ethan what she'd read in her mother's journal.

"I feel so betrayed. Also, angry and sad."

"You've had so much thrown at you this week. Of course you're confused. I knew some of it, but now hearing it from your perspective . . ." Ethan trailed off as they entered back into the forest. The leafy canopy high above them acted as a protective barrier, making Joey feel safe to open up to Ethan.

"It is a lot. I can't absorb it all. I feel like I'm reading a book about someone else's life."

Instead of answering, Ethan stopped walking and gently tugged on her hand until they stood facing each other. His other hand reached up to touch her cheek, and the look in his eyes made everything fall away.

"Ethan." His name came out as a whisper. Her heart pounded and she felt faint.

"I don't want to add to your stress." Ethan's voice was low, but Joey heard every word. "But I can't help thinking about what you said, how I made you feel so bad you hadn't wanted to come back to Kauai all this time. I'm so sorry."

His thumb ran down her face, just grazing the side of her mouth, and all the tension inside her eased. She didn't know what was happening, if he was only apologizing or if there was more behind his words. She couldn't speak, waiting to see what he would do. Without realizing she was doing it, she took a step closer until their bodies touched and heat ignited in a way she hadn't ever felt for anyone. Not even Oliver.

His eyes softened and then he was leaning down, his hand resting against her cheek as his other arm looped behind her and drew her closer. Her breath catching, Joey's eyes fluttered shut. When his lips touched hers, she almost let out a whimper. She'd dreamed of kissing Ethan again so many times over the years, but the reality was nothing like her daydreams. He was real, his lips soft, lingering over hers, breathing new life into her. Her fingers dug into his shoulders as their kiss deepened. The reality was so much better than the dream.

When they finally pulled away, he pressed his forehead against hers, and they stayed like that for a moment, both slightly out of breath. His hands stroked down her back, bringing goose bumps to her flesh. She wanted to stay here in this magical forest and not deal with everything she'd learned about her family. With Ethan, everything felt possible. In Ethan's arms, she felt like she could survive anything.

"Does this mean you've forgiven me for how I acted all those years ago?" Ethan's voice rumbled, making her lips twitch.

She pulled back so she could look him in the eye. "Maybe. But you might have to work a little harder to convince me."

"Well, at least Sam can't kill me now," he said with a straight face, which made them both burst into laughter.

"But seriously, are you sure you're okay with this? I care about you, Joey. If this is too much right now, I understand. I don't want you to think I'm taking advantage of you because you're vulnerable right now."

"First of all, let's get one thing straight." Joey put her hands on her hips. "You're not taking advantage of me now, or back then. I was eighteen, legally an adult, and I knew what I was doing. I wanted to kiss you. And what I do now has nothing to do with my brother."

Ethan widened his eyes in mock fear. "Okay. Got it."

She stepped away and looked down at Wonton, who sat patiently at her side. "Secondly, I really don't know what I'm doing right now. What I do know is that I've been semi-infatuated with you for most of my life."

He chuckled and the look he sent her made her blood hot. "We don't have to decide right now what this is. You have a lot to sort through, and I want to help you with that, not hinder your process."

She nodded, her heart swelling with tenderness. She couldn't deny everything felt less intimidating with him at her side. "I'd like that."

"Okay." He leaned in and gave her a sweet kiss before taking her hand. "Let's get you through this, losing Sam, everything you're discovering about your family. I'm here for you. However you need me."

"Thank you." She leaned her head against his shoulder for a moment, then they started walking again, back toward the entrance of the trail.

For another twenty minutes, she didn't think about anything except Ethan, Wonton, and the beauty of Kauai all around her. For that, she was grateful.

⁂

When Joey got back to Sam's apartment after her walk with Ethan, she felt calmer. He'd gone back to his clinic to deal with paperwork, but they would meet again at three o'clock in Kapaa for happy hour. She smiled, flopping back against the couch, thinking of their kiss. Her fingers traced her lips where Ethan's had been, and she couldn't help the beam of happiness that was radiating through her body. It felt good to finally clear the air with Ethan. Even better, it felt great that he returned her feelings.

She wanted to tell someone, call Maggie, but Maggie was in the air on her way to Kauai. She had a lot of friends all over the world from her travels, but she hadn't told any of them about Sam's death. It felt like too much to explain when all she wanted to dwell on right now was what was happening with Ethan. Yet she also didn't want to obsess over what was going to happen. It was too soon to get ahead of herself. Not while she was wading through all the family secrets that had been kept from her all her life.

Instead, she decided to go through her emails, responding to everything that she'd put off in the past few days. First, she needed to tell the project she had been working on in Malaysia that she wasn't going back. Kauai was pulling her back in, and she was listening. This was where she needed to be, not just for Sam but also for herself. The sister of a friend of hers who was renting her apartment in NYC would be overjoyed to hear that she could have it for a couple more months. Joey would call her in a bit.

Second, she needed to check in with her literary agent. Reading about her family's past had sparked something within her—a desire to set her next book in Taiwan during the martial law era. Ideas had already formed in her head, a dual timeline story about redemption and coming to terms with the past, much like what she was experiencing right now. She'd never done a book like this, though, and wanted to run the idea by her agent.

She worked at the dining table for the next hour, taking care of the details of her life that she'd neglected since hearing about Sam's death. When she finally looked up, it was with a sense of satisfaction that at least one aspect of her life was in order. Her heart and mind, on the other hand, were another story. But she couldn't begin to process everything without finishing her mother's journal. Looking at the fruit trees in Sam's backyard, she decided to have a papaya as she read.

Getting up, she went outside and picked a papaya off the tree with the picker. When she had it washed, sliced, and the seeds scooped out, she sat on the lanai with the journal. She and her mother had loved papayas and mangoes when they had lived in Thailand. It was too late for mangoes here, as the season ended in October, but the papaya was making her remember the fruit her mother used to slice for her every morning in Bangkok. She closed her eyes as she put the first bite in her mouth, searching for any remnant of memory of the mother she'd lost so long ago.

19

Ah-Hui
1996, Bangkok

It had been a long day, and I couldn't wait to get home. Sometimes Zhi Wei and I took care of patients together, and sometimes we separated, depending on who needed us. I'd gone to help deliver a baby and then went swimming at a local pool afterward. When my son had left for college in New York four years ago, right as Zhi Wei and I had decided to become traveling physicians in southeast Asia, Sam had encouraged us to learn how to swim. Like a lot of Taiwanese, neither of us could swim and were fearful of water. But because our travels would take us to coastal locations in Thailand, Malaysia, and Vietnam, Sam was worried for our safety.

"It's important." Sam stood in front of where Zhi Wei and I sat on the sofa, relaxing and watching TV after a long day at the primary care clinic we worked at in Lihue on Kauai.

"Sam, move." Zhi Wei tried to shoo our son from where he blocked the TV.

"Baba. This is important." Sam crossed his arms over his chest and glared at his father. "You're going to have to take boats to some of your patients. What if one tips over? You need to be able to swim to safety."

Zhi Wei waved a hand in the air, a frown on his face. "Nothing's going to happen to us."

"How do you know?" Sam's face was set in that stubborn way I knew well. Ever since he was a baby, if he didn't want to do something, his brows would draw together and his lips would purse as he figuratively dug his heels in. I loved my son, but I knew how stubborn he could be.

"You really think a boat could tip over?" I worried my bottom lip with my teeth. It hadn't even occurred to me that we could be in danger just traveling to patients in remote areas.

"Yes." Sam turned his direct gaze on me. "Those boats aren't the sturdiest. Some are downright leaky and shouldn't even be on the water. Please, Mama, talk sense into Ba. You need to know how to at least tread water until someone can get to you."

I stared at my son, his words running through my mind because I was terrified of water.

"Stop this nonsense. And get out of my way. I can't see the TV." Zhi Wei's words were impatient, and he made a shooing motion with his hand.

"Ba."

"Son. Get out of the way. Now."

Sam heaved a sigh and moved, but I knew the subject wasn't closed. I was right. When Zhi Wei was in the shower, Sam approached me where I sat reading in bed.

"Mama, please. If Ba is too stubborn to take swimming lessons, at least put my mind at ease and you take them." Sam sat on the side of my bed, and my face softened at the earnest look on his face.

"You really think it's important?" My fear of water battled with his insistence.

"Yes. It could save your life. Please?" His eyes beseeched me and my heart melted.

"Okay. I think the YMCA in Lihue gives adult swimming lessons." Even though we both worked in Lihue, we had rented a house in Kapaa, about twenty minutes north of Lihue, so that we could have a bigger yard.

"Thank you, Ma." Sam blew out a breath, and I could see how relieved he was. "Can you try to convince Baba too?"

I gave him a wry look. "I'll try, but do you think he'll listen to me?"

Sam's expression darkened. I'd always wondered whether he knew about his father and Ren Ren. He'd been only five when it had started, and not quite six when I'd given Zhi Wei the ultimatum. I chose to believe my children were too innocent to know what had been going on back then. And I chose to believe that my husband hadn't started up his affair since, but I always wondered. I hated feeling suspicious of my husband when he'd tried over the years to show me how much he loved me. But I couldn't help it. And as I stared at my son now, I realized he was almost a man. He was seventeen and graduating from high school a year early. He would soon leave for New York and live his own life, far away from us.

"Mama." His voice was low but vibrated with intensity. "Leave him. Come to New York with me. I'll help you with Chiao-Yi. You can start over."

My breath hitched as I stared at my son. He knew. He had to. But how? I felt my body go hot, then my fingers started to tingle, and a ringing sounded in my ears. For just a brief moment, I let myself imagine leaving with my son for New York with my daughter. I would be free. No longer living and existing in the same house as them. No longer tortured by every look, every touch between them, wondering whether they'd started again, the anguish that spread through me, thinking about them together when I wasn't home. My husband claimed the affair had ended years ago, but the emotional stress and the devastation of the past sixteen years of living with them had taken its toll. I longed to be carefree and happy again.

I almost said yes. The word was about to slip out of my mouth, but then I thought of my daughter, and I knew I couldn't go.

"I can't," I finally said, not meeting Sam's eyes. I knew he'd be disappointed in me. "He won't let Chiao-Yi go, and I can't leave her behind."

"Mama." Frustration made Sam's voice come out like a growl, and I flinched, hating myself. I knew what he was thinking. That I was weak and couldn't stand up to my husband.

"I'm sorry. I can't leave Chiao-Yi behind. And he would never allow me to take her." I pleaded with my eyes for my son to understand. "When she's old enough, when she's ready for university like you, then I'll leave him."

Sam didn't speak, but his jaw clenched. He didn't believe me, that I'd ever leave his father, but saying those words out loud, I knew I would. Once my baby girl was old enough to fend for herself, I would leave.

"I'll take swimming lessons." I reached out and placed a hand on Sam's forearm. "I promise. And I'll try to get your father to take them too."

His jaw worked and then he finally spoke. "I only care about your safety. If he won't listen to me, then that's his problem. But I'm glad you're going to take my advice."

And I had. I'd signed up for private swim lessons at the YMCA without telling Zhi Wei. He'd scoffed when I'd suggested them to him, saying he didn't need them. My husband used to listen to me, used to value my opinion, but ever since he'd started working with Ren Ren for a free Taiwan and started the affair, I no longer had any influence over him. It made me sad, made my heart shrivel up at how far we'd come from that day we'd shared stinky tofu together at the night market. But there was nothing I could do.

So I signed up for the lessons, terrified to death that first time getting into the pool. But my instructor was patient, a young man who seemed to realize my visceral fear was so very real, and he didn't patronize me or talk to me like I was a child. He let me slowly get used to the water, and over the next three months, I met with him twice a week. Slowly, so slowly, I learned to put my face in the water. I learned to tread water and swim freestyle and breaststroke. I liked breaststroke the best, because I could see where I was going, my terrified gaze focused on the opposite wall. And slowly, I got over my fear of water and started swimming at least three times a week, always finding a pool wherever we landed so that I could keep it up.

I was tired after my swim here in Bangkok after delivering a baby, so I was hoping to take one of the new pink microbuses that were air-conditioned back to our place. But a fight broke out at the bus stop when someone tried to jump the queue. The people who had been waiting a long time were angry, and one man threw a punch. Someone else retaliated and then they were brawling, fists flying as one of them struck an old woman on the side of the head by accident. The woman slammed into me.

"Are you okay?" I asked in my rudimentary Thai as I tried to keep her upright.

She moaned and collapsed against me, and I held her up while trying to assess the damage. I wished I had ice because I could already see a contusion forming on the side of her head. Another woman noticed my predicament and came to help.

"Come," she said. "I know the shop owner there. He can get us some ice and let her rest." The stranger helped me hold up the old woman on the other side and together, we half carried, half dragged her to a little store that seemed to sell a little bit of everything.

The store's owner came running up when he saw us and helped the old woman into a chair as his wife went into the back to get ice.

"I'm a doctor," I said in Thai as the old woman sipped from a cup of water that the shop owner fetched for her. "Okay for me to check you?"

She nodded and I began to examine her, running my fingers lightly over the bump on her head and checking for any other injuries.

"Do you know what today's date is?"

She answered correctly and I continued to ask her questions to assess her mental state.

"Do you have a headache?"

"Just where he hit me." She pointed to the bump.

"Look here." I held up my pointer finger. "Follow my finger with your eyes only." I'd learned how to say all this in Thai since I needed it so much when examining patients. "Good." I gave the woman who had come to our aid a nod. "Her eye movement is smooth, and she doesn't appear to have double vision or neurological issues."

I turned back to my patient, who was now holding a bag of ice wrapped in a towel to her head. "I think you just have that contusion on your head, which should subside in a few days. But if your vision changes or the headache gets worse or doesn't go away, you should see your doctor." I patted the woman on her hand because she was gripping mine tightly.

"Thank you." Her voice was stronger now and she looked at me with gratitude. She said something else in Thai that I didn't understand.

The stranger who had helped us translated for me. "She said your husband is very lucky to have such a smart and beautiful wife and doctor."

I felt my cheeks redden, and I looked down. If only my husband still felt that way about me. And only me.

The shop owner, who turned out to know the old lady, came over to us. "We'll keep an eye on her. I called her grandson, and he's going to come and escort her home." He handed me a bag of papayas and mangoes. "He said to give you these from him. To thank you for helping his grandmother."

I peeked in at the green and yellow fruits, my mouth already watering at the sweetness. Chiao-Yi loved papayas and mangoes as much as I did, and I couldn't wait to share them with her.

I thanked the man and left the store, sighing when I saw the long line at the bus stop. I decided to walk home, even though it would take twenty minutes and it was so hot out. But I didn't want to get involved in another altercation, and I could see tempers were still high in the queue. Better to keep moving. I'd probably get home faster walking at this rate.

By the time I made it to the guesthouse Zhi Wei and I had rented for our mission, I was drenched in sweat. I mopped my face with the hem of my cotton shirt and couldn't wait to get into the air-conditioning and cool off. I sighed in relief when I opened the door and rushed in, standing still for a moment. The cool air felt so good after the mugginess outside, and I was already envisioning a quick rinse off in the tub when I heard a sound coming from the bathroom down the hall that Ren Ren shared with my daughter.

I frowned, remembering a similar situation years ago when I'd arrive home with my son to our New York City apartment. They couldn't be in the bathroom together, could they? But then the sound came again, and I recognized it as someone retching. Alarmed, I put the fruit in the kitchen and walked toward the bathroom. Was that Ren Ren? Was she sick?

I usually avoided being alone with her, but now concern made me rap lightly on the door.

"Ren Ren? Do you need anything?"

The toilet flushed and a few seconds later, the door opened. Ren Ren stood there, her face so pale she looked bloodless, and she had a hand on her stomach.

"I'm fine," she said. "Must have been something I ate."

I studied her carefully, noting the roundness of her face, more so than usual. Her breasts looked fuller and there was something about her that looked like—no. My mouth dropped open as I realized what I was thinking. Ren Ren looked *pregnant*. Was it possible?

She met my eyes and then turned away. Brushing by me, she headed for her room. "I'll be fine. I just need to lie down for a minute."

She closed the door to her room before I could say anything. I stood there for another moment, my quick bath forgotten as my mind raced. Could Ren Ren really be pregnant? If she was, it had to be Zhi Wei's. She'd never had a boyfriend since she'd come to live with us. And if she was, that meant they had started their affair again. When? The stone in my stomach grew heavier, and I had to close my eyes, the grief so powerful that I thought it would swallow me.

Disgust and anger flowed within me, and a rage I hadn't known I was capable of began to build within. I'd believed my husband when he said he would leave Ren Ren alone. I'd believed him when he told me over and over again throughout the years that he loved me and only me, that Ren Ren had been a mistake. Why had I been such a fool?

My son had tried to tell me. But I hadn't wanted to believe him, hadn't wanted to believe that Zhi Wei had gone back on his word. Four years ago was when Zhi Wei and Ren Ren had gone back to Taiwan together. A memorial for her father, they said. It was safe for Ren Ren to go, now that Taiwan was no longer under martial law. Victor would be with them, Zhi Wei had told me. There was nothing to worry about.

But now I wondered if I'd been naive. *They had gone to Taiwan for two weeks together.* And if I was honest with myself, there had been signs since then that they might have started their affair again. But now, even thinking there might be a new baby on the way, fury filled me in a way that had eluded me before.

I could not allow another child, a child who wasn't mine, to jeopardize my children's future. They were the most important people to me. If Zhi Wei knew he'd fathered a child, he would provide for the baby, taking away from my children. I couldn't allow that to happen. But I had to make sure I was right first, and if I was, then I needed a plan.

When Zhi Wei got home later that night, I studied him closely. He was tired, fatigue pulling at his eyes, making them droop, and he barely looked at Ren Ren, much less treated her with the awe and respect he'd plied on me both times when I was pregnant. To him, children were everything. He'd been so overjoyed when I was with child, and I felt sure if he knew Ren Ren was pregnant with his child, he would be treating her like delicate glass, making her sit and put her feet up, bringing her food, and making sure she was resting. But he did none of that.

"What would you do if there was another baby on the way?" I asked him when we were alone in our room. We still slept in the same bed, even though he rarely touched me anymore.

"What?" He sat up and snapped the light back on. "Are you pregnant?" His face lit up in hope, and he put a hand on my flat stomach.

I pushed his hand away. "No, I'm not." I turned so that I could look into his eyes. I'd learned to tell when he was lying to me. "But what would we do if there was another baby on the way?" I was about to turn forty-six, and while that was considered geriatric in the medical world, it wasn't out of the realm of possibility for me to be pregnant.

"I would be so happy." A grin split his face. "Is it possible? Do you want another baby?"

"No," I said flatly. I did not want another baby to tie me to him for even longer. I'd already decided that when Chiao-Yi went off to college, I was leaving him. Leaving him to Ren Ren and getting out of this farce of a marriage. I was counting down the days until my youngest child was old enough for me to go.

"Oh." His disappointment was evident by the way his mouth turned down and the light in his eyes dimmed. I knew then that he didn't know about Ren Ren's baby. Yet.

I had to make sure she really was pregnant. The next day, when Ren Ren took Chiao-Yi to meet with her tutor, I searched her room. I didn't know what I was looking for and thought it would take a while to go through her stuff, but in her underwear drawer, I found a box of pregnancy tests, with only one left. I looked through her garbage, hoping to find the evidence of a positive test, but there was nothing. Even still, I was pretty sure Ren Ren was pregnant. Why else would she have taken a pregnancy test? I wondered for a brief moment if she had a boyfriend or someone she'd met and slept with. I asked around the neighborhood, but no one had ever seen her with a man. She was almost always with Chiao-Yi. And on her one day off, she'd often disappear with my husband, working on pro-democracy stuff, I'd assumed. Now I wondered.

I kept an eye on her closely for the next couple of weeks and heard her throwing up again on more than one occasion. When she knew I was in the house, she tried to disguise it by flushing the toilet or running the bath water, but I knew and recognized the signs. And then one day, I heard her whispering with a friend outside of our guesthouse. I'd cracked my window open the night before to get some fresh air and had gotten up to close it before the heat of the day made us turn on the air-conditioning. Zhi Wei had already left the house, and it was my day off. I would spend it with my daughter. Ren Ren must have slipped outside to meet her friend because I could hear her voice if I listened carefully.

"You have to tell them." Her friend was urging her. "It's his baby. He'll take care of you."

"I can't," Ren Ren whispered back. I leaned closer to the open window, staying out of sight. "He told me he told her that he wouldn't touch me again. I know it's wrong, but I love him so much. I couldn't say no when he came to my bed. I love her too. I don't want to hurt her."

Her friend made a most unladylike sound. "If you love her, why are you sleeping with her husband?"

There was silence and I leaned so close to the window I almost fell into it. But I managed to catch myself and when I could focus again, their voices were fading, as if they were walking away. I chanced a peek out of the window and saw their backs just as they reached the end of the alley and disappeared.

Ren Ren was pregnant with my husband's child. I slumped to the floor, stunned at this confirmation. I had been right. And when my husband found out, he would be overjoyed. He would treat this new baby as his own, an equal to Sam and Chiao-Yi. The thought of Ren Ren's bastard child getting the same attention and rights as my children incensed me more than the affair ever had. I couldn't allow this baby to jeopardize my children's future. There was no way I was going to let Zhi Wei provide for this child.

When I'd heard the phrase, "I would kill for my children" in the past, I always thought it was so melodramatic. How could anyone ever think of killing someone else, even for their own children? But in that moment, standing in my bedroom alone, Ren Ren's words still echoing in my head, all I could think of was killing her. The rage that welled up inside me was bigger than myself, and I wanted to go out there and strangle her until she was no longer breathing, taking her child along with her. My hands fisted at my side and I was literally seeing red. I took a step toward the door and then I stopped. Rational thought came back, and I knew I couldn't react, couldn't do what I wanted because I would go to jail.

Drawing in a deep breath, I blew it out, trying to control my temper. I had to plan carefully and make it look like an accident. I couldn't get caught because it would defeat the whole purpose of taking care of my children. They needed me. I paced my room, thoughts flitting in and out of my head as I examined my options. Poison? Accidentally pushed in front of a bus? Allergic reaction of some kind?

The next few days passed in a haze of fury and plotting. I could barely focus on my job through the fog of my murderous thoughts. I couldn't give my daughter my full attention like I usually did, and I found her quietly studying me one night when she thought I wasn't looking. I was going to say something to her, but then she jumped up and ran to her bathroom. I followed her, intending to tap on the door to make sure she was okay when the phone in the living room rang.

I turned, about to go back to the main room to answer it, when I heard the front door open and quick footsteps. Ren Ren answered the phone, and I knew it was my husband by the way her voice changed, became softer. She giggled at something he said, and I wanted to march out there and scratch her eyes out. Rage filled me again and suddenly, I realized I was capable of killing. I'd heard that everyone had a point that, if pushed, they could commit murder. And it appeared that point for me had come.

As I listened to Ren Ren's one-sided conversation with my husband, the ugliness and fury built within me once again. I used to be a brilliant, kind doctor whose mission was to heal those who were sick or broken. But now I was no better than someone who murdered people with no remorse. Because in that very moment, I would have gladly strangled her with my bare hands.

I couldn't live like this anymore. Something had to give. I had to change it because it was obvious Zhi Wei never would. He was content to have a wife and a mistress, all living under one roof like a happy little family. Maybe he'd stopped the affair for years, but sometime recently, he'd started up with her again. It had always been ingrained in me from the time I was a small child that the husband was the head of the family, that what he said goes because that was the way our Taiwanese culture dictated it. But it was 1996 and I no longer lived in Taiwan.

"Zhi Wei!" Ren Ren's girlish voice squealed out his name. She dissolved into giggles again and that's when it hit me.

Ren Ren wasn't the problem. She had been an innocent girl, only seventeen when she came to live with us, and twenty-two when my husband first bedded her. She was as much a victim as I was. *Zhi Wei* was the problem. He was the one who seduced a guileless virgin. She'd confessed that fact to me about a year after she came to us, when I still felt affection toward her, before she started sleeping with my husband. She'd told me she'd never kissed a boy, didn't know anything about sex. I'd been the one to educate her, to tell her what happened between a man and a woman. She'd been horrified. But no longer horrified a few years later when she started sleeping with my husband.

I'd been going about this all wrong. I'd been trying to get rid of Ren Ren, tried to convince Zhi Wei to leave her behind when we moved to Kauai, and then again when we moved to Southeast Asia. I'd loved Zhi Wei so much that it hadn't occurred to me that *he* was the problem. It was easier to blame Ren Ren. But now, standing in the hall, listening to Ren Ren laughing at whatever my husband was saying, my heart hardened, and for the first time since I met him, I felt nothing but contempt and outrage toward *him*. He was supposed to be my husband. He was supposed to love me and only me. He'd disrespected me and he wasn't sorry about it because I'd let him. I'd let him walk all over me, let him do whatever he wanted.

My old neighbor Pippa had been right. I should have left a long time ago. I didn't have to live with his actions. I'd basically given him permission to carry on with Ren Ren by not putting my foot down.

I bit hard on my bottom lip. My eyes were finally wide open, and I saw my husband for who he really was. I couldn't believe how stupid I'd been. He was the one who needed to be gone. *He* needed to be punished. And I was going to be the one to make him pay, to get rid of him so that my children would be safe and I would finally be free.

Now I just had to figure out how to kill him without getting caught.

20

Joey
Present Day, Kauai

"Oh my god." Joey's mouth hung open at what she'd just read, and her entire body went hot and then cold. Her mother had been plotting to kill her father? She didn't think things could get much worse, yet here it was.

She looked up from the journal, her eyes unfocused as she stared into space. Was this the secret Sam had alluded to? Had their mother killed their father? But then how had she ended up dead too? So many questions bombarded her mind, and she felt as though bees had taken over her body, making her buzz and vibrate with nervous energy. This was the last thing she'd thought she'd read.

She jumped off the chair on the lanai, needing to move. She couldn't imagine the kind, gentle mother she vaguely remembered as someone who would kill anyone, much less her own husband. Could she have done it? Was that why they'd drowned?

A pain started in her chest and Joey pressed her hands over the spot. She'd grown up mostly in the United States, where women had as many rights as men, and where powerful influential women were her role models. She'd never have tolerated having someone cheat on her, much less live with the offending person. It made her feel even more guilty for her part in destroying Oliver's marriage. It didn't matter that she hadn't known he was married; the results were the same. She was just as bad as Ren Ren, and she wanted to bury her face in her pillow, so ashamed of that chapter of her life. But Oliver had lied to her. He'd deceived her.

And now, finding out how much her own mother had suffered because of a situation similar to what Joey had found herself in, however unwittingly, skewered Joey's heart. It bled for her mother, and she knew her mother would be ashamed of her if she knew Joey had been "the other woman."

"What happened?" Joey said out loud, not sure if she was asking about her mother's situation or her own. She'd always thought she was so smart, so intuitive when it came to other people's intentions. So how had she believed Oliver for eight months and never suspected he was married?

Wonton jumped off the couch and came to pace at Joey's side. She stopped and stared down at the little dog.

"Are you helping me worry?" They walked the length of the living room together before turning around and heading back to the other side.

She wished she could talk to Sam but he was gone. And Maggie was still on a plane. Joey could have texted or emailed her, but this wasn't something she wanted to discuss digitally. She'd tell Maggie when she saw her later today. Joey was about to pick up the journal again when her text alert sounded.

She looked at her phone and read the message from Ethan.

See you at 3. I made a reservation under my name.

Right. She was supposed to go to happy hour with Ethan in Kapaa. She checked the time. The reservation was in forty minutes, and it would take her at least half an hour to drive there, so she should leave now. Ethan had suggested a place closer to her, but she'd said she was fine with meeting in Kapaa, as Maggie would be arriving shortly after their meeting and she could go right to see her best friend from there.

"Wonton, you'll be fine here by yourself?" She leaned down to scoop up the dog into her arms. She carried her over to the dog bed next to the couch and placed Wonton in it after giving her a kiss. "I'll be back soon, before dinner, okay?" Maggie had said she would sleep over in Princeville with Joey and let Kristy have her grandparents all to herself.

Grabbing the car keys, Joey left the condo, heading for her rental car. She would return it tomorrow with Maggie and use Sam's car, now that they had it back. She drove down to Kapaa, something still niggling at her. What was it that was bothering her about what she'd just read?

She wrinkled her nose in frustration when the thought eluded her. Before she knew it, she was pulling into the parking lot of the resort where the restaurant was located. Her heart skipped as she walked down the pathway toward the restaurant situated by the water. And then there he was. Ethan, sitting at a table on the edge of the lawn, looking so handsome in a light-green short-sleeve button-down as he studied the menu. She took a moment to drink him in before she made her way to his side.

"Joey." His smile was warm, and he stood, giving her a quick hug before she sat down.

She gave him a shy smile even as her body leaned toward him.

Stop it, she admonished herself. *Focus.*

To Ethan, she said, "I just found out my mother wanted to kill my father."

"Oh." His eyes widened but he didn't look surprised.

"I take it you knew about that?" Joey narrowed her eyes at him.

"Yes. Sam told me just recently. After he got his diagnosis." Ethan looked directly into her eyes, which she appreciated.

"So it's true." Joey sat back, the fact hitting her even more now that Ethan had confirmed it. "Did Sam tell you what happened? How did my mother end up drowning too?"

"He didn't really give me details. He told me he left that for you in a video, but he wanted me to know so that I could be there for you if you needed it." Ethan moved closer to her. "Did you find out what happened?"

She shook her head, trying to ignore the way her body was waking up by being in his presence. "Not yet. I only just read about her thinking she needed to kill him." She looked around, hoping no one had overheard her. "God, that sounds so terrible."

"I know." Ethan sat back as the waitress approached to take their drinks order. Once she'd left, he focused on her. "Are you okay?"

"Why do people keep asking me that?" Joey took a long sip of her ice water, not realizing how dehydrated she was until she'd drunk most of the glass. "I'm as okay as I can be, given everything that's happened this week and everything I'm learning about my parents." She stopped, realizing how bratty she sounded. "Sorry."

"It's fine. I'm sorry you're going through all this." Ethan's quiet voice soothed her irritation.

"Thanks." The waitress placed their drinks in front of them, and when she'd left, Joey picked up the martini she had ordered. "I just want to forget about all of it for a bit." She blew out a breath and took a sip.

"I'm fine with that." Ethan held up his glass to her. "We'll enjoy our meal and pretend we're tourists here for happy hour and nothing else."

"That would be perfect." Joey was grateful that Ethan got it.

They ordered and then Joey relaxed, looking around at one of the restaurants she used to come to with Sam. It wasn't fancy, but there was a view of the ocean with palm trees swaying overhead and the crash of the waves a soothing backdrop to the ambience. They used to love coming here on Wednesdays for happy hour when there was a live performance by one of the best ukulele players in the world.

She and Ethan were sitting side by side, their chairs angled to get the best view. They held hands, and Joey tried really hard not to overthink this. Yet a part of her couldn't believe she was sitting here with

Ethan, and when he picked up her hand and kissed the back of it, she had to work really hard not to let out a squeal of elation.

As they ate (Joey was sorry they had to let go of their intertwined hands), her mind kept going back to the section of her mother's journal that she had just read. It wasn't until the waitress was clearing away their dishes that Joey finally realized what was bothering her about it. If her mother was right and Ren Ren had been pregnant, what had happened to the baby? Joey's eyes widened and she turned to Ethan, her mouth dropping open. He angled toward her, concern evident on his face.

"What is it? You look like you saw a ghost."

"The baby." Joey stared at Ethan. "If Ren Ren really was pregnant, what happened to the baby? Did she have it? If she did, that means I have a half sibling out there somewhere."

"Oh." That was all Ethan said, but the look on his face made the adrenaline in her body pick up and her stomach churn.

"What? What do you know?" Her eyes stayed on Ethan.

"Another thing Sam kept from you." Ethan gazed at her, one hand raking through his hair. "I'm so sorry." He sighed.

"What else did he keep from me?" Joey's voice rose, and she saw someone at the next table glance over at them.

Ethan looked at her for a moment before speaking. "You have a half brother."

Her whole world tilted, and the words hit Joey like a physical blow. She collapsed back into her chair. She had a half brother. Someone who was related to her by blood. Why had Sam never told her? And how did Ethan know and she didn't?

"I'm sorry, Joey." Ethan's voice brought her eyes back to his face, and she could see that he was truly sorry. Yet that didn't make her feel better.

"I . . ." Words failed her and the poke she'd just eaten threatened to come back up. She had a half brother and Ethan knew. She couldn't help the stab of hurt that spread through her body.

"Joey. Look at me." He reached for her hand and folded it between his. "I didn't keep this from you on purpose. Sam found out back in 2001 because Ren Ren had reached out to him after the September eleventh attack. She told him about her son and wanted both of you to know him. Sam refused. He wouldn't let her contact you."

"Wait, wait, wait." Joey took her hand back, Ethan's words crashing over her. "He knew all the way back in 2001? And neither of you thought to tell me in all these years?"

"I told him he should tell you about your father's affair with Ren Ren and give you the choice whether you wanted to know your half brother. You were sixteen at the time, old enough to understand. He told me he would tell you." Ethan swallowed, his face twisted in concern. "I thought he did. And that the reason neither of you ever brought him up again was because you'd decided together that you didn't want anything to do with him. It wasn't until right before he passed away that Sam told me he never told you the truth about any of it."

"Why didn't he tell me?" Joey cried, the hurt washing over her as if someone had thrown a bucket of ice water on her. "He didn't give me the chance or the choice." She pushed her chair back and stood, grabbing her purse. The betrayal from Sam, her father, Ren Ren, and now Ethan was too much, and she had to get out of there. "I have to go. I'm sorry."

She turned and walked as fast as she could toward the exit. She heard Ethan calling out her name, but she didn't turn around. By the time she finally got to the path that led back to the hotel and into the parking lot, she was running, tears streaking down her face and all these secrets shattering her heart.

21

An hour later, Joey was parked on the street in front of Maggie's parents' house in the Wailua Homesteads, up toward the mountains and to the west of the Wailua River. Maggie's father had picked her up from the airport, and Maggie had texted that they'd be arriving in less than three minutes. Joey couldn't wait to see her and Kristy, couldn't wait to unload everything she'd discovered. When she'd left Ethan at the restaurant, she'd driven to Lydgate Beach, a family-friendly place with its two protected coves, and sat in the sand, her arms around her legs. She'd stared off into the ocean, watching the waves crash against the rocks and the ocean disappearing into the horizon far, far out. It had calmed her but didn't put to rest all the unanswered questions this latest bit of information had conjured up. Ethan had called and then texted, and she'd sent back a text that she was fine but needed some time. She told him she'd call him the next day.

When she saw Maggie's father driving down the street, she got out of her own car. Maggie waved from the passenger seat, and Kristy rolled down the window in the back and yelled out, "Hi, Aunty Joey!"

Maggie threw her door open before the car had come to a complete stop, and she barreled at Joey, arms outstretched.

"Maggie." Joey caught her, then they were hugging, both squealing and talking so fast that neither could understand what the other was saying. Kristy joined them soon after, wrapping her little arms around them both. When Joey finally pulled away, she found Mr. Estrada standing there grinning at them, Maggie's and Kristy's suitcases at his side.

Maggie's hands gripped Joey's upper arms. "It's so good to see you." Her eyes roamed over Joey's face. "How are you? I mean, how are you, really?"

Joey blew out a breath. "Not good. I have so much to tell you."

"Okay, later. When little ears aren't listening." Maggie went to get her suitcase from her father.

"I can carry my own suitcase now, Aunty Joey." Kristy showed Joey how she could drag it all by herself up the path to the house.

"Good job. You've grown so much," Joey said.

Kristy beamed at her as Mr. Estrada gave Joey a hug.

"It's good to see you, Joey. We haven't seen you in so long."

"You too, Mr. Estrada." She knew his words weren't meant as a reproach, but she couldn't help feeling embarrassed that it'd been a long time since she'd come to visit Maggie's parents. She'd spent almost as much time in this house during high school as Maggie had at hers.

"It's Joe." Mr. Estrada grinned. "You don't have to call me Mr. Estrada anymore."

"I can't help it." Joey grinned back. People had always teased them that they had the same name. "It's a habit."

The front door opened, and Maggie's mother, Akiko, came out, her face lighting up when she saw her daughter and granddaughter.

"You're home!" She ran to Kristy and wrapped the little girl in her arms.

"Hey, what am I, chopped liver?" Maggie stood with her hands on her hips but a smile on her face.

Akiko reached out and pulled Maggie into the embrace as Kristy squealed and beckoned to Joey. "You too, Aunty."

When they finally pulled away, Akiko looked at Joey. "We're so sorry about Sam."

"Thank you."

In avoiding Kauai, Joey had forgotten that this family was hers, too, ever since Maggie had befriended her on her first day of high school. Joey had felt like a sore thumb, starting at a school where most of the kids had known each other all their lives. But being Asian helped, and with Maggie being half Filipino and half Japanese, Joey had felt right at home in the Estradas' house where she'd often go after school to do homework while Sam had been working at the clinic with Ethan.

Akiko put out a plate of mochi malasadas, and Maggie's eyes rolled back into her head as she took a bite of an ube one.

"I miss these so much." She held the purple donut in her hand, studying it before popping the rest of it in her mouth. "They don't have these in Alaska."

"I made you some pancit and salmon onigiri for you to take up to Princeville with you." Akiko smoothed a hand down Maggie's wild, wavy dark hair.

"Me too?" Kristy brightened at the mention of the Filipino stir-fried noodles and the Japanese ball of rice wrapped in seaweed.

"Of course." Akido pulled Kristy's ponytail.

"Thanks." Joey nodded her appreciation. She'd had many meals with the Estradas because they often invited her to stay for dinner before Sam picked her up on the way home from work.

After their snack, Joey helped Maggie unpack her suitcase in her room while Akiko did the same for Kristy, who would sleep in Maggie's room by herself tonight.

"You can go now, Mommy." Kristy surveyed the room. "I know you have a lot to tell Aunty." She lowered her voice and whispered, "About the divorce stuff."

Maggie rolled her eyes, making Joey and Akiko laugh. Akiko ushered Kristy out so that Maggie could pack a small bag for her sleepover with Joey in Princeville. They kept their chatter light, talking about people they once knew and how Maggie's flight had been. There would be time later to get to the hard stuff, the things Joey had discovered about her family.

When they were ready to go, Akiko handed a reusable shopping bag filled with their dinner to Maggie. "See you tomorrow, Mags."

Maggie hugged her parents and opened her arms to Kristy, who was jumping around the living room on a bouncy ball. "Excuse me, can I have a hug goodnight?"

Kristy reluctantly left the ball to give Maggie and then Joey a squeeze before running back to her toy. Maggie rolled her eyes again, then they were out the door, heading for Joey's rental car. As soon as they were buckled in and Joey was turning out of the road where the Estradas lived, Maggie pounced.

"Okay, talk."

Joey glanced over at her friend, smiling a little at the bossy tone in her voice. Maggie had always been able to pry whatever it was that was bothering Joey out of her. When her parents had died, Joey had turned into a quiet kid, where once she used to talk all the time. But losing her parents had made something dim within her, and she'd grown accustomed to keeping so much inside because she didn't want to burden Sam. Maggie was the one she'd spilled everything to, often after Maggie had coaxed Joey to open up.

"My mother wanted to kill my father." The words spilled out before Joey could stop them. *Damn.* She'd wanted to wait until they were back at Sam's place before getting to the heart of what was bothering her.

To her surprise, Maggie laughed. "Well, she wouldn't be the first wife to want to kill her husband. I mean look at me and Ben."

"What's the latest on that?" Joey was glad to turn the attention on Maggie.

Maggie sank into her seat, arms crossed over her chest. "It's so ridiculous. My lawyer says we now have to file a motion or something stating that $1000 is not enough of a jump in income to warrant me paying Ben anything." She shook her head in disgust. "I mean, like, what the fuck? Ben wanted this to be amicable. He wanted to use a mediator instead of hiring lawyers. But then he lets his family do bullshit like this? I ended up having to hire a lawyer, which is costing a lot of money."

"That's terrible. I'm sorry." Joey reached out to touch Maggie's arm briefly.

"You should be so glad you never got married. And that you don't plan on it ever." Maggie's voice was bitter.

Joey's heart dropped. That was not what she wanted Maggie to say. Not when she'd recently confessed her feelings to Ethan, kissed him, and then had their first fight, all in one day.

"I'm sorry." Maggie must have caught the look on her face. "I didn't mean to hijack the conversation or discourage you from marriage. Marriage is great." And she gave an exaggerated grin, making Joey laugh.

"It's fine. I want to know what's going on in your life too."

"Now's not the time for me." Maggie sat up straighter and turned to face Joey. "Tell me about your parents."

"My mom wrote in her journal that she was going to kill him. Like, she was plotting my father's murder." Joey looked straight ahead, out the windshield as she said this, but she heard Maggie's sharp intake of breath.

"What?" Maggie's jaw dropped in disbelief. "I thought you meant it figuratively."

Joey swallowed the lump in her throat before she continued. "The last entry I read said that she'd found out Ren Ren was pregnant, and she realized it wasn't Ren Ren she needed to get rid of. It was my father. She meant that literally."

"No."

Joey glanced at Maggie and saw the shock in her eyes. "Yes."

"Okay. Hold that thought." Maggie held up a hand. "We'll talk about that more when you're not driving. What's going on with Ethan?"

Joey's eye twitched as she thought about running out of the restaurant earlier. "Well, apparently, he's known since 2001 that I have a secret half brother that Sam never told me about. So I'm kind of mad at him too."

"Wait, what?" Maggie's voice rose. "What has happened since I spoke to you last night?"

Joey sighed. "A lot. I might have also kissed him."

"What?" Maggie screamed, making Joey wince. "What the heck?" She waved her hands in the air. "No, never mind. Don't tell me. Focus on getting us there safely. We have all night to dissect everything."

And they did. Once they'd arrived back at Sam's unit and Maggie had fawned over Wonton and received many kisses and tail wags, they settled on the couch with the feast Maggie's mom had made spread on the coffee table in front of them. Joey had poured them each a glass of cold sauvignon blanc, and Wonton was settled by Joey's side with a chew bone. When Joey had told Maggie everything she knew, Maggie put her glass of wine down on the table and fell back against the cushions.

"Whew. You weren't kidding about it being a lot."

"It's crazy. I'm still getting used to the fact that Sam, who I thought was my only family all this time, is gone. And now I find out that I have a half brother out there somewhere." Joey took a sip of her wine. "Oh, and my mother might have murdered my father."

"It sounds like a soap opera." Maggie shook her head. "Not to mention you and Ethan!"

"I know." Joey looked down. "I wish Sam had told me all this when he was alive. I can't even process Ethan because my mind is spinning with everything else."

"What are you going to do?" Maggie's voice was full of concern.

"Finish reading the journal tomorrow. I can't right now. I feel like I got run over by a truck." Joey tried to laugh but it came out as a half sob.

"No, I mean, what are you going to do about your half brother?" Maggie reached across Joey to pull Wonton into her arms when Wonton tried to eat the last bite of onigiri in Joey's hand.

"I don't know." Joey swallowed. "I'm all alone now."

"You're not. You have me and my family." Maggie grabbed her hand, holding it tight. "And Ethan and the Kellys next door."

"I know." Joey gave Maggie a grateful smile. "Ethan said the same thing."

"Hmm." Maggie rubbed Wonton's ears, a thoughtful look on her face.

"What?" Joey turned to her friend. She knew that tone. Maggie was contemplating something.

"You've been shielded all your life by Sam. Maybe it's not such a bad thing that you have to stand up for yourself now." Maggie put up a hand. "I don't mean that it's a good thing Sam is gone. Just that now you can make your own decisions."

Joey took a moment to think about it. Then she nodded. "There's one more video from Sam. He said to watch it when I've finished reading our mother's journal. I want to see it now, but I'm also dreading it because I know it will be the last thing he left for me before he died. It's like, if I don't watch it, I'll still be able to look forward to seeing him again, you know?"

"Yeah." Maggie reached out and squeezed Joey's shoulder. "I'm going to miss Sam. He was like my big brother too. I can't even imagine how you're feeling right now."

Joey rubbed her hands over her face, willing herself not to cry. Maggie kept her hand on Joey's shoulder, and Joey reached up to hold it with both her hands as if hanging on from a cliff. They stayed like that for a few minutes, the only sound in the room coming from Wonton, who was licking her leg.

Finally, Joey dropped her hands and turned to Maggie. "Thanks for being here."

Maggie nodded, a small smile on her face. "What about Ethan?"

"What about Ethan?" Joey tried to keep her voice calm even as her heart thudded a bit too loud in her chest.

"You've had feelings for him all your life. So much so that you avoided Kauai after he got married." Maggie didn't let the frown on

Joey's face deter her. "Now you find out he's divorced and single. And has feelings for you."

Joey set her mouth, not sure if she wanted to answer since she didn't quite know what to do about him.

"I know that look, Joey. You're being stubborn." Maggie shoved her gently in the shoulder.

"I am not stubborn. That's Sam's specialty." Joey pretended to glare at Maggie.

"Well, some of his stubbornness rubbed off on you." Maggie's voice was teasing, and Joey knew she was trying to lighten the mood.

"Okay, yes, I still have feelings for him. But I can't add one more thing to the pile."

Maggie plunked Wonton into Joey's lap so she could refill their wine glasses. After taking a sip from hers, she looked over at Joey.

"You're right. You do have a lot to deal with. But maybe the time is finally right. Maybe now is right for you and Ethan."

Joey shook her head. "I've wasted so much time in the past because of him."

"You don't have to be alone for the rest of your life." Maggie's brows arched.

"Says the person who just told me I was lucky not to be married," Joey shot back at her.

"I didn't mean it." Maggie shoved Joey on the shoulder. "If I hadn't gotten married, I wouldn't have had Kristy."

"That's true." Joey would allow her that.

"All I'm saying is, maybe now is finally the time for you to be open to a relationship. Maybe Ethan had backed off before because of Sam."

"Maggie." Joey gave a look. "My family is obviously not good with relationships. Maybe we're better off alone."

"That's fine, if that's what you really want." Maggie held Joey's glance, then she looked away and picked up the remote for the TV. "Let's watch something mindless. I think you need a break from all this drama."

Joey gave her a grateful look as Maggie started flipping through the channels. She'd get back to reading her mother's journal in the morning, but for now, she was content to snuggle on the couch with her best friend and her brother's dog, watching a romantic comedy or some stupid reality TV show where people made even worse decisions than she did. Tomorrow she would finish the journal and find out what her mother had really done when she found out that Ren Ren was pregnant.

22

Ah-Hui
1996, Bangkok

"Here, I made some ginger tea with honey for you."

Zhi Wei handed me the mug, and I accepted it with a grateful smile. I was sitting propped up by two pillows in bed, trying to get through paperwork while recovering from bronchitis. I was finally feeling better after two weeks of constant coughing, but my throat was still raw, and the hot tea was soothing.

"What are you up to tonight?" I asked, my eyes on the papers in front of me.

A month after realizing that I needed to get rid of my husband, I'd come up with the perfect plan. But then bronchitis had sidelined me, and I'd had to put my plans on hold. Now that I was feeling stronger, it was time to finally put it into motion.

"Ren Ren is taking Chiao-Yi to the weekend market. We'll have time to ourselves tonight." Zhi Wei ran a hand down my arm, and my gaze shifted to him.

"Oh." I couldn't keep the surprise out of my voice. Even though I knew Zhi Wei still loved me despite sleeping with Ren Ren, he hadn't tried to spend any time with me, just the two of us, in a long time. We were always with either Ren Ren, Chiao-Yi, or both.

"I asked Anan to make spaghetti and meatballs before he left. It's ready and waiting for us." Zhi Wei looked at me, a half smile on his lips.

"Really?" Our private chef, who came in four times a week, was a genius. I'd told Zhi Wei yesterday that I was craving good old spaghetti and meatballs from America, and my heart softened, thinking how Zhi Wei had heard me and asked Anan to make it.

"Do you want me to bring it to you in bed, or are you feeling up to eating at the table? I thought we could watch a movie together after." His gaze didn't waver. "In bed."

I blinked, caught off guard. When I had first arrived in New York from Taiwan, Zhi Wei had thought watching movies would be a good way to improve my English. We used to nestle together in bed and watch everything from emotional dramas to romantic comedies and action pictures. Zhi Wei would sometimes pause the movie, making me repeat iconic phrases from popular movies. He'd laugh at my pronunciation, but never in a mean way, and we'd often collapse in a fit of giggles, which would quickly turn into lovemaking.

Was that what he was suggesting? It had been a while since we'd been together, and I'd grown accustomed to it. Why now? Did he know what I was going to do and was trying to soften me up? But how was that possible? I'd told no one about my plans.

I narrowed my eyes slightly, but he only gave me a crooked smile in return. It had been so long, and I was craving his attention, his touch. But no. I shook my head slightly. I had a mission, and I was going to carry it out. For my children.

"Come on, Ah-Hui. Sit with me for dinner." He reached out a hand and without thinking, I took it in one of mine.

I let him put the papers aside, then I got out of bed and followed him into the main room. I was silent through dinner, allowing Zhi Wei to carry the conversation and only nodding or answering in one-word syllables. I was too busy trying to make sense of why he was suddenly making an effort in a relationship that I thought was already dead.

"Don't forget, we're going to that village down the river in two days, to do exams and vaccinations for the children." Zhi Wei took the last bite of meatball from his plate and reached for his water glass.

I looked up sharply, because that was the trip that I'd decided would end my husband. It was the perfect plan. Zhi Wei thought we both couldn't swim. He had no idea that I could. I studied his face for any indication he knew what I planned to do, but his expression was relaxed.

He finished his glass of water and then held out the glass for me to refill from the pitcher sitting right in front of him.

I looked at it, wondering what would happen if I refused. But I'd always done whatever he needed, including filling his water glass because he was too lazy to do so. Or I'd been too accommodating in the past and this was what I had trained him to do. As I stared at his outstretched hand with the empty glass in it, something within me snapped. Who did he think he was, treating me like a servant, expecting me to cater to his every whim? Why had I thought that was acceptable—an educated, smart woman like me? Why had I let the culture we'd grown up in make me believe that I had to do whatever my husband told me to? When would this tyranny ever stop?

"Ah-Hui?" My husband's voice was more confused than commanding as he continued to hold out the empty glass.

"No." The word came out softly, so I said it again, louder. "No."

"No, what?" Slowly, his hand came down until he'd set his glass on the table. "What's going on?"

"No." I said it again because it felt good. I was done being the docile wife. "I know you're sleeping with her again. Have been for some years." My voice grew stronger with each word. "You told me you would never do that again. You told me you loved me, that I was the most important woman to you in the world. But that's not true, is it?"

I stared into my husband's eyes, part of me wanting him to tell me he was sorry, that he did love me, only me. And that same part of me knew that if he did, I would cave again and accept him for what he was, even if it killed me.

But he didn't say any of that. He stared at me, his gaze stricken, and then he looked at the floor as if he was too ashamed to look me in the eyes.

And I knew then. He would never give her up. Whatever it was that drew him to her, he couldn't say no, not even for me. As much as he claimed to love me, he was addicted to her. To her and the rush from fighting for a cause they both passionately believed in. A cause I wouldn't even let him talk about in our home, in front of our children.

I stood, our romantic night suddenly ruined. If I had been wavering in my decision to carry out my plan, I no longer waffled because my husband had just shown me how he truly felt. I wasn't the most important woman in his life. I'd been replaced. For some reason, Ren Ren had yet to tell my husband he was going to be a father again. And before she did, I was going to end this, once and for all. In two days, when we would go by boat to that remote village. Two more days until I'd finally be free from the threads that bound me to him in a way I never imagined.

⁂

It was almost time. Zhi Wei and I were about to leave in twenty minutes. We would work in the village, seeing as many patients as we could. It would be a long day, and I knew we'd both be exhausted on the boat ride back, so it wouldn't seem out of the ordinary for me to fall overboard.

For that was my plan. I would "accidentally" fall into the river on the way home in the dark. I was positive Zhi Wei would jump in to save me. Because despite the affair, despite his refusal to kick Ren Ren out, I knew without a doubt that he still loved me. As much as he wouldn't let Ren Ren go, he felt the same for me. Despite everything, I firmly believed we were tied together by a red thread of fate. And that thread, that binding love, was going to be what led to his death. He will drown trying to save me, and I will swim to safety, pretending that I was exhausted from fighting in the water because I couldn't swim. I loved Zhi Wei, I always will. But I loved my children more, and I knew I had to do this.

I would hug my daughter tight before we left for this trip, because she was about to lose her father. I knew she would grieve as she loved him so much, but I knew she'd be better off in the long run. I would do anything for her. I would be there for her, help her get over losing her father. And one day, she won't remember much about him. She never has to know what I'm about to do. Because I will burn this journal as soon as I get back, without my husband. No one will ever know the truth, and they will help me mourn the loss of my husband.

It's finally time to end this once and for all.

23

Joey
Present Day, Kauai

"No. There has to be more."

Joey turned the pages of the binder desperately, searching for more of her mother's words. That couldn't have been all that was in the journal. There had to be more. Didn't there?

But there wasn't. That was the end of the translated pages.

Joey sank back against the cushions of the couch as if she were boneless. Her mother's last words rang through her head, and she kept shaking it, trying to believe that her mother had planned to murder her father. Now she understood why Sam had been so adamant about keeping this from her. As a young child, she knew she would have been devastated, unable to process the news, if she had known the truth. She was devastated now, and utterly appalled, but as a child, it would have completely ruined her.

It was early and Maggie was still sleeping in the guest room. They'd both squeezed onto the queen bed, neither wanting to disturb Sam's room upstairs. Joey had yet to manage to strip Sam's bed and wash the sheets because she wanted to keep as much of her brother as she could.

She longed to wake Maggie up, to talk about what she'd just read, but Maggie had been exhausted by her travel and needed her rest. Joey looked at Wonton, curled up next to her on the couch.

"I wish you could talk." She stroked a hand down the dog's back, and Wonton licked her arm. "Okay." Joey took in a breath. "I'm going to watch Sam's last video." As much as she wanted to save the very last one her brother had made for her, she needed answers. There was no way she could go about her life until she finally knew everything her brother had kept from her.

She was glad she'd left the laptop on the kitchen table last night so that she didn't need to go back into the guest room and risk waking Maggie. She hoped Sam had the answers to her questions. Like, if their mother had planned to kill their father, then how had they both drowned? It didn't make sense.

Joey sat at the table and went to the video. Putting her wireless earbuds in, she started it and braced herself for whatever Sam was about to tell her.

"Joey. Here we are again." Sam smiled in the video, but Joey could see the strain behind his eyes. "I know you're probably completely shocked right now. Do you see why I never wanted you to know the truth?"

Joey nodded, her eyes fixed on her brother.

"You're probably wondering what happened, why our mother drowned if she'd planned on swimming to safety." Sam let out an exhale. "They found a contusion on the back of her head. I think she must have hit her head when she went over and blacked out. Just like she thought, Ba went in after her even though he couldn't swim. I think she accidentally drowned. She had every intention of coming back to you, of getting rid of the journal like she said on the last page. But she never made it."

"Oh my god." Joey covered her mouth with a hand, the horror of her parents' last moments paralyzing her. Whatever had happened, it was tragic. And Sam was right; it was not something a child should have to be burdened with.

"I wanted to tell you as you got old enough to understand." Sam clasped his hands together in front of him on the video. "I started to so many times, but every time I brought up our parents, you would talk about a memory you had of them, and I just couldn't disillusion you. You idolized our mom so much, and you were our father's special girl. How could I tell you that our mother tried to kill our father because of an affair with your nanny, and ended up killing both of them instead?"

Joey shook her head, thinking about the turmoil Sam had lived through. She knew she would have done the same, had the situation been reversed.

"I'm sorry, Sam," she said out loud. "That you had to carry that burden by yourself all these years." She'd known her brother was strong, but now she realized exactly how strong he had been. He'd lived with this knowledge for most of her life as he'd shielded her from the worst of their parents' actions.

"I'm sorry, Joey," Sam said on-screen, making a small laugh burst out of her that they were both apologizing at the same time. "I'm sorry I never told you about our family drama, but I don't regret it." He glanced down at his clasped hands for a moment before looking back up. "Ren Ren gave birth to a boy. We have a half brother who lives in Taiwan. I never wanted to have anything to do with him. I should have told you about him when you were old enough, let you decide for yourself if you wanted to contact him." Sam stopped and pressed his lips together before continuing. "I know I was being selfish. I didn't want you to have another brother. I blamed Ren Ren and transferred that blame to the boy. If he hadn't existed, would our mother have come up with that outlandish plan and killed both of them?"

"Oh, Sam." Joey's heart was breaking for the grief in her brother's voice.

"If you want to know him, I left his contact info on my computer." Sam's eyes bore into Joey's. "In 2001, Ren Ren reached out to me after the 9/11 attacks. She wanted to make sure we were both okay, even though we had moved to Kauai by then. She told me I had a half brother who was almost five. She wanted to talk to you, but I said no. You were sixteen at the time, going through the regular teenage angst, thinking about college and telling all your secrets to Maggie. I didn't want Ren Ren to set you back when I felt you were finally moving on with your life, getting over the death of our parents."

Joey didn't react because this was so like her brother. He took everything on his shoulders, whether that was right or not. Was she mad that he hadn't told her Ren Ren had reached out to them? At this point, Joey's mind was frozen, and she had no idea how she felt about anything.

Sam continued speaking on-screen. "Ren Ren told me she blamed herself for coming between them, but that it wasn't her fault, the accident." Sam ran a hand through his hair. "I do blame her. If she hadn't been sleeping with our father again, after he'd promised our mother that he had ended the affair, if she hadn't gotten pregnant, none of that would have happened. I refused to let her contact you. And right or wrong, I blamed her son too."

Joey nodded, knowing how loyal Sam was and understanding why he'd felt this way. She had already forgiven Sam in her heart for keeping this from her. Now that the truth was staring her in the face, she knew she wouldn't have been able to handle it as a child, and not even as a young adult. She'd had nightmares for years, well into her early twenties, about her parents' drowning, and to have known all this would have been too much.

"Ren Ren's boy, Yao, reached out to me when he was in California for college." Sam looked back into the camera. "He told me that his mother had passed away recently. He'd known about us his whole life and had always wanted to get to know us." Sam blew out a breath. "I told him he wasn't family, that he couldn't talk to you either. I asked him to leave us both alone, that he's not our brother. And I never heard from him again, even though he gave me his email address to pass along to you in case I changed my mind."

Joey clasped a hand to her mouth, trying to process what Sam was telling her. Another loss taking a piece of her heart. Deep inside, no matter how angry she was at Ren Ren, she had held on to the hope that maybe she'd get to see her old nanny again. That Joey would get to ask her why. Why had she done what she did? Had it been worth it, destroying her family like that? And now that would never happen.

"What are you doing? Are you okay?"

Maggie's voice made Joey jump, and she dropped her hand and turned to where her best friend stood in the doorway of the guest room.

"I'm . . ." Joey trailed off as she reached out to pause the video, pulling the earbuds out of her ears. "I'm watching Sam's last video. It's . . . a lot."

"Oh." Maggie's eyes widened and she gestured back to the guest room. "I'll leave you to it."

"No, it's okay. I need you." Joey gestured to the couch next to her and Maggie came to her side. "Watch the rest with me. Or rather, let me rewind it and you can watch the whole last video." She explained to Maggie what she'd just read in her mother's journal, and then they watched the video together.

Maggie held Joey's hand the entire time, and when they got to the part where Joey had left off before Maggie joined her, Maggie squeezed her hand hard.

"I love you, Joey. I know you're probably mad at me for keeping all this from you and not telling you in person." Sam's face was filled with sorrow. "I know some people won't agree with the way I went about it. But this was what I thought was best. I made mistakes and yes, I can be selfish and stubborn, but you know everything I've done has been with your well-being in mind. I know Ethan and Maggie, and even Victor will be there to help you pick up the pieces as you decide what you want to do. I couldn't ever make myself reach out to our half brother, but maybe you will want to. And I know you. If you do, you're going to feel so guilty that you're doing something I never wanted and kept from you. But please don't worry about me. I was selfish, and now it's your turn to be selfish. If you want to seek Yao out, do so with a clear conscience because I fully support whatever you decide."

Sam reached out and touched the screen on his end and Joey put her fingers against Sam's on the laptop. They stayed like that for a moment until Sam pulled his hand away. "Be well. I love you." And with one final look into Joey's eyes, he turned off the camera for the last time.

Joey let out a sob and fell against Maggie. Her friend held her, rubbing her back as Joey fought with all the emotions roiling inside her. No matter what Sam had done, she knew he spoke the truth, that all he'd done was his best to protect her. It might not have always been the right thing to do, and yes, part of her was angry that he'd kept so much from her, but she couldn't fault Sam. He'd suffered, too, with no one to guide him as Sam had done for her.

"What can I do?" Maggie asked, continuing to rub her back.

"Nothing. You being here is enough." Joey's voice was muffled as her face was buried in a cushion. After a moment, she wiped the tears away with the back of her hand.

"Then I'm glad I'm here."

They stayed like that for a long time. "We should get breakfast." Joey finally moved, breaking the peaceful spell that had come over the condo.

"You want to get an acai bowl at The Spot?" Maggie drew back, her eyes searching Joey's face.

"Sounds good." Joey managed a watery smile.

With Wonton in tow, they drove the short distance to the Princeville Shopping Center. Once they got their acai bowls with fresh Kauai fruit, they took them over to a picnic table in the courtyard, both sitting on the same side to take advantage of the mountain views.

"What are you going to do? Spend time on island?"

"Yes." Joey stared out at the red ginger flowers around the courtyard. "I've missed Kauai. I told my renter in New York she could have it for another few months. She's paying month to month, so I'll see what I'm going to do after that."

"I'm glad you're staying for you, and not just to sort out Sam's affairs." Maggie nudged her with a shoulder. "We'll plow through some of that today."

"Thank you." Joey's head rested on Maggie's shoulder for a moment before she straightened and took another spoonful of acai.

"What about your half brother?"

Joey heaved a sigh. "I have to reach out to him." As she said this out loud, she realized she'd made up her mind as soon as Sam had confirmed that they had a half brother. Unlike Sam, she didn't hold a grudge against Yao. Even though Sam had said he wouldn't mind if she wanted to know Yao, guilt twinged through her even just thinking of reaching out to Yao.

"I knew you were going to say that." Maggie took her last bite and pushed her bowl aside.

"I miss Sam so much." Joey tried to articulate what she was feeling. "But how can I not want to meet another brother that I'd just found out existed?"

Maggie nodded. "Exactly." She was going to say more but then her text pinged. She looked at her phone and her mouth dropped open. "No way."

"What?" Joey turned to her, alarmed at the shock on Maggie's face. "Everything okay?"

"Yes." Maggie looked up, disbelief on her face. "Ben is finally doing the right thing. He contacted my lawyer, said things have gone too far. He's calling off his parents, telling them to leave me alone."

"Wow." Joey looked at the phone Maggie held out to her and then back up at her friend. "It's about time he grew a spine."

"I wish he'd done it while we were still together." Maggie sighed, staring out at the landscape. "Maybe we would have been able to make things work."

"Do you still love him?" Joey studied Maggie's face. "Do you want to get back together?"

"No." Maggie shook her head. "Too much has happened. Things I can't forgive him for. He never put me first. He didn't stand up for me against his parents' racist comments. He didn't stand up for Kristy. I'd rather be alone than with a man like that."

"I'm glad you're going to get closure then." Joey put an arm around Maggie.

"And I'm glad you're going to reach out to your half brother." Maggie smiled at her.

"I am. I'll email him as soon as we get back to the condo. Thanks for being here," Joey said. "I needed you."

"Anytime." Maggie leaned her head against Joey's. "I've got your back. Always."

24

Joey sat in front of her laptop, trying to figure out how to start the email to a half brother who was sure to be shocked when he saw the message from her.

"Dear Yao, I'm the half sister you thought didn't want to know you," Joey said out loud. "No, that's terrible." She deleted what she'd written and tried again. "Dear half brother. No, better to use his first name." She deleted it. "Okay, Dear Yao. It's me. I'm the problem."

She groaned and deleted that, too, and then stared at her blank screen for several seconds, chewing on her bottom lip. Maggie had taken Wonton for a walk, giving her space to compose the email. She'd show it to Maggie before she sent it but had needed time to come up with something that wouldn't scare the poor man. She also had to tell him about Sam's passing, which was going to be a lot to put into an email.

She started typing again, and this time, she listened to her heart and just wrote what she hoped he'd want to hear if she were in his shoes.

> Dear Yao,
>
> I know you've known about my existence your whole life, but I only found out about you yesterday. I'm sorry to tell you that my brother, Sam, passed away

> recently. He'd never told me about you but left some information, including your email address, if I wanted to reach out to you. I hope you don't mind that I'm writing now after all these years.
>
> I think you're about twenty-eight years old? Sam told me that you live in Taiwan but had come to the States for university. I know our family history is complicated, but I would really like to get to know you. I completely understand if this is not something you want, given how Sam has treated you and your mother when you've both reached out to him. I don't blame my brother; he was only trying to protect me. But in my own defense, I had no idea until yesterday that you existed.
>
> If you do want to reach out to me, you can reply back to this email. I sincerely hope I'll hear from you, but if I don't, I'll respect your decision and will not bother you anymore.
>
> Your half sister,
>
> Joey Zhang

Joey looked over what she'd written, thinking it was the best she could do. She'd wait for Maggie to approve it before sending it off. In the meantime, she called Victor.

"Joey," Victor said when he answered after three rings. "Everything okay?"

"Yes. I want to get started with whatever I need to do for Sam."

For the next half hour, Victor went over everything until her head spun. All the little details, like contacting Social Security, canceling his prescriptions and subscriptions, canceling unnecessary insurance, and a host of other tasks that threatened to overwhelm her. But she took a deep breath and continued to take notes as Victor talked, grateful that Maggie was with her and would be able to help with the many tasks.

"Thanks, Victor," Joey said when he finally wound down on his instructions.

"It's a lot for you to deal with by yourself. Do you have anyone you could reach out to?" Victor's concern was clear. "Maybe Ethan?"

"Yes, Ethan said he would help, especially with stuff related to their practice. But Maggie's here."

"Oh, good." There was relief in Victor's voice. "I'm glad you won't be alone."

Joey pressed a hand to her forehead as the loss of Sam surged through her again. "I just found out I have a half brother. Which is kind of nice, especially as I thought I have no family left."

Victor was quiet for so long that Joey wondered if they'd been disconnected. But then he said, "You actually do still have family. Besides your half brother."

"What?" Joey's grip on her phone loosened, and she had to catch it with the other hand. "Who? Where?"

"Your mother came to me a couple of years after you were born, and asked me to help her find her mother and grandmother. I felt like I owed it to her, and I told her I'd try."

Another long pause.

"And?" Joey couldn't take the suspense. "Who did you find?"

"Her grandmother had passed away soon after her husband was taken by the KMT. And then it took me many years, but I finally found her mother, your grandmother."

"My mother was reunited with her mother?" Joey's heart leaped at the thought that maybe her mother hadn't died completely heartbroken over her family.

"No." Victor stopped as if searching for words. "I didn't find her until after your parents drowned. Literally a few days after their deaths."

Joey's mouth dropped open. "What?"

"I'm sorry, Joey."

"That's so sad. You found her mother a few days too late." Joey shook her head, sorrow for her family making her heart ache.

"I know." Victor was quiet for a moment. "Your grandmother had gotten remarried and was using a new name. That's why I had a hard time tracking her down. But the irony of finding her a few days too late . . ." He trailed off. "Anyway, I have your grandmother's most recent contact information if you want it. She still lives in Taiwan. In Keelung."

"She's alive?" Joey whispered. Her heart pounded and goose bumps broke out over her skin. How was it possible that she just found out she had a brother and a grandmother?

"Yes."

Joey fell back against the chair, her eyes closed. Her grandmother was alive.

"Joey?" Victor's voice made her eyes snap open.

"Will she talk to me? I want to meet her." Her heart raced but she knew this was what she wanted.

Victor was silent for a moment. "I thought you might say that. You and Sam have always been so different."

"We are." Joey understood why Sam had cut himself off from their remaining family members. But for her, she needed, no *craved* the connection.

"Okay. I'll call her."

"Thanks, Victor." Joey cleared her throat and then continued. "I'm going to email my half brother too. Sam left me his email address."

"Good." There was a pause. "I'll be in touch."

"Thank you." They said goodbye and hung up just as Maggie walked into the condo with Wonton. "Oh, good, you're back." Completely deadpan, she said, "My grandmother is alive."

"What?" Maggie unclipped Wonton from her harness. "Why do things always happen to you as soon as my back is turned?"

Joey told her what Victor had just said and then pushed her laptop in front of Maggie. "Is this okay?"

Maggie scanned the message and then gave Joey an encouraging smile. "This is perfect."

Joey reached across Maggie and hit the "Send" button. "Done."

"Whatever happens, I'm here for you." Maggie touched Joey on the shoulder.

"I know he might not respond. Or he could take weeks to respond." Joey took her computer and walked to the couch, collapsing onto it with the laptop still clutched in her hands.

Before Maggie could answer, Joey saw that she had a new email. She sat upright when she realized it was from Yao.

"He replied already." Joey blew out a shaky breath. "He's glad I reached out to him."

Maggie took the laptop and read out loud. "Dear Joey, I'm so happy to find an email from you. I've wanted to know you and Sam my whole life, and it is a miracle to get your message. I'm so sorry to hear about Sam. I understood why he was so angry, but it has always saddened me that I couldn't be a part of your family. I'd like to talk with you. Perhaps through Zoom or FaceTime if you have an iPhone? I look forward to hearing from you."

"He wants to talk to me." Joey couldn't help the way her voice shook. The brother she didn't know she had wanted to talk to her. It made her feel like a traitor toward Sam to say this, but she knew Maggie would understand. "I lost one brother, and then out of the blue, found another one."

"It's okay." Maggie put the laptop down and turned to Joey, wrapping her arms around her. "You're okay."

They stayed like that until Joey got her emotions under control. She blew out a breath even as she wiped away the tears. "I haven't cried this much since my parents drowned." She gave Maggie a tremulous smile and finally put into words what she was feeling. "I feel like I'm betraying

Sam, but I really want to get to know Yao. And my grandmother, if Victor can find her. They're all I have left in the world."

"Sam would be happy for you." Maggie's voice was forceful. "I have no doubt."

"Okay." Joey took in another deep breath. "Then I'm going to set up a video call with Yao."

Maggie nodded and something finally loosened in Joey's chest. For the first time since finding out Sam was gone, she thought she'd be able to go on with her life.

25

"I got this." Joey sat in front of her computer, about to talk to her half brother for the first time in her life.

It was the day after she had reached out to Yao. Joey wiped her sweaty palms on her shirt and then reached out a hand to accept the FaceTime call on her laptop.

A second later, she saw her half brother's face. She'd been expecting him to look like Sam but sighed in relief when she realized he looked nothing like her brother. Sam was long and lean and wiry, and while she couldn't tell how tall Yao was from the screen, his face was rounder than theirs, more like Ren Ren's, and his shoulders were broader than Sam's.

They stared at each other for a moment, neither saying anything. Yao spoke first. "Hi, Joey. You have no idea how long I've looked forward to meeting you." He brought a hand up to his mouth. "It's so great to finally talk to you."

"I'm sorry I never knew about you. But I'm glad to meet you now." She grimaced. "You must hate us."

Yao shook his head. "No." He paused, staring at her. "My mother told me what happened."

"Oh." Joey gazed back at him, wondering exactly what Ren Ren had told him. "My brother, he's very protective. He kept a lot of things from me. I've only found out the truth this week. After he passed away." She'd told Yao over email about Sam's illness and death.

"I'm sorry I'll never get a chance to know him." Yao looked pensive. "I've heard about both of you my whole life. My mother longed for us to meet. She never forgot you."

"I never forgot her either," Joey said softly. "I missed her so much after Sam brought me back to New York. I couldn't understand why he made her go away. I was so mad at him. I only found out about—" She stopped before saying the word "affair." She still harbored a lot of resentment and anger toward her father and Ren Ren.

"The affair with your father." Yao didn't flinch as he said this, as if he was resigned to the fact.

"Yes."

"You must have been so angry at my mother when you found out." Yao's expression didn't change.

"I was. Am. I don't know." Joey let out a sigh. "I've missed her so much ever since Sam made her go away. Now finding out what she and my father did . . . I want to understand."

"Why didn't you ever reach out to her then?" There was no accusation in Yao's voice.

"I had no idea where she'd gone. Sam refused to tell me." Joey pressed her lips together, remembering the drama of that time. "I was so upset when he wouldn't tell me how to get hold of her. I cried, threw a shoe at him. I went on a hunger strike, refusing to eat until I couldn't take it anymore." Joey shook her head. "Sam was more strong-willed than me. Eventually he wore me down, and we never talked about it again. But I did try to find her myself." She let out a laugh. "The problem was, I never knew her full name. Can you believe that?"

"What?" Yao looked at her like he didn't believe her.

"I'd called her Ren Ren Ayi since I could remember. No one ever told me her full name. I had no idea what her family name was, or anything about her. It's hard to do a Google search when all you have is a nickname."

"Huh. So that's what happened." Yao nodded. "She told me she had a special bond with you. She thought you'd reach out to her once you were an adult. She waited every year, hoping this was the one when she'd hear from you."

"That's so sad." Joey met Yao's eyes. "I did try to find her. I even asked Victor for her name. Asked him to reach out to her for me. Sam must have gotten to him because he told me to leave it alone."

"Chen. Our surname is Chen. I wish—" Yao cut himself off. "It's no use wishing. What's happened has happened. I'm just glad you finally reached out to me."

"Sam and I are very different." Joey smiled at that. "As you probably already figured out, Sam is very stubborn. When he makes up his mind about something, it's almost impossible to get him to change. I'm more open than he is, more willing to forgive, to forget."

"I reached out to him once, did you know that?"

Joey nodded. "What happened? I mean I know the results but . . ."

"I had gotten into the Herb Alpert School of Music at UCLA. For music and composing. I called Sam my first day on campus. My mother had just passed away the month before. Stage 4 brain cancer. It was quick. I was feeling lost."

"I'm so sorry." Joey brought a hand up to her mouth. Even though she knew that Ren Ren was gone, hearing how she'd passed brought the grief front and center again.

Yao nodded. "She was supposed to be there with me on my first day of college. She'd told me about you and Sam and your father, how you were all musical and used to play together, sometimes duets, sometimes solo." Yao's smile was sad. "And that you all have beautiful singing voices. Like me."

Joey closed her eyes for a moment and then opened them to find Yao studying her, kindness on his face.

"Sorry. Keep going." She took a deep breath and then blew it out.

"I thought maybe when he heard my mother had passed away, he'd be willing to talk to me. Maybe meet me." Yao spoke with no emotion, as if reciting lines out of a book. "It was only my grandfather and me then, my mother's father. When I mentioned my grandfather, that was the only time Sam showed interest in our conversation. It was known that my grandfather had been captured and killed by the KMT."

"Yes." Joey didn't know much about Ren Ren's family. "Can you tell me more about him?"

"My grandfather was a major leader of the democracy movement." Yao paused for a moment. "Unknown assailants broke into his home one day and killed his wife and two sons. My mother was injured, too, but she survived."

"I read that—in my mother's journal. Poor Ren Ren." And the reminder made the anger at her old nanny dim a little bit.

"My grandfather's friends came up with the story that he was captured and killed by the KMT and then smuggled him out of Taiwan in 1976. He was granted asylum and lived in Sweden for many years before finally being able to return to Taiwan in 1991." Yao spoke again as if he were reciting lines from a history book and not relating what had happened to his family. "My mother was still living with you then. Sam said he hadn't heard that my grandfather was alive and had returned to Taiwan. He said he stayed away from politics."

"I never knew your grandfather was still alive." Joey shook her head. "What happened after Sam made your mother leave?"

"She went back to Taipei to my grandfather. Had me soon after and the three of us lived together." Yao gave a soft smile. "My mother and I, when I was old enough, took care of my grandfather because he suffered many physical ailments from the torture that was inflicted on him during his imprisonment."

"What your family's been through." Joey couldn't comprehend the words Yao was saying. Yes, her brain understood but her heart couldn't take in what had happened to Ren Ren's family. "I'm sorry Sam was rude to you," Joey said softly. "But after hearing what happened between your mother and my father, I understand why he was like that."

Yao nodded. "I know. My mother finally told me everything when I graduated from high school."

Joey leaned toward the screen. "What did she say?" She was curious as to how Ren Ren had justified what she'd done to Joey's family. "I mean, if you don't mind telling me."

"I don't mind. You deserve to know." Yao dropped his gaze. "She knew it was wrong to fall in love with your father, but she said her love for him was as necessary to her as oxygen is needed to stay alive. She said she was powerless, that she needed him in order to breathe. To live." Yao looked up, meeting Joey's eyes. "They worked together, fighting the fight my grandfather had been doing before he'd been captured and his body broken, his spirit destroyed. She said she did it for her father, for all the people out there that were brutally murdered or wrongly imprisoned and tortured."

"But it wasn't right." Joey couldn't help saying this. "She hurt my mother."

"I know." Yao sounded on the verge of tears. "And she knew that and was so ashamed of herself. She tried to stay away from him. When he ended the affair the first time, she thought of leaving them, finding another family to nanny for or maybe going to university and getting an education. But she couldn't. She couldn't leave him, and she couldn't leave you. She loved you so much."

Joey felt the tears gathering in her eyes. "I loved her too. But I don't know if I can forgive her for how she destroyed my family."

"I know. That's why I wanted to get this out, to clear the air between us." He swallowed. "I know why Sam rejected me. But if you and I are going to have any sort of relationship, I needed to tell you how my mother felt. When your parents drowned, she wanted to die too."

"Oh no." Joey sucked in a breath. All that tragedy.

"She said the only reason she didn't die was because of me. Me and my grandfather. And the thought that she might see you again." Yao's voice was hoarse.

"She never did." Joey wanted to put her head down and cry. Cry for Sam, and Yao, and Ren Ren. "I didn't know everything was such a mess."

"Well." Yao swiped at his eyes and gave her a smile. "On that maudlin note, I want to know everything about you." He stopped and Joey could see the way his cheeks reddened. "I mean, not right now obviously. I just can't believe I'm actually talking to you."

Joey let out a laugh. "I hope you're not disappointed."

"No, no." Yao was quick to say. "Not at all. You're even better than I imagined." He blushed again. "I didn't mean it like that. I mean . . ." He trailed off, obviously searching for the right words.

Joey jumped in to save him. "I know what you mean. Why don't we start with the basics. Get to know each other."

Yao sighed in relief and for the next forty-five minutes, they traded stories about their lives. He told Joey he was a music composer for TV shows and movies.

"Two years after returning to Taiwan when I'd graduated from UCLA, I decided to do my master's in music at a nearby university. I didn't want to leave my grandfather again to study abroad. I'd been working as an assistant to a music supervisor for a popular Taiwanese TV show, and it made me realize I wanted to learn more about the world of film composing."

"You're the only one of us who went into music." Joey's voice was wistful. "Our father would be proud."

Yao's mouth dropped. "You just . . . You said 'our father.' Sam said he wasn't my father."

"Sam was wrong. As much as he wanted that not to be true, our father is also your father."

Yao's face shone with gratitude. "Thank you for saying that." Then he shook his head. "Anyway, I loved my job and when that show closed, someone recommended me for a new one. I was able to juggle my studies with working, and my interest in composing for TV shows and movies increased. The circle of film composers in Taipei is surprisingly small, and I learned so much from my mentors as well as at the master's program."

"That's amazing." She was glad he was telling her about his life. "I did consider going into music, but writing called to me instead."

When it was time to hang up, Joey felt as though they'd barely scratched the surface.

"I look forward to talking to you again." Yao looked down as he said this, as if not wanting her to see how much the call had meant to him.

"Me too."

They made plans to speak again in a few days, then Joey hung up, staring off into space for a few minutes. How she wished Sam had told her about Yao sooner. But he was gone and there was no point playing the "what if" game. She sighed, her eyes landing on Sam's urn. Where was she supposed to scatter his ashes?

A thought popped into her head, and she turned back to her computer, pulling up Google on her browser. She typed something into the search box, and after reading the results, she nodded and picked up her phone to call Ethan.

26

He answered on the second ring.

"We should do it tomorrow night." Joey didn't even bother with a greeting. "It's going to be a full moon. A supermoon, to be exact."

"Does that mean you're not mad at me anymore?" Ethan's tone was light.

"I am but it wasn't your fault. Sam should have told me." Joey tried not to let the emotion take over. She needed Ethan's help. Sam was the one she should be mad at, but Sam was gone and it didn't feel right being mad at a dead person.

"I'm glad you forgive me," Ethan said softly.

"Okay, now that we got that out of the way. Tomorrow night?"

He laughed and the sound went straight to Joey's heart. "Do what? What're you talking about? And what's a supermoon?"

"It's the closest that the moon comes to Earth in its orbit. And I'm talking about Sam's ashes." Joey swallowed hard, still having a hard time describing her brother as ashes. "I think he would have liked it if we scattered his ashes in the ocean under a full moon. My family is a bit obsessed with the moon, in case you didn't know."

"I do know that." Ethan was quiet for a moment. "Okay, let's do it then. Which beach?"

"Kalapaki." Joey was suddenly sure. Before today, she'd assumed Sam wanted her to scatter his ashes at Anini Beach where his body was found. But then she remembered something he'd said to her the last time she was here.

It was the day Sam had watched her paddleboard at Kalapaki Beach from shore, and she'd asked him why he didn't have a serious relationship. Even though he hadn't answered that question, he had said, "There's something about this beach that just speaks to me. It feels like forever."

"Okay. Do you want to meet me in Kapaa, and I'll drive us down?" Ethan's question brought Joey back to their conversation.

"No. I'm going to drive Maggie to the airport tomorrow night. Let's meet at the back parking lot at Kalapaki Beach."

"Sounds good. I'm glad Maggie has been there for you."

"Me too."

When they hung up, she stretched her arms overhead, yawning. Wonton trotted over to her, looking for affection.

"Let's go find Maggie, shall we?" Joey leaned down to scratch Wonton behind her ears.

Wonton barked in answer.

Joey couldn't wait to tell her best friend all that had happened, and that she had a "date" with Ethan (and Sam) the next night. She could get through this, one day at a time.

⁂

Joey and Ethan strolled in the sand at Kalapaki Beach as the sun began to set. Sam held Wonton's leash, and Joey cradled the urn in her arms. She was grateful for Ethan's company, even though she was painfully aware of him as a man. She couldn't help it. Was this how Ren Ren had felt about her father? An uncontrollable urge to be near someone no matter the consequences?

They walked all the way to the end of the beach by the cliffs, and Joey finally turned to Ethan.

"Do you mind if we sit for a while? Wait for the sun to go down?" For some reason, she could only picture scattering Sam's ashes in the dark under a full moon. They had decided to do it from the cliffs up above, where they had to climb down on the side of the golf course and out to the lighthouse at the end of the bay.

"Of course not." Ethan spread out the large towel he was carrying, and they sat shoulder to shoulder, their feet buried in the sand. Ethan put an arm around her. "Okay with this?"

She turned and smiled at him, and he pulled her closer until her head landed on his shoulder. Wonton made herself comfortable against Joey's leg, and a peaceful calm came over her as the crash of the waves reverberated and the orange, pink, and purple rays of the setting sun lit up the sky. They didn't speak until the sun had gone down.

"My parents drowned under a full moon." Joey looked out over the water as she spoke. "The day my parents died, I remember looking up at the sky. The moon was so big it looked like I could touch it. I called it a ghost moon, because I imagined my parents as ghosts, going up to heaven. Do you know about Ghost Month?"

Ethan shook his head. "What's that?"

"In Taiwan, the entire seventh month of the lunar calendar is dedicated to the dead. It typically falls between August and September." As Joey spoke, the darkness descended, bathing them in shadows. "During Ghost Month, it's believed that the gate of the underworld is opened, releasing spirits to wander the living world. It's also known as the Hungry Ghost Festival because it's believed that these spirits who died without proper offerings, or those who suffered a tragic death, are thought to seek food and comfort from the living. People leave out offerings of food and burn incense and joss paper, also known as ancestor money, outside their homes and stores for the hungry ghosts." Joey turned to Ethan. "Ghost Month used to scare me when my parents told me about it. I envisioned all these ghostly white apparitions taking over the world for a month, trying to steal our souls. But as an adult, it comforts me somehow. I always wondered if my parents had come back to visit us, if they'd sought us out during Ghost Month. And now Sam too."

Ethan reached over and touched Joey's hand. Without thinking, she entwined her fingers with his. She stared up at the moon, imagining she could see Sam's ghost up there looking down at them. Would he approve of whatever was happening between her and Ethan? He'd known about Joey's crush on his best friend and had never made her feel bad about it. And after the humiliating kiss with Ethan when she graduated from high school, she'd gone on a dating spree, going out with any boy who so much as looked at her, trying to erase Ethan from her mind. She'd like to think her brother was okay with her and Ethan being together.

Ethan's hand was warm but dry, and a searing heat traveled slowly up Joey's arm until she felt as though she was lit from within. She turned to him and then they were kissing, this time more urgently than their first kiss in the forest. He cupped her face with his hands, and she wound an arm around his neck, pulling him closer. His lips parted and his tongue sought hers. He kissed her so intensely that she forgot her own name.

"Joey," he whispered against her lips.

She smiled, the longing she'd felt for Ethan for most of her life finally satiated. They would have continued kissing if Wonton hadn't wormed her way between them and popped up to lick their mouths.

"Wonton." Joey pulled away, laughing and trying to avoid the canine tongue.

"I guess her patience is up." Ethan picked up the dog so Joey could stand.

"She's right. It's dark and time to do what we came here for." Joey brushed the sand off her shorts.

"You mean we didn't come here to make out like teenagers?" Ethan teased.

Joey groaned. "I can't tell you how many times I'd sit on this very beach and daydream about making out with you."

"Really?" Ethan lifted a brow.

"Come on. You must have known about my crush." Joey crossed her arms over her chest.

"When you were younger, it was cute. But then when you were in high school . . ." Ethan shrugged. "I tried to stay away. I didn't want to inadvertently lead you on."

Joey gave a knowing look. "Uh-huh. And then I made a jackass out of myself."

They smiled at each other, and that long-ago day no longer seemed as embarrassing. Joey reached down to pick up the urn that she'd placed on the towel when they had sat down. They took Ethan's car to drive up to the cliffs and then picked their way carefully down the stairs on the side of the golf course, guided by the light of the moon. Once they reached the rocks, Ethan picked up Wonton, cradling her in his arms, and they made their way carefully over the giant black rocks until they stood at the end, facing the ocean.

Joey stared out at the water, the waves frothing against the rocks and the roar so much louder in the night. It was beautiful in a terrifying way. The darkness was all around them, but the glow of the moon was enough to see by. The ocean pounded and crashed as the waves broke over the rocks, reminding Joey how beautiful but also how deadly the ocean could be. Her entire family had died by drowning. She could never forget the danger and balanced now carefully as she opened the urn. With one look at Ethan, who gave her an encouraging nod, she upended the urn and let the ashes fly out, carried away by the wind into the water and out to sea.

They stood there watching the ocean's performance. Joey didn't want to move, to break the spell. She'd thought she would cry, but a sense of peace overcame her, and she could only smile, imagining that Sam had found their parents and that they were together again.

"Goodbye, Sam," she called out into the ocean. "Take good care of him."

Ethan echoed her words, then they stood like that, neither speaking, for a long time.

Finally, Joey turned to Ethan. "Want to go back up and sit on the golf course?" She didn't want to go home yet.

Ethan nodded and they made their way carefully over the rocks and back to the stairs, climbing to the top of the course. Ethan laid out the towel on the grass, and they sat together, Wonton huddled between them.

"Thank you for being here." Joey leaned against Ethan and looked up at the giant moon. It was so bright, the light shining down and enveloping them.

"I'm glad to be here." He wrapped both arms around her and pulled her close so that her head rested against his chest.

She could hear the beat of his heart under her ear, feel the warmth of his body and the hardness of the chest that cushioned her head. She closed her eyes, wanting to remember every moment of finally being in Ethan's arms. She didn't let herself think of her aversion to relationships, the disaster that was her parents' marriage, or the fact that she didn't know what she was doing with her life. None of that mattered in this moment, and when she felt his lips on the side of her head, she looked up.

He leaned down and then they were kissing again, kissing as if they'd never kissed before. Hungry, needy, urgent. She wanted to wrap herself around Ethan, feel every part of his body, and she ran her hand down his chest, eyes closing at the reality of him. This wasn't a dream. She was really sitting at one of her favorite places on the island, high above Kalapaki Bay, kissing the one man she'd never been able to forget.

Her eyes opened and she looked at him. Really looked at him. Whatever had been in her heart spilled over, and she wished Sam were alive so she could tell him how she felt about Ethan.

"Okay?" Ethan asked, rubbing away the tear rolling down her cheek with his thumb.

She nodded, putting her head against his chest. "I'm just missing Sam."

"Me too." He wrapped her in his arms, and they stayed like that, Wonton content between them, until Joey's leg started to fall asleep.

He laughed as she shook it out. "We should get you and Wonton home. You've got a drive back up to Princeville."

She nodded, knowing she had to leave but wishing they could stay here. She stood and watched as Ethan folded up the blanket, then they headed back to the car, the now-empty urn clutched in her hands. They didn't speak until Ethan had driven her down to the lower lot where she'd left her car. She got out and Ethan did, too, putting Wonton in Joey's back seat. Then Ethan turned and gave her a lingering kiss that made her toes curl.

"Sleep well, Joey."

He got in his car before she could think of what to say, then he was gone. She stared after his car lights long after it had disappeared from view, until she finally got into her own car and drove toward home, her heart both happy and heavy.

27

Three days after Joey had scattered Sam's ashes, Victor called her while she was at Kealia Beach, just south of Anahola, with Wonton.

"I finally tracked down your grandmother."

Joey held her breath. "And?"

"Let's just say she was reluctant to be in touch," Victor said.

"What?" Joey's jaw dropped. "She doesn't want to be in contact with me?"

"She did ultimately decide it was fine. If you ever go to Taiwan, she'll see you."

"Oh." Joey's brows rose. "She'll see me? What is she, royalty?"

Victor was silent.

Confusion jumbled Joey's brain. This wasn't the result she'd been expecting. She'd thought her grandmother would have been overjoyed to hear about her, that she'd want to see her. Now she didn't know what to do.

"I'll send you her email and physical address. Should you decide to reach out."

"Thanks, Victor."

She got up off her towel, needing to walk after that revelation. This beach was a favorite of locals. To the west, kids boogie-boarded, sliding into shore with shouts of joy. Surfers went out to her right, braving the high waves with a grace and ease she wished she had. The beach was long, and she walked south with Wonton, wondering what she was going to do now. She'd done what she came here for: scatter Sam's ashes and start all the paperwork involved in his death. She'd been talking to Yao almost daily, and Yao had mentioned this morning that he'd love to have her visit him in Taiwan.

Part of her really wanted to see Taiwan. Sam wouldn't take her. But now? She yearned to see all the places her mother and Ren Ren used to reminisce about. She wanted to eat at the night markets, see where her mother had lived, experience the culture. Yet something held her back. She felt like she would be betraying Sam. Lose one brother and jump right into knowing another one who happened to show up?

She shook her head, focusing on Wonton trotting ahead of her.

"Wonton, what do I do?"

Wonton turned back as if she'd understood Joey's plea. *Go to Taiwan.*

Joey stopped and stared at the dog. Had Wonton just spoken to her? Wonton took that moment to scratch her ears with her back leg, looking as undignified as she possibly could. Joey laughed and looked out at the water. Maybe she should. She had nowhere she needed to be, and any deadlines she had could be accomplished anywhere.

"You're right." Joey squatted down next to her dog. "I need to go to Taiwan." Meet her grandmother, find out why she was reluctant to be in touch with Joey. Meet Yao. The only time she'd been to Taiwan, she had been a baby and couldn't remember anything.

"Come on." Joey turned around and headed back to her towel. "We have to get home. I need to call Yao."

⁂

"Joey, hi!" Yao was grinning broadly when he picked up the FaceTime call. His face was flushed, and Joey could see someone moving behind him.

"Is this a bad time?"

"No, no." Yao was quick to say. "We just got back from open mic night at a pub."

"He was magnificent." An older man who looked so much like Ren Ren that it took Joey aback for a moment, poked his head onto the screen, speaking in English like Joey and Yao.

"This is my grandfather." Yao gestured to the man. "Ah-Gong, meet Joey."

"Oh." Joey was awed into silence for a moment. She'd done her research on Yao's grandfather after they spoke that first time and now knew he was something of an icon in Taiwanese politics. He was a symbol of hope, a hero to the Taiwanese, someone who had fought for their freedom. "It's an honor to meet you."

He nodded. "Same."

Joey stared at him for another moment, thinking about his murdered wife and two young boys, taken in retaliation for his refusal to cooperate with the KMT when he was imprisoned. She'd read that he'd been tortured beyond belief, yet stayed strong and didn't cave under the cruel interrogation of his jailers. He was a brave man who stood up for basic human rights and was a quiet leader among those lobbying for a more democratic political system on the island. He'd suffered greatly and yet here he was, still full of life. Joey couldn't fathom everything he'd endured and felt like she'd just met the Dalai Lama.

Finally, she turned her attention to Yao. "What did you play at the open mike?"

"Something I'd been working on." He ducked his head as if embarrassed. "I like to play around sometimes, compose music for myself."

"Don't be shy, Yao," his grandfather chided him. "Why don't you play it for her?"

"Yes." Joey's eyes lit up. "I'd love to hear you play."

"Oh, I don't know." Yao looked away.

"Come on, Yao." Now Joey really wanted to hear his music. "Please?"

He looked at his grandfather and then back at Joey. "Really?"

"Yes." She nodded.

Without another word, he handed his phone to his grandfather and walked to the piano behind them. He sat and Joey saw the way he took a deep breath, as if tuning everything out except the piano in front of him. When he began playing, the notes were soft and spare, each one separate, no chords yet. Then he added his voice to the song, and Joey's heart contracted. She realized he was singing about his grandfather in Mandarin, the man who had taught him to be a man.

It was a clever melody. Yao had combined the intricate arrangements of a classical piece with a catchy hook on the refrain that gave off a visceral, energetic feeling that made a delicious shiver go down Joey's spine. His voice grew stronger, hitting a high note as his right hand went up an octave and cascaded through a complex sequence, going faster and faster until his fingers were a blur and his voice carried the last note impossibly high. He cut it off into a moment of silence. Then his fingers crashed back down onto the keys, flying through the last chords until there was nothing.

Joey sat in stunned silence, realizing her half brother was a musical genius. That was the most moving and all-consuming piece she'd ever heard. When Yao finally turned around to face the camera, she clapped, loud and long. When he came closer and took his phone back, she saw he had a huge grin on his face.

"That was absolutely fabulous. Best thing I've heard, ever." Joey couldn't help staring at Yao. "Our father would have been so proud."

Yao flushed, but Joey could see the pleasure that lit up his eyes when she said that.

"My grandson." Yao's grandfather looked like he was almost in tears. "You are going to be famous one day."

Yao turned to his grandfather. "What if I don't want to be famous?"

He raised his brows. "I didn't want to be, either, yet look at me." He patted Yao's cheek. "Sometimes you don't get to choose. You just do what feels right to you, what moves you. What you have is raw talent. You can't buy that or learn it. It's within you."

"I agree completely," Joey said.

"You're a good boy." Joey could see the emotion in the old man's eyes. "Your sister said your father would have been proud. Ren Ren would be very proud of you too."

Yao blinked fast, as if not wanting to cry. "Thank you," he whispered.

"You're going to do great things." Yao's grandfather's voice was soft yet full of conviction. "Do what you love, what you believe in."

"Like you did." Joey couldn't help putting in.

The old man sighed, a heavy sound that carried so much weight. "Yes, I suppose. Although for me, it came at a great cost and many years of my life lost."

They were quiet for a beat, and then Joey broke the silence. "I'm coming to Taiwan. I'd like to meet you, both of you. And my grandmother."

Yao turned to her, his eyes lighting up. "When?"

"That's why I was calling. I wanted to see what works for you?"

"Today. Tomorrow," Yao said, making them all laugh.

Yao's grandfather spoke into the camera. "I'll leave you two to sort out the details. I'm going to lie down."

"Need help, Ah-Gong?"

The old man shook his head. "I'm fine." He turned to Joey. "I look forward to meeting you in person."

"Me too." And Joey realized it was true.

Once he was gone, Yao threw out some dates and they made tentative plans, contingent on her checking for flights and getting in touch with her grandmother. They spoke about what she wanted to see when she was in Taiwan, and then he looked at her, excitement brightening his face.

"Guess what?" He didn't wait for Joey to answer. "I got a job offer to be the film composer on a new project in Hollywood."

"That's amazing." Joey's eyes widened in surprise.

"It is. I couldn't believe someone liked my music enough to want me to go to Hollywood to meet them. It's beyond my wildest dreams."

"Have you already gone to LA?" Joey asked.

"Yes, last week. And I just got the official offer yesterday." Yao beamed at her.

"Will you have to move there?"

Yao's eyes clouded. "Technically, no. I could do most of it from Taiwan remotely, but if this is what I want to do, work in Hollywood, I'd have to move there eventually to make contacts, stay relevant. But I don't want to be so far away from my grandfather."

"I get it." Joey looked at Yao in sympathy.

"He's the only family I have left." Yao paused. "Well, besides you. He's been declining lately, and I want to spend as much time with him as I can. I can't fathom a life without him. He means so much, not just to me but also to our country."

Joey nodded and they were quiet for a moment.

"I'm glad you reached out," Yao said.

"Me too."

And she really was. Whatever doubts she'd had about a half brother she hadn't known existed had faded with each phone call she had with Yao. She had a *feeling* he was about to become an important part of her life.

28

A few days later, Joey and Ethan drifted down the Wailua River on Ethan's paddleboards. He had two, one for Rory when she came to visit. It'd been a long time since Joey had gone stand-up paddleboarding, and she thought with nostalgia about when she and Maggie used to come here during high school.

Joey and Ethan had paddled about halfway to the start of the hike to Secret Falls, which was a big hit with tourists, and now they were sitting on their boards enjoying the beautiful day. Ethan used his paddle to keep her close when she started drifting away.

She turned to Ethan, admiring his tanned and toned body, muscles firm and heart-stoppingly gorgeous. They'd spent every day together since scattering Sam's ashes, and she'd cherished the moments with him. But it was time to return to reality.

"I'm going to Taiwan." She'd booked a ticket to leave tomorrow and hadn't told him because she didn't want to think about what would happen once she left Kauai.

He nodded, looking at her. "To meet your half brother and grandmother. I knew you'd go eventually."

"Yes." She trailed a hand in the water. "I need to go."

"You do." Ethan's legs dangled off his board. "I'll be here, waiting for you."

Joey's heart cracked and she looked down at the water, willing herself not to cry. She took a moment to compose her emotions, her gaze rising to the greenery on either side of the river, the kayaks and paddleboards going by them.

This was what she'd wanted almost her whole life. For Ethan to look at her the way he was now, to share her life with him. Yet here they were, and she knew she wasn't ready for a relationship. She needed time to sort out her feelings on everything she'd learned about her family, to figure out how she was going to deal with it and how it would affect her life.

She didn't want to hurt Ethan. They'd spent the last three nights together, and they were everything Joey had ever imagined being with Ethan would be like. He was a tender, yet skilled lover, and she couldn't get enough of him. He made her feel protected but also loved and cherished, and he looked at her as if she were the most beautiful person in the world. But she couldn't lead him on when something inside her believed they were doomed before they even started.

She knew she should tell him not to wait for her. But she couldn't make herself say the words. She wanted to absorb the time they had left, to imprint Ethan onto her mind, into her soul. So instead, they drifted for a while and then finally stood to paddle back to shore.

They picked up food in Kapaa, and then Ethan drove them up to Sam's apartment. Conversation was light, Ethan asking about what she would do in Taiwan. With each word that came out of his mouth, her heart grew heavier, knowing she should break this off with him before she left. She didn't know what she'd find in Taiwan, couldn't see what the future held. Yet she couldn't make herself say the words.

When Ethan went to use the bathroom, Joey sat at the piano, drawn to it again ever since hearing Yao play. She'd tinkered every day, playing Sam's favorites, going through Sam's sheet music and sight-reading songs from musicals as well as classical pieces. Now, without thinking, she began playing her favorite Rachmaninoff piano concerto, her fingers remembering the notes even though she was rusty. She poured all the longing, conflict, shock, and sorrow into the music, her fingers releasing the emotions she couldn't express. There was only her and the music flowing out of the piano, and she was surprised she still remembered this complicated concerto after all these years.

She looked up to find Ethan leaning against the wall, his eyes on her, hunger and passion evident on his face. She didn't speak, only stood and walked to Ethan, who never took his eyes from hers. She wanted this last night with him, needed it. Tomorrow, she would tell him the truth, that she couldn't be in a relationship right now, not when everything in her life had been turned upside down. She knew it was selfish, but she couldn't help it.

Her hand reached out to touch his face; he brushed a hand down her side, making goose bumps break out on her skin. They drew together until they couldn't stand it any longer, and then they were kissing, the need for each other taking over any rational thought. All Joey knew was that she needed him, wanted him. She put every other thought aside, focusing solely on Ethan because she knew things were going to change the minute she left Kauai.

⁂

The next morning, she awoke to an empty bed. Her hand reached out and brushed only the sheets, still warm from where Ethan had been all night. She pushed herself to sit up in bed, the smell of coffee wafting in through the partially closed door. She got out of bed and walked into the kitchen, finding Ethan making them omelets for breakfast.

She went up behind him and wrapped her arms around his waist, putting her cheek against his back. She inhaled, wanting to remember everything about him. For she knew she was about to say goodbye.

He took her hand and turned her to face him, giving her a gentle kiss on the lips.

"Breakfast is ready. Then you can pack. I'll drive you to the airport." He leaned in to kiss her again, but she pulled away before he could.

They stared at each other in silence as Joey struggled to articulate what she was feeling.

"Don't," she finally said, even as it broke her heart.

His brow furrowed. "Don't what?"

"Don't wait for me. I don't know what's going to happen. I don't know what I'm doing with my life." She paused, and then said what was perhaps the truest thing in her heart. "I'm no good at relationships. My whole family has been the same way. It feels like it's not something we're destined to have."

"Joey, what happened to your parents has nothing to do with you." He reached out to touch her on the shoulder. "I know there's something between us. I can wait until you get back from Taiwan to figure it out."

"No. I don't know." She shook her head. "I'll mess it up. I don't want to hurt you."

"You won't, if you're honest with me. With yourself." His gaze was intense.

"I can't, Ethan." She met his stare and felt tears welling in her eyes. She didn't want to cry. She wanted to be stoic, to convince him that hoping for a relationship with her was just an exercise in futility. But she couldn't find the words and only stared at him, helplessly.

"Joey. Are you telling me everything that's happened these past few days means nothing to you?" Ethan raked a hand through his hair and looked away from her.

"No. They meant something. They meant everything." Joey looked at him, pleaded with him silently to understand something she herself couldn't even comprehend. "I just know that I'll end up fucking it up. My mother tried to kill my father. Sam swore off long-term relationships. And my own track record doesn't exactly inspire confidence."

Ethan didn't speak. His jaw tightened, but he didn't try to convince her otherwise, for which her heart dropped even though she knew it was for the best. They stood like that for long moments, until Ethan finally spoke.

"I'll respect your wish. Don't worry about me." He looked straight ahead. "Do what you need to do, put the ghosts of your family to rest. Figure out what you want, and if that still includes me, I'll be here."

"Ethan." She put a hand on his chest, and he put his over hers for a moment before dropping his hand. "Thank you for understanding. You do what you need to do too. And if the stars align . . ." Joey stood there, trying to memorize his features.

He drew her close. He wrapped his arms around her, and they clung to each other as if they were drowning. Joey moved and then they were kissing, a fierce desperate kiss as though they'd never see each other again. Joey wanted to sear this moment in her brain to bring back out when she was missing him in Taiwan. She didn't want to let go, yet she knew she must. When they finally broke apart, they stared at each other until Ethan gently tapped her forehead with his own.

"Bye, Joey. If you need me for anything, anything at all, you know how to reach me. Call me. Okay?"

She nodded. "I will."

He let go and with one last soft kiss, he left, closing the front door softly, leaving her with the untouched omelets he'd made as a parting gift. She stood there in the kitchen, the tears sliding down her cheeks. They came, faster and faster, until she couldn't see. She stayed like that for a long time.

29

Taipei, Taiwan

Thirty-four hours later, Joey stood outside of Yao and his grandfather's apartment. She'd come straight here after dropping off her bags at a hotel nearby, and taken the stairs instead of the elevator up to the third floor. She took a breath and then whispered, "I'm sorry, Sam," before knocking softly. The door immediately opened.

Yao stood there, a tentative smile on his face. Joey looked at the face she'd been getting to know and wondered if she should hug him. Yao solved the problem by sticking out his hand.

"I'm so glad to finally meet you, Joey."

She took his hand in hers, and the smile on his face grew bigger.

Joey gave his hand a squeeze. "I'm so glad to meet you too."

Yao stepped back, opening the door. "Come in."

There were a few awkward moments as she settled on the couch while Yao bustled about. He put water on for tea and placed a tray of snacks on the coffee table.

"This is a nice apartment." Joey looked around at the cozy living room filled with photos of their family and paintings of flowers and birds.

"My grandfather bought it when he returned to Taiwan from Sweden. It was important to him to be in a doorman building with twenty-four-hour security." Yao perched on the edge of a chair facing Joey. "It's not huge, but we love it. And more importantly, my grandfather feels safe here."

Joey stood and went to look at a group of photos arranged on a table. She picked one up and stared at her old nanny, who was much older than the Ren Ren Ayi she remembered in her mind. "Your mother hasn't aged at all in my memory." She glanced over at Yao and then back at the other photos. "I wish I had gotten to see her again before she passed away."

"I know." Yao gestured to the paintings on the wall. "She did these. When we first came back to Taiwan, she started painting as a way to ward off the grief of losing your parents and you and Sam."

"They're beautiful." Joey studied the paintings and then looked back at Yao. "Where's your grandfather?"

"He should be out soon." Yao lowered his voice. "It takes him longer to do everything these days. He's slowing down."

Joey nodded. She was about to say more when she heard a shuffling noise. Coming down the hallway was Yao's grandfather, his figure slightly hunched over his cane. Yao jumped up and went to his side, but the old man waved his cane in the air.

"I can walk to the couch by myself."

Chastened, Yao stepped back and allowed him to go ahead until the man stopped in front of Joey.

"You must be Yao's sister." The old man gave her a warm smile.

She nodded. "It's such an honor to meet you." She reached out a hand, and he took it in both of his. She felt as if she was in the presence of greatness.

Yao's grandfather let go of Joey's hand and settled on the couch, Yao hovering anxiously nearby. "I've heard so much about you," he said, resting his cane between his legs. "My daughter had never forgotten you."

"I never forgot her either." Joey's voice was low.

"She grieved for years after Sam banished her." The old man let out a heavy sigh. "I know she did wrong to your family and Sam had every right to do what he did, but in her defense, she was so young when she went to live with your parents. She'd survived the massacre of our family. No child should ever have to see something like that. And when she fell in love with your father, she didn't have a mother to guide her, or me to give her advice." His regret was evident on his face. "I blame myself for what happened to them. To Ren Ren."

"It's not your fault." Yao reached out to pour his grandfather a cup of tea.

A scowl crossed the old man's face. "*Aiya,* it is my fault. But I can't change the past." He accepted the cup of tea with a nod. "Let's not get into that right now. This is a joyous occasion."

"It is." Joey turned to Yao. "I'm meeting a half brother that I never knew existed. And I'm meeting you," she gestured to his grandfather, "who has done so much for Taiwan."

"And I finally got my lifelong dream of meeting you." Yao gave Joey a shy smile.

She smiled back. "I want to hear more about being a film composer."

"Basically, I compose the music for TV shows and movies and work with the director and showrunner to get the right tone and theme for each episode or film."

"Sam and I are musical too. Like our father. He cultivated our love for music. I used to play duets with him on the piano. Sam would sing or accompany us on guitar." Joey nodded at Yao. "You must have gotten it from Baba."

"I've always loved music." Yao looked at his grandfather. "My mother and Ah-Gong encouraged me. This is my dream job."

"I'd love to hear some of your compositions." Joey leaned forward.

"He's so gifted," Yao's grandfather put in.

Yao blushed, red tingeing his cheeks. "You really want to hear what I'm working on?"

"Yes. The glimpse I got on FaceTime wasn't enough." She rested her elbows on her thighs and cupped her chin with one hand. "I thought of going into music but somehow fell into writing instead."

"Go on, Yao." His grandfather made a shooing motion toward the piano.

Yao thought for a moment and then shook his head. "Let me play you a recording I made recently. It has an orchestral backup with me on electric piano and will give you a better idea of the kind of things I compose for film and TV."

He picked up his phone and scrolled through until he found what he was looking for. He hit play and then put the phone on the coffee table in front of them.

Joey closed her eyes, letting the music take over and hold her captive. Yao was right. The use of the virtual instruments really elevated the experience and felt like she was listening to a whole orchestra. When it was over, Yao's grandfather clapped, and Joey followed suit. Yao's eyes darted back and forth between them.

"You're brilliant." Joey opened her eyes.

"He is." Yao's grandfather had a proud look on his face.

Yao dipped his head in a slight nod. "Thank you."

"Our father loved music so much. He would have been absolutely blown away by this." Joey felt a lump in her throat as she said this.

Yao's breath caught. "That means everything to me." He paused for a beat. "What about you? Tell us about your work."

They listened intently as she told them about her travels, the pieces she was commissioned to write, her volunteer work. "I really want to write a book set in Taiwan. I'm going to do research while I'm here, see if anything inspires me. I feel as if many Taiwanese Americans, myself included, don't know enough about what Taiwan has been through in the last century."

"I'll help you." Yao sat forward eagerly. "My grandfather can too. He knows more about Taiwan's history than anyone I know."

The old man nodded. "I do. I'd be happy to tell you anything you want to know."

"That would be great." Joey sent them a grateful look.

"I'm sorry to hear about your brother's passing." Yao's grandfather's eyes shone with sympathy, and Yao nodded too.

"Thank you." Joey looked at her fingers. "I wish he'd told me about Yao years ago."

Yao's grandfather inclined his head. "It was a delicate situation. I don't condone what my daughter did, yet I couldn't denounce her either. She loved your father. Too much. And with what happened to our family, she had so much fire inside, so much drive to defeat the KMT and fight for Taiwan independence that it overshadowed everything else in her life. I think in her mind, your father and her work got entwined."

Joey studied his face, wondering if he'd meant it when he said she could ask him anything. "You've had a hard life too." Her voice was soft. "Can you tell me about any of it? How you got involved?"

A wry smile came over Yao's grandfather's face. "Are you sure you want to hear an old man's stories?"

"Yes," Joey and Yao said at the same time. They turned to each other and shared a smile.

"Well." Yao's grandfather settled back on the couch. "I was getting my bachelor's degree in political science at National Taiwan University when the February 28 incident occurred in 1947."

"The same university my mother went to." Joey's voice was hushed.

"Yes." Yao's grandfather nodded. He settled back on the couch, and his eyes took on a faraway look, as if transported back in time. "I was studying at the law library when the incident that sparked the massacre happened."

Joey leaned forward, a chill going through her as she braced herself for this legend's story.

30

Yao's Grandfather
1947, Taipei City

When the incident that sparked the 228 Massacre happened, I was at the College of Law Library on the NTU campus, about seven kilometers away. I was oblivious to the chaos happening not that far from me, when agents of the Tobacco Monopoly Bureau struck the widow for selling contraband cigarettes. Some of my friends had been there and told me later how the crowd had retaliated at the brutality of the agents when the poor widow was only trying to make money selling both legal and contraband cigarettes. The agents had confiscated all of her stash, including the small amount of cash she'd made, as she pleaded for them to give it back to her. Instead, an agent beat her with the butt of his pistol, and witnesses retaliated by destroying the agents' vehicles.

"Come on, get your head out of your books," my roommate pleaded the next day, upon finding me studying at my desk in our room. "You won't believe what's going on out there."

"I have to finish this assignment." I barely looked up from my work. I was focused on becoming a lawyer and was not involved in any way politically back then. I was part of a group of students of law, economics, and political science who devoted ourselves to our studies with books, theories, and abstract discussions. Even though we weren't politicized yet, it was hard to miss the evidence of a mounting crisis in our country. But at that moment, my studies were more important than the uprising I had no idea was about to turn into a full-fledged massacre of our people.

"Really?" My roommate gave an exaggerated huff. "You'd rather be holed up in here with your books than out there where history is happening?"

"You go." I waved a hand at him. "Tell me about it later."

He left, slamming the door louder than was necessary. I had no idea at the time that my disinterest would later save my life.

It was a terrifying time, a tense few weeks after the incident. Even I finally looked up from my books long enough to hear about how a great confrontation between the Formosans (The Portuguese named the island Formosa, meaning "beautiful island," back in the 1500s. After World War II, the Chinese government, especially the KMT, pushed for the name Taiwan. Calling us Formosans was just a tiny bit of rebellion for me.) and the occupying Chinese had begun. Formosans burned down the offices of the Tobacco Monopoly Bureau and beat up its employees in retaliation. Demonstrators marched, eventually in front of the governor's offices, where they were gunned down.

"We're drawing up a petition for reform," my roommate said one day as we shared a simple meal of rice porridge mixed with sweet potatoes and sides of pickled vegetables in our room. "Do you want to join us?"

"Isn't that dangerous?" I stared at him, surprised he would be willing to stand up to the government. He had seemed like such a mild-mannered person when I first met him.

"We're not going to say anything to provoke the government. We're exercising restraint while getting our point across. The more people we can get to sign the petition, the more power it will have." He looked at me imploringly.

"I . . ." I trailed off, not sure what to say. Something was warning me against putting my name on that petition. "I don't think so," I finally said.

His face dropped in disappointment. "Well, if you change your mind, you still have a few days to join us. And if you know anyone else who would be interested, send them my way."

I nodded and the subject was dropped until he found me in our room the next week.

"They took our petition." He was practically jumping up and down with glee. "The governor's officials said it was very useful advice and that they would discuss it seriously. They asked us to write down our names and addresses so they could find us in case they have questions."

"Huh." I looked at him dubiously. Why would the governor's officials track down mere university students for advice? Didn't they have whole committees of important people for that? But I didn't want to dampen his enthusiasm, so I just congratulated him.

He might have been optimistic but within a few days, I could tell Formosans were in danger. Despite the governor's proclamation that they would listen to the people, form committees to settle the incident, and draw reforms for consideration, troops were sent into the port town of Keelung and a reign of terror began.

"Did you hear what's happening?" My roommate and I were rushing to class, and he was whispering to me. "They're shooting and bayoneting men and boys, right and left in Keelung." He was breathless, his chest heaving with exertion. "They're raping women, grandmothers and young girls alike, and they're raiding homes too. My uncle said they're even putting people into bags and throwing them into the ocean."

"What?" I turned to stare at him, my mouth open in horror.

He nodded, his eyes wide. "My uncle says they're coming here, too, to Taipei. Things are going to get bad. I can feel it."

And he was right. In the next weeks, people started disappearing. Prominent men, some women, were targeted. Editors and teachers, lawyers, and doctors who had dared criticize the government were killed or imprisoned. Nobody knew exactly how many Formosans died in the following weeks, but some estimated up to twenty-eight thousand.

And then one day, I came back to our room to find the other students of our dorm in an uproar. Many were hysterical, speaking in high voices, while some slumped to the ground, their heads in their hands.

"What's going on?" I asked the boy who lived in the room next to ours.

"They were here, a few hours ago." His face was ashen, and he looked like he was about to keel over. I led him to a chair in his room and closed the door, waiting for him to calm down.

"Who was here?" I was pretty sure I knew, but I had to ask.

"You know." He shook his head as if trying to dislodge something from his brain. "They just strode in like they owned the place and started seeking out the ones on their list."

My heart sank when I heard that. "What list?"

"The one your roommate was so enthusiastic about and tried to get me to sign." He turned and the look in his eyes made my legs shake. "They took your roommate. And several others that had signed the petition."

"Oh no." My heart dropped in terror. "Where did they take him?"

"No one knows. That's why everyone is so hysterical right now. Some think they've been thrown in jail. One person thinks they're going to be killed."

My heart pounded and I was ashamed that my first thought wasn't for the safety of my roommate. My first thought was that thankfully, I was not a member of any politically active group at the time, and my name wasn't on any manifestos or petitions like the one my roommate had signed. But then reality set in and I was terrified for him.

"What're we going to do?" I asked.

The boy shrugged helplessly. "I don't know."

"I have to find him." But where to begin? Did I have the courage to march into a police station and demand to know where my roommate was taken? I was just a student studying law and had had no experience with any of this.

I went back to my room, trembling with emotion. What was happening to our country? Where was my roommate? In my worrying, I finally started to become angry. Angry about what was being done to Taiwan and to our people. I took a deep breath, knowing I had to find out what happened to my roommate. I was about to leave my room, go out to search, when another student I knew well rushed into my room, slamming the door behind him.

"Where're you going?" he asked. He had a look of horror on his face that made my stomach drop.

"I need to find my roommate."

"You're not going anywhere." He sank onto my bed, and the despair on his face made me want to throw up. "Your roommate is dead. They killed them. All the students they rounded up earlier. They're all dead."

"What?" I didn't believe him. My next-door neighbor had said they'd only been taken a few hours ago.

"I was walking back here and took a short cut." The boy blew out a breath as if trying to steady his nerves. "I'll never forget what I saw."

"What? What did you see?" I was frantic now, my gut telling me nothing would ever be the same again.

"I don't think I was supposed to see that. It was . . ." He closed his eyes for a moment. "They had all these students lined up in a row. And they shot them in the back, one by one, each falling down like dominoes." His voice hitched and he brought a hand to his mouth. "I recognized some of them. Including your roommate."

"No." I stared at him in disbelief, not wanting to believe my roommate was gone.

I couldn't speak after that, caught in a spiral of thoughts and feelings and hopelessness. When I woke up the next morning, I knew that

I couldn't just sit by and let innocent people like my roommate be executed for no reason. I had to do something.

I tried to gather as much information as I could in the coming weeks. I went home to visit my family, having long discussions with my father, who'd been appointed chairman of the settlement committee in our hometown. But one day, just as I was preparing to return to Taipei, he was seized along with other committee members.

How my mother worried, wondering what was happening to my father. I tried to find him but was told no one knew where the men had gone. My brothers and I reached out to anyone we knew who might have political ties, but no one knew anything. Until a week later, a committee member who had been taken along with our father came limping up the path to our house. The minute I saw him I knew the worst had happened.

"He's gone," the man said, as soon as we had ushered him into the house and settled him in a chair. "I'm sorry." He broke down, burying his face in his hands. "I wish I could have stopped them, but there was nothing I could do."

"What happened?" Our mother cried, gripping my sister's hand.

"They bound us with ropes, threw us in a room. I don't know where." The man looked down at the floor as if too ashamed to face our mother. "I don't know why, but they took your husband, separated him from us. They looped ropes around our necks, and I thought that was it, they were going to kill us. But they didn't."

My other sister pressed a mug of tea into the man's hands and he took a grateful sip before continuing.

"When they brought your husband back, they had bound wires around his hands and ankles, and used pliers to tighten the wire—" He choked on his words, his hands shaking so badly he had to set the mug down. "I'm sorry. I wish I didn't have to tell you this."

"Tell us." My oldest brother stood over the man with his arms folded across his chest.

"Your father screamed in agony, and they didn't care. They kept doing it, tightening the wire tighter and tighter—" The man gasped as a sob escaped. "After a few hours, they shot him. Right in front of us. They made us watch."

My mother screamed and fell to the floor. My sisters were at her side, along with my younger brother, as I stared at this man in shock. I couldn't believe my father was gone. What was happening to our country, that good people like my father were being tortured and killed for no reason? My heart hardened and I knew I had to do something, to prevent another family from feeling the grief we were suffering. That was the moment I knew I had to get involved and speak out against the government.

31

Joey
Present Day, Taipei

Joey's heart was in her throat as she tried to digest everything Yao's grandfather had just told her. Her stomach clenched and she doubled over on the couch until she was sure she wasn't going to vomit.

"It's one thing to read about what happened in Taiwan during the martial law era, but another thing to hear about people's actual experiences." Joey was finally able to speak.

"It is, yes." The old man nodded. "Before martial law was lifted, the atmosphere was so horrible that it was an extremely scary thing to take part in any political activity. Some people would even refuse to have anything to do with you if you were involved in any way."

"That's why so many Taiwanese Americans don't really know what happened." Joey shook her head. "Their parents were afraid to talk about it."

"You were born in America?" he asked.

Joey nodded. "I've only been in Taiwan once, when I was about a year old, so I don't remember anything. And my brother refused to utter a word about Taiwanese politics. The only things I knew were what I read in the news or when our friend Victor would try to draw me in."

Yao refilled Joey's mug of tea and she took a grateful sip.

"Our country has been through so much. Everyone was afraid to say anything about the government that could be construed as 'rebellious' or supporting the communists. That's why so many people chose to stay silent." Yao's eyes were on his grandfather as he said this.

Joey turned to the old man. "Yet when your father was killed, that was when you started being very vocal about your stance on the government."

"It was." He nodded slowly. "But it was years later before I publicly denounced our government. I lived a dual life for a time, having been appointed by the president to high political positions once I graduated from law school. But I knew what the government was doing was wrong. They killed my father, and thousands of other men like him. I wanted to overthrow this system of authoritarian rule." His voice hardened, and Joey saw the way he clenched one hand. "Under this rule, the character of the Taiwanese people was destroyed. I had to stand up for my beliefs." His eyes focused on Joey's. "And it cost me my family."

"I'm so sorry," Joey said again. She leaned toward him, wishing there was something she could do to comfort him.

"Ach." He shook his head. "All this was so long ago."

"I never knew any of this about you. Ren Ren only spoke of you as her baba and how much she missed you. She spoke as if you were gone, dead."

He gave a sad smile. "That was what we had to let the world believe so that I could escape from Taiwan. And that included letting my daughter think the KMT had killed me."

"My grandfather was imprisoned for months," Yao interjected. "Then released and then imprisoned again for over a year. The things they did to him. His body is broken."

"Why you tell her that?" The old man scolded Yao in Taiwanese.

"It's okay," Joey put in, also in Taiwanese, making him turn to her in surprise. "I understand. Yao's proud of you. I speak Mandarin and Taiwanese, but I don't read or write it anymore."

Yao nodded. "What you did for Taiwan was very brave."

The old man pursed his lips and shook his head. "It's not about being brave. I believed strongly in independence for Taiwan, rather than unification with the mainland, which was favored by the Nationalists. I only did what I believed was right."

They were quiet for a moment, the only sound the whir of the fan overhead.

"How did you escape Taiwan?" Joey finally asked.

"Ah, I can't tell you that." But then he chuckled and the tension in his shoulders eased. "Let's just say I had friends in high places who managed to get me out of jail. I wrote a letter to the Stockholm Amnesty International representative for help. And with a forged passport, I was able to escape Taiwan and was granted political asylum in Sweden for many years." The smile slipped from his face. "My friends spread the story that I was killed in prison. I wanted to reach out to Ren Ren, but I couldn't, not without putting her or me in danger. I escaped in 1976, and it wasn't until 1991 that I was able to return to Taiwan and get word to Ren Ren that I was alive."

"Oh." Joey brought her hands up to her heart. "Poor Ren Ren."

Yao's grandfather started to speak, but a big yawn came out instead.

"Are you tired, Ah-Gong?" Yao was immediately on his feet.

Joey looked up and saw the fatigue in the old man's eyes. "I'm sorry. I didn't mean for you to relive such a hard time in your life."

He waved a hand in the air. "I wanted to tell it. It's time people know what we went through, what Taiwan has suffered. If you want to write a book about it, then I'll help you."

"Thank you." Joey hoped he understood the depth of her gratitude with those two words.

Yao jumped to his feet. "Let me help you into the bath." He turned to Joey. "Can you wait for me to get out? I'm just going to get him situated."

"Of course." Even though she'd been conflicted about meeting Yao, she was so glad she had. She knew it was a rare opportunity to also meet his grandfather, and she was grateful for it.

Yao's grandfather bade her farewell, and the two of them disappeared down the hall while Joey stayed on the couch, thinking of all that he'd told her. She shuddered, the atrocities Yao's grandfather and others like him had endured during the White Terror making her sick. It was unimaginable, and she sent up a prayer of thanks that this was no longer the world he'd lived through.

Ten minutes later, Yao was back.

"Is he okay?" Already Joey felt something for the old man, a kinship or a protective need to shield him after everything he'd been through.

Yao nodded. "Because of all the broken bones and the stress his poor body has been through in his imprisoned years, he needs to soak in a hot tub every night to alleviate the severe aches and pains."

"Oh."

"He's ninety-seven." Yao looked down. "I need to be here to take care of him. When he gets out of the bath, I have to apply ointment to his ankles, which are still chafed from where they'd shackled him. And to his damaged ribs, and the burn marks on his back. I have to prop three pillows behind his back because his broken ribs don't allow him to lie down comfortably."

"I don't know what to say."

"Don't worry." Yao gave her a soft smile. "It's hard to fathom when you haven't lived through it. But we have a good routine."

"I'm glad." She studied her half brother. "I wasn't sure how I'd feel, meeting you. Sam was so against it, and it felt like going behind his back. But I'm glad I came."

"Me too."

They shared a smile and then talked some more about their lives until Yao's grandfather called out to him.

"I'll get out of your hair." Joey stood and slung her purse over her shoulder. "I'm going to Keelung tomorrow to meet my grandmother, but I'll be back the next day."

"I'm glad."

"Thank you. Really." Joey reached out to touch Yao's forearm.

They exchanged a look, and with one final goodbye, Joey walked out their front door while Yao went to tend to his grandfather. Her mind was buzzing with ideas for the book, and she couldn't wait to get back to her hotel room and begin jotting down notes and making an outline. It felt good to be productive again, and she knew she needed to do the book justice. It had become important to her.

32

The following day, Joey was on a train from Taipei to Keelung, where her grandmother had lived for the last twenty-plus years with her second husband. Joey was nervous because when she'd called, her grandmother hadn't sounded enthused that Joey had found her.

"You want to come to Keelung?" Joey's grandmother's voice had been full of doubt.

"Well, yes." Joey paused, at a loss for words. "I mean, I didn't even know you were alive. When Victor told me he'd found you years ago, I guess I . . ." She'd trailed off, unable to articulate her needs.

There had been silence on the other line for so long that Joey wished she hadn't reached out. But then her grandmother finally spoke. "Call me when you get to Taiwan. We'll figure it out."

So now Joey sat on a train that would get her to Keelung from Taipei in forty minutes. She passed the time by researching and expanding on the notes she'd taken as she'd listened to Yao's grandfather. So many thoughts crowded her mind, and her fingers flew on her keyboard, recording them all. For the first time in years, she was excited to write again.

By the time they pulled into the Keelung station, Joey had a loose outline for the book. Buoyed by her progress, she got off the train with a bounce in her step. But then she stopped in surprise, because standing in front of her was a woman who looked so much like her own mother. Joey knew immediately this was her grandmother. She'd expected to take a taxi, since her grandmother hadn't offered to pick her up. The woman hadn't seen Joey yet, giving Joey time to study her.

She was taller than Joey had expected, since her own mother and she herself were just barely five feet, two inches. Her face was stoic, not a trace of a smile or softness. Her posture was ramrod straight, and she wore tailored tan slacks and a white silk blouse—so much more elegant than the green sundress Joey had on. Feeling frumpy compared to her refined grandmother, Joey smoothed a hand down her skirt, squared her shoulders, and strode toward her. As she approached, her grandmother turned in her direction, and her eyes lit in recognition.

For just a moment, Joey thought everything was going to be okay, that her grandmother was going to welcome her with open arms and they would have a wonderful reunion. But then the light shuttered over her grandmother's eyes, and that stony look settled over her visage again.

"Ah-Ma?" Joey reached out a hand.

Her grandmother squeezed Joey's hand briefly and then let go. Her eyes swept over Joey's face. "You're very pretty." It didn't sound like a compliment—more of a comment.

"Um, thank you?" Joey stood awkwardly at her grandmother's side.

The older woman nodded and then turned on her heel. "Come. Let's have lunch by the water. There's a sushi restaurant I like near here."

Joey stood still for a moment, watching her grandmother's retreating back. She hadn't even asked whether Joey liked sushi. (She did, but that was beside the point.) Joey had envisioned that she'd be welcomed into her grandmother's home (she'd given her the address, after all), that she'd meet her grandmother's second husband and whoever else lived in their household. She hadn't thought they'd have lunch near the train station.

Her grandmother was almost out of sight, and Joey darted forward, running to catch up with her. They strode side by side without speaking. Joey looked around her at the steep hills on one side and the ocean on the other. A fine mist sprinkled her face, and the gray sky looked like it would open with rain at any moment. She considered herself to be in shape, but she could feel her breath coming in short gasps as they practically sprinted down the sidewalk. Her grandmother finally stopped in front of a door and opened it, not holding it for Joey, who had to catch it with her foot before it slammed in her face. By the time they were seated at a table facing each other, Joey was starting to think this was a mistake.

"So." Her grandmother sat back after the waiter put ceramic mugs of hot tea in front of them. "How are you?"

"Good." Every question she'd wanted to ask flew out of her head. "Um . . ."

They stared at each other until the waiter came back.

"I'll order for us both?" her grandmother asked, one brow raised.

Joey could only nod. When the waiter left their table, she finally found her voice. "I have so much to ask you." She cleared her throat. "Did you know my parents passed away in 1996?"

"Yes."

Joey waited, but that was all her grandmother said.

"Did you ever . . ." She cleared her throat again. "Didn't you miss your daughter? Did you ever search for her?"

Her grandmother sighed. She took a sip of tea before answering. "Ah-Hui made her choice. She chose your father over her own grandfather and family." The mug thumped down on the wooden table a little too loudly. "My father was thrown in prison and killed. *Killed.* Because my daughter wouldn't marry the man we matched her with. We lost everything after that." Her mouth set into a firm line. "Everything."

Joey's heart hurt at the thought of all that loss. "I'm so sorry. I'm sure my mother didn't know the sorrow her actions would cause."

"How do you know?" Her grandmother stared at her, as if daring her to challenge the question. "She only thought of herself. What *she* wanted. And her actions resulted in the death of my father."

Joey was silent, not sure what to say. She could see where her grandmother was coming from, but at the same time, how could she just cut her own daughter out of her life like that?

"It was like reliving my past all over again." Joey's grandmother spoke with intensity. "Just like when my husband disappeared. I went to Taichung to search for my father. I asked everyone I knew, went to police stations, tried to get anyone who had connections to the government to intervene. I even begged the family of the boy who your mother was supposed to marry. Do you know how humiliating that was?" Her eyes glittered like cold, dark stones in the dim light of the restaurant. "My father was an old man when they took him, and when I think what he must have endured before they shot him—" She broke off and looked away.

"I'm sorry," Joey whispered. It was a similar story to the one Yao's grandfather had told her. She couldn't fathom a world where an old man was thrown in jail and tortured before being murdered. "Didn't you ever want to find her, though, and find out what happened to her?" *Didn't you ever want to know you had a granddaughter and a grandson?*

Joey's grandmother lifted her eyes to stare into Joey's. "Life is full of disappointments. Yes, I missed my daughter, but she made her choice. She wanted to be with him, your father. She turned her back on us, got my father killed." She shook her head. "No, I never wanted to find her. I was too busy in the months after my father was taken, searching for him. After he died, I had to take care of my mother. We lost the house, we lost everything. I spent months—years—picking up the pieces. When one of my brothers got married and moved to Tainan, my mother went to live with him until she passed away a year later. I left, traveled around Taiwan. I needed to be away, to grieve in my own way."

"That must have been so awful for you." Joey's heart broke for her grandmother and her family, yet she felt for her mother, too, stuck in an impossible situation. What a choice to make, between who she thought was the love of her life and her family. Joey didn't know what she would do, had she been in that situation.

They were silent as the waiter put platters of sushi on the table. When he left, Joey's grandmother continued her story.

"I finally got a job with a friend in Taipei whose family owned a bridal boutique. I worked as a seamstress." She sighed and picked up her chopsticks. "I was there for five years. And then I met my second husband, a software engineer who lived here in Keelung. He'd come to Taipei on business, and we met through friends."

Joey nodded, feeling encouraged that her grandmother was telling her about her life. "Are you happy?"

Her grandmother frowned. "What is 'happy'? I do well enough. I married my soulmate the first time, and look how that ended up. This time, I married a practical man, built a nice life with him. I have everything I need; I suppose you could say I'm happy."

Joey thought about this as they ate. She barely tasted anything, even though she knew the food was good. As cold as her grandmother turned out to be, Joey couldn't help admiring her a little bit. She'd lost everything, yet here she still was with a second chance at life. In a way, Joey was in a very similar situation to her grandmother, although hers wasn't as dire. She felt as if she'd lost everything too.

When the waiter cleared away the dishes from their first course, Joey looked at her grandmother. "I had a brother. Sam. Your grandson. He recently passed away." The words made her throat clog, and she took a sip of tea to wash down the lump.

"I'm sorry." Her grandmother's face softened, but she didn't ask what happened to Sam.

"I found—" Joey cut herself off. She'd been about to tell her grandmother about her half brother but realized her grandmother already didn't think highly of Joey's father.

"Found what?" Her grandmother frowned.

"I found that I needed to come here. To finally visit Taiwan." Which was true, just not the whole truth.

Three more plates arrived, each more beautiful than the last. The fish was so fresh, but Joey barely noticed. Would her grandmother invite Joey to her home after lunch? She hadn't realized how much she longed for her grandmother's approval, her acceptance. She'd even packed some things in her tote bag, just in case her grandmother invited her to stay over.

When the waiter had cleared their last plates away, Joey's grandmother wiped her mouth with the cloth napkin and placed it on the table.

"Thank you for coming to see me."

Joey stared, wondering whether this was the end of their visit. "Of course. I would have come sooner if I'd known about you."

There was an awkward silence as they contemplated each other, and then her grandmother let out a deep sigh. "Look, I have the sense you want to get to know me, to be in my life. But the truth is, I have a new family now. They don't know I'm here, meeting with you. I don't want to do anything to upset them."

Joey's jaw dropped and she couldn't speak.

"I wish you well." Her grandmother folded her hands together primly on the table. "And I'm truly sorry about your brother. But this is how life turned out. I hope you understand."

Joey stared at her grandmother for another moment, so many emotions cycling through her body. Disbelief, shock, grief, anger. Joey put her napkin down and stood, pushing her chair in with care. She wouldn't let her grandmother leave her. *She* would be the one to leave first.

"Thank you for meeting with me. I'll take care of the bill on the way out." Without another word, Joey walked past their table, heading for the front of the restaurant and willing the tears to stay away until she was out of sight. But her grandmother reached out and took hold of her arm just as she passed.

"Wait." Joey's heart leaped with hope, but then it dropped at her grandmother's next words. "Don't worry about the bill. I've got it."

Their eyes met for a moment, and then, with a nod, Joey walked away. Joey could still feel the impression of her grandmother's fingers on her skin as she went out the front door. She headed down the street as a tear trickled slowly down her cheek. She had no idea where she was going, but she knew she needed to move.

She walked, tears blurring her vision, refusing to allow any more to fall. She would not cry for a grandmother who didn't want her in her life. She would survive this and focus on the family she *did* have. Maggie and her family and the Kellys. Maybe even Ethan. And now Yao and his grandfather. With each step she took, Joey's resolve to not let this turn of events affect her life grew stronger. Her grandmother's rejection would not define who she was. She was a strong woman, she had her life ahead of her, and she was going to live it to the fullest. After the deaths of her parents and of her beloved brother, she knew she would never take life for granted again. She only had so much time left on earth, and she would go after her passions, spend it with people who made her happy and who *wanted* to be with her. And if someone didn't want that, well, then Joey would accept it and move on. After she let herself wallow for a bit.

With resolve, Joey decided to stay in Keelung for the night so that she could walk through the famous Keelung Night Market. She would take in the sights, and then tomorrow, she'd return to Taipei and hear more of Yao's grandfather's story, perhaps get to know Yao better. She would not waste her energy crying over a grandmother who didn't want her.

She lifted her chin and walked on, in search of a place to stay for the night. Even though her meeting with her grandmother hadn't gone as she'd expected, she knew she would be fine. Because she came from a family of strong women.

33

Joey got back to Taipei at five thirty in the afternoon the next day, after spending a night and a day soul-searching in Keelung. She'd wandered the Keelung MiaoKou Night Market by herself after checking in to a hotel, awed by the rows of yellow lanterns that lit the night everywhere she looked. She sampled Taiwanese street food for the first time by herself, wishing Sam were at her side. Or Yao. That thought surprised her. She wanted to get to know Yao better. She tried hard to tamp down the guilt that this desire brought up. In her heart, she knew Sam would understand. It was much harder convincing herself.

The next morning, she'd walked along the Keelung Port, looking out at all the cranes and shipping containers, thinking about how brave her mother had been, believing in love so much that she'd estranged herself from her family. Her parents' tragic end didn't instill confidence in relationships, though. Did she—Joey—have the courage to pursue what was happening with Ethan? She thought of Sam, of what he'd done to protect her, and forgave him for all he'd kept from her. Now knowing the truth, she knew why he'd done it, even though she wished he'd given her the choice to know about their family when she became an adult.

She'd gone up the hill to the Big Buddha Temple and stared at the giant white statue of Guanyin, the goddess of mercy. When Joey googled the name, she read that Guanyin embodies compassion and is associated with protection, healing, and mercy. She thought of Yao and his grandfather as she took in the magnificent statue, which looked down at the children's playground with motorized cars and scooters for kids to ride.

When she got back to her hotel room in Taipei, Joey threw herself on the bed. She'd talked to Maggie earlier on the train ride back to Taipei, but the urge to talk to Ethan, to share everything she'd experienced in Taiwan so far, was strong. She reached for her phone but then stopped herself from dialing. First, because it was almost midnight on Kauai. And second, because she'd told him not to wait for her, and it wouldn't be fair for her to call him just because the whim struck her. She sighed, forcing herself to think about the night to come. Yao had agreed to accompany her to the Shilin Night Market when the sun went down. After lying there for another half hour, she finally got up to start getting ready.

It was late November, and there was a nice breeze in the air (Yao had told her how stifling hot it was in the summer) when Joey met up with Yao under the 3D tiger at the night market. She was proud of herself for finding her way without getting lost. She was staring up at the 3D tiger as it came to life and pounced on a roasted corn on a stick when Yao came up behind her.

"You found it." He stood there shyly, his hands in his pockets and looking down at his feet.

"I did." Joey swept an arm around her. "This is amazing." It was much like the night market in Keelung, but bigger and filled with so many lights from signs and lanterns that the streets sparkled and it almost felt like daytime. She looked back at Yao, realizing this was the first time they'd been alone together. "Thanks for joining me."

"Of course." He flashed her a quick smile and then gestured ahead. "Shall we?"

"Lead the way."

They strolled slowly, stopping to buy food at different stalls when something caught her eye. Joey tried oyster omelets, pan-fried buns, roast corn on a stick, and a Taiwanese sausage wrapped in a rice sausage. She wished she had a bigger stomach, as she wanted to try everything.

She stopped in front of one vendor. "Is that stinky tofu?"

"Yes." Yao got in line.

"My parents met here at this night market at a stinky tofu stand." She looked around as if they would appear in front of her eyes. "Over fifty years ago."

"Really?" Yao's eyebrows rose. "Tell me about them?"

She glanced at him and then began to tell her parents' story once they got their tofu. As she spoke, her heart loosened a bit, her anger at her father lessening just the slightest bit. Even though she hated what he'd done to her mother, she didn't know the whole story. Didn't know how he was feeling or thinking when he'd embarked on an affair with Ren Ren. And if they hadn't, then Yao wouldn't be standing here next to her.

When she was done, Yao walked into a side alley, which was less crowded. "I can understand now why Sam had such animosity toward my mother. And me."

"I'm sorry," Joey said.

Yao shook his head. "Don't be. It's not your fault."

They stood there, silent, in the middle of the crowded and lively market, not making eye contact, not sure what to say.

Yao finally broke the silence. "This is considered the most touristy night market. I'll take you to Tonghua Night Market another day."

Joey nodded, and they continued walking.

⁂

The next day, Joey was back in Yao and his grandfather's apartment. She'd come armed with her laptop, as his grandfather had said he would tell her more about the past. But the old man was taking a nap and hadn't gotten up yet, so Yao was tinkering on the piano for Joey.

"Won't you wake up your grandfather?" She asked as she settled on the armchair facing the piano.

"He's used to me playing at all hours of the day. And he sleeps soundly." He played a scale with both hands, his fingers flying up the keyboard. "You want to hear what I'm working on?" He turned to meet her eyes. "I could use another set of ears."

"Of course."

Yao turned back to the piano and began to play. The melody rang out through his right hand while his left replicated the bass notes of the strings section. The music flowed until he got to a crescendo moment and stopped.

"There's something off here." He played the notes again with one ear cocked.

Joey came to his side. "Play that again."

He did, and then she reached over and played the same notes, but instead of going down the scale at the end, she went up, giving the tune a more hopeful feel.

"That's it!" He turned, eyes wide. "But wait, I think it needs this at the end." He played some notes, adding to hers.

"Yes." She grinned at him, then he reached for the eraser, rubbing out the notes and replacing them with the ones they'd created together.

When he finished the piece, he turned to find Joey with tears in her eyes.

"It makes me sad that our father never got to hear you play. He loved music so much. He was always singing, playing when he had an instrument."

"I wish I'd known him."

Joey let out a breath. "Our family was so screwed up. What our parents did affected you, me, and Sam in different ways. I wish we could have grown up together, or at least known about each other."

"Me too." Yao looked down as he said this. Before he could continue, his grandfather walked into the room to the armchair Joey had vacated.

Joey greeted Yao's grandfather, who smiled at her. "Thank you for being willing to tell me more about Taiwan."

He nodded. "It's not often I get a rapt audience anymore. You're saving an old man from boredom."

They all laughed, then Joey got out her laptop, ready to take notes. For the next hour, Yao's grandfather told her story after story, giving her a condensed history of Taiwan, but with so many intimate details that she wouldn't have been able to get just through research. Yao went into the kitchen and brought back snacks, making sure his grandfather ate and drank while he talked. Joey watched them closely, the bond between them so endearing.

"My daughter followed in my footsteps," the old man said. "She became a DPP Taipei City Councilwoman two years after she and Yao moved back to Taiwan."

"DPP?" Joey tried to remember what that stood for.

"The Democratic Progressive Party," Yao said.

"Right." Joey remembered that the DPP was the dominant party in the Pan-Green Coalition, in opposition to the KMT.

Yao's grandfather studied her for a moment. "You have every right to be angry with Ren Ren. She did harm to your family. But she had a hard life."

Joey nodded. "I know."

"I'm not referring just to the massacre of my family." Yao's grandfather frowned. "She was kidnapped in 1998, soon after the election. They sent me a ransom letter, along with one of her pinky fingers."

Joey gasped, horrified.

"They didn't take her because of her political views." The sorrow was deep in Yao's grandfather's voice. "They took her because of me. They were criminals, out to extort me for money because they believed I was rich."

"Were you . . ." Joey trailed off, uncertain whether to ask the question.

"Was I rich?" Yao's grandfather gave a dry laugh. "No. While I'd made good money as a lawyer, I was certainly not a rich enough man to come up with the $3 million they demanded within the next few days." He shook his head, a mournful look on his face. "A journalist had recently written a hit piece on me, denouncing my work in fighting for a free Taiwan as that of a greedy politician. He implied that I had a hidden bank account in Switzerland, where I'd squirreled away millions of dollars when I'd been in Sweden. It was so preposterous that I'd laughed when someone showed me the article and promptly forgotten about it. But it seemed someone had taken the journalist seriously and thought they could extort me for money by kidnapping and torturing my daughter."

Joey drew in a breath but didn't respond, mesmerized by the words Yao's grandfather was saying.

"I can suffer all the torture they've heaped on me over the years, but Ren Ren's kidnapping almost broke me. If I could, I would have traded myself and endured what they did to her instead."

34

Yao's Grandfather
1998, Taipei City

When I opened the box that had been delivered to my apartment, all the blood drained out of my face. My hands trembled as I reached for the plastic bag that contained a part of a finger, and when I read the ransom note, demanding $3 million USD, bile rose in my throat. But it was the photograph of Ren Ren, bound and gagged on the floor, that made my knees give out. They had taken my daughter, and rage enveloped me until all I saw was red. I had to get her back.

I didn't go to the police because they said they would kill Ren Ren if I did. I wouldn't jeopardize my daughter's life. Instead, I showed up at the ransom drop spot, a coffee shop in the middle of a bustling shopping center and ordered a coffee. I sat at a table in the back as directed, putting the bag I'd filled with as much money as I could on such short notice under my chair, also as directed. I tried not to look around, tried not to appear as though I was worried or searching the crowd for the kidnappers. The newspaper in my hand shook and I slapped it on the table, realizing my hands were giving away my fear. Staring blindly at the paper, I sipped the coffee slowly, waiting for something to happen.

By the time my coffee was almost done, anxiety had taken over. Why wasn't anyone approaching me?

Just then, a commotion outside the coffeehouse caught my attention. A man was arguing with a policeman, and someone with a camera was taking pictures. The man was pointing into the shop, and years of being hyperaware of my surroundings made the hairs on my arms stand up. I rose, picked up the bag at my feet, and made my way to the exit. I had hoped to slip out unobserved, but the man saw me and shouted, "There he is!"

The police officer turned and approached me before I could escape. "Are you okay?"

I looked at him, my heart pounding, wondering what he meant. "Yes." I turned to leave but the first man blocked my way.

"Is it true? Someone kidnapped your daughter? Are you here dropping off the ransom?"

My mouth gaped and I stared at him. How had he known? When the camera behind him clicked, I realized he was with the press. I hadn't told anyone what I was doing. So who had leaked it to the press?

I pushed past him and was able to evade his outstretched arm, as he tried to grab me while shouting out questions. I ran when I got free and jumped on a bus that had just pulled up on the corner. I didn't know what to do. Should I have stayed and gotten the police involved? Had the kidnapper seen the press and policeman and gotten spooked? What were they going to do to Ren Ren?

I made my way to my closest friend Frank's apartment building. I realized I needed help, and I knew I could trust him. His face fell when I relayed the story of Ren Ren's kidnapping.

"You need to go to the police."

"No." I didn't trust them, not after what I'd been through.

"This isn't good." His voice was low.

"I know. Let me think." But before I could decide what to do, my cell phone rang. I picked it up, every nerve in my body prickling, sure it was the kidnapper.

"We told you not to go to the police." The male voice on the line growled.

"I didn't. Who are you?" My voice came out much more powerful than I thought. My ears strained for any clue that would tell me who was calling and why.

"We'll give you one last chance." He named a location close to my apartment and said to be there at the same time the next day. He disconnected before I could ask another question.

Frank and I stared at each other. I didn't want Ren Ren to endure another night and day with her kidnappers. But what could I do? I had no idea who had taken her.

"We need to call Liu." Frank's voice was solemn.

I looked up sharply at the name. Liu was a criminal, someone whom I had once saved unintentionally. He'd been on trial for a drug-related incident, and I'd gotten him off on a technicality. He'd told me to call him if I ever needed anything, as he cast a wide network in the criminal underworld. But I didn't want to associate with the likes of him, especially as I was trying to lie low ever since my return to Taiwan.

"He could help," Frank argued. "He may know who has your daughter."

I turned away and stood, walking to the window and gazing out on the busy city street below. I knew Frank was right. I needed Liu's help.

Frank contacted him and Liu asked us to meet him in a bar on the other side of Taipei. When we got there, we found him in a back booth. We walked through the dimly lit, smoky bar to where he sat, a cigarette dangling out of his mouth.

He stood and slapped me on the back before doing the same to Frank. Once we sat facing Liu, he put his cigarette out and rested his elbows on the table.

"I'm glad you finally called me." He leered at me, his version of a smile. "I could have helped you so many times over the years."

I didn't smile back. "My daughter is in danger. If you know anything, please tell me. I have to get her back before they kill her." I told him about the ransom note, the severed finger that I'd determined was a pinky, and the photo. "Do you have any idea who's behind this?"

Liu leaned back, his eyes narrowed. "I heard about this on the news. That stupid journalist." He cursed in Taiwanese, a vulgar slang that had Frank raising his eyebrows. "He's slime, has contacts in the underbellies of Taipei."

I didn't meet Frank's eyes, for if we did, we'd burst out laughing, as Liu was one of those contacts living in the underbellies.

"How did he find out?"

"Apparently someone who knows the kidnappers told him, and he wanted to be the first to break the story." Liu spit on the floor in disgust.

"You know who did this then?" I watched Liu's face carefully, wondering whether I could trust him.

He nodded and pulled a pack of cigarettes out of his shirt pocket. "I'll help you get your daughter back."

My heart leaped with hope, but I tempered it, not wanting to get ahead of myself. "How?"

"Don't ask." He lit the cigarette and blew a cloud of smoke away from us. "I don't ask how you got me off when I was on trial, you don't ask how I go about my business."

"What can I do? Is she okay?"

"As far as I know, she's still alive. As for okay?" He shrugged and took another drag on the cigarette. "That I can't guarantee."

I narrowed my eyes at him. "Are you behind the kidnapping?"

He threw his head back and roared in laughter before shooting me a stare that would have made a less desperate man quake. "How many times do I have to tell you that you can trust me? I am forever indebted to you." He put a hand over his heart. "That actually hurts my feelings, that you don't trust me."

I gave him a look, and he let out another snort of laughter. "Okay. Fine," I said. "I trust you. I trust you to get my daughter back, then we're even. You don't owe me anything anymore."

He nodded, throwing back the shot of whiskey in front of him. He tapped it on the table twice when the waitress walked by and she nodded. "You two want anything?" He pointed at us.

"No." I'd come here for my daughter, not to have a drink with a notorious criminal. "I just want my daughter back."

"Give me a few days." He would have said more but I interrupted him.

"A few days?" I half stood in dismay. "I can't leave her with those people for a few more days." I didn't realize I'd hoped Liu would go now and bring my daughter to me.

He squinted. "It's going to take time. Delicate negotiations." He laughed again and then almost choked on the smoke swirling around him. "I'll get her out as soon as I can." He tapped the table with his fingers. "Wait to hear from me. Don't do anything in the meantime. Don't go to the police. If you do, I won't be able to help you."

We stared at each other for a moment as my thoughts raced. Was I making a big mistake? Should I go to the police instead of counting on Liu? But I didn't trust the police any more than I trusted Liu. And at least with Liu, he felt like he owed me something. He had connections that the police didn't.

Mind made up, I stood and put out my hand. He remained sitting but shook my hand. "I'll bring her back to you, hopefully alive."

My eyes widened and I was about to make a retort when he roared with laughter again. "Kidding! Just kidding. I'll bring her back alive."

Frank stood and with a nod at Liu, we left, his laughter trailing after us. I hoped he would make good on his word. My daughter's life depended on him.

⁂

Three days later, a knock came at my door. I flew to it, eyes on the peephole, as the doorman hadn't called up to say anyone was here to see me. What I saw made me gasp and I threw open the door.

"Ren Ren!" My daughter stood before me with Liu next to her, holding her up.

Her hair was disheveled, and it looked like someone had hacked a hank of hair out of one side. Her face was swollen, lips caked with dried blood, and a dirty handkerchief was wrapped around her left hand. She was wearing a giant T-shirt over the gray pants that I'd remembered her wearing to work the day she disappeared, and when she walked forward, I was alarmed to see that she was limping.

"Baba." The word came out strangled and she collapsed in my arms. I held her up, murmuring into her ear, trying to soothe the choking sobs that racked her body.

I was so thankful I'd already put Yao to bed. Yao, my innocent grandson who couldn't understand where his mother had gone and had asked me a million times when she would be coming home.

I nodded at Liu over her head, thanking him without words. He tipped his head once and then turned and went back down the stairs. I closed the door after him and led my daughter, my poor, poor daughter to the couch, helping her to sit carefully. She slumped back against the cushions and then I rushed about the apartment, gathering the things I needed to tend to her wounds, clean her up, assess the damage. When I unwrapped the handkerchief from around her hand, the smell that came off her mangled limb made me want to gag, but I held it in. She needed a doctor. I could already see the infection setting in, pus oozing out of the bloody stump that used to be her pinky. She didn't speak a word while I ministered to her, cleaned her up as best as I could. And then I called my driver to take us to the hospital.

She huddled against my side, my arm around her, holding her close. When we were almost at the hospital, she picked her head off my shoulder to look at me. "They didn't break me. I'm still here."

I nodded, not trusting myself to speak.

"I am your daughter. I stayed strong. I knew you would get me out." Her head dropped back on my shoulder as her good hand went to her mangled one. "I will never stop fighting for our country."

"I know." I squeezed her closer and I whispered into her hair. "My brave, strong daughter."

And we stayed like that, bound together by all we'd endured, until we arrived at the hospital and the driver opened the door for us.

35

Joey
Present Day

Joey stared at Yao and his grandfather, her heart bleeding for all that her old nanny had lived through. Her feelings were conflicted; she was still angry with Ren Ren for what she'd done to Joey's family, but how could Joey not feel for Ren Ren after hearing this story? There was silence as she struggled to comprehend what this family had been through, even after martial law had been lifted in 1987. She couldn't imagine the bravery and strength they had within, so convinced about a cause that they'd risked their lives and endured unimaginable torture for it. She searched her soul, wondering if she'd ever believed in something as passionately as Ren Ren and her father had.

"I am so sorry this happened to Ren Ren."

Yao's grandfather sighed. "Me too." He looked at Joey. "She spoke of you often. She loved you."

"I loved her too."

"She longed to see you, to beg your forgiveness for how she wronged your family." The old man shook his head. "She blamed herself for your parents' death. She told me what Sam said to her, and she took full responsibility. But she was just a young girl when she went to live with your family. She didn't know any better."

But Joey's father had. She didn't say this out loud. Her father had taken advantage of a young girl grieving for her family, a young girl who had looked up to him.

"Did she ever . . . marry?" Joey was curious about her old nanny.

"No." Yao spoke up, a faint smile on his lips. "But she had a gentleman friend, as my grandfather called him."

The old man snorted, making Yao smile.

Joey looked back and forth between them. "Who was it?"

"Liu's son." Yao's grandfather practically spat out the words.

"He was good to my mother, Ah-Gong." Yao turned to Joey. "After Liu helped rescue her, he sent his son to check on her a few days later. He was a respected man, unlike his father. My mother and he were a good pair. They never married but I was glad she found someone to stand by her up until her death."

Yao's grandfather's face softened. "He was good to her, even though I still don't like it that it was Liu's son."

They continued talking, but Joey tuned out for a moment. Even with all the tragedy in her life, Ren Ren had found happiness with a man. If she could do that, what was stopping Joey from giving her heart to Ethan? For the first time since hearing about the affair between her father and Ren Ren, Joey's heart relented a bit, no longer so angry at her old nanny.

⁂

Joey spent the next three days with Yao and each time, she felt more comfortable in his presence. He took her sightseeing, to see the skyscraper Taipei 101, and for soup dumplings at Din Tai Fung. They visited with his grandfather again, and she started writing the book, words flowing out of her like they hadn't in a long time. She helped Yao with the piece he was working on, the two of them playing a duet on the piano while they sang the words together, his grandfather their captive audience.

One day, they were strolling through Longshan Temple, and Joey was admiring all the dragons that adorned the roof when Yao's phone rang. He pulled it out, a frown on his face.

"Wei?" Yao put the call on speaker.

"Yao." It was his grandfather's caretaker, a man in his late twenties. "You need to come home. Now."

Yao's eyes darted to Joey's. She froze, her attention on him.

"What is it?" Yao was already walking even as he spoke. Joey ran to catch up.

"It's your grandfather. He fell. He won't let me call for an ambulance."

He kept talking, but Yao had broken into a run with Joey right behind him. When they finally got back to Yao's building after hailing a cab, they ran up the two flights of stairs to the third-floor apartment. Yao entered the apartment first, and she bolted in after him, following him to his grandfather's room.

"Ah-Gong!" Yao cried as he practically threw himself onto his knees at his grandfather's bedside.

The old man lay in bed, propped up by pillows and a blanket covering his thin frame. At the sound of Yao's voice, his eyes opened. He blinked a few times and then reached for Yao's hands.

"What happened?" Yao's eyes scanned the scene, frantic.

His grandfather gave a faint smile. "I'm fine. I just got dizzy for a moment and lost my balance. Everything is fine."

Yao's eyes darted to the caretaker, who was sitting in a chair on the other side of the bed. "Is that true?"

The caretaker shrugged. "He seems stable. All his vitals are fine. No signs of distress. But I still think he should go to the hospital just in case." The man locked eyes with Yao. "He refused."

"Ah-Gong." Yao turned to his grandfather. "Does anything hurt? Your heart? Your head? We should go to the hospital."

"No." His voice was low but firm. "I don't want to go to the hospital."

"But . . ."

"No." His grandfather spoke louder. "Listen to me. I want to stay here. I have . . ." He trailed off. A few seconds later, he continued, ". . . things to say to you."

They stared at each other until Yao reluctantly nodded.

He looked over at Joey who moved to his side.

The caretaker stood. "I'm going to go, since you're all here. Unless you need me?" He turned to look between Yao and his grandfather.

"Go, go." Yao's grandfather made shooing gestures with one hand. "I'm fine. I promise. Yao can handle it from here."

The caretaker patted him on the arm. "You gave me a scare. Get some rest. I'll see you tomorrow." With a nod at Yao and Joey, he walked out of the room.

Joey spoke at Yao's side. "I'll get out of your way too. I'm sure you need time together."

Yao's grandfather waved a hand at her. "No, please stay. I have things I want to tell Yao. I'd like you to be here."

Her eyebrows shot up but she nodded.

"Sit." The old man gestured for Yao to get off his knees and draw two chairs to the bedside. They sat, waiting for him to speak.

"You're going to be fine." The words came out slightly garbled, as if he had spoken with water in his mouth. "I've lived a long life. Almost ninety-eight years." The old man sighed, his chest going concave at the exhalation. "They weren't easy years, and I suffered a lot of loss. My whole family gone." His eyes fluttered and he struggled for breath, making Joey lean forward, her eyes wide in alarm.

"Are you sure you don't want us to take you to the hospital?" Her intuition told her something was wrong.

"No, dear girl." He turned to her. "It's time. I'm ready to go. I've hung on because I needed to make sure Yao wasn't all alone in the world." The last few words came out as a whisper. He tried to smile but his lips were dry, and they cracked.

Yao took an ice cube out of the container that the caretaker had left by the bed and ran it over his grandfather's mouth. The old man licked his bottom lip, sending his grandson a look of gratitude.

"Don't say stuff like that." Yao's voice was fierce.

"Yao, listen to me." His grandfather reached out to clasp Yao's hand. "I don't want to argue with you. I have too much to say." He paused to catch his breath and then continued, his voice so weak Joey had to lean forward to catch his words. "Go to California. It's time you started your own life. A life filled with music and joy and happiness. What happened in this country, what happened to my family, to your mother and to your father, it has all cast a shadow over your life." He stopped to cough, and Yao picked up the cup of water and held the straw to his lips.

"Are you sure you don't want to be alone with Yao?" Joey felt like an interloper.

The old man turned to her. "Please stay. Yao will need you." His voice was reedy, as if he didn't have the strength to fully use his diaphragm. "Please help him." He reached out a shaking hand, and Joey took it. "I can go now because I know he will be fine with you in his life. He won't be alone any longer." He fell back against the pillow and closed his eyes, his fingers loosening their grip on Joey's.

"Ah-Gong!" Yao cried, reaching to touch his grandfather's face, his eyes darting in panic to Joey. "We need to call an ambulance."

"No." The word was weak, but they both heard it. The old man's eyes slowly fluttered open. "No. I want to go peacefully, in my own bed, with you both here." He took a breath and then continued. "I've waited a long time to see my wife and sons again, to reunite with Ren Ren. I've given up my life for Taiwan, and now I want to go. Here at home. Not in a hospital."

"No." The word came out of Yao, pitiful and small, as tears streamed down his cheeks.

Joey's heart hurt so much it felt as if it would crack. She put a hand on Yao's shoulder and squeezed, wanting him to know she was there.

"You're a good boy, Yao," his grandfather whispered. "You weren't given much of a chance in life, but now it's your turn to shine. Go to California. Make a name for yourself. Let them see how brilliant you are. Your mother and I, we'll be watching you from up above." His cloudy eyes turned to Joey. "Your father will be watching you too. Both of you."

"Don't leave me." Yao put his forehead down on his grandfather's hands, his voice muffled as sobs shook his shoulders. Joey fought back her own tears. "I can't do this without you, Ah-Gong."

The old man put his other hand on top of Yao's head, gently stroking his hair. Then his hand stilled and he whispered, "You'll be fine. You have a sister now."

Yao froze, his head unmoving under his grandfather's hand. Joey watched with grief as the old man took a final breath and then his body stilled. Yao let out a wail as his grandfather's spirit left his body, and Joey moved in, putting her arm around her grieving brother as he kept his forehead on his grandfather's still form.

They stayed like that for a long time, the only sound in the room coming from Yao's choked sobs and the loud ticking of the grandfather clock in the corner. Finally, Joey gently took Yao by the shoulders, forcing him to lift his head. The look in Yao's eyes broke her, and she reached down to draw her brother up. When he was on his feet, she took him in her arms, holding him tight, sending him the message that he wasn't alone, that she was here and wouldn't leave him. He clung to her like a koala to its mother, and when he finally spoke, he said only one word.

"Stay."

Joey nodded, knowing what he was asking for.

"I won't leave."

⁂

A week later, Joey and Yao stood at the funeral home, where his grandfather's body had been taken and preserved for the seven-day wake that followed his death. Because they had no other family left, Yao chose not to go the full Buddhist tradition of keeping the body at home for family to watch over. Instead, he spent most days at his grandfather's coffin, accepting the condolences of the hordes of Taiwanese who came to pay their respects. A geomancer had chosen an auspicious day for the cremation, which would take place today.

Joey stayed by Yao's side for most of the mourning period, except when she went out to run errands or get food to make sure Yao ate. She finally broke down and called Ethan, who comforted her when grief and tears overcame her.

"I'm here, Joey. Call me anytime, okay?" Ethan said just before they hung up.

"Thank you." Her heart and body missed him so, but with everything happening in Taiwan, she couldn't focus on her feelings for Ethan yet.

Maggie offered to fly to Taiwan to be with her. But Joey declined. This was a time to focus on her new brother. She now believed she was meant to be here to help him with the loss of his grandfather.

Yao was going to play a piece today. He hadn't told Joey what he would be playing, but he sat alone now at the piano in the main observation room, barely acknowledging the crowd. His gaze was on his grandfather's casket. After his performance, the casket would be taken to the crematorium. The funeral home was packed. Pro-democracy advocates, politicians from the DDP, supporters from all over Taiwan had shown up to pay their last respects to this formidable man, filling the room, which was as large as half a football stadium.

Joey made her way to the front, where a chair had been reserved for her. She sat down, her gaze on Yao as the man from the funeral home welcomed everyone. It was standing room only, with people scattered along the edges of the room and at the back spilling out the front door. When the room hushed and the slight coughs and rustling of the crowd had diminished, Yao finally turned from the coffin and faced the piano. He didn't acknowledge the crowd, didn't say anything, only stared at the keys of the piano. And then he raised his hands and brought them down on the gleaming instrument, his fingers flying.

Joey smiled when she recognized the piece right away. It was the one she'd helped him with, the one they'd played together for his grandfather. It was powerful, the chords ringing as Yao's right hand flew through the passage Joey had helped him perfect. And then, after a moment of silence, Yao started to sing.

The words were simple, but they told a story of heartbreak and loss, of terror and unthinkable tragedy. Yet they also told a tale of strength and power, of the determination never to give up on what you believed in. Joey's hands were gripped into fists as she sang along with Yao in her head, the music building and building. She could hear the intakes of breath all around her as the audience was swept away by the magic of the music coming from Yao.

But all of a sudden, his voice stopped, right as it was about to hit the high note. His fingers followed a few beats later, the beautiful music suddenly ending in a discordant clash of notes. Joey stared at Yao, willing him to continue but seeing that he couldn't. Her brother had lost his fight with grief, and his shoulders shook silently as he bowed his head.

Without thinking, she stood and went to his side, standing on his right as her fingers played the progression they'd written together. She began to sing, going back to the buildup of the song, repeating the words:

You will find the strength, you will rise and be strong because you're not alone.

Yao looked over at her and she nodded at him. Without taking his eyes off her face, his left hand started playing the chords again, and then it was as if they were back in his grandfather's living room, performing the duet for the old man. By the time they hit the high note, their voices rang together, strong and powerful, rising above the crowd and up into the heavens.

When the last note faded away, there was a moment of silence, so hushed that it was as if they'd all lost their hearing, before the audience burst into applause and everyone was on their feet. This was an unprecedented funeral. Yao had wanted it to be a celebration of his grandfather's life, and the song he'd just played truly was. He stood from the piano and took Joey's hand, and they turned to everyone, all the people who had shown up to honor the man who had done so much for Taiwan and her people, the man who had suffered immeasurably but who had never faltered in his beliefs. Joey squeezed Yao's hand, and together they turned to receive the hundreds of people whose lives had been touched by the soft-spoken yet passionate man who was Yao's grandfather.

36

"Yao."

Joey leaned against the doorframe of Yao's room, looking at her brother lying on his bed, giant headphones on his head. She'd left him alone for almost two weeks as he'd processed the loss of his grandfather. He hadn't wanted to talk, hadn't wanted to do anything Joey had suggested. So she'd provided food, made sure he showered, and got out at least once a day. If he wanted to talk, which wasn't very often, she was there to listen. If he wanted to hide in his room, she let him.

But now she was about to go back to Kauai the next day, having stayed longer than she'd intended. She needed to put the rest of Sam's affairs in order, to decide where she and Wonton would live. Most of all, she needed to finally talk to Ethan. She'd been so sure when she'd left Kauai that she would mess up any relationship between them. But now, having heard Yao's grandfather's stories, having met her grandmother who had also risen from nothing to have a second chance at life, and Ren Ren, who had found happiness with a man despite everything she'd gone through, Joey knew she couldn't hide anymore. She needed to confront what was between her and Ethan, and how she would move forward with her life.

Yao took the headphones off and pushed himself up. "Hi."

She walked in and sat on the chair at his desk, turning it around so that she faced him.

"I'm leaving tomorrow."

"I know." She'd told him when she'd booked the ticket a few days ago. His face was drawn, his cheekbones pronounced, as he'd lost weight since his grandfather's passing.

"I looked up apartments in Fairfax, the area you said you'd want to live in if you moved to California. There are a few that might fit your needs. Maybe one of your friends there can FaceTime you while they tour the apartments." She stopped, waiting for a reaction.

"What?" Surprise tinged his voice.

"It's your dream. Your grandfather wanted you to go." She put her hands on her thighs and leaned forward. "He'd want you to live."

He nodded again and looked down at his hands. Joey waited, an arsenal of responses at the ready if Yao protested. But he surprised her.

"Okay."

"Okay?" Joey's brows rose.

"Yes." Yao raised his head. "I was already thinking about it. I just haven't made myself do anything yet." He inclined his head. "Thank you."

Joey nodded at him.

"What about you?" he asked. "What will you do?"

"I don't know." She shrugged. "I'll figure it out when I get back to Kauai. Maybe I can help you move, once you find a place."

"You'd come visit me?" He blinked at her.

She looked at him. "If you want me to. There's a reason we found each other now."

He reached out a hand, and she took it in hers. When he squeezed it, she nodded at him, knowing any anger that might have lingered at Ren Ren was gone. Her son, Joey's brother, was now a part of her life. So much had changed in the last month, so much loss but also so much discovery. She'd come to Taiwan confused, grief-stricken, searching for something. And she was leaving with a newfound strength, a new outlook on life, knowing life was too short to dwell on the things that weren't so important in the long run. It was time to go after what *she* wanted.

37

Kauai

Two days later, after almost twenty hours of traveling, Joey finally arrived back on Kauai. She took in a deep breath of the sweet Kauai air and knew she was home. It felt so different from when she'd first arrived over a month and a half ago, shocked by Sam's sudden death. She knew Ethan was waiting for her on the curb outside Baggage Claim A, and her heart picked up in anticipation of seeing him. Would they still feel the same way about each other? Had he meant it when he said he would wait for her? She'd been so stupid, trying to push him away just as they'd discovered each other. She'd come to understand that she'd done that because she was scared. Scared that whatever was happening between them would fail and he would be one more person to leave her. But on the long flight home, she'd realized she'd much rather risk that than not take the risk at all. And it was time to tell him.

The first thing she saw once she got her suitcase and walked out of baggage claim was Ethan leaning against his car. A smile lit her face, and she picked up her pace. He met her halfway, then she was in his arms, his embrace tight and his familiar smell making her feel like she'd come home. They stayed like that for a moment, and Joey realized how much she'd missed him.

"Hi," he said when they finally pulled away.

"Hi." She grinned at him, and then he was leaning down, and their kiss was so sweet and so perfect that Joey wanted to cry with happiness.

"You look beautiful," he murmured against her lips.

In answer, she pulled him even closer, her heart feeling so full she was afraid it would burst from her chest. She closed her eyes briefly, letting her cheek rest against the warmth of his T-shirt, feeling his hard chest under the cotton. All her doubts deserted her, and she knew this was where she belonged—in Ethan's arms.

They could have stood on the sidewalk for the rest of the day as far as she was concerned, but Ethan eventually reached out to take her suitcase, and she reluctantly let go of him. He drove her up to Princeville, their conversation light, but always in physical contact throughout the ride. His hand on her thigh; hers on his neck, his shoulder, leaning in to kiss him on the cheek during a red light. They would talk later, but for now, she was drinking in his presence, wondering how she'd ever thought she could live without him in her life.

When they got back to the complex, they headed straight to the Kellys' front door. It opened after they rang the bell, and Wonton came flying out, jumping on Joey's legs with joy. She leaned down to scoop up the little dog.

"I've missed you, Wonton." She buried her face in the dog's side while Wonton tried to lick and kiss every inch of her face.

When Joey looked up, Mac and Linda stood there grinning at them.

"You look good, Joey," Linda said, her eyes appraising Joey.

"I feel . . . better." She put the dog down to face the Kellys. "Taiwan was good for me."

"We're glad." Linda patted her on the arm.

"I've missed Kauai." She looked behind her at all the lush foliage and bright flowers.

Mac stepped forward. "Why don't you come over for dinner? You must be tired after that long flight."

Joey smiled, looking over at Ethan. "Ethan said he made plans for us."

Linda raised an eyebrow at them. "Ooh. A date."

"Yes." Ethan's voice was firm even as a smile played on his lips.

Linda winked at them, and after a few minutes of catching up, the Kellys sent them on their way, saying they'd see Joey for lunch the next day.

They went into Sam's apartment—hers now—where Joey took a shower and changed while Ethan sat on the couch with Wonton. It was the day before New Year's Eve, and while she still had a Sam-size hole in her heart, she'd gained so much more. She'd found Yao. She'd spoken to her grandmother, and although it was painful, it had helped her see a new way forward. She'd gotten closure there even if it hadn't turned out as she'd wanted. Her parents' marriage hadn't been perfect. They'd had flaws just like she did, just like Ren Ren, and just like Sam. But in the end, she knew they all loved her, and she couldn't change the past. She could only go forward the best she could.

And now there was Ethan, and the possibilities no longer scared her. If Ren Ren could find the courage to share her life with someone after all the brutal incidents in her life, then Joey surely could.

Forty-five minutes later, she, Ethan, and Wonton got out of the car at a beach in Kapaa after stopping by Ethan's place, where he picked up two bags he'd packed. His daughter, Rory, was visiting him for the holidays but was out with friends, and had said she wanted to meet Joey. Wonton strained against her harness, her tail wagging furiously as she smelled the ocean air. The wind blew, ruffling her fur as it made Joey's hair dance around her head. Ethan reached out and tucked a few wayward strands behind her ears, and she leaned into his hand, closing her eyes for a moment.

Ethan grabbed the bags out of the back seat and pointed down the beach. "Let's move in a bit so that if tourists come explore, they won't be on top of us."

Nodding, she kicked off her flip-flops and bent down to get them after unclipping Wonton from her harness. The little dog rarely strayed too far from her people and trotted at their side. The sun was low in the sky and the temperature was comfortable, still hot but with a constant breeze that kept everything cool. Once they were about halfway down the beach, Ethan put the bags down and spread out the blanket. Then, gesturing with his hand, he waited until she'd settled on it before placing the bags on one end and sitting down.

"I picked up ginger fried chicken and shrimp from Konohiki Seafoods and made an Asian cucumber salad to go with it," he said, taking out containers and setting them on the blanket between them. "Maggie's mom brought over a large portion of pancit, so there's that, along with fresh fruit and a bottle of prosecco." Ethan pointed to the other thermal bag that was keeping the wine cool. "Should we open that first?"

"Yes." Joey had brought the cups, utensils, and napkins, and pulled them out. Once Ethan had popped the top off the prosecco, he poured them each a cup.

"To Joey. Who went through so much these past few weeks, but whose strength never fails to amaze me." He raised his cup in the air, and Joey tapped hers against it. "And to Sam, and Yao's grandfather. May they be reunited with the people they loved."

Joey looked at him, her heart full and appreciation for Ethan's thoughtful sentiment chasing away any last doubts she might have had. She raised her glass to him, her eyes signaling all that she was feeling.

"You know how I feel about you. How I've always felt about you."

He nodded and she tried to control the blush that was creeping over her cheeks.

"I told you not to wait for me because I was scared. In my experience, relationships destroy people. They destroy the trust, love, and whatever it was that drew two people together. I didn't want to do that to another person. I'm almost forty years old, and I've fended for myself for so long it's hard to place that trust in someone else."

"I get that." Ethan nodded. "I've done marriage before."

Joey looked off into the ocean, knowing she had to tell Ethan what was on her mind, even if it was scary. "You know I've had a crush on you since I met you." Her lips twitched when Ethan nudged her knee at that. "I'd be lying if I told you I don't want to pursue this with you. Because I do." She finally turned to look at him. "I just don't know how that would look. I've been independent for so long I'm not sure I can change my need to travel, to go where the wind takes me."

"I don't need a traditional relationship." Ethan held her gaze, his eyes warm, his face open. "I only want you."

Her eyebrows quirked up, but she didn't interrupt him.

"I've done traditional, and it didn't work out so well, except we got Rory out of it. I want to enjoy life, spend it with someone who makes me happy, someone I love." He reached out and laid a hand over one of hers. "That person is you."

She bit back a smile even as her heart filled and her breath quickened.

He continued, "We don't need labels or an official document or any of those traditional rules tying us down. We can make our own rules, as long as we're both in agreement on what happens between us going forward."

"I'm not sure I completely understand." Joey's heart was suddenly pounding out of control. She needed him to be clear, to spell it out for her. "Do you want an open relationship? Where we're together but can also be with other people?"

"Absolutely not." Ethan let out a laugh—more like a snort, which made Joey laugh despite the way her nerves were suddenly making everything inside her stand at attention. "I meant we make our own rules. We get to know each other, be together however much or little we want. I know you have an independent life, and I do too. But why can't we share that life, even if we're not stuck together like glue?"

Joey gave him a skeptical look, yet her insides had awakened and were jumping up and down with glee. Could Ethan really feel the same way as her? Were they really that in tune with each other?

She decided to be brave. The women who had shaped her life, however peripherally, filled her mind for a moment, giving her strength. Her mother, Ren Ren, even her grandmother. "I've decided to stay here for at least the next six months, to give us a real chance. I told my tenant in New York she can have the apartment for now. I want to see what we can build together."

"I'm glad," Ethan said. His gaze never wavered from hers.

Joey held up a hand. "But I have some travel plans too. Not just for work, but to California to see Yao and help him with his move. I'll go back to Taiwan with him for his grandfather's one-hundred-day celebration after his death. I'm just not sure if I am capable of staying in one place for too long."

Ethan raised his brows at her. "That's fine. Maybe I'll come with you for some of it, if you want."

"You'd be okay with that?" Hope leaped within Joey. Could it really be as simple as this?

"Yes. I love you," he said. "As long as we're honest with each other, why couldn't it work? Planes are a marvel these days."

Her mouth curved as he intertwined their fingers together. They fit perfectly, like the last piece of a puzzle, clicking with satisfaction into place.

"I'm in awe of the woman you turned out to be. You flew to Taiwan to see your brother even when you were hesitant, and you met your grandmother. You did what Sam never could in all his years." Ethan's fingers were warm and strong, and she moved closer until they were touching. "You forgave your parents for what they did. You forgave Ren Ren and, by extension, her son. Sam let all that anger fester within him, unwilling or unable to let it go."

"I did." Tears gathered in Joey's eyes, but they were happy tears. "Poor Sam." She felt for her brother, who'd had to grow up way too fast with no one to guide him.

"Before he passed away, he said to me that he thought he got cancer because of all that anger and hatred he kept inside. He realized too late that he should have let it go. Forgiven Ren Ren and Yao." Ethan's smile was sad, and he pulled Joey closer until she was sitting in his lap, her back against his chest. He wrapped an arm around her from behind while keeping the other in her hand. "Love doesn't have to follow a script; it doesn't have to be just like everyone else's. As long as we communicate, are honest with each other, we can do this, Joey." He tipped his head down, kissing her on the neck.

She melted against him, love for him filling her heart. She never thought she'd be here, wrapped in his arms, feeling his heart beating against her back. Before she could express her feelings, he spoke again.

"I love you, Joey. Let me love you. I want you to get to know Rory. She's been dying to meet you. We'll figure it out."

She turned in his arms and gazed into his beautiful, kind eyes. "Ethan." She thought of all that she'd learned since Sam passed away, all that had prevented the people she loved the most from finding happiness with another person. In that moment, she let go of all her doubts, all her hesitation, and let herself live in the moment. "I want to meet Rory too." And she realized she really did.

She pulled him close and then they were kissing, a coming together of not only their lips but also their hearts and minds. She knew without a doubt that her parents and Sam would have approved of her being with Ethan.

When they finally parted, she looked at him. "I love you. I've loved you for a very long time. I want to be with you."

And the smile he beamed back at her healed any last wounds that still lingered in her heart.

ACKNOWLEDGMENTS

This was the hardest book I've written to date, and if it weren't for my agent, Rachel Brooks, I don't think it would have seen the light of day. Our eighth book together (although technically it was the fifth book we worked on together), which went through so many revisions and changes, I think I made poor Rachel's head spin. It had so many R & Rs and rewrites that eventually we had to put it away. Enter my brilliant editor, Pippa White, who finally gave me the insight to understand the essence of the book and pulled it out of me like taffy.

Thank you to Rachel and Pippa for all your hard work on this book and for helping me get it to publication. As I've joked to both of them, I thought *Ghost Moon* was trying to make a ghost of me, but we did it!

Thank you also to Andrea Hurst, developmental editor extraordinaire, whom I've been blessed to have worked with for four books. Your genius brain made all my books so much stronger. To the Lake Union team—author relations manager Darci Swanson; art director Kimberly Glyder; marketing manager Brittany Morris; production manager Angela Elson; cover designer Amanda Kain; and editors Shuja Khan, Karen Brown, Jill Schoenhaut, and Jessica Poore—you all were the best to work with!

Thank you to Wu Li-pei, Gene Wu, and Julie Lee. Without you, I wouldn't have been brave enough to write about Taiwan and what the Taiwanese people have been through. Also, a big thank-you to my fellow

Taiwanese American authors, Shawan Yang Ryan, Ed Lin, Julie Wu, and Charles Yu for inspiring me to continue the path you laid for us.

As always, my family makes it possible for me to disappear for hours while working on a book. Thank you to my parents and my husband and son for putting up with me when I pull out my laptop during bouts of inspiration, even at happy hour. And to my constant writing companions, Cash and Hanna—the best doggy writing assistants ever.

To all the readers out there who have discovered my books, the biggest *thank you* to you all. Your support, enthusiasm, and sharing of my books are what make it possible for me to continue my career as an author. From the bottom of my heart, I appreciate you all!

BOOK CLUB QUESTIONS

1. Family secrets play a big role in this book. Does your own family have secrets as big as Joey's that would change how you think of your family?

2. Joey was brought up by her brother, who was ten years older than her. Do you know anyone who was also raised by a sibling?

3. Did you know anything about the martial law era of Taiwan before reading this book? If not, has it helped enhanced your understanding of what the Taiwanese people have been going through?

4. Did the Taiwanese food descriptions in the book make you hungry, or are they too foreign for you? Would you try any of the food described?

5. Sam makes a hard decision to take his own life after his cancer diagnosis. What do you think of his decision? What would you have done in his shoes?

6. There are many heavy topics in this book: suicide, torture of political prisoners, kidnapping, infidelity, a murder plot, etc.

Were you able to navigate them in the book and understand what the characters were going through?

7. Joey has suffered from unrequited love for many years, so much so that she doesn't return to Kauai after college because of Ethan. Have you ever had an unrequited or lost love like that?

8. Ah-Hui's mother and grandparents cut her off completely after she chooses to leave for New York with Joey's father. Would you have been able to do that if you were Ah-Hui's mother?

9. Joey ultimately finds two family members whom she didn't know about, one who wants her in their life, another who doesn't. Would that have devastated you if you were Joey?

ABOUT THE AUTHOR

Photo © 2020 Dave Cross Photography

Lyn Liao Butler is the Taiwanese American author of eight novels, including *The Fourth Daughter*, *The Deadly Book Club*, *What Is Mine*, and *Red Thread of Fate*, which was a finalist in the WFWA Star Awards for 2023. Before becoming an author, Lyn was a professional ballet and modern dancer and is still a fitness and yoga instructor. She and her family, including two rescue dogs and a myriad of foster animals, divide their time between Kauai and New York. For more information, visit www.lynliaobutler.com.